Rebel Unbound

First Book of the Promissa Trilogy

E. R. Phoenix

REBEL UNBOUND: FIRST BOOK OF THE PROMISSA TRILOGY

Book Cover by Christian Bentulan © Covers by Christian.

Edited by Miranda Miller © Editing Realm

First edition 2024

Contents

Trigger Warning

The dystopian romance Rebel Unbound takes part in a society where injustice, persecution, and brutality are rampant. Some of the incidents depicted may be disturbing to some readers. A few scenes depict rape and sexual assault. There are also instances of gore, alcohol consumption, weapon use, and explicit sexual content.

To all who had a dream but put it on wait due to life.
May you find your way back and never let go of it.
It's never too late to pursue and fulfill what you desire.
Believe in yourself.

"Hope" is the thing with feathers
That perches in the soul
And sings the tune without the words
And never stops at all

And sweetest in the Gale is heard
And sore must be the storm
That could abash the little Bird
That kept so many warm

I've heard it in the chillest land
And on the strangest Sea
Yet never in Extremity,
It asked a crumb of me.

—Emily Dickinson, "'Hope' is the thing with feathers"

Chapter 1

Abi

November 6, 2210

Faces from another time pierced my soul. Dad gazed into my mother's green eyes, a smile on his handsome face. His ebony skin contrasted with Mom's alabaster hands as they held each other. Mom's beaming expression said more than words ever could. It was the last family photo we took before my parents were murdered.

"Abigail, are you done with your bags? Dinner's ready."

I sighed. "Yes, Aunt Annie. I'll be right there."

I trailed my fingers across my dad's image. I appeared so small next to him...

My oldest sister, Sarah, stood next to me, grinning. My eyes prickled with tears. It had been a long time since I'd seen that smile, her face now hollow and empty. She took after Mom, her long blond hair braided to the side.

Deb stood next to Mom. Her hazel eyes beamed with joy, much like mine.

Our bronzed skin, a wonderful mix of their love.

Such a beautiful picture.

My chest tightened as I put it inside the backpack. I had no option other than to enter a New World Government facility tomorrow. Turning eighteen came with that obligation, but that didn't mean I'd forget what they did to us. How they destroyed my family.

Blood rushed into my ears, and my heartbeat quickened at the thought of getting closer to my goal. I would follow their rules, be an obedient citizen, and then have my vengeance. They wouldn't see it coming.

Deb stepped inside and leaned against the doorframe. "How's it going, sis?"

"It's going..." I put the backpack on the floor and sat on the bed.

Deb was twenty-four and had gone through the process already. She was a PE teacher, as was her boyfriend, Connor. In the facilities, the government assigned each citizen a job and trained them for three years, but that was not the only thing that happened there.

I clenched my teeth at the thought of what they'd do to me once inside. All residents got their eggs and sperm extracted. Females were subjected to tubal ligation, while males had a vasectomy.

Since my early years, I'd dreamed about having my own family, a partner to come home to, children to cherish and raise. But that dream was gone. The NWG would soon take it all away from me.

This was all part of the Population Control Initiative that was implemented seven years ago with the NWG regime. Everything the government obtained from these procedures became their property and was stored in the Reproductive and Genetic Investigation Center in Electi. An in vitro pregnancy was an option if you wanted a kid. Every family could have one child only. If the NWG granted their approval, that is.

After graduation, everyone was relocated where needed. Deb was an exception, as she got to stay with us. Sarah was never the same after what happened to my parents and needed constant care. Uncle Scott had friends in high places and got Deb a special permit to work part time and help care for Sarah while he and our aunt worked.

Deb sat opposite me on her bed and played with her silver bracelet, a gift my parents had given her on her sixteenth birthday. It was lovely with a golden heart in the middle.

"A family heirloom passed on from generation to generation," Mom had said.

Deb took it off and held it out. "Take it."

"What do you mean? That's... No, Deb. Keep it. She gave it to you."

She grabbed my hand and clasped the bracelet around my wrist. Her eyes sparkled, and she smiled slightly. "I want you to have it."

I touched the golden heart and closed my eyes. Mom's beaming face came to mind as my throat tightened.

When my parents died seven years ago, Deb and I were left alone to cope with their deaths.

Sarah, after witnessing our parents' murder, was a shell of her old self, receiving psychiatric care from the government, regular visits at home, and medications to keep her sane.

Aunt Annie and Uncle Scott took us into their home, but other than his sharing my father's blood, it never felt like a true family.

Sometimes I'd catch him watching us, his eyes glossy, a hint of a smile on his face. But just as fast, his smile would waver, and his usual disregard for us would take its place.

As for Aunt Annie, her face was always tight, her posture rigid, and her tone stern toward us. No love, no sympathy.

From time to time, Uncle Scott's jaw would tighten at my aunt's berating comments, and I'd hear them arguing afterward. I couldn't grasp it, but sometimes, even for a second, his softened features and comforting gaze reminded me of his younger brother's expressions. Of his loyalty and love.

How I missed Father.

They traveled by train to Electi daily, part of the few Promissa residents selected to work behind their walls. She was a nurse to the elite, and he, a lieutenant assigned to train elite soldiers.

"Abigail and Deborah Davis! Come right this minute, or the food will get cold. It's less than two hours from lights out."

Deb sighed. "She never has dinner with us. I can't even remember the last time she cooked. I guess she's excited about your advancement."

I rubbed the back of my neck as I stood. "Let's just go. She'll have a fit if we're not there, and I don't want to deal with her right now."

We sat to eat spaghetti and meatballs. Everything was systematized, and every morning rations were distributed based on each citizen's job and performance. We got more than other residents, who got the bare minimum, just enough to sustain themselves.

My parents shielded me from most of the injustice, but after their death, Deb showed me the real face of our beloved New World Government and the man behind it all—Minister Jordan Niles.

Many rebelled against the regime at first, but those who did were either imprisoned or killed. After a couple of months of the NWG shutting down all insurgent activity, fear took hold of Promissa's citizens, and no one dared oppose him or his policies.

We dined in silence, just the three of us. Uncle Scott mostly arrived late at night and had dinner alone, while Sarah ate in her room.

For half an hour, I had to listen to my aunt tell me how grateful I should be for the opportunity the government was about to give me. My insides twisted at how she defended them. To admire them as if they were our saviors. It was just crazy.

Deb and I cleaned up after dinner while we still had water. Everything in Promissa was regulated—utilities, food, the freedom to roam around the city. I was convinced they never dealt with this in Electi, the fortified city to the east.

My aunt loved working for them. She longed to one day be accepted into their society. Even though the government assured us that citizens could go up the system depending on their performance and dedication to their pledge, I suspected we would never reach their level. They'd never see us as equals.

Elites came from afar and settled in our city, creating their own little world. They seized control of our land, its resources, and everything we built, making it their own.

Did she honestly believe they'd ever see her as an equal? We were nothing to them, just pawns to use as needed.

Before going to bed, I went to Sarah's room to say my goodbyes. I walked in as she was finishing her meal. If you timed it correctly, you might be able to have a little talk with her while the medicines wore off. Otherwise, it was like talking to a zombie. No emotions. No presence.

She patted the bed. "Hello, Abi. How are you doing?"

I sat beside her. "Good. I...I came to say my final goodbyes. I'll be heading to the facility tomorrow. Uncle got me into the advanced group. He wants me to work for Electi since my teachers said I showed promise."

"You're turning eighteen already?" She clasped my hands tight, and her expression darkened. "Don't go. Don't let them take you away like they did my baby. I'll never see you again if they do. Please. Stay."

I jerked back and stiffened at the urgency behind her words. Again, talking about her "baby."

Seven months—that's how long it took for her to be stable enough to be discharged from the hospital. Post-traumatic stress disorder. That was her diagnosis. A couple of months after my parents' murder, she convinced herself she'd had a baby and the NWG took it. But it never happened. The doctors explained it was a scenario she'd created in her mind after losing our parents. That's the reason she was medicated, to help her deal with these hallucinations. They said we needed to be careful not to encourage them.

I squeezed her hands. "Sarah, there's no baby. It's just us."

She shook her head violently and held my face. "No, Abi, you need to believe me. Please." Tears fell freely down her pale face. Her lips trembled. "How can I make you understand? They took everything away from me! Please don't let them take you too!"

A heaviness settled in my chest as I saw truth in her words for a moment. Could it be possible? Could the baby be real?

A sound at the door warned me someone was listening in just as I was about to reply.

My aunt watched us with a grimace.

"If you've already said your goodbyes to your sister, go get some sleep. The officials will be here to get you by dawn." Her tone was stern, her features pinched.

"Can you give us a minute, please?" I needed more time with her. I just wanted to reassure her everything would be fine. That I would not let them change me. That I would somehow avenge our parents. Avenge her.

My aunt shook her head. "No. It's time for Sarah's medicines, and, clearly, your presence makes her anxious." She walked into the room, holding a syringe.

I stood stiffly near Sarah's bed, my teeth clenched. I had no idea what was wrong with Aunt, but she was always this way. Blaming us for Sarah's panic attacks. Keeping us away from her.

I kissed my sister on the cheek. "Everything's going to be fine. I'll be back in no time."

She gripped my shoulders with trembling fingers and began to sob. "No! Don't leave! I can't lose you too!"

My aunt grabbed her arms and pulled her away from me. "See what you do? Go! Now!"

My heart sank for Sarah. I hadn't seen her this distraught in a long time.

I backed away and paused at the door, wincing as Aunt Annie injected her. Sarah's cries followed me down the corridor until everything fell silent.

When I arrived in our room, Deb was getting ready for bed. We talked about the future we dreamed of until we fell asleep. One without the regime.

"Abi, wake up. You need to go now." Deb shook me hard.

I opened my eyes at the urgency in her voice. "Deb? What the hell?"

"Come on. They'll be here soon. Please hurry."

I rubbed my face and sat up. It was pitch black, but I could make out Deb putting stuff in my backpack.

"We knew they would come. There's nothing we can do about it."

She shook her head. "I won't allow them to take you." She handed me the backpack and pulled me from the bed. "You need to leave. Now."

I tried to open the bag, but she grabbed my hand.

"There's no time for that. I added enough to last you a couple of weeks. That should give us enough time to get you out. I'm sorry I can't go with you, but it's the only way."

My heart thundered in my ears. "Are you crazy? I can't go to the streets." I bit my lip. "What the hell am I going to do out there without you?"

Her eyes misted. "Oh, Abi... I know." Her voice thickened. "If I had any other choice, I'd take it, but I don't."

I gripped her fingers. "But if they find out you helped me, they'll arrest you. You know what happened to Christina and Jimmy." Nausea churned in my gut. Losing him, my best friend, had been hard. I couldn't lose Deb too. "I can't let that happen."

She touched my cheek. "That's for me to deal with, not you. I'm willing to sacrifice everything for your freedom. If you go to the facilities, they'll arrest me anyway when I try to break you out."

"Why did you wait until now to tell me this?"

"I couldn't risk telling anyone before today, not even Sarah." She glanced around as if expecting someone to leap out of the shadows.

"Okay. Okay. Let me get this straight." My hands shook. "You just want me to parade through the front door and never come back?" I frowned. "This is insane."

She crossed her arms. "Insanity is for you to go willingly to the facility." She leaned toward me and stared into my eyes. "I'm not allowing that. Ever. You may be too young to remember, but before this said 'reform,' we had complete control of our lives and bodies. No matter what situation the world was in, it should never have come to this. And, yes, I want you to go out the back door and find somewhere to hide. Abandoned buildings around the city may work. Be careful who you trust. In a week or so, my people will find you. Don't approach them until you trust they're the real thing."

Her gaze darted around. "There's a code we use to prove you're one of us. It's in my journal. Memorize it." She patted the backpack. "Read the journal. Guard it. I'm taking a big risk by giving it to you, but you need to learn about us and what we're doing. There's a letter inside the journal. Give it to my people. It's your ticket out."

I threw up my arms. "What people? Who are you?" Deb was only a teacher as far as I knew, but from what she was telling me, there was a lot more about her I didn't know.

"I'm part of the council of the People's Revolutionary Front, a group that lives outside the system. We're trying to get as many people out as we can, people who oppose the regime. This is where my friends will take you."

I widened my eyes. "This...is a lot to take in." I raked a hand through my hair.

Deb was like a mother to me and wouldn't do this unless it was the only way. I had to trust her and her community. Going out there alone was terrifying, but I choked down my fear.

"Okay, tell me what to do."

She handed me clothes and a flashlight. "Put this on, and try to be as quiet as possible."

I changed quickly into black cargo pants. In its pockets, I found a pocketknife and pepper spray. I pulled on the black tank top, hoodie, and combat boots, then put my hair up in a ponytail.

Deb opened the door, wincing as it creaked.

Sarah's door was closed, as was our aunt and uncle's bedroom. We tiptoed through the house to the back door. We were privileged to have a house of our own, as most people lived in apartment buildings.

Deb hugged me tightly. "I'm sorry I can't go with you now, but I need to get Sarah out too. Don't try to return. If something goes wrong, hide. Survive. I know you'll find a way. You're a Davis, after all."

She kissed my cheek, then helped me put the backpack on. "I love you. Now go and don't look back. We'll see each other soon. Trust me." She closed the door behind me.

And just like that, I was alone.

Chapter 2

Abi

May 2211

"January 2203: There's no greater feeling than being in Connor's arms while watching the stars. But as good as it feels to me, a sense of dread is growing among our group. So much talk of change all over the internet about a new regime has us worried. Will we be able to have moments like this in the future?" (Deborah Davis's journal)

After a couple of months, when no one came to get me, I accepted my gruesome reality. I was stuck on the outskirts, inside enemy lines, with nowhere to go and no one to trust.

The first months after my escape were hard, but I learned to survive. Deb's journal kept me going. I read it constantly and learned about how it all happened.

The government began by attacking education at its core, closing all schools, and creating a new curriculum with a government-approved homeschool system. Social gatherings were outlawed as well as leisure activities. The government-approved channel was the only source of news available since computers, cell phones, and any kind of technology were outlawed and access to the web restricted.

It was surprising how much you could do by instilling fear. The policies of Minister Niles kept people in line. Anyone who disobeyed or talked against the NWG was beaten and taken in, never to be seen again.

The threat of it and the mystery of what happened once they had you in custody brought terror to everyone. And this was the outcome. A fractured society with a privileged class, while true citizens struggled to survive. My skin crawled from the injustice of it all.

As for me, I believed they were using us. But for what purpose? That was one of the things I wanted to know, especially after losing Jimmy four years ago.

His image popped into my mind as he kissed me tenderly. His dirty-blond hair, his deep-blue eyes, almost as if you were peeking into the heavens. I could still feel the warmth of his embrace and smell the woodsy aroma of his hair.

Our friendship had changed into something more, but then his sister and he tried to escape and were taken by the government.

Why didn't he tell me about it? Why didn't he say goodbye?

My body protested each move, and even waking up was a struggle. It was only a matter of time till I was caught. Would I be taken to the same place they took him?

Darkness seeped into my soul, drowning me slowly. Death would be a welcome reprieve.

"Hey, do you want some more?" Paul's voice interrupted my thoughts as he offered me a piece of beef jerky.

I took it. "Sure. Thanks."

He nodded and ate his ration.

Paul and I found each other a month ago by chance and helped each other ever since. He was already settled in this huge storage room when I arrived, so I stayed on a small office space across the floor. We both enjoyed our privacy but always made time to eat together and chat.

A year ago, his father was arrested for distributing anti-government propaganda. Paul only had him, and after his father's arrest, he decided to flee. He was just fifteen when he started searching for the People's Revolutionary Front, the same rebel group I was waiting for.

He claimed there was talk about the rebels in Promissa and that residents were searching for them. Some were looking to escape, others to provide information to the government and get more resources.

"How was your day?" Paul asked.

"Nothing new. I tried to get some water from that apartment complex two blocks west, but I had to get back. Too many patrols in the area. And you?"

Paul rested sideways on the floor, still munching on his jerky. "I followed a couple of escapees like us. They went into the abandoned shopping street to the southeast." His brown eyes settled on me. "I was thinking we should join them. The more of us, the better."

My heart skipped a beat at his news.

He sat straight and gripped my hand. His eyes were bright. "Don't you think it's time to act? If we get together and find a good hiding spot, maybe we could do something about all this. Even if it's small, anything's better than just sitting in wait."

I let go of his hand and got up, then paced back and forth.

Could this work? Perhaps in numbers we could find a way out, some way to evade the patrols and get out of the city. I still hadn't told Paul about my sister, about what I knew. True, the journal didn't give a location, but it did say they were deep in the forest. If we could get enough rations and water for the journey and more people to guard our way out, maybe we could make it.

"Stay here. I have something to show you."

I went back to get my stuff. I'd show him the journal, the proof that the PRF existed. It was time to act.

Something thudded against the door from Paul's side of the floor, followed by a huge smash that echoed all around me. I jumped. Officers on patrol. I dashed to my room and backed up against the wall.

Paul. Fuck.

"What have we got here?" The man gave a mocking chuckle.

I peered back through the doorway. Two patrol officers in NWG uniforms approached him. Their menacing grins turned my legs to lead.

"Please. I beg you. I'll go without a fight." Paul's voice shook.

One of them squatted close to him. "Oh, but that takes away all the fun. Come on! Fight us!"

He reached out, but Paul crawled back. Paul was smart but not much of a fighter. His frame was thin and weak, and he appeared much younger than his sixteen years.

"No. Please." Paul tried to flee, but the guard caught him by the hair.

Paul cried out, arching his back.

In one swift move, the officer punched him in the nose. A hollow cry filled the room. Blood splattered all over Paul's face and clothes.

The man snickered and pulled out his baton. "Did you wet yourself, boy?"

I winced as a solid blow connected to Paul's stomach.

My blood froze at the horrifying scream, and I clapped my hands against my ears.

"Come on! Scream for us!" He slammed the baton against Paul's jaw.

Crack!

Paul's head snapped back, and blood gushed from his mouth. "Please." He gurgled and doubled over as the officer continued beating him mercilessly.

I shook uncontrollably, locked in place, as his pleas for mercy fell silent.

"Hey, maybe you should stop," the second officer said.

"Is that all you've got?" The guard spat on Paul's face. "You fucking escapees. Do you think you can run from us?" He snarled and choked Paul, then drew his fist back.

"I said stop!" His partner grabbed his arm in mid-strike. "You're going to kill him!"

"And what's the problem with that? Isn't it better to kill them right away? Why do they even want them alive?"

"I'm not about to question General Lavigne's orders!"

The officer wrenched his arm free and stepped back. "Fuck. There's blood all over my uniform. White's a pain to clean up. Get him up!"

The second guard approached Paul, who was covered in blood. "Are you okay?" He leaned in to assist him.

Paul's leg hung limp as he gripped the officer's arm for support. He grunted and flinched as the man scooped him up. His black hair was soaked with blood, and his face was a wreck. His eyes were so swollen you couldn't see their brown irises, and his jaw rested at an unnatural angle.

"We need to process him like the others," the officer holding him said. "Let's call it a day."

After a few moments, everything grew quiet, and I stepped out with my rucksack. I paused midstride as I took in the scene before me.

A pool of blood drenched the floor. At the sight, I puked. Its stink, combined with urine, permeated the room.

I swallowed hard, my throat tight.

How could they do this? Where were they taking him?

We hadn't known each other for long, but his heart was good. His intentions true.

This had to stop. We were nothing but numbers to them. Pawns for whatever they had in mind.

I crouched and, choking down a sob, took Paul's blue cap. Rummaging through his rucksack, I found his dagger and stashed it in my pocket. It was a hunting knife. His father used to hunt before the regime, and after he was arrested, Paul took it with him.

My chest constricted at the unfairness of it all, and I vowed to find him. Someday I'd get him out.

It was night by the time I made my way out through an alleyway. Except for the typical pattering of feet and clattering of trash cans, everything was quiet. Rats, dogs, and humans. Hunger drove us.

My supplies were running low, so I headed south to where Paul told me he'd seen the escapees. Streetlamps flashed on and off as I walked through an old neighborhood. Voices rang out from decrepit dwellings, while other buildings stood shuttered with barred windows and doorways. I jolted to the left as patterned footsteps alerted me to the presence of a small patrol. Maybe two blocks away.

I glanced left and right and dashed over to an old shed. A rusty padlock held the door shut. I slammed my shoulder against it with all my might—once, twice. It shattered, and I walked in, closing the old wooden door behind me. The area was crammed with gardening tools and equipment. I spun around and crawled into a corner behind a bag of leaves.

"I'm sure this is where the sound came from."

They were here.

I strained to keep my breathing under control. As I drew Paul's knife, my heart pounded against my chest, and my hands trembled.

"This lock's broken."

I held my breath as the door clattered open. Out of the corner of my eye, I saw the guard shifting things around, gun in hand. Sweat beaded at the back of my neck as his footsteps approached. A loud crash outside made me jump, and he twisted around.

"What the hell was that?"

Gunshots boomed.

"There. Down that alley. Come on!" someone yelled from the street.

"I'm right behind you!" The officer darted out of the shed.

My adrenaline came crashing down. My body shook.

I banged my head against a shelf.

Fuck, that hurt.

I turned on my flashlight and moved stuff around. There had to be something hidden.

The government sometimes cut down the number of resources to be distributed, and many prepared for this by storing goods.

Salted dried beef and raisins. That would do.

"Hey. Are you okay?"

I slashed at the space behind me. The woman caught my arm. My dagger and flashlight crashed to the ground as she shoved my face to the wall and locked my arm behind me.

"Let me go!" I thrashed.

"Calm down. If you keep screaming, they'll find us," the man said.

I paused. Who were these people?

"We're here to help," the woman whispered close to my ear.

A scraping sound caught my attention.

"If I give this back, will you hear us out?" His voice was calm, smooth.

I could hardly make out his profile as he offered me Paul's dagger. I swallowed hard and nodded.

The woman let go, and I took the dagger.

I scurried to a corner, holding it in front of me.

They both stepped back.

The flashlight illuminated part of the shed. I could make out a woman much taller than me and stronger. Her face was gentle, auburn tresses hanging at her waist.

As for the guy, he was tall with a slim frame and dark skin. He adjusted his glasses and smirked. "I like her! She's got spunk."

"Who the fuck are you?" I tensed every muscle as I kept my stance.

The woman pursed her lips. "We'd feel much better if you put that blade down. We saved your ass. A thank-you would be perfect."

I frowned. "What do you mean?"

"I'm Jacob. This is Bonnie. We were searching for food when you broke into this shed. You were loud as hell. I kicked a trash can to distract them. We know this part of town, so we led them away and ran back."

They were the ones who distracted the patrol. I lowered my hands slowly, and they relaxed.

"You're runaways?"

"We wouldn't be helping you otherwise. Now, you have our names. How about yours?" Bonnie lifted an eyebrow.

Could they be the ones Paul saw? I narrowed my eyes. *Should I trust them?*

My instincts urged me to run, but I was alone, and my need to survive another day won overall. I still had my dagger. At the first sign something was off, I would run.

"Abi."

She nodded, picking up the flashlight. "Nice to meet you, Abi. Now, how about getting out of here and going somewhere safe?"

I stepped back.

Jacob got close and raised his hoodie. "If we wanted to hurt you, we would've done it already." His gaze never left mine. In his waistband was a sheathed blade. "We want to help you. Will you trust us?"

I stowed my knife and put my hands in my pockets.

Jacob's mouth twisted into a wry grin. "Come on."

We walked a block east, Jacob leading the way. An abandoned grocery store lay before us. The glass windows were shattered, the racks empty. Trash covered the floor. Jacob looked around before removing an old wooden panel on the floor.

I couldn't believe my eyes as he uncovered a dark stairway. An abandoned subway station. I thought the tunnels were all sealed by debris after the war. The government had created a solar-powered train system because of it.

Bonnie used her flashlight to guide us down the tunnel. There were crumbled walls and garbage everywhere. Graffiti decorated the walls with mocking depictions of Minister Niles and phrases like "NWG sucks," "Fuck the regime," and "Free Promissa."

"Welcome to our home." Jacob extended his arms. "It's not much, but it's safe."

Flattened cardboard crates were scattered throughout the area. The air was stale, but at least it was bearable.

Bonnie dumped her stuff out of her backpack and onto the ground. Canned food, some beef jerkies...

"Your home?" I asked.

"Bonnie found this place a few months ago."

Noises echoed down the dark tunnel.

I stiffened. "Who else lives down here?"

"There are five other runaways. We mostly keep to ourselves, but we keep an eye out for one another. Anyone who sees or hears a patrol whistles to alert the others. But it's never happened." Jacob took a canteen of water from his rucksack.

At the sight, I licked my chapped lips.

He handed it to me while cocking his head. "Take this. I've got more."

I swallowed and coughed. "Where?" I managed to say between swigs.

"When people go to work, we go into their houses and fill our bottles." Jacob drank from his canteen before putting it away.

"But aren't you afraid of being seen?"

He shrugged. "I'm terrified of dying all the time, but it won't stop me from living. I won't allow myself to be bullied."

I furrowed my brow as he fixed his piercing gaze on me. Something stirred within me. A sudden awareness of the man in front of me caught me off guard and turned my skin to fire.

Chapter 3
Abi

June 2211

"*March 2203: The implementation of laws to exert control over resources started without people having a say in it. Each day more resistance grows among the young. Four new people joined us tonight at our usual spot in the forest north of the city. I got a feeling this meeting would be important, as someone among the new faces would make everything more real. I hope he's here to help us, not to turn us in.*" *(Deborah Davis's journal)*

"Again!" Bonnie said.

Jacob offered his hand to help me. He pulled me up, his hand lingering on my arm after I flinched. "Are you good?"

"Yeah, just a little tired." Bullshit. My entire body ached, but I wouldn't give up.

He lifted an eyebrow and released my arm, leaving a tingling sensation on my skin.

I stretched. The weight from hours of training seemed as if a train had run over me and I miraculously survived.

"Maybe we should stop for the day," Jacob said.

Bonnie folded her arms across her chest. "We've been training for weeks, and she still needs to improve."

"Let her decide."

I shrugged. "Let's try it again."

I convinced Bonnie a couple of weeks ago to show me how to defend myself.

Jacob was my attacker in all my drills and won every single time. He didn't like playing the bad guy, but it had to be him. He was much taller and stronger than me.

I kept trying even though my body was starting to bruise.

Jacob stepped behind me. His hold was so strong I couldn't move an inch. He pressed his lips to my ear. "Remember the technique we talked about yesterday. Use your body."

Goosebumps rose on the nape of my neck, his deep voice distracting me. I focused, trying to remember everything they'd taught me. Keeping my elbow low, I tried to hit his abdomen, but he gripped me tighter. He was crushing me.

I shifted my weight toward the front, causing him to loosen his grip, and tried the low elbow strike again. This time it connected. I twisted and used a knee strike, hitting his groin. Jacob hollered and fell to his knees.

My heart skipped a beat, and I covered my mouth. I couldn't believe it. I'd actually done it!

Bonnie applauded as Jacob doubled over in pain. She crashed into me, and we jumped and hooted, celebrating my victory.

"I'm so proud! I knew you could do it!" Bonnie said.

We continued talking excitedly.

A groan warned us of Jacob's state.

I held my hand out. "Oh, I'm sorry!"

He waved me away. "Don't worry about my wounded ego. Go celebrate." His voice was low.

"Did I hurt you?"

While holding his groin, he looked up at me, his eyes glazed over.

I couldn't keep myself from laughing.

Bonnie followed suit. The moment was priceless.

Later that day, as Jacob scouted the tunnel, Bonnie and I sat by the fire.

"What's going on between you two?"

I stiffened. "I don't know what you're talking about."

She huffed. "Oh please. Don't try to hide it. You're always going around each other. Whispering in each other's ears. Your glances and smiles are nauseating. You need to get over it and tell each other how you feel, or I will."

I widened my eyes. Was it that obvious? "I thought you two were—"

"Hold it right there, my friend. Don't even finish that thought. First, he's like a brother to me. Second, I don't even like boys. So...what are you gonna do about it?"

I dipped my chin and rubbed my nape. "Nothing. I'm not going to throw myself at him. I don't even know if he's into me."

"Oh, but he is. If I were you, I'd tell him and enjoy life a little. It's a blessing to find happiness in this hellhole. I'd take it in a heartbeat."

"I don't know."

"Hey. What are you up to?" Jacob sat next to me. He leaned back, his leg grazing mine.

"Oh, just talking about girl stuff. You wouldn't understand." Bonnie stood. "I'm off to bed. You two can keep watch."

I sat still, trying to think of something to say.

"How's everyone?" I asked.

"They're worried about the food going scarce. We're going to have to go on food runs more often. Some of them are weakening from hunger."

I grimaced at the thought. They were kids, no older than fifteen. This wasn't the kind of life they deserved.

His fingers brushed my back, and a flush of warmth spread throughout my body. "Come here and relax. There's nothing we can do to fix that tonight. We might as well enjoy the warmth of the fire and talk about other things."

I leaned back, and we stared into nothingness. The fire our only light.

"Sometimes I like to think I'm outside in the forest, free. It helps me sleep better, thinking everything's just a bad dream."

My chest lightened at his words. So much hope amid all this darkness.

He took my hand, and our fingers entwined. My pulse quickened.

"Abi?" His deep voice slid through me like a caress.

He touched a stray strand of my hair and gently laid his palm on the back of my neck. His stare swept over me, stopping on my lips before returning to my eyes.

"You're beautiful." He skimmed his thumb slowly down the center of my collarbone, and I closed my eyes to savor the sensation.

His lips met mine. Soft. Gentle. It was a sweet kiss, our lips lingering. Exploring.

My heart thumped against my chest, and the need to have him closer grew stronger. I instinctively put my hand on his back and drew him to me. The kiss became desperate as his body pressed against mine.

He tasted like honey, each stroke of his tongue sweeter than the last. It was addictive, and I couldn't get enough of it.

He held his palm against my cheek and pulled his lips away from mine. "I'm sorry."

"Don't be." He was so handsome, intelligent, loyal, and dedicated. It was foolish to deny it. I'd fallen for him, and like Bonnie said, finding someone who made you feel this way in all this chaos was a gift. One I was going to take head on. "I really like you, Jacob. It was amazing."

A fire rekindled in my heart as we leaned back and relaxed into each other. Maybe life was worth living after all.

September 2211

Four months had passed already since I moved in with Bonnie and Jacob. We came down from our weekly food run and went directly to Bonnie.

"Hey. How are you feeling? We didn't find much." I gave her my backpack.

"How am I? Useless as always." She huffed as she divided the goods.

Lately, Bonnie wasn't going out at all, not strong enough to hold herself upright for long periods of time. On our last run, she fainted on the way back, and Jacob had to carry her. Since then, she'd been getting worse. She wouldn't eat unless we made her and couldn't keep the food down. We didn't know what was wrong.

I reached for her shoulder. "Don't say that."

She raised her head. "It's the truth. I'm a burden for both of you." She dipped her head and finished sorting our food, then went to sleep.

Jacob touched my shoulder. "Let her be. It must be difficult for her, but she'll be fine."

I leaned into his touch. "I just wish we could do more."

"I know." He grabbed my hand. "C'mon."

I followed him to our space on the other side of the tunnel. He pushed the covering to the side, and we entered. A blanket lay in the middle, and a lantern sat in a corner. He lit it and placed our rations on top of a small box we used as a table.

He turned toward me and brushed my cheek with the back of his hand. He put his arms around me, hugging me tight, then peppered kisses from my mouth down to my neck.

I gasped. An ache flooded my body all the way to my core.

"Sometimes I dream of taking you on a date. A real one." His deep voice promised so much.

I found my own voice after a moment. "This is perfect."

He stepped back and held his hand out. "Let's eat some gourmet jerkies and nuts. It's the specialty of the house."

I giggled, accepted his outstretched hand, and sat with him on the floor.

With each passing day, we'd grown closer and had gotten to know each other.

He told me about his father, Abraham Jackson. He used to be a history professor at the university before it all changed. He continued teaching at the facilities but had grown depressed, no longer able to teach real history, only that of the magnanimous New World Government and how they saved Promissa from a dark and uncertain future. A strategy used to brainwash citizens into believing they were our protectors. After years of learning this shit, most kids fell willingly into the hands of their "saviors."

Jacob couldn't take it anymore, so one night he took his father's knife, the one he kept for protection, and left their apartment to search for ways to fight the government. To reclaim the city and return his father to his previous self.

I thought about the past battles and everything that had been stolen away.

"You seem lost." His dark eyes fixed upon me as he pushed up his glasses.

My breath caught. He was so attractive and full of life, ready to take on anything.

I touched Deb's bracelet. "Just thinking about all we've lost. How we came to this..."

He nodded.

"I get that resources were low, but our ancestors fixed that. They even created innovative technologies and policies to protect what was left. New ways to get resources. What I don't get is why. Why did the wars take place? There was no reason to fight."

Jacob shook his head. "Power. Power destroys everything. Countries fought for control over places rich with technology and resources. These wars went on for decades, moving from one place to the next. That's how the NWG took control of Promissa and some other cities, and with the money of the elite, they were unbeatable. Now we're left with this."

I lowered my gaze. "The regime..."

The NWG. Those assholes. They took our city and made it their own.

Promissa was immense, with communities scattered throughout the area. Now it was bordered by government facilities, most for education and training, others for medical purposes, military exercise, food, and energy development.

Jacob clenched his jaw. "We need to get our city back. I'm sure we have a chance if we remain together and recruit."

I gripped his hand. "We'll find a way to get it back."

There was a fire in Jacob that pulled me to him. A magnetism I couldn't fight. He was a natural leader.

He squeezed my hand. "You never say anything about your past."

His warmth soothed me, and I interlaced my fingers with his.

"I haven't been completely honest with you." I hesitated. It was now or never. "My sister, the one who helped me escape. She's the leader of a group. I waited for them to find me, but they never did. Then we met." I looked into his eyes. "Perhaps we can escape together, make our way through the forest, and find them. They have a base hidden in the mountains."

He clutched my hand tighter, his eager eyes holding me. "Is this for real? Are they the rebel group people keep talking about?"

I nodded. "As real as can be. I'm just too scared to go alone. But if I had you two..."

He shifted closer. "You know you have us. We'll make it out of here. I promise."

There was a brief pause. Suddenly, the space between us became too small. Our breaths mixed, and warmth built between us. I stroked his thigh, traveling up to his waist.

He leaned into me, his fingers running through my hair. "I'm so glad we found you."

I trembled as he closed the gap between us and kissed me. We'd kissed before, but this was different. It was feverish, intense. He broke the kiss and trailed a finger down my neck, moving it ever so slowly to my cleavage while keeping his eyes on me.

I anchored my fingers through his belt and pulled him close, arching my back as he pushed his lips against my breastbone. His smoldering mouth burned wherever it touched. Tasting. Nipping.

He moved his hand up my thigh and reached my core. He rubbed gently against it, and I gasped at the sensation, pressing myself to him. My core throbbed, flooding with pleasure, pleading for more.

We were both out of breath, our foreheads brushing.

"I don't know if I'll be able to stop if we go on." His gaze explored me. Dark. Penetrating.

I gripped his shirt, drawing him close. "I want this, Jacob. I want you." I pulled him in and kissed him with all the passion I'd been holding for the past few months.

He softly pushed me down, pressing his body against me. He linked his fingers with mine and pinned my hands to the ground, trailing kisses from my neck to my mouth. "I love you, Abi."

My heart swelled at his words, and every corner of my body ignited. I was so lucky. "I love you too."

We let everything go. All our fears. All our worries. And we basked in each other.

Our limbs entwined, our mouths explored every inch of each other until our bodies became one.

It was raw. Intense.

And it was beautiful.

The first time for both of us.

When it was over, we held each other. And we just stayed there. Dreaming of our future.

Another failed food run. For the last two weeks, we'd been rummaging around the neighborhood without luck. We even entered another area in our desperate search but still had nothing to show for it.

Once we were back underground, my stomach protested. My arms hurt, my legs were heavy, and I was cold. So cold...

Jacob hugged me, and I leaned into him. He was doing everything he could to keep the three of us alive, but we were losing the battle.

Bonnie's condition deteriorated by the day, so we couldn't risk venturing into the forest in search of the rebels. She didn't talk much and wore a blank expression on her face. Sometimes we'd catch her walking aimlessly and would guide her back. She was lost to us.

Jacob helped Bonnie settle for the night.

He took my hand. "Let's go to sleep. We need to save our energy. Tomorrow we'll search the western sector."

Even though my entire body hurt, sleep continued to elude me night after night.

"What's going on in that head of yours?" He spooned me and peppered kisses to my neck.

I closed my eyes. "I'm worried. We can't keep up like this. Bonnie's weak, and we're starving."

"I know. It feels as if we've already lost her." His hand went to my side.

As he stroked my ribcage, I grimaced.

"You never say anything, but I know you're in pain. I worry about you. You're not sleeping, and you've lost more weight."

I twisted into him and touched his cheek. His eyes were sunken and heavy. He was eating even less than we were, but he never complained.

"I'm all right."

He pulled me to his chest. "Have you noticed the streets lately? They're suspiciously empty. Don't you think it's odd?"

A chill ran through me. "I've noticed." Two whole days without seeing an officer. Something was off.

"I told the others to keep watch. Let's hope it's nothing and try to get some sleep."

I nodded, and he kissed me softly.

A high-pitched sound echoed around us.

A whistle! The signal!

For a moment, I couldn't move, my body glued to the ground.

Someone shook me violently, and I heard my name.

"Abi. Come on. We need to move."

I bolted up and got my stuff ready.

Jacob turned in a circle, his gaze darting around the tunnel. "Where's Bonnie?"

Her space was empty.

Fuck, this was the worst moment to lose her. We moved down the tunnel and stopped in place. Bonnie was maybe twenty feet from us.

I covered my mouth as Jacob pulled me behind a crumbled wall. We peered from the side.

"Hey, look what I found here."

Bonnie's shrill scream boomed through the tunnel as a man dragged her to a corner.

Two other patrol officers tied up the rest of the runaways.

"Come here, guys. I bet we can have some fun with this one."

"No." Her cries were heartbreaking.

Coldness spread through my body down to my feet.

Jacob pulled me back, face-to-face. Nostrils flaring, he drew his dagger and clenched it. "I'm going to get her. Stay here."

I shook my head, gripping his arms. "No. Please don't go. They'll kill you."

He hugged me and kissed my temple. "I'll make it back. I promise. Do you have your knife?"

I nodded and took it out of my pocket. A shudder ran through my limbs as a stone-cold fear settled deep inside. He closed his eyes as I caressed his cheek, taking in all of him.

He squeezed my hand gently. "Stay here no matter what happens. I love you."

I pressed a kiss to his lips. "Come back to me."

My whole body trembled as he crept toward the guards, using the shadows as his allies. When he was close enough, he attacked the officer who held Bonnie, aiming for the back of his neck.

Bonnie's eyes widened. In a split second, the officer moved, and the blade only grazed him.

"You fucking bastard!" His shout alerted the other two.

Jacob slashed at the officer's stomach. Blood seeped through his uniform as a boom rang out. I covered my mouth to muffle my scream.

"Jacob!" Bonnie yelled, scurrying toward him.

I stumbled back, clamping my hand to my mouth as a silent cry left me.

No, no. This couldn't be happening. The entire world fell around me as Jacob collapsed to his knees, his shirt drenched in blood.

A sharp pain hit my chest as if I'd been physically attacked. I couldn't move.

His gaze flew to mine, eyes welled up with tears. He looked at Bonnie, gurgling as he attempted to speak. Blood streamed down his chin.

As Bonnie thrashed behind him, the injured officer pointed his weapon at Jacob's head. "You thought you could take me down." He touched his belly. "This is nothing."

Crying, Bonnie tried to reach Jacob, but another guard grabbed her.

The wounded officer chuckled. "Is this your friend, princess?" He pushed his gun against Jacob's temple. "Say goodbye."

Jacob's bulging dark eyes met mine as a piercing boom rippled down the tunnel.

I covered my ears and crumpled to the ground. I clawed at my chest, nails scratching my skin.

Time seemed to stand still as Jacob's body jerked sideways. Blood oozed from the side of his skull, and his limp body slowly hit the ground. Black spots covered my eyes, and my vision blurred.

He...he was gone.

I wanted to run to him, but I was numb. Blood pooled around his body.

With a sneer, the officer approached Bonnie and trailed his fingers down her cleavage. "You'll pay for what your friend did. Now, how about some fun?"

As the other officer held her, he pulled off her jeans, and the third fondled her, wetting his lips. Bonnie tried to fight them off, but they punched her and held her in place.

Bonnie... My stomach twisted, nausea hitting me as one of them flipped her over and forced himself into her while the others watched. Her gut-wrenching scream made my insides turn.

I closed my eyes tightly.

This can't be happening. This isn't real.

Her cries for help kept coming as the bound runaways begged for mercy.

I clutched at my throat, trying not to retch as they tore her clothing, laughing as they took turns to break her. I desperately wanted to help her, to beat them off, but my body wouldn't cooperate. The light from her eyes faded as they continued, her cries muffled by their assault. After a while, the only sound I heard was their grunting echoing across the tunnel's eerie quiet.

"Fuck! Do you think she's dead?" One man pulled away from her while another felt her pulse.

He shrugged. "Well, she was fun while she lasted."

My chest burned as I bent forward and sobbed quietly.

For Bonnie. For Jacob. For our hopes and dreams.

"Leave them here. No one has to know about these two," the one who killed Jacob said.

They took their time putting themselves together.

"Come on. Let's take the others away. We hit the jackpot tonight."

An unnerving silence haunted the tunnel.

I knelt beside Jacob and hugged him tight, his blood drenching me.

"Ah!" A burning cry ripped through my soul. Every breath was suffocating. He was my everything. My strength. My light. And now he was gone. I clung to him until my tears dried up, and I kissed his temple.

An emptiness settled in my heart when I laid him down, then touched his face with the back of my hand. His skin was ice cold. I closed his eyes, and my heart crushed to pieces, his dark gaze lost to me forever.

I unbuckled the leather belt from his waistband and closed it around me, then sheathed his dagger on one side and Paul's knife on the other.

His blood-splattered glasses had fallen a few feet away, and I stuffed them into my pocket.

Bonnie's body lay to the right. My friend. My sister. Her empty eyes stared right at me.

"I'm so sorry," I choked out as I held her battered body.

Proof of the attack soiled her clothes and skin. I threw up beside her, unable to contain it any longer.

After cleaning her, I placed her next to Jacob, draped a sheet over her, and closed her eyelids. I took her thread bracelet, which she always carried, and placed it next to Deb's, promising never to forget her and the horror she endured before dying.

I shed my final tears after a silent prayer. Neither of them deserved this.

Before I left, I kissed Jacob for the last time, his cold lips so far from the warmth he gave me daily. I clenched my fists, blood pulsed in my ears, and a desire for vengeance raged in me.

I grasped their hands and made my vow.

"I will not stop until they're destroyed. I swear."

Chapter 4
Davon

August 2212

The city of Electi buzzed with activity. I stared out onto the entertainment district from my penthouse as I loosened my bow tie and unbuttoned my shirt. Laser lights blazed from the performance hall. People moved out of the district, swaying and dancing their way into the train station. Drunk, satisfied, and without a care in the world.

Matt stood by the dining table with our map, an *X* marked on each location we'd already searched.

Promissa was massive, and finding Abigail Davis seemed like an impossible task. After many failed missions, we were sent here without a return date, and eight months later, we still had nothing. Nonetheless, I promised Deb I'd find her, and I would.

My phone rang, and my father's name appeared on the screen. What on earth could he want? I'd just said my goodbyes.

"Hello."

He chuckled. "You always sound so happy to hear my voice."

I rolled my eyes. "What do you want now?"

"Come to dinner tomorrow. Bring Matt."

I looked at Matt, and his green eyes focused on me. He arched an eyebrow.

"Dad," I mouthed.

Matt muttered something and shook his head. Most likely a curse. He despised the man as much as I did, and dealing with him was the most difficult part of the operation.

"We'll be there." I hung up.

My shoes clicked on the black marble floor as I stepped closer to Matt. We'd just returned from one of my father's political parties.

"Dinner?" Matt asked as I stood next to him.

"Yes," I grumbled.

"Fuck. I don't want to see that jerk again. Wasn't tonight enough of a torture?"

"Sometimes I think he does it just to piss me off. But there's no option. By the way, is the fake checkpoint ready?"

"Jimmy handled it." Matt kept marking the *X*s.

What are we missing? What's she up to?

I pointed to the east, and Matt's eyebrows furrowed.

"We already checked the west. How about these slums south of the prison system? We're missing something, but I can't put my finger on it."

Matt hummed as he double-checked his work.

We both scanned the map for a few minutes.

He traced his fingers along the area where Promissa's shopping district stood before the war. "Wait a second. Could she...?" He smacked his palm against the table. "That's it. This must be it." He grinned at me. "The old subway system!"

Adrenaline rushed through me as I doubled over the map, holding my hair back. "How did we miss that? I bet she's been hiding there all this time."

I tapped the map just south of Promissa's industrial park. "We'll start here." From there, the subway tracks moved south and then east. "And finish here." I marked the train tracks that bordered Promissa's government center.

"With all the destruction down there, it could take months to search the tunnels. We should get started right away." Matt circled his shoulders back and tipped his head up, briefly closing his eyes. He rubbed his face and combed his blond hair back. "I'm done for the night. See you tomorrow." He walked out. His flat was one floor down.

I sank down onto my black leather sofa and gulped what was left of my drink.

Abigail Davis, where are you hiding?

Matt and I arrived at my father's palatial estate around eight o'clock. Its marble balustrades and columns resembled those of ancient Greece. My pulse rose just thinking about how Promissa citizens lived while we basked in our wealth.

When we entered the foyer, the world constricted around me. No matter how much I tried to control it, that sharp stab in my chest and the need to catch my breath caught me every single time.

Matt clasped my shoulder, and I straightened. He understood better than anyone what I was going through.

This house, once filled with love and happiness, was a mausoleum for many memories now lost.

All the moments I had with my father came back, but my steps quickly drowned each one in shadow. Every smile, every hug, every deep conversation with Dad had been shattered by his ambition to mold me into what he believed was a better man. A ruthless and unbeatable soldier. I had no love for him left in my heart after all the years of training and beatings. His presence only brought back all the faces I destroyed, the bodies I broke, the lifeless eyes of each of my victims.

The ringing cadence of my mother's heels as they tapped the marble floor upstairs announced her presence.

I cracked my neck and massaged my jaw to dispel the roaring in my ears and the rigidness of my muscles, then hid my clenched fists in my pockets.

"Davon, Matt, I'm glad you could come." Her melodic voice settled the restlessness within me. She beamed as she walked down the central staircase, bringing me back to my senses.

Regal and stunning as always with a black minidress and her long dark hair styled to one side. She looked much younger than her forty-seven years.

Her love for me was unconditional. Her only flaw—loving my father. She never knew of the atrocities he did to me in my teenage years, and I didn't have the heart to tell her.

Mother knew the government's actions were wrong. When I lived here, I'd sometimes hear her arguing with Dad in their room, but he always convinced her it was all important to preserve balance. And she always believed him, her devotion blinding her.

I approached her and held her tightly. If there was one person I was always glad to see, it was her.

"My boy, I'm happy you made it." Her eyes glistened as she smiled warmly. She touched my cheek, making me feel like a child again even though I was twenty-six.

She brushed her hands down my gray long-sleeved shirt and held my hands. "Are you okay? You seem tense."

I was so tall I had to bend over to kiss her cheek. Being her only child, we were very close, and I became her confidante. The person she went to when she was feeling down or excited to share her moments of sorrow or happiness.

But as years passed, I'd become reserved, not wanting to burden her with what I was subjected to.

I squeezed her hands. "I'm okay, Mom." I shook my head. "Just a lot of work and not enough rest."

She humphed. "I'll talk to your father. He needs to give you a break. You both work too hard."

She moved toward Matt and hugged him. He spent most of his youth here, so he was like family. "I'm glad you could come too."

"Me too, Rebecca," Matt said.

She tipped her face toward Dad's study. "Honey! The boys are home!"

My father's echoing footsteps resounded down the corridor as he exited his study. His broad steps and steady gate projected power.

A rolling heat tore through my belly as I resisted the violent impulses that rushed through my mind.

He pulled my mother by the waist to kiss her as she grasped the open collar of his white shirt to draw him closer. They were always like this, crazy about each other. Their deep devotion never faded.

He brushed his fingertips down her jawline. "You're as beautiful as ever, love."

She blushed.

I offered him a tight smile and bit the inside of my cheek as he embraced me and patted my back.

"Thanks for coming."

His dark hair and olive skin matched mine. Twenty-four years my senior, he was an older version of me. If it weren't for his short salt-and-pepper hair, you would think we were brothers.

He shook Matt's hand. "Glad you could join us."

We followed Mom as she motioned toward the dining room. Servants laid out the table while we talked about trivial matters. That is, until my father brought up his favorite subject—capturing the insurgents.

"Davon, did you hear about today's feat? We captured a rebel faction in one of the facilities. One of our spies aided us. Ms. Gibson has been a vital component of our operations recently, and I expect great things from her. We dispatched a team of operatives throughout the system to see if the rebels would take the bait, and they did. She just went in."

I choked, then sipped my wine.

Matt's eyes widened.

How many did he send in?

"By the way, she thinks highly of you. You spent about a month training her class. Do you remember her?"

It would have been more than a year ago. I recognized most of the faces, but I had no idea who she was by name.

"Her name doesn't ring a bell. I've trained so many."

"Long black hair. Blue eyes. Average height with a small frame. I'm kind of shocked you don't remember her. After all, she was in the top five last year."

Yes. How could I forget? Leslie Gibson. I would never forget her skills, especially with computers. She hacked every single system without a hitch and was top grade in her stealth and observation skill training. A true genius and incredible asset. She was able to pass undetected and obtain highly delicate intel from the NWG archives, the first student in years to achieve this. No one saw her go in or out, not a single flaw in her mission.

"What kind of facility did you raid?" My pulse quickened as I waited for his answer, wondering who'd been caught and how many lives had been lost.

A server offered him more wine, but he waved him away. "It was a food storage warehouse. Ms. Gibson oversees our operational technologies and obtained video footage of their activities. They were stealing small quantities of food daily and illegally distributing it in the slums to the north. Some escaped, but we're working on capturing the rest."

Another insurgent group we were unaware of.

The system was flawed, and many struggled to survive. The number of resources that reached the outskirts was ridiculously low. The people living in what everyone called the slums, settled in the northwest, received the bare minimum.

We noted a few years ago that some citizens began acting covertly against the NWG, assisting these marginalized groups. The injustice enacted by the regime over time had reawakened feelings of hatred in Promissa. We were actively searching for a way to communicate with these factions, as they could be vital for our mission.

"And what's your game plan?" I said, hoping to get more details.

Mom reached for his hand. "Can't we just enjoy dinner with our son?"

He glanced at her. "I'm sorry, love."

The moment was lost. I'd have to bring it up later in his study.

"By the way, Rebecca, Mom sends her regards. She plans to contact you soon," Matt said after a moment of silence.

Grinning, Mom leaned forward. "Oh, that would be wonderful. Lisa hasn't visited me in a long time. How's she doing?"

"Good. Working in the hospital as usual."

Dad cleared his throat.

Mom squeezed his hand. "I know Frank's your friend, but the divorce was years ago. You can't hold a grudge against Lisa."

Matt stiffened, his jaw clenched.

"I'm not going to put myself between you two, but her rebellious ideas are dangerous." Dad held her gaze while kissing the back of her hand. "Promise me you'll be careful."

"I will. You don't have to worry about it."

"Thanks, love." He smiled affectionately at her and then at me. "I'm happy you came, son. You too, Matt. This moment, all of us together away from politics and work, is all I hoped for tonight. We need to make more time to just dine as a family and talk."

My breath hitched. A lightheartedness grew within me as memories flooded my mind, reminding me of him when I was a child. We talked about history back then and went on and on for hours.

Mom would leave us because she was bored with the subject.

I, on the other hand, was never tired.

This glimpse of his old self made me question if he still had some good in him. If only there was a way to bring him back.

I locked my hands together below the table. As soon as the thought entered my head, I buried it. He was rotten to the core. These were only fleeting moments. I couldn't let myself forget who he really was or what he'd done to me, or he'd have me in his clutches.

After an uneventful dinner, my mother said her goodbyes, and we headed to his study. In many ways, my home at the rebel base reminded me of this place.

I looked through the books and took one about the Ottoman Empire.

"An excellent choice. Constantinople's conquest is remarkable. Are you taking it with you?" Dad asked.

I nodded. I often borrowed books from him. His collection was priceless.

My father and I both shared interests in history and battles and collected relics, mostly blades, from history's most memorable wars.

His most valuable object, the Mikazuki Munechika, was prominent in his collection. Sanjo Munechika, one of Japan's most skilled swordsmiths, created this katana. Its name referred to the crescent moon. It was placed in a mahogany katanakake with the tsuka facing right, symbolizing battle preparation. An exquisite blade.

"Tell me. Do you have anything special for me?" My father sat back on his leather chaise lounge and casually crossed his legs.

I walked to the bar to serve whiskey. One for me and the other for Matt, who leaned against a wall. Knowing him, he'd keep to himself. My father wrecked his family, and he only endured his presence for a short amount of time.

"Davon, I asked you a question."

I cast him a glance. He wasn't used to being ignored.

I sat on his settee after giving Matt his drink and mirrored his pose. Two could play this game.

"So...?"

I swirled my drink. "I have a location for you. We overheard some residents at Matt's clinic discussing people fleeing through the forest. There appears to be a checkpoint to the west. We got out there and saw soldiers scouting in gray uniforms. They were well armed."

Dad clenched his fists. "They're becoming more daring. We deployed scouts to that area after we took their base a year ago. I knew there had to be more out there."

My fingers twitched. I squeezed my glass and sipped my whiskey, relieving the dryness of my throat, trying to contain my rage as I remembered that day. Hundreds of souls were lost as Lavigne's forces stormed our import base. We believed they wouldn't find a building so far west. It was the only community that wasn't underground, and they destroyed it. Nobody survived, and the people fought to the bitter end, choosing to die fighting rather than be captured. Because of that attack, Deb's sister couldn't be rescued in time since our entire forces were sent to safeguard the other bunkers.

"I'll send the military to get them and call on you as soon as we have them in custody."

I clenched my jaw as I recalled the endless drills, tortures, and killings. I despised this man for what he forced on me and wouldn't forgive myself until I honored the oath I made when I joined the People's Revolutionary Front.

I'd free Promissa and remove the threat. It was the only way I could atone for my sins.

The sins of my father.

Chapter 5

Davon

October 2212

No sign of Abigail after two months of exploring the ancient underground subway system. I sat next to Matt's desk, where he studied a map of the city. We'd been at his clinic for hours, trying to figure out where to look next.

Matt was a general practitioner and served the people of Promissa. Everyone in the city thought we were regular citizens working illegally to aid the less privileged areas.

I ran his clinic, which served as our nerve center. We'd converted a small residence near the northern slums into a welcoming space for citizens in need of medical assistance. As Matt desired, it was open and free to all to provide them with equal access to health care. It was small but functional.

My father was against this kind of establishment since there were health-care facilities for that, but most people in our area preferred a more personal space where they were valued as human beings, not as just a means to an end. He approved of the clinic because he knew it was a good base of operations, a way to keep our identities hidden and the intel coming.

One of my duties as his spy was to infiltrate the city and gather intelligence on potential rebel factions. The other was to train his elite soldiers in espionage, fighting, and torture techniques at least once a year, the latter being my area of expertise. One he'd drilled into me since I was sixteen.

As memory after memory of my victims rushed through my head, a terrible fog swallowed me whole.

The foul smell of pee and feces. Agonizing screams and pleas for mercy echoed around me as I selected the next tool with my blood-splattered hands. My soul sealed away while I methodically did my job. I was a monster created for a sole purpose. To torment. To kill.

"Hey." Matt touched my shoulder. "Are you all right?"

"Sorry, I'm good." I faced him. "What were you saying?"

"We should search this area to the south." He pointed to the map.

"You're right. We need to get down there. The problem lies in finding an entrance to those tunnels. That area was heavily bombarded years ago, and most parts are unreachable. We'll check later tonight."

I rubbed my eyes and went to take a bath. I needed to get my mind back in the game.

At 10:00 p.m., we walked down a desolate district in Promissa, full of abandoned stores and deserted alleyways. The wind scraped trash along the streets as streetlamps flashed. We'd already encountered two patrols that saluted and moved forward without wasting a second glance. All the officers knew my face, and no one dared question my actions, which was why Connor, the general of the PRF's army, sent us in. He knew we were his only chance of getting Abigail back.

A hollow sound beneath our feet stopped us. We both looked down. A wooden plank.

I stepped around it as Matt crouched and slid it to the side. "This is it."

We turned on our flashlights and started down the steps.

The hairs on the back of my neck stood on end as we entered the darkness within. At the bottom, there was a large, abandoned space. Its walls were covered in angry graffiti. We found two abandoned rucksacks lying in a corner and moved forward.

A moldy scent mixed with the smell of something rotting hit me as I stepped farther in. I darted my eyes from left to right, then halted. A chill ran through my body. Dark patches covered the floor, and two bodies lay close to each other in the center of it all.

"What the hell?" Matt knelt to get a better look.

One of the bodies was exposed. Its clothing was mostly intact, covering what was left, skin patches and bones. The other was wrapped in a blanket.

Matt's hands trembled as he removed the sheet hiding the second body and inspected each. "This must have happened about a year ago. It's a man and a woman. He was shot in the head." He pointed at the bullet hole in the skull.

I moved forward, each step heavier than the last, then crouched to get a better look at the woman.

Please don't let it be her.

Long auburn hair, maybe five and a half feet in height. "It's not her."

Matt glanced up and nodded, then continued examining beneath the man's shirt.

My stomach twisted at the state of her clothing. Ripped and stained. I took her clenched fist and opened it forcefully, its crunching noise making me flinch. If my suspicions were right, I needed to examine the nails. Bile rose to my mouth when I saw the dark stains and dried flesh trapped within them.

The room became smaller and the air heavier. This woman was probably violently raped. It wasn't unheard of, as soldiers would sometimes boast in the locker rooms about their "conquests." We imposed severe penalties for such actions, including incarceration, a drop in military rank, and expulsion from the armed forces. Nonetheless, it was no-man's-land out here, and there was no way to supervise their behavior.

An eerie silence enveloped us as we stayed there, motionless. No one deserved to die this way. No one.

I pushed myself up. "There had to be someone who escaped. The care they took with these bodies and the blanket covering the female... Someone left after paying their respects."

Matt stood, his expression vacant. "It sure looks that way. Let's explore further."

I found an ancient subway cart at the end of the tunnel. I walked ahead, his dragging footsteps trailing behind me.

Blood streaks covered the floor.

"Someone was dragged out," I said while Matt entered the cart.

Five backpacks lay across the seats.

"They must have been taken." Matt's voice cracked as he picked up an abandoned toy car.

I tensed, and my fists shook.

How did you recover from something like this? The patrols, citizens like the rest, attacking their own people. Their minds convinced they had a right to impose, beat up, rape, kill...

I smashed a window and let out a guttural roar. The sharp pain and bloodied knuckles were a small reprieve from the raging turmoil that burst through my body.

"Fuck this! They were just kids." I turned to Matt, nostrils flaring as I tried to contain myself.

Matt pocketed the toy and tipped his head back. He moved his lips with his eyes closed, and after a long exhale, he faced me. "We'll avenge every one of these souls, but for now, we need to focus on our mission. We keep moving and find Abigail before they get to her."

Matt and I sat on my sectional sofa, drinking, and listening to rock music in the background.

Back to square one.

We returned to Electi to rethink our strategy. After checking the apartment for bugs and searching my video feed, we started going through everything we'd done and the areas covered.

"Almost a year and still nothing to show for it. Do you think she's still out there?" Matt asked, his feet resting on the ottoman.

I took a swig and nodded. "Something tells me she is. Last week I checked the files on the runaways who were captured, and no one matches her description."

Matt sighed. "I get you, but we've searched everywhere."

I ran my hands through my hair, pausing midway.

What if?

I rushed to the map to see the places we had searched already and the timeline.

Matt followed.

"A year ago, we searched the western outskirts and moved north six months later. We didn't take long there because the prison facilities were already open and there weren't many areas left to hide in. We've been searching in the tunnels nonstop since August."

Matt frowned. "And...?"

"What if she's always been a step ahead of us? What if we've been searching in the wrong order? If what I suspect is right, she fled the north last summer as the jail facilities were opened, and the only area large enough to hide in today would be..."

"The western outskirts," Matt said.

With a grin, I placed my palms on the table. "She's there. I just know it. We need to go back and search again. This time we're not leaving without her."

The meeting with Father went smoothly. We convinced him we needed to relocate to Promissa to a makeshift flat we had there and investigate potential areas for more rebel checkpoints.

Lavigne's team discovered the fake checkpoint around a month ago. They scoured the region but had little success. Only a chest of weapons and some charred papers were found, leading them to believe they fled abruptly and torched the records to protect their group. This gave us the ideal cover and enough time to complete the rescue.

Matt left after the meeting to say goodbye to his mother, and I stayed at home to do the same.

"Please be safe out there. I always worry while you're off on your assignments." Mom embraced me. "Do you have to leave so close to your birthday?"

I took her hands in mine. "Yes, Mom, it's important for Dad that we do this."

She let out a sigh. "All right, give me a second. I'll be right back."

I waited in the foyer as she went upstairs.

Dad unlocked the door to his study and stepped out.

I put my hands in my pockets and looked upstairs, silently pleading with Mom to hurry so I could leave.

"Are you leaving already?" He wore slacks and a white unbuttoned shirt, more relaxed than his usual suit.

"Yeah. I'm just waiting for Mom." I shifted my feet.

"She's probably looking for our gift. She's sad you'll not be here for your birthday. We had a party planned. I'm pretty bummed myself, but I understand, and I appreciate your efforts."

I looked up to find him staring at me, his eyes glazed.

He drew me into an embrace. "Happy birthday. Come back safe."

I stilled, trying to ignore the sense of calm that built within me. My treacherous body hugged him back. The safety of his arms and the sense of protection transported me back to my childhood. In that instant, I knew he loved me even if it was in his own twisted way.

Dad broke the embrace and held my arms. "I'm proud of you, son. Of all you've become."

An urge to run swept through me. Reality barging in.

What I've become? What you made of me...

I stepped back, trying to put as much distance between us as possible.

This mind play, it wouldn't work.

My dad squished his eyebrows as my mother came down the stairs.

Just in time.

She handed me a small black box. "This is from both of us. Happy twenty-seventh birthday."

"Thanks." I glanced between both my parents.

I opened the box. An obsidian ring rested inside, crowned with my initials in silver. It was stunning, elegant.

I didn't like gifts. They reminded me of the injustice out there. But this came from Mom, and I wouldn't deny her. I put it on, a perfect fit.

I kissed her cheek. "It's perfect."

Dad patted my back. "Be careful out there. Don't let your guard down."

I nodded as Mom pulled me in for one last hug. My chest tightened. I always missed her.

I swept her into my arms, her feet leaving the floor, and leaned into her neck. She was so small compared to me that it felt like holding a child.

"I love you, Mom," I whispered next to her ear.

She giggled as I put her down. She caressed my cheek down to my chin. "I love you too."

We reached the apartment by midafternoon. It was about a mile south of the city's western limits, near Matt's clinic. The apartment would serve as our headquarters.

We packed MREs, water, clothes, and weapons and set off into the night for an abandoned region on the western edges. This time we would hide like the other escapees and avoid patrols.

Matt had his guns ready. As for me, I was fine with my khukuri, my blade of preference. A gift from my father. I couldn't part with it no matter how hard I tried.

Half-destroyed buildings with melted rebars and shattered windows spread all around us. What was once a highly industrialized zone now lay in ruins, a warning that everything we'd accomplished could be easily destroyed by our own greed. A step back from all the progress we could have made, shattered by our own insatiable hunger for power. Out here, the gloom of the war era felt as present as ever.

Over forty years ago, wars for resources erupted all around the globe. This country's government was decimated after years of wars as different nations sought to claim control of its riches.

The cities were left to fend for themselves, using what little of their military forces remained. Some were completely annihilated, while others, such as Promissa, continued fighting. After several years of fierce battle, Promissa fell under the control of the NWG, an outside government formed by an alliance of power-hungry politicians, businesspeople, and upper-class citizens.

I didn't recall anything about my birthplace. We migrated here after the NWG took over the majority of the East Coast decades ago. The city of Electi was established, and we settled there more than fifteen years ago after the war ended.

Many Promissa residents left, but the vast majority, who were impoverished, were forced to accept the new rule. Everything was good for a few years until the new laws were enacted and the regime was put in place.

My chest constricted, and I struggled to breathe. This place must have been full of life before the wars, but now it was merely a tomb.

Only the wind and a dog's howl broke the night's calm as we entered an abandoned apartment complex. The squeaking of metal from the fire escape steps caused me to jolt sideways before we entered. Glass and drywall crunched beneath us as we walked upstairs.

Once we found a spot to settle in, Matt straightened. "I think we should help more this time. Many people rely on us."

We were like brothers, yet I was his general, second only to the general of the army, Connor Harris. I could make the call.

I cast him a sidelong glance as I drew out my cot. "You want us to help other runaways? Guide them to safety?"

Matt nodded, his jaw set. "Yes. This place must be swarming with them."

I knew this to be true, and most were children orphaned by the government or abandoned when their caregivers were imprisoned. We could do more, and when I looked into my friend's eyes, I realized we had to.

"We'll do it."

April 2213

The area was indeed full of escapees, and we spent over six months helping dozens of them go safely into our system while we actively searched for Abigail.

There was still no sign of her, but a woman matching her description was seen by a runaway. She headed east after nearly being captured by a guard. The girl who gave us the intel said the woman fought the guard's grip and, while freeing herself, stabbed his inner thigh.

If this was true, we needed to be cautious in our approach because Abigail Davis would most definitely be difficult to catch.

August 2213

August's weather was agonizing. I rubbed my neck with a wet towel as sweat trickled down my face. The heat was unbearable.

"You should rest. You're on edge," Matt said as I stood guard by a window.

We moved to another abandoned apartment complex a month ago while following Abigail's lead. Exposed pipes were visible through plaster gaps in the ceiling, and crumbled debris could still be found in some places. After removing the rat feces and mold, we settled in an old flat.

Some places were chosen to be renovated for government use in the future, and this must be one of them since it had an acronym painted on the entrance: NWRDA. It stood for New World Reconstruction and Development Agency. They oversaw rebuilding.

We were already looking for alternate locations in case they took over the area.

I tied my hair back and shook my head. "My instincts rarely fail me. Someone is following us, and I don't like it."

"You're just paranoid." Matt rubbed his brow.

My calm snapped. "We have three months left to find her. We can't let anyone put the mission in jeopardy. You really don't feel it?"

"No. I don't." Matt rolled his eyes and went about cleaning his gun.

"Whatever, man." I sighed.

We learned about Deb's capture by the government during our most recent check-in via our checkpoint system.

The news shook me to the core and, more so, the knowledge of what she could be going through.

Maybe if I was there to help... I shook my head.

No, I need to focus on the mission.

Three months. Connor ordered us to get back to our base, Janus Peak, by November. Whether we completed our mission or not, he needed us urgently to get Deb back. But I couldn't face him empty-handed after all these years.

I'd find Abigail and then get Deb back.

Chapter 6

Abi

2213

"June 2203: Last night we had a meeting. Our group is growing, almost twenty-five now. People from all classes and ages are joining. There was a pattern in the laws implemented by the government. Every year they took something more, strangling us little by little. Snatching away our rights. They were setting up their pieces, preparing them to strike." (Deborah Davis's journal)

Days became months, and months became years. I slowly lost track of time. My nights were filled with terror, as memories of the past plagued me. Ending my life crossed my mind countless times, but the promise I made to Paul, Jacob, and Bonnie kept me going.

Before leaving the abandoned subway station, I found an old leather journal among the runaways' things. It had been my travel companion ever since. At night, I'd write in it, describing as much as I could to keep me sane.

I was forced to move to the western outskirts more than a year ago when the government inaugurated two facilities north of the city. Facilities surrounded by barbed wires and towers.

Out here, remnants from the wars were everywhere, some buildings ruined by explosions, others half destroyed. The government was salvaging and renovating structures, gradually taking control of the area. For what purpose, I couldn't say, but it was something big.

I stayed near a less advantaged suburb in the periphery of the city, hiding in vacant rooms inside the flawed system. Most of the time, I gathered what I needed to survive. If I was lucky, I'd get to wash and eat, but that rarely happened.

I touched my daggers. My pocketknife was safe in my backpack, forgotten there ever since that night. I could still smell and taste the foul, acrid taste of his cigarette. His cruel touch. The metallic taste of his blood. Nausea hit me, but I pushed the thought away and focused on the task at hand.

Finding food and water. I hadn't eaten or drunk anything for two days.

I made my way through the alleys, gripping the walls for support. NWG patrols' constant presence in this area made it almost impossible to get supplies lately, and my body was running low on fuel. Sometimes I couldn't even hold myself upright, but I kept pushing, I couldn't give up.

After another failed food run, I went back to my building. Heavy footsteps shuffled downstairs.

For a month now, two men were living downstairs and scouted the area daily. They were armed, and their muscular builds showed they trained heavily.

At first, I thought about leaving, suspecting they were undercover agents from the NWG, but there was something off about them. The government rotated its soldiers every couple of weeks, but these two never shifted, and I hadn't seen or heard anyone else or any radio transmission.

I sneaked down the steps as they left, their clothes blending flawlessly with the darkness.

Where are you going every night?

I trailed behind them and followed them into a building two blocks east, jolting as a loud bang broke the eerie calm.

One of them turned on a flashlight, and I backed into a corner, straining to hear their voices.

"It came from the basement," the blond one said.

The other signaled down the stairs. "You go down and check. I'll stay here in case they try to run." His strong voice carried authority.

The other crept toward the stairway, gun in hand.

The air stilled around me as I watched the man now standing a couple of meters away tighten his fist around a huge, curved blade. His muscles bunched below his shirt as he let out a long exhale and got into a wide stance, ready to pounce on whoever came up.

The room went pitch black as his companion descended.

I wobbled as my eyes adjusted to the darkness, and my foot caught just in time to keep me from falling. It dragged, making a scraping sound, and I winced.

He glanced back. "Who's there?"

I froze, beads of sweat running down my brow. I knew he couldn't see me, but his eyes were on me nonetheless. I could make out dark stubble covering his clenched jaw as his eyes moved frantically, searching the darkness. I held my breath and stayed as quiet as possible.

In that moment, two sets of footsteps treaded up the stairs.

The man turned, his posture rigid. "Matt? Is it her?"

I scampered back into the shadows and peeked out as Matt stepped into the room, flashlight in hand, with a boy at his side.

"I'm sorry, Davon."

His shoulders dropped.

Where had I heard that name before? I searched through my memories. His name flashed in on a journal page. Davon, part of Deb's group. Could he be the same guy?

Matt squeezed Davon's shoulder.

Davon shook his head and sheathed his blade, regarding the boy. "It's okay. What's your name?"

The boy bit his lip. "Richard...Richard Michaels."

"You don't need to be scared anymore, Richard. My name's Davon. You already met Matt. We're here to help."

Richard nodded, then slumped against Matt.

"He's just dehydrated. I found him on the floor downstairs with no food on him. Living in his own filth. He wouldn't have lasted in this state."

Davon picked him up as if he weighed nothing. "Let's get him to check-point four. A runner can get him to a safe house and treat him."

I followed them from a distance, swaying.

They made their way north toward the forest.

I shifted my gaze to the left and crept up to a concrete barrier on the alley's side. A block away, a patrol was scouting. I clenched my muscles as I watched the trio.

Matt and Davon glanced sideways and, without hesitation, darted away, disappearing before my eyes.

Were they evading the patrol?

I clutched my chest and willed myself to believe they could be it. My way out of here.

A while later, when they didn't reappear, I hobbled back to the building. Once inside, I leaned back against a wall, grimacing. I cradled my stomach and winced at the way my ribs protruded. I sighed. My eyelids were so heavy.

I woke with a jolt, and my heart leapt. Voices downstairs. Were they back?

For how long had I dozed off?

I still had my daggers with me as I tiptoed downstairs, using darkness as my ally. They sat near the kitchen in the area they lived in.

Taking tentative steps, I reached a counter and crouched behind it, gripping Jacob's dagger. At this rate, I didn't know how long I had until my body gave out. If they were the real thing, I needed to know. They were my last hope.

Sweat dripped down my face, my heartbeat roaring in my ears like a frightened animal. This was the closest I'd been to anyone in a long time.

"I know you want to keep searching, but it's been two years already and still no sign of her. She might have been taken already. You know the lists aren't that reliable. Remember the tunnels? Some names are never recorded," Matt said.

"We can't just give up. I get the feeling this girl is much stronger than you give her credit for. If she's anything like her sister, she's alive."

"You just refuse to accept it. Abigail Davis is as good as dead."

A gasp escaped me. I covered my mouth.

Both chairs screeched.

Bile burned the back of my throat. I crawled back, dagger in hand.

"Stay right where you are!" Davon yelled.

I pointed my blade at him, my hand trembling at its weight.

Be strong.

Both men towered over me a couple of feet away. Davon held his large blade and Matt a gun.

Davon's unwavering brown gaze studied me. Tattoos covered his arms, and his dark hair fell to his shoulders. His stance was rigid as he aimed his blade at me.

Matt had shorter, wavy hair. His green eyes fixed on me. Suddenly, he made his move. I swung my blade at his legs, failing miserably as he caught me and took my dagger. He pulled me up, then reached to pat me down.

I responded on instinct, using what Bonnie had taught me, and kicked him in the groin with all my might. As he went down with a groan, I took Paul's knife out. I'd never let a man abuse me again.

Within seconds, Davon was on me. I slashed at his chest, and he jumped back, dodging it just in time. With both hands on the dagger, I took a defensive stance against him. He pivoted right, and as I reached to stab him, he diverted left and, in an instant, had me locked in front of him. He squeezed my wrist till I dropped the blade.

"Listen very carefully." His voice sounded low and menacing. "You'd better not try anything like that again. Now, be still."

I flinched at his touch but stood my ground.

Matt pushed himself up, a grimace passing across his face as he adjusted himself, then passed Davon a rope and took my other dagger.

I fought as Davon tied my hands to the back of a chair, followed by my ankles.

"If you keep this up, you'll hurt yourself," he mumbled.

I stopped fighting and pressed my lips together as he crouched in front of me, blade in hand.

His dark eyes focused on me. "Who are you?"

I tested the rope around my wrists and challenged his stare. "I was here first." I coughed, my bravado failing as my voice became hoarse. I hadn't talked for a long, long time. "You're the ones invading my building. You first!"

Davon's eyebrows flashed up, but he didn't put his dagger down. Instead, he moved into my space and held his blade to my throat. In a low, steady voice, he said, "Well, as we're the ones holding you captive, I think the honor of talking first goes to you. Now, who are you, and why are you here?"

I inhaled deeply as the cold touch of his knife pressed against my neck. But I didn't flinch and held his stare, searching inside those two dark pools. I didn't know what I wanted to find, but I couldn't read him. It was like staring into a dark void, one impossible to escape if you fell into it.

I shivered. "I'm Abi...Abigail. I've been hiding out here for years. I'm not sure how long." I swallowed, my mouth as dry as a desert.

He stepped back. My body trembled as his piercing gaze searched into my very soul. But I kept still and didn't shift my eyes from him. I pushed my shoulders back and held my head high, wincing as the ropes strained against my wrists and burned my skin.

For a second, his eyes flitted toward the ropes, then returned to me.

Matt came closer. "Do you think it's her?"

Davon tilted my chin up. I expected his touch to be coarse, painful. But it was strong yet soft, almost caring. I tried to jerk back, but he held me still. In that moment, it was only him and me, as if the rest of the room darkened and we were in the spotlight.

His commanding voice broke the silence. "Tell me more."

I didn't know if it was his gaze or the intensity that emanated from him, but words just spilled out, and I wasn't able to stop them. "I'm alone. I've been hiding since my sister helped me escape. Someone was supposed to get me but never came."

I darted my gaze between them. Matt stood just behind Davon.

"Are you with them? The PRF? Is that why you helped that boy today?" My belly fluttered. They could be the ones I'd been waiting for.

Davon let go of my chin and paled. "What's your sister's name? When did you escape?"

"Deborah Davis. I escaped in 2210."

He and Matt exchanged a look.

Matt shook his head and pressed his lips together in a hard line. "How do we know this is really her? She could be a spy."

"So could you," I said, getting back their attention.

"How old are you?" Davon's voice grew quiet.

"Twenty. Twenty-one. I don't know for sure."

His shoulders relaxed, and he sheathed his blade. "I think it's her."

Matt tilted his head. "We need to be sure."

"I'm telling the truth!" Hot tears stung my eyes. It had been too long. Alone. I couldn't take it anymore. I couldn't go out there again. These men were my only hope.

I remembered the letter and widened my eyes. "I have a letter! Deb told me not to open it ever and to show it to whoever found me. It's in my backpack. Upstairs."

"And how do we know someone isn't waiting for us?" Matt asked.

I ground my teeth. "And how do I know you aren't here to harm me? I don't even know who you are." I sighed audibly, forcing down a lump in my throat. "Please. Just go and check. Take your weapons with you if you want. It's the only thing I have that may confirm who I am."

Davon's features softened. "Stay with her. I'll check upstairs and bring what I find back with me."

Matt moved a chair and sat in front of me, holding the gun in his lap. "If what you're saying is true, I've never seen anyone stay so long in hiding without dying of starvation or getting snatched by the patrols. We've been searching for you for nearly two years." He raised an eyebrow. "How did you do it?"

"I don't know. I just held on to hope, I guess." I choked back tears as I remembered the people I'd lost. "I've been watching you for almost a month now. I only came forward because I saw you take that boy out of the city and away from a patrol. When you came back, I needed to know if you were for real, so I hid and listened. That's when you said my name."

He leaned forward. "Wait. You've been watching us for a month now? How the fuck did you slip by us?"

I flexed my fingers behind me and drew them into fists, confronting his gaze. "Look. I've been through hell. I know how to be invisible."

"But still…"

I glared at him. "You know what? I don't care what you think. I still slipped by you. Deal with it."

"That you did." He chuckled and cocked his head. "We'll wait for Davon and see what he brings back."

A couple minutes later, Davon stepped into the room with my backpack and stopped in front of me. "Where is it?"

"Open the front pocket. You'll find a leather journal. Inside, there's a blank, sealed envelope."

He rummaged through it and pulled out the journal, then removed the old, stained envelope.

"Is this it?" He showed it to me.

"Yes."

Hope filled me as he opened it and took out the letter. He read it, his eyes intent, occasionally glancing at me. I bit the inside of my cheek and tasted blood.

When he was done, he studied me.

"I hold the key," he said and waited in silence.

Wait. I knew this. The code Deb told me to memorize long ago. I read it so many times.

I closed my eyes, searching my mind for the right words. It had been too long since I'd read it. There.

I glanced back. "Over beginnings and endings. I hold the staff."

"Over the passage of time." Matt's eyes lit up. "It's really her."

Davon nodded. "Welcome to the rebellion, Abigail Davis."

My heart stammered the second those four words left his mouth, and joyful tears streaked down my face. This was it. This nightmare was over.

Safe at last.

Chapter 7
Abi

2213

"*August 2203: I still struggle to get by. It's been a month since it all happened. My parents were killed. God knows how I miss them. Too many questions have gone unanswered, but the government officials stay silent. We're nothing to them. If it weren't for Connor, I don't know how I'd be.*

"*Now I was not only a sister but a mother to Abi. An orphan at ten. She was hanging on, but as for Sarah, she wasn't coping well and was still secluded in a psychiatric ward. The poor thing was with them when it happened.*

"*The government has finally achieved what we feared. Total control of our lives. Being strong is the only option, as our fight is just beginning.*" (Deborah Davis's journal)

Was it happening at last?

Matt put his gun away and freed me. I stood and rubbed my hands to recover the blood flow but slumped back. His arms were around me in an instant, and he helped me sit.

He retrieved a canteen from his bag and held it to my mouth. "Here."

I gulped down as much as possible. Once I got my fill, he put it by the table and went to the kitchen counter, leaving me with Davon.

He was tall, more than a foot taller than me. He rubbed his dark stubble, then buried his hands in his pockets and locked his gaze on me. "I'm sorry for how we treated you. We needed to make sure who you were. I hope you understand."

Was this the same man who held a blade to my neck moments ago?

I raised an eyebrow, never taking my attention away from him. This world was cruel, and trust had to be earned. He'd just threatened to kill me, and it would take some time, but I understood his actions. I would have done the same thing in their shoes. "I do."

His face relaxed as the tension in the room ebbed. Now that he wasn't threatening me, I couldn't deny how stunning he was with his rugged looks, chiseled jawline, and deep, dark eyes that pulled you in. His olive skin contrasted nicely with his long, wavy dark hair. His black shirt clung to him, and his muscles bulged beneath it.

I coughed, and he passed me the canteen back.

My throat was dry as hell. "By the way, who the hell are you?"

Davon chuckled. "I'm sorry. I guess introductions are in order." He shifted his weight. "I'm Davon. We're part of the People's Revolutionary Front and were sent here to find you. You've been our mission for the last couple of years."

Last couple of years? If they'd found me earlier, maybe... I closed my eyes and shook my head slightly. Better to not dwell on what-ifs. It happened, and that's it.

I glanced at Matt, who leaned against the counter, watching our exchange.

He flicked his gaze between us and touched his chest. "Oh, it's my turn now." He grinned and bowed, keeping his eyes locked on me. "My name's Matt, and for the record, I don't trust you much."

Davon glared at him.

Matt threw his hands up. "Relax, big guy. I'm just saying. I don't trust easily, but if you say she's okay, I'm good with that."

I suppressed a smile. Matt seemed like a down-to-earth guy. Almost comical in his own way.

"You don't give last names?" I asked.

Davon shrugged. "We don't."

He looked through his possessions and passed me a bag of nuts and dried fruit. "Here. Take it."

"Thanks." I ate a handful and gave it back.

His brow wrinkled.

I waved him off. "I'm okay. Save some for later."

Davon sighed. "Whatever you lived through these past years is over. We have enough. Eat." His voice was warm. He offered it back. "You need to get your strength back."

My face burned as I processed the meaning of his words. I scratched my tangled, matted locks. "I know I look like shit, but I'm okay."

His eyes narrowed as he came closer and sat on the chair Matt left earlier. "Never look down on yourself for what you've been through."

I leaned my elbows on my knees, touching Bonnie's thread bracelet, then raised my head and nodded, accepting the food.

His lips softened into a warm smile.

"I forgot to tell you. The girl's been stalking us for a whole month."

Davon's gaze shifted from Matt to me, and he quirked his eyebrows. "How's that possible?"

I pursed my lips. "First of all, I have a name." I offered Matt a hard smile. *Did he just wink at me?*

I shook my head. "Second, why is it so impressive that I slipped past you guys?"

Davon stood and folded his arms across his chest. "Well, Miss Davis, we're trained for this, and it should be difficult to sneak by us."

I smirked. "Obviously, many people have probably slipped past you. You just haven't noticed till now. Maybe you aren't as good as you think you are."

Matt laughed. "She's got a point."

Davon scowled at him, then regarded me, his body relaxing. "You're good. I'll give you that."

I grinned, liking this new side of him.

The guys moved the table to me. Davon sat opposite me, while Matt leaned against a wall.

"So when are we getting out of here?" I touched Mom's golden heart, the one fixed to the bracelet Deb gifted me the night I escaped. I was ready to see my sister again.

"As soon as we can," Davon said. "When we came back from the forest, a huge patrol was entering the area. We were lucky to get that boy out. Maybe in a day or two it'll be safe again."

"I think we should wait longer." I knew how patrols worked in this area.

Davon furrowed his brow. "You're saying we should stay put. For how long, Miss Davis?"

"I don't know. When patrols come in high numbers, they usually stay for a week or so." I took another sip of water, a blessing for my parched throat. "And call me Abi."

"That sounds good, *Abi*."

The way his voice deepened as he said my name made my pulse beat faster. I gazed at his lips, then up to find his eyes rooted on me.

His face jerked, and he pushed his chair back and stood. "I'll grab the food."

I followed his figure as he retreated to the kitchen. Why was I so drawn to him? I shook my head.

Matt's presence offered a reprieve as he took the seat next to me while Davon prepared our MREs.

The thought of eating something decent made my mouth water. My sister did leave some food in my backpack, but it lasted about two weeks. After that, I just ate what I could find.

At first, it was terrible. My stomach ached, and my body weakened. But after a couple of weeks, I got used to the pain and began to fast for longer periods of time. I learned to survive with what little I could get.

Davon set a chicken Alfredo pasta in front of me. "Enjoy."

I took a tentative bite with my fingers and moaned. My tongue tingled at the warmth and rich flavor. "This is glorious. Thanks."

"Um, here." He handed me a fork.

I dipped my chin, my face growing hot. I was used to eating with my hands and didn't think twice about what they'd think. "Sorry for that."

"Don't worry. Just eat." Davon moved back to the counter to get his food.

Matt ate next to me.

I peered up to find Davon's eyes on me. I coughed as a piece of pasta went down the wrong way.

Davon was by my side in an instant, pushing the water toward me. "Sip some and eat slowly. The food won't run away."

With a nod, I drank and laid a hand against my breastbone to calm myself, then continued my meal.

"Take your time. After you finish, we can get to planning. There's much to talk about." Matt took a bite from his dinner.

Afterward, Matt passed me a warm blanket. It was getting chilly, so I was grateful.

Matt sat by me, cleaning his gun, while Davon practiced moves with his blade a couple of meters away.

Now that I wasn't scared shitless, I studied his weapon. It had a black wooden handle with a semicurved sharp blade. He moved it from hand to hand, controlling it like it was part of him. I got a rush of adrenaline just thinking about one day using a weapon like that.

The silence was deafening.

Enough of this.

"How's this going to work?" I pressed my lips together. "Are you going to answer my questions?"

Davon sheathed his blade. "We'll answer what we can." He brought in a chair and sat with us.

I had many questions, but there were some that had troubled me from day one. "Where's Deb? Did she get Sarah out? Why didn't you come to get me sooner?"

They glanced at each other.

Davon shook his head. "I can answer one of those questions. Deb couldn't get you as she planned because one of our communities was attacked. All of our forces were deployed to defend the rest of the PRF bunkers." He lowered his gaze and swallowed. "As for your sisters, we can't divulge anything until we get back."

My blood boiled, and heat flooded my chest. This was all I wanted—to know about my sisters and get back to them. I bunched my hands underneath the blanket, and my whole body tensed. I had waited three years for some kind of signal that my sister was still looking for me, and I worried every day about Sarah. They were all I had.

I gritted my teeth. "What? It's a simple question. Are they okay? Did something happen?"

Davon sighed. "Abi, you need to understand. Please. You'll get an answer when we get to the base."

My rage burst free of its chains like a wild animal. *Fuck this.* I slammed my fists on the table, then stood and shoved my chair back. "I will not calm down! I thought you trusted me."

Matt jumped, his eyes huge.

Davon didn't look at me while he fidgeted with a black ring on his right hand, but then his gaze met mine. "I do trust you. But we have orders."

"Fuck your orders!" I closed my eyes and took a calming breath. This wasn't going to get me any answers. "Can you at least tell me if they're okay?"

His gaze didn't waver. "Deb sent us here to get you."

"And what about Sarah?" My vision blurred. I hoped she was already out.

"She's safe."

I searched his eyes for the truth, then sank back into my chair. *They're safe.*

Matt walked to the table. His warm, expressive eyes reminded me of Sarah's.

He sat. "Do you have other questions?"

The next question had plagued me ever since that horrific night. "I guess you can answer this. What's today's date?"

"Today is September 30. Year 2213."

"Three years out here..." My voice broke as I remembered all that had happened. Jacob's face before he died. Bonnie's screams as she slowly lost her light. Two whole years since I'd left them in that tomb and never looked back. One since... I covered my face for a moment, taking shallow breaths.

My hatred toward Minister Niles had grown tenfold over the years. He was the brain behind it all, the man responsible for every single event I'd experienced outside. He took Paul and murdered Jacob and Bonnie. Then...

I shook my head. I wouldn't let fear bring me down. I wouldn't let him win. He and everyone close to him would pay for their crimes.

That meant regaining control of my life. To become stronger and reclaim what was stolen from me.

I held my head in my hands.

"Are you good?" Matt's voice was low.

I nodded but stayed quiet until my heart steadied.

I flinched as Davon's hand grazed mine. A brief, soft touch.

He pulled back and softened his features. "I just... If you need to talk about it, let me know."

I straightened. "Don't worry. I'm okay."

Davon slumped back in his chair.

Matt took some cards out and shuffled them. "How about a game of hearts?"

We both stared at him as he removed the two of clubs from the deck and started dealing the cards.

After two failed attempts and a lot of explaining, we got to play. The mood changed drastically. Matt smiled often, and Davon was at ease. They acted like brothers, and I wondered how long they'd known each other.

Matt played the jack of spades, and Davon grunted in annoyance. It was obvious he had the queen of spades and was due to lose this game. It had been forever since I'd relaxed like this.

"Have you guys known each other long?" I asked as I broke the hearts.

Both inhaled sharply at my play.

"We've known each other since childhood. Obviously, I'm the wiser of the two." Matt winked at me.

Davon threw the queen of spades, taking the trick. "I don't know about that. Being older than me doesn't make you wiser but definitely annoying as fuck."

Matt chuckled as he wrote a fourteen next to Davon's name.

"And how old are you?" Both appeared to be older than me, but I couldn't put a number on it.

"I'm twenty-eight, and Davon's twenty-seven."

"Twenty-eight in less than a month." Davon threw an eight of hearts.

Matt pointed at himself with a mischievous grin. "Still, I'm the most fun to be around."

I giggled as they continued their banter. I took the trick by throwing the ace of hearts.

"Now you know our age. How about you? Is it twenty or twenty-one?" Davon asked, taking me back to our first conversation.

"I thought it was November already, but, no, I'm still twenty."

We decided to move to the floor after we finished the game. Davon lost horribly.

"We joined the PRF ten years ago. One of our goals is to get the fugitives to safety before the government tracks them down. We developed a system of several checkpoints at the city's borders that aid the process. From there, another team takes over and relocates them to a secure place." Davon lay on his side.

We'd been talking for some time about the rebellion. Janus Peak was the name of their base as mentioned in Deb's journal. It had been in operation since 2204. They were off the grid, using only renewable energy and hiding in a bunker system beneath the mountains. I was rendered speechless by all they'd accomplished. They had food, water, and electricity. Everything outside the New World Government's radar. I couldn't wait to see it.

"Is that where you took the boy? To a checkpoint?" I asked, sitting cross-legged between them.

"Richard." Matt nodded. "Yeah, he's safe now. We found dozens of escapees during this mission. Some we found dead, but we were able to sneak out most of them." His demeanor sobered after he mentioned the dead runaways.

This wasn't new for me. I'd seen plenty. Just dead in alleys, starvation, or cold the major culprits.

"You mentioned a system. How many bunkers do you have?"

Davon sat with his legs crossed. "Well, Janus Peak is the center of operations since the command center rests inside, but we have five bunkers in total."

"And how many people does the rebellion have?"

Davon grinned. "Thousands."

I lifted my eyebrows. Thousands of people were preparing to reclaim their homeland.

We continued talking until my eyelids got heavy and I couldn't keep awake. I went to sleep with hope in my heart. It was the first time I'd slept soundly in a long, long time.

Chapter 8

Davon

October 2213

We found her at last.

I stared at the ceiling after a good night's sleep, something I hadn't been able to have in what felt like ages. The back room we slept in had just enough space for the three of us. Abi groaned, obviously disturbed by Matt's God-awful snores.

She seemed fragile at first, but after seeing her kick Matt and fight me, I could tell she was tough.

I had to make up for how I'd treated her. I tried to fight the desire to dominate everything, the harsh nature that was instilled in me after years of rigorous training, yet I sometimes acted just like my father. I was a jerk.

Abi resembled the photos Deb showed me years ago. Her changes were probably caused by her hardships throughout the years outside. Matted hair. Eyes and cheeks hollowed out. Blotchy skin with raised welts on her arms. Flea bites. Many people came into the bunker with similar marks.

Last night, she kept licking her badly split lips, taking little sips of water while we talked. Her body trembled as she struggled to stay upright.

Curious, she'd asked what seemed like a million questions before drifting off. She had strolled languidly into the room, leaning against the walls for support. Her feet were shaky and her steps sloppy. She nearly passed out as she got to her cot. When I helped her down, it was like holding a feather.

An urge to protect her took root within me at that moment. I needed to talk to Matt and have him examine her.

"Morning. Did you sleep well?" Matt sounded bubbly as always. A morning person through and through.

"Not thanks to your snores." I grunted.

"I don't snore." Matt took his gun and went to the door. "I'm going to check if the floor is clear."

He'd never accept he snored. I bet Aoki just got used to it because how on Earth someone could sleep next to him for eight years and not go crazy was beyond me.

I sat up and checked on Abi. She was sound asleep when Matt came back and gave me the all clear. I went to the kitchen to get some jerkies and cheese ready for breakfast. We didn't have much left, but Matt was heading to our apartment today to grab more.

"How's she doing?" Matt asked from his chair as I divided the food.

"I don't know, man. I think she needs a checkup. Did you see how she was trembling last night?" I moved to the table.

"That's expected. But I'll examine her after breakfast."

We both turned as Abi stepped out of the room. She swayed sideways.

Matt hurried to her. "Hold on. I'll help you."

She waved him off. "Don't worry. I can do it."

"Morning, Davon." She sat by me and bit into the jerky and cheese. "I haven't eaten this in a long time. I really like it."

"I'm glad you do. Here, take this." I passed her a bottle of water, and she took a mouthful.

"How did you sleep?" Matt asked.

"It's the best sleep I've had in a long time. Other than your snores, it was perfect." She grinned as Matt put a hand to his chest.

"I can believe that sort of comment from this Neanderthal but from you?" Matt's face was comical as he acted hurt.

Abi giggled. It was a beautiful sound. Her hazel eyes came alive as she smiled. In the light, I could see the coppery strands in her dark hair.

"I'm just telling the truth. When I first heard you, I was so scared I almost ran out, thinking a wild animal had entered." She winked at me.

This was a new side of her. I grinned back since tormenting Matt was one of my favorite things to do.

"You two are making it up. Aoki has never complained about my snoring."

"Ha! You accept it at last!" He'd never admitted as much.

"Okay, you got me. I snore. But it can't be that bad."

We both raised an eyebrow, and he shook his head.

"Who's Aoki?" Abi asked.

"Oh, right. We didn't talk about him last night. He's my husband. You'll love him." Matt's eyes brightened whenever he mentioned Aoki. They were inseparable and my two best friends.

Abi beamed. "I can't wait to meet him."

After we finished our breakfast, I went to the rooftop and took out my binoculars to check the area.

Patrols inspected on a regular basis, looking for runaways. Every hour, we took scouting shifts. If they came in, we had to be ready to hide or go to another location.

Because it was a ten-story building, the roof gave us a vantage point from which to watch for patrols. One lurked a few blocks west. Matt had to go soon, or he'd run into them. When I got to the sixth floor, I peered inside. Matt was tending to Abi.

At least we'd have a better idea of her present condition.

Half an hour later, after I checked the rest of the building, Abi was resting, and Matt was getting ready to leave.

"How is she?" I asked.

"Not good. As I suspected, she's been in a state of starvation for a few years now. Her muscle mass is extremely low. Her pulse is weak, and she's heavily dehydrated. She's alert, but I think she's not getting enough sleep." He closed his bag and put it on.

"She may recover in a few days from her dehydration if we treat her intravenously. But coming back from malnutrition may take weeks, if not longer." He raked his hair back. "There's something else. I think there's emotional trauma also. Even after explaining I was a doctor, she kept jerking away from my touch during the examination. Her pulse jumped numerous times, and her breathing became short, ragged. These are all symptoms of a panic attack."

"Fuck." I didn't even want to think about what she went through out there. We needed to get her out of the city as soon as possible.

Matt grabbed my shoulder. "She's strong, Davon, and her will to live even more so. I'm sure she'll make it with our help. I'll stop by the clinic and grab some IVs, supplements, and antibiotics for her flea bites. I'll also bring extra supplies so she can wash herself."

I nodded. "I hope she recovers faster than expected. The longer we stay, the greater the risk."

"Agreed." Matt reached the door. "Take care of her. I'll see some patients at the clinic and try to make it back before dusk."

Abi awoke about two hours later, taking me by surprise as I was looking out a window.

"Hey. Everything okay?" She crossed her arms. "Have you seen any patrols?"

I touched her hand lightly as she scratched her right arm. "Don't scratch those. They'll get infected."

She covered her arm and pulled away. "Sorry. I'm a wreck." She watched the streets, her eyes darting frantically in different directions.

"Come on. Let's have a snack."

A ravenous look entered her eyes. "Sure."

She sat at the table as I went to the back room to get our backpacks. I passed over the bag of nuts and dried fruit we started eating yesterday and a water bottle.

"Drink more. Matt said you need to hydrate. How long have you gone without it?"

She took it. "I have a sip or two every day. These last months have been very hard to get by. You've been here. You know how it's been."

"I do."

Patrols actively moved around. If I were to guess, something had happened. New intel maybe. I would have to contact my father soon to find out what changed but after Abi's extraction.

She watched me curiously as I retrieved from my bag the belt and two daggers Matt had taken from her yesterday.

I handed them to her. "Take them."

She touched the black dagger, closing her eyes as she exhaled. "Thank you." She stood and put it on.

I motioned to her blades. "Do you know how to use those?"

"Not really. Not like you."

"But you do know how to fight. What you did yesterday—that's self-defense. When did you learn it?"

Her eyes narrowed, and she hesitated before answering. "My friends taught me."

"Your friends?"

She sat back. "I've never told anyone about it."

Something bad happened. I could see it in her eyes as they glazed over. I stayed silent. Some things were better left unspoken, especially those you wanted to forget.

She reached inside the backpack and pulled out a pair of glasses. They were dark, stained with blood. She unsheathed the black dagger and placed everything on the table. "These belonged to Jacob. It's all I have left of him."

She pointed to a white-and-pale-blue thread bracelet I'd seen her touching yesterday. "This belonged to Bonnie. They rescued me from a patrol two years ago and led me to their hideout. The abandoned tunnels. Bonnie showed me how to fight." She closed her eyes briefly. "I spent three months with them. We thought we were safe..."

"What happened?" I tightened my fists and tried to keep my voice steady, but the thought of what she could have gone through set my skin on fire, wrath bursting within me.

Her eyes flashed as something dark passed through them. "They were murdered."

Her lower lip trembled as a single tear, then another escaped her eyes. I remained silent until she calmed down. She set her jaw and tightened her grip on the dagger.

"Will you teach me how to fight like you?"

Her unblinking stare caught me off guard. A look I knew very well.

No doubt a lot more had happened out there. What she confided in me just skimmed the surface. "Once you get better, I promise to teach you."

I remembered what we saw in the tunnels. Could they be her friends? Could she be the third person who survived? I wouldn't push her to tell me more because I knew how difficult it could be.

The rest of the morning passed quickly. She watched as I showed her how to clean her blades and slash at an enemy.

"Can I see it?" She pointed at my khukuri.

I took it out and gave it to her.

She touched it reverently with care. "It's beautiful. Where did you get it?"

"My father gave it to me on my fifteenth birthday. It's a khukuri, a *cha aklo*.Considered a warrior's blade in Nepal. It's been with me for thirteen years. It can slice through bone, highly effective in battle."

She slid the khukuri back toward me. "And your father?"

I clenched my jaw. "I don't want to talk about it."

She brushed the top of my hand as I retrieved my blade. I inhaled sharply as my nerves fired up all at once.

"I understand. You don't need to say anything. My parents were killed when I was ten. *He* took them from me." She squeezed my hand and slowly pulled away as her face transformed. Nostrils flaring. Body tense. She murmured, "Jordan Niles."

I cringed as she said his name. She pinched her eyebrows together, and her chest heaved. I could see the hate in her cold stare. A killing intent behind it. Her reaction mirrored my own.

My skin crawled at what he'd done to this city. The terror his regime instilled in each citizen, the families he'd broken apart, the homes he'd destroyed. All for what? To make a "perfect" country, to live at the expense of others and enrich his own compatriots while trampling over those he deemed unworthy. To create his own twisted utopia.

How could anyone forgive him? How could I ever hope for redemption?

After lunch, I stayed vigilant as she went to rest. I'd let her make her own story about my father. I was positive she'd run once she realized who I was.

I'd seen it in the bunker, where some still gave me a cold shoulder and a harsh gaze. Living among them, a mirror image of him, leading them against my own. Even though I was the second-in-command, some found it difficult to accept me. No matter how hard I tried, his name would always overshadow all my actions, leaving me needing to do more, to fight harder in hopes that one day all would be forgotten.

As for Abi, whatever trust we'd built would vanish the instant she knew. I had to make sure she knew me for whom I truly was, not what my name carried. Because maybe, just maybe she'd see I was not like him.

I jerked sideways. Someone was downstairs. In an instant, I shook Abi's form. Her eyes widened as I covered her mouth, putting a finger to my lips. She nodded, and I let go, gesturing for her to get her stuff and follow me.

We exited through a broken window that led to a fire escape. As we crouched outside, a patrol entered the floor.

"Hey, look in here. There's a bedsheet. It's still warm. Search around. They can't be far," a soldier said.

I signaled down. We needed to get out.

We climbed down very slowly. As we reached the ground floor, a commotion sounded from above.

Someone shouted, "Over here! They're going down the fire escape."

When I glanced up, a soldier emerged, followed by three others.

A shot hit above us, ricocheting away. Abi crouched and covered her ears, her trembling form frozen in place.

"I know you're scared, but we need to move." I helped her up.

Her eyes were wide, and her chin quivered, but she nodded and continued her descent. Their hurried footsteps pursued us, clanging on the metal floor, the sound echoing around us. A little bit more, and we'd hit the street.

Another shot struck the rail behind us as we rushed around a corner and went east down an alley. I ran for the building where we found the boy last night. The basement could serve as a hiding place.

Taking Abi's hand, I headed downstairs, then ducked into a corner next to what appeared to be an old heater. The area was pitch black and reeked of urine. I forced back a gag, and Abi covered her nose.

She trembled beside me, her hands sweating.

"Get your dagger out. Be ready," I whispered in her ear.

After a couple of minutes, we heard shouts from the street.

"Search the block. They must be close."

I squeezed her hand as footsteps thudded down the stairs to the basement. My heart pumped against my chest as I tried to control my breathing. Abi did the same.

A flashlight lit up the space.

A soldier entered. "Fuck. What's that smell?"

We pushed back as light illuminated the room. He was almost upon us when a woman came down.

"Is there anyone down here?" She grunted. "What the hell? This place smells awful!"

"Yeah. Fucking escapees must have hidden here. Let's check this area just in case and then move upstairs."

We huddled together as they began kicking things around. One pointed his flashlight at us, but the heater hid us.

He crossed to the opposite side of the room.

"Let's go. I don't think they're down here. Just a bunch of engines and heaters."

"Sure," the woman said.

They exited the room.

We both exhaled. I reached inside my backpack and pulled out a shirt. I ripped it in two and wrapped one part around Abi's face and the other around mine. The ammonia stench was so strong it hurt my eyes.

We waited till it was dark and tiptoed upstairs, blades in hand, until we reached the top floor.

This structure was some form of factory, a manufacturing center if I were to guess. Inspecting stations as well as tools and industrial machinery filled the room.

I set my backpack down and removed the cloth from my face.

Abi stood by the window, her hands trembling uncontrollably as her dagger fell to the ground. She swayed sideways, almost falling over.

I caught her in time and helped her to the floor. "Rest. We're safe for now. They won't come back for a while."

"Are you sure?" she asked as I removed her face covering and propped her head up on her backpack.

I nodded, and she slowly dozed off.

Matt and I had a plan in case we got separated. We'd mark the location with a circle in the right-hand bottom corner of the building's entryway.

It would be undetectable unless you looked for it very carefully. I went to the front of the building and scratched the sign with my pocketknife, then did the same upstairs. After barring the door behind me, I took my chaaklo and waited by the window, watching for Matt.

A tapping noise jolted me awake. The orange hues of dawn peeked from the horizon. I must have dozed off. The tapping continued, following a pattern I recognized. Morse code for PRF. Our code. I rushed to the door.

"Brother." I hugged Matt. "I'm glad you found us."

"Me too." He dashed over to Abi with his medical equipment. "What happened? It took forever to find you. Patrols were stationed across the area. They went west around an hour ago."

"They discovered us after lunch. We barely escaped. After a couple of hours, they left, and we found this space." I helped him get everything ready.

Abi's eyes fluttered open. "Matt?"

"I'm here. How are you doing?" His voice was gentle.

She shifted, trying to sit, but slumped back.

"What's happening?" I asked him.

Abi was pale, her eyes sunken.

"Her blood pressure is dropping. She's still dehydrated and after last night, weaker than before. Once I place the IV, she'll start to get better."

She jerked back when she saw the needle. "No, get that away from me!" She scrambled away, shaking all over. "Please don't do it, Matt. I hate them."

I crouched next to her. "You need this. We're trying to help."

She grabbed my arm, her panicked eyes pleading. "Give me more water. Please. I'll do whatever you say. Just don't inject anything into me. That's what they did to Sarah, and she was never the same."

I raised my eyebrows and blinked at Matt.

He shook his head and took her other hand. "Abi, please trust me. Whatever they did to Sarah will not happen to you. We need to treat you with intravenous fluids. You'll get better faster. What happened last night could happen again."

Abi stopped fighting and held my hand.

I smoothed her hair back, hoping to calm her down. "He's good at this. You won't feel a thing. Everything will be over in a minute."

She turned her focus on me and nodded. Matt fixed the tourniquet and inserted the needle. She flinched.

Once the catheter was in, he removed both the needle and the tourniquet and connected the tubing.

"It's done." Matt taped the IV to her arm.

She gazed at me, her eyes soft. "Thanks."

My heartbeat quickened. Where she still clutched my hand, my flesh warmed. She squeezed it gently before letting go.

Matt huffed. "So that's how it's gonna be around here. After I search all night to get to you, not even a thanks." He touched his heart. "You hurt me, Abigail Davis."

We both laughed and relaxed into a smooth chat. No words about the government or the rebels. Just a pleasant conversation over breakfast.

Chapter 9

Abi

"*O*ctober 2203: The government implemented checkpoint stations, but some geographical sites were difficult for them to control. Those were the ones we used to move around. Many wanted to escape the regime, but no options were available. We made it our mission to find a location to make our own, a place far from the government and their facilities." (Deborah Davis's journal)

After three days of Matt's treatment, I was much better. My muscles didn't cramp as often, and I could walk without support. With so much time to kill, we got to know each other.

Davon had a deep sense of commitment toward others, like it was his sole job to keep us safe. He made certain I'd eat my food and drink the water I needed, keeping watch so I could sleep at night. Ever since they found me, my nightmares had dwindled, but sometimes I'd wake up in the middle of the night, drenched in sweat, to find Davon shaking me awake. He never asked about them but always assured me I was safe now.

Matt was more relaxed. He was a great physician, always checking if I was all right. His humorous personality came through more every day. He teased Davon when things got too serious and made it impossible not to laugh at random stuff.

Matt approached me with his medical bag. "Hey. I think we can pull that out for good."

I grinned. "For real!"

At last!

He crouched next to me on the floor and began removing it. I jerked. The sensation was odd. It wasn't painful, but it was uncomfortable.

As Matt finished, I glanced to where Davon was preparing our lunch on top of a working bench. He raised an eyebrow.

I mouthed, "I'm okay."

Nodding, he continued prepping.

Lately, it was like this between us. It started after we were almost caught, a sort of connection. A sense of being there for each other. I couldn't explain it, but it was almost as if all my problems and worries faded away with him by my side.

Matt approached him. "I'll check the building." Taking his gun, he left us.

Davon sat beside me. "Are you all right?"

"Yeah. Happy to at last be free of that torture device."

He chuckled. It was a deep and beautiful sound.

"Do you feel better?" He checked my arm.

I grinned. "I do. I feel more awake. Do you think I can start moving a bit more? Maybe even some training? If I stay one more day resting, I'll die of boredom, and all this would be for nothing."

The corner of his mouth curved up as he nodded. "I'll talk to Matt to see if we can start walking more inside the building and maybe go up and down the stairs. He told me in a week or two you should be strong enough for the trip to the base."

"I will be. The sooner we get there, the better. I want to see my sisters so bad." And I wanted to get the hell out of this city.

He remained silent, clearly deep in thought, then interlaced his fingers. "We'll do our best."

I scratched the back of my neck. Something about the way he acted whenever we talked about going to the base made my stomach clench. Was he hiding something? I asked him about it once, and he said it was nothing. But still...

I shut my eyes and shook any negative thoughts away. Perhaps I was just imagining things. I reined in my need to know more and decided to put it aside for the time being. I could tell from our chats he had experienced trauma. He couldn't bring himself to talk about his family without hesitation, as if there was something truly upsetting about his past. I'd give him as much time as he needed. He'd done the same for me.

I reached into my backpack for my journal. I froze as Jacob's glasses fell out, then picked them up with care and put them back inside.

"Was he important to you?"

I faced him. His chin was propped on his hands.

I never thought I would ever be able to feel safe around a man again. But there was something special about Davon. His soothing voice. His unwavering attention while we chatted. I was able to talk to him. Really talk to him.

"I loved him. When all I could see was darkness, he was my light." I closed my eyes. I could almost see him, his beautiful smile, his caring gaze, his hands as he cradled mine. The heaviness that nestled within me every time I thought of him and that terrible night suddenly lightened. And I knew I had to let it all out.

"In many ways, Bonnie and Jacob saved my life. I learned how to find food and water and to fight. I regained my trust in others. In myself." As a knot grew in my throat, my voice broke.

He grasped my hands. I thought I'd jerk away, but I relaxed into his touch. I studied his calloused hands, the result of years of training, as he held mine with so much care.

"If you don't want to talk about it, you don't have to." He gently squeezed them, and I couldn't help doing it back.

"They came in the middle of the night. Three officers. Bonnie was ill, and they seized her. They intended to..." I shook my head, gathering strength to continue. "Jacob went to defend her and asked me to hide. He was shot."

Hot tears streamed down my cheeks.

He brushed his thumb over my hand. "You don't have to—"

"I do. I need to get this off my chest. This fear. That's what they want." I curled forward and dropped my head. "They killed Jacob and raped Bonnie until she died. Her screams continued until there was only silence. And all I could do was hide."

I gulped. I could almost hear her.

Hear myself.

Pain. Powerlessness. Anguish.

It was suffocating.

Davon drew me to him while I sobbed. Holding me until I let it all out. Until there was nothing left.

I pulled back just enough to see his face.

His gaze was fixed on me. "I'm sorry this happened to you. There are no words."

"I promised them and myself I would take the government down. Avenge them."

He stayed silent. Unblinking. Then he squeezed my hands and brought them between us. "Abigail Davis, I vow this to you. We'll defeat them and retake the city at any cost."

I exhaled.

He would not abandon me. We would take it all back.

Davon started training me two days later. My body was very weak, but my strength came back slowly. We worked on balance and coordination first, then started to build my resistance by using the stairs.

After a week, I could endure longer trainings. He never left my side, monitoring my form and heart rate. He told me he'd been training the PRF military force since it was created nine years ago.

We sought each other's presence, spending most of our time together. While I was with Davon, Matt would keep watch and vice versa.

Matt oversaw my health, always checking in on me. I'd gained a pound or two in the last couple of weeks and was getting healthier. Hopefully, we'd be able to make the journey soon.

I was leaning on a workbench, writing in my journal, when Matt offered me a protein bar.

"Hey. How are you feeling?"

"Good." I started eating it. "Thanks."

"Your color has improved." He grinned as I took a big bite of the bar. "As well as your appetite."

"I feel much better."

"That's what I wanted to talk to you about. The patrols could recheck this building at any moment, and we can't risk it. I think we should start preparing for the journey. How do you feel about it?" He wrinkled his eyebrows.

I dropped my pencil. My heart pounded so hard that I could practically hear it. To finally leave this place and see my family. That's all I'd longed for.

I clasped Matt's hands. "Let's do it."

"Perfect. I'll talk to Davon as soon as he's back so we can start planning."

Blood rushed through my body at the realization that we'd finally make the journey. I couldn't wait to see them!

Chapter 10

Abi

"*D*ecember 2203: A couple of months ago we took our first step to- ward reaching our goal. Davon brought a map with the location of an underground bunker system constructed during one of the many wars that came before us. The system needed some repairs to the infrastructure that were already underway.*" (Deborah Davis's journal)*

We started early and prepared everything before sunrise.

As I was organizing my stuff, I double-checked it, making sure every- thing was packed and ready. I took my family picture and studied it. So much had changed.

Three years ago, Deb gave me this backpack and sent me on my way. Soon I would get back to her.

Would I be able to live a normal life?

Friends. Family. A new, fresh beginning.

These past weeks had been unbelievable. Sharing my time with Davon and Matt made me hope for more. I not only found a new sense of kinship in them, but I'd also watched them spar, and they were incredible. The way they fought, their focus and determination in every move. I wanted that—to join their fight.

I was already a rebel in my own right, but I wanted to be much more, and I knew they could teach me to be strong and become like them. Unstoppable.

I jumped as Matt touched my shoulder. "Hey, sorry to scare you. You zoned out for a bit. Are you okay?"

"Sure. Sorry. It's just..." I shook my head. "I can't believe I'm leaving this city. It's surreal."

He leaned sideways and peered at the picture. "Is that your family?"

I beamed at him. "Yes. These are my parents, Douglas and Elizabeth Davis."

"They look like they adored each other."

I swallowed hard as hot tears pricked my eyes. "They did. They were the best." I put the photograph away.

He squeezed my shoulder. "Soon you'll be surrounded by people who will become your family." He took my backpack. "Let's go. Davon says it's safe outside."

I followed him downstairs. Davon turned as we approached.

Every time I saw him my heart skipped a beat and his smile warmed me inside.

Clouds covered the skies as we moved through the alleys. We all donned gray clothes to blend with our surroundings.

I glanced around and clutched my hoodie.

This isn't right. Where are the patrols?

Not a single one for more than half an hour. My thoughts drifted to that night.

No.

I shook my head and hurried to keep pace with Davon while Matt watched our backs.

"Keep close," Davon muttered at me, then looked behind me.

I twisted in time to see Matt change his stance and cock his gun.

He nodded and moved to the front, peeking around a corner of a building. He gestured for us to follow, and we rapidly crossed another alley.

After some time, the wind picked up, and we entered a charred structure. A storm was brewing.

I shivered. A chilly gust of wind hit me as I peered outside, and I pulled
my hood over my head.

Davon passed around some protein bars and took the map out of his
pocket.

Gritting my teeth, I went to his side. "Davon?"

He fixed his gaze on me, giving me his undivided attention.

"Don't you think it's strange we haven't encountered a patrol?"

Davon flicked his gaze between Matt and me and scraped a hand through
his hair. "I know. Something's off. But we need to keep moving." He
pointed at the map. "We'll reach checkpoint four soon. Just one more mile
to go. Once we get there, we check in and continue north. We can stay the
night at the safe house so Abi can rest and continue the journey tomorrow. We should reach the peak tomorrow night." He pointed toward the
mountains where the base was.

We started moving again. After half an hour, Davon abruptly halted,
extending an arm out to stop me.

A woman screamed, followed by two gunshots.

Davon jumped in place and twisted around. He took me with him inside
a building. His hands shook. "Fuck." He kept me in place with one hand
while gripping his hair behind his head with the other.

When I looked up, tears hovered in his eyes.

"What the hell's going on?" Matt walked to the front. His face grew pale.
"Is that Carlos and Christina?"

I moved away from Davon. A patrol of ten heavily armed soldiers stood
guard. Two of them went to open the back of a white NWG van. Behind
it, a man and a woman lay on the street, a pool of blood beneath them.

No, no, this isn't happening.

"What the fuck?" My voice was too loud.

One of the guards signaled another and started moving toward us.

We're going to die here. I'll never see my family again.

The musky scent of Davon's palm filled my nose as he softly covered my mouth and took a step back.

He let go of my mouth and slipped his hand down to my stomach.

I flinched at his touch on instinct.

He took his hand away and rested it on my shoulder.

The soldier's footsteps drew near.

Another shouted, "Hey, guys. A little help here. These bodies are heavy."

"We heard some noise coming from this building!" the one approaching yelled back.

"It must have been a stray or a rat. You can come back later to guard the perimeter, but, first, we need to get these two in the van and clean up this shit."

Davon pressed my back to a wall and bent forward, his face only inches from mine. "I won't let anything happen to you. Do you trust me?" His voice was strained, and he flattened his lips into a hard line.

An invisible force tightened around my chest. The world spun around me, and I fisted my hands onto his shirt to keep from falling. Everything was hazy.

Davon held my face in his hands. "Breathe."

I nodded. He was so close I could feel his warm breath. I followed it, finally able to catch my own.

His touch was gentle as he tipped my chin up so our eyes met. "We *will* make it out. I promise." He pulled me to his chest and whirled his head toward Matt. "We need to find another route out of the city. After sundown, we'll walk half a mile east and run toward the next entry point."

Matt nodded and bit his quivering lip.

Davon recovered, his emotions now under control. But Matt had a vacant expression. It was obvious the two people lying out there were their friends.

Once it was dark, Davon guided us to our next exit point, using small storage buildings as cover. We faced a two-lane highway with a raised sidewalk on the other side. A wall separated it from the forest.

Matt went out to check for patrols. Everything was clear.

The wind howled around us.

Davon brushed my arm. "We're going to need to run from now on. The next point of entry doesn't have cover. We'll follow that sidewalk for about a quarter of a mile. There's a break in the wall that will get us into the forest. Once we get through it, we'll be safe."

I shuffled back. I had an empty feeling in the pit of my stomach. What if something went wrong? What if we were caught? "I don't run that fast."

He softly grabbed my shoulders. "You're ready for this, and I'll be right beside you. Don't let go of my hand, okay?"

His rough hand gripped my own, and I squeezed hard.

The weather got even worse. As we stepped outside, heavy rain drenched us.

Davon cocked his chin at Matt. "Go front. Don't look back. Just run and lead the way."

With a nod, Matt went ahead, his gun ready. "Okay, guys. We go in three, two…"

Davon pulled me as we dashed across the highway. We jumped to the sidewalk and continued uphill as rain poured on us, drowning my vision. The strong winds hit us, masking all sounds and making the climb more difficult. My lungs burned, but I kept running as fast as I could.

I slipped, but Davon broke my fall. A cracking noise echoed around us. Two guards ran toward us. Firing at will.

"Shit," Davon said. "Run!"

We bounded forward, but the soldiers were gaining on us, and gunshots kept coming.

"We're almost there," Davon shouted, urging me to go faster.

We ran side by side. A splitting noise, followed by an impact to my right thigh made me fall. I released an agonizing scream. The searing pain in my leg made it impossible to stand.

"Abi? Fuck!"

Nausea hit me fast, and I retched.

Davon picked me up. He ran and talked to me as the rain gushed down mercilessly on us. "Stay with me."

My vision started to blur.

The rain washed away my tears, and I clenched my eyes shut, wishing this was all a bad dream. My leg went numb, and a cold chill slithered up my spine.

"We're almost there." Davon's strong arms drew me closer, and I clung to his warm, soothing voice.

Footsteps approached fast. Two gunshots fired next to us as my mind was shrouded by darkness.

Two voices talked frantically, and I grunted as someone tugged at my pants, pressing hard against my thigh.

"Fuck, Matt! Be careful! She's hurting."

Davon...

"Keep the pressure. We need to stop the bleeding," Matt said.

I opened my eyes. Davon knelt beside me, holding my thigh as Matt tied a cloth firmly around it. The pain was unbearable.

"Davon!" I cried out. "What's happening?"

He leaned toward me. "I'm here. Everything will be okay."

"Keep her still," Matt said.

I lifted my head. Blood oozed from my thigh, and Matt's hands were drenched with it. Davon's clothing was also soaked.

I felt lightheaded, and everything grew hazy. "Davon?" I gripped his arm. Was I dying?

"Stay with us." Davon's voice was urgent. Pleading.

But I couldn't stay awake and fell into oblivion.

Leaves crunched beneath my hands. We must have reached the forest.

"I can't believe they're dead," Matt muttered.

"It's happening, Matt. If we do nothing about it, they'll find us. We need to talk to Connor." Davon's voice was deep, and it sounded like he cracked his knuckles. "Thanks for coming back for us. If not for you, those guards would've killed us. Did you hide the bodies?"

"Yeah. All done. I checked the area. There's no one else. I recognized one of them. He was the one who heard Abi. He must have stayed to check the area."

"Still, we need to get to a safer place." He paused. "Is this normal? Why isn't she waking?"

I'm awake.

I wanted to let them know, but my eyes wouldn't open.

"Don't worry. Let her body rest and recover. The bleeding stopped a while ago, and I sutured the wound as best as I could under the circumstances. Her body is just responding to blood loss and stress." Matt's voice sounded far away.

"How did this happen?" Anger lurked in Davon's clipped tone.

"It just did. You can't control everything."

Footsteps receded.

"I need to take a piss," Matt said. "I'll check her wound when I get back, see how it's doing."

I willed my eyes open, and I saw stars.

Davon clutched my hand, his eyes closed. "Please come back to us."

I squeezed his hand, and he jerked his head up.

"Hi there," I murmured.

He held my hand to his chest. Bending toward me, he exhaled and threaded his fingers through my hair, which sent comfort all over my body.

"How do you feel?" His dark gaze centered on me.

"It hurts like hell." I coughed and recoiled at the shooting pain. "What about you? Are you hurt?"

"You just got shot, and you're asking about me?" He shook his head, put his canteen close to my mouth, then held my head up so I could drink.

"I'm just glad you're awake. We'll make sure you heal and get you back on your feet. This shouldn't have happened." He touched my cheek.

I leaned into his touch and closed my eyes. "How long was I out?" It felt like hours.

"When you got shot, we were very close to the entry point. We reached the forest in about two minutes and stopped to take care of your wound. That's when your body went into shock." He let out a hard sigh. "We walked until the rain stopped. You've been out for over an hour."

☐His eyes glazed over. "I thought I lost you."

I smoothed his wrinkled brow, then brushed the stubble on his cheek.

"I'm here. I'm okay now."

I'd never seen him this way, this lost. He looked so fragile. Broken.

He took my hand and kissed the palm tenderly, softly. It was a simple, intimate act. One that sent a jolt through my body and made me realize how much he cared for me.

"Hey, you're awake!" Matt emerged from behind a tree, breaking the moment.

We both centered our attention on him.

"Hey, Doctor," I said as Davon made room for him beside me without letting go of my hand.

Matt brushed my shoulder. "How are you doing?"

I looked down at my thigh. "It hurts...a lot." My voice was small.

He sighed and undressed my wound. I dug my nails into the ground as he removed the last piece of bandage.

"The bullet went in and out. No bones seem to be affected, but the muscles are definitely damaged, and there's a lot of inflammation." He rewrapped it and gave me a pill and some water. "Take this. It's for the pain. It's all we have for now."

He regarded Davon. "We need to get to the safe house and get some antibiotics and stronger pain meds into her system as soon as possible."

A pained hiss escaped me as I tried to sit up, but I slumped back and grimaced.

"What do you think you're doing?" Davon frowned down at me.

I huffed. "What does it look like? Trying to get up. We need to move." I cursed, attempting to sit up again to no avail.

"Not on your own you're not."

"But..."

Before I could protest, he scooped me up.

Umph. My breath hitched, and I bit my lip.

Fuck, it hurts.

I squirmed as I tried to get into a comfortable position.

He glanced at me. "I'm sorry. I know you're hurting."

I relaxed as he massaged the back of my neck. His touch was slow and careful.

"Try to rest."

I nodded.

He started walking deeper into the forest. "Let's go, Matt."

Matt followed behind with our rucksacks.

A sheen of sweat covered Davon's forehead as he shifted me up. Everything faded in and out of sight, and I grasped his shirt, struggling to stay awake.

He held me tight. "Don't worry about me. Please. Just rest."

My eyes drifted shut, and I fell into a deep sleep, cocooned in his warmth.

Chapter 11

Abi

"*January 2204: We left everything to Davon. Three years to endure until we could get back to our mission. We got into the same facility, which felt like a prison. Same routine daily—wake up, eat, take classes, eat, study, eat, and sleep. Solitary quarters for everyone and not much time to make friends. This was going to be exhausting.*" (*Deborah Davis's journal*)

Bright light surrounded me as someone laid me down. My eyes adapted, and I saw white all around me and then him.

Davon's heavy eyelids revealed the journey had been difficult.

He brushed my hair behind my ear. "We're here." His voice rolled through me like honey.

Matt rummaged around a kitchenette, opening and closing cabinets. Davon went to a water container and got some. No windows, just a light-bulb in our area and one illuminating the bathroom. A bunk bed to my left.

"Found it." Matt got something out of a small fridge hidden inside a cabinet. He approached me with an IV bag, two small vials, and some medical supplies that included syringes.

I shifted and winced at the ache coursing through my leg.

He came to my side and pierced one vial, filling a syringe.

Not again.

On impulse, I covered my arm.

Davon stood beside me. "Abi, you know we have to do this."

I blew out a breath and glanced at Matt, whose eyes were red-rimmed.

Had he been crying?

"Okay. Do your worst."

"I'll put an IV in your arm and then inject penicillin directly into your thigh. You should feel better by tomorrow morning." Matt prepared my arm for the IV.

Davon moved to my left side. I flinched as the needle stung my arm. He took my hand in his, taking my mind off the pain.

God, I hate needles.

Davon held my gaze. "It's almost over."

Matt stripped the wound, and I jerked back in pain. It was like someone was stabbing my thigh mercilessly, and I quivered at the force of it.

I squeezed Davon's hand and stayed as still as possible.

"It's over." Davon's thumb moved languidly along my palm, soothing me.

"Sorry about that. I had to inject the penicillin as close to the wound as possible." Matt collected his equipment. "We'll rest here until you heal properly."

Davon helped me up and passed me a cup of water.

Matt injected some stuff into my IV.

We both glanced at him.

"These are pain relievers. They'll drown the pain so you can sleep." Matt went back to the kitchen.

I stroked Davon's dark stubble with my thumb, caressing his cheek, wanting to comfort him. "You should rest as well. You look like hell."

"Thank you for your kind words." He chuckled as he leaned into my touch. "I'll rest as soon as you're asleep."

I would have to trust him on that one since I was already feeling the effects of the meds. The world started to shift as everything went out of focus.

As I drifted in and out of sleep, Matt and Davon talked.

"Are you okay?" Matt asked in a low voice.

"I am. It's just..." Davon exhaled. "I thought I'd lose her, same as Elaine. I can't explain it, but I feel protective of her. I..."

I struggled against the sleep threatening to claim me.

"Will not happen again. We're better prepared. Her wound will heal."

I tried to hear all Matt was saying but kept slipping in and out of consciousness.

"Was strong too. I just can't bear if anything happened to..."

Davon's voice was muted as I fell into nothingness.

When I opened my eyes, the main room was pitch black, but the bathroom was brightly lit.

Davon slept on the bottom bunk bed as Matt snored loudly on top, his foot dangling from the railing.

Davon's brow creased. Even though his eyes were closed, he moaned as he tossed and turned.

I frowned. This wasn't the first time I'd seen him restless during the night. Could he suffer from nightmares like me?

He shifted a bit and relaxed. I sighed.

He wore only his cargo pants. One hand hovered over his obliques, while the other was arched behind his head.

I moved to a sitting position on the bed, hissing in pain, and froze, hoping not to wake him.

These short glimpses of him were rare.

He was always the protector. Strong but gentle. Always on guard. Sheltering me from my demons.

He breathed languidly, ragged and gorgeous. All muscle, not an ounce of fat on his body.

I focused on the phoenix tattoo that adorned most of his pecs and the left part of his abdomen. Flames covered the feathers, ranging from orange to red to black. A work of art.

I shook my head. Nature was calling me. Not wanting to wake anyone, I silently pulled the sheet off. I wore only my T-shirt and my underwear, nothing else. Had I been like this the whole way here?

My cheeks burned, and I hugged my arms around myself.

Had they seen them? My scars... The shirt was long enough that it reached my midthigh. Maybe they didn't notice.

I took a steady breath. I needed to focus.

Inching toward the side of the bed, I put my weight on my left leg and stood, gripping the bed for support. When I reached the end, I took a tentative step toward the bathroom and hit the floor with a thud as a surge of pain tore through my leg. I grabbed my thigh, suppressing a scream as I tried to reach for the bed.

Strong hands encircled my waist and hoisted me off the ground. I froze in place, too scared to move, but Davon's unique musky scent brought me back to my senses.

"What the hell do you think you're doing?" His tone was sharp as he turned me around to face him.

I glared at him. "I need to pee, and I didn't want to wake you. My leg hurts, and I really don't need you scolding me right now."

"I'm sorry. It's just that..." He clenched his jaw. "It drives me crazy how you always want to do everything on your own and never ask for help."

"You're right. I'm stubborn. But I've told you before, I'm used to dealing with everything by myself. This whole thing of having you around is all new to me."

His features tightened. This was one topic we'd fought about before. He always wanted to do everything for me, and I wanted to do it myself.

"Okay. But at least let me help you." He offered me his arm.

I accepted it, and he lifted me enough that my right foot didn't touch the floor.

"Can you manage from here?" He let go of me as I took hold of the sink.

"I think so. Thanks."

He nodded. "Let me know if you need help getting back."

As soon as the door closed behind him, my body returned to its emergency status. I noticed Matt had taken out the IV, making it easier to manage the job.

I called out softly to Davon after finishing.

He held me close to his chest and helped me slide into bed. "I'm going to let go now." His voice was smooth, comforting.

A groan came from the bunk bed. "What time is it?"

Davon stepped back and looked at his watch. "It's 5:30 in the morning. I'll make coffee."

Matt yawned. "Thanks, man."

My memory of the rich taste made my mouth water. "Wait. Coffee? It's been years since I last had coffee! Can you make one for me too?"

His low chuckle stirred something in me, and he winked at me. "As you wish, Miss Davis."

Breakfast was unbelievable. Davon made eggs and sausage and served me a huge cup of coffee.

"Where do you get all this food from?" I bit into a sausage.

Matt drank his coffee. "Sometimes our hunters bring back fresh meat, but most of our food comes from the farming and engineering bunker. They have laboratories that prepare synthetic meat and protein-based foods and an underground greenhouse where they grow all our fresh produce."

"It's still difficult for me to imagine all you've created. It's surreal." I sipped my coffee. Strong, just the way I liked it.

The throbbing pain in my thigh took me back to yesterday's events. I couldn't stop picturing the bodies, and that name kept flashing in my mind. Christina.

"Davon?"

He ate a bite of eggs. "Hmm?"

"There's something clawing at my mind about what happened yesterday."

"You mean two nights ago. You've been asleep for more than a day," Matt said.

I gasped. I slept through an entire day.

"What did you want to know?" Davon asked.

I shook my head. "It's about your friends."

Davon stopped eating. "Two great soldiers and good friends."

Matt rubbed his face. "Jimmy will be devastated when he hears about Christina."

I gulped. "Jimmy?"

No way. It couldn't be.

"You remember him?" Davon said.

I narrowed my eyes. "How do you know I've met him?"

How could he possibly know about us?

"He talked about you all the time. He's the captain of the runners and wanted to be on this mission from the beginning."

"But I thought he and Christina were caught while trying to get away."

Davon shook his head. "They got out safely. Some stories about the escapees are twisted so others don't get the wrong idea."

Oh my God, it's truly him. He's alive and well.

My heart swelled, but then I remembered. I bit my lip. "He'll be devastated. Christina and he were very close." I wanted to be with him so badly, to comfort my friend. "And what about the other soldier? What was his name?"

He let out a heavy sigh. "Carlos."

The name hinted at a memory, but I couldn't grasp it.

"You don't need to say more. I'm sorry about bringing this up during breakfast." I stared down at my food and continued eating.

"No worries. It's normal to have all these questions, and if we can answer them, we will." Matt patted my free hand. "I almost forgot." He went to the kitchen and gave me some pills. "Pain meds. These won't cause drowsiness."

I swallowed them and continued with my meal.

Davon glanced at me. "How's the pain?"

"Not as bad as before, but it still hurts like hell."

He looked down, a pained expression on his face. "It's my fault. It shouldn't have happened."

I covered his hand, and he inhaled sharply. "Don't say that. You had no idea soldiers were going to be there."

He closed his eyes. "I should've known. I was supposed to protect you, and I failed. You could have died."

"But I didn't."

He shook his head and let go of my hand before returning to his food.

Matt mouthed, "Let him cool off."

Davon eventually helped me to bed while Matt washed the dishes. He put gloves on and checked my thigh wound. It appeared better, but the area was still red and raw to the touch.

"Do we have any more antibiotics? The wound looks infected," Davon asked.

Matt approached with a syringe. "This is the only one left. By the way it looks, she'll need at least two more shots." He held my thigh. "Take a deep breath."

I ground my teeth and gripped the mattress as the syringe pierced my skin.

Fuck, that hurt.

Davon dressed the wound, then took out the map. They went to the table and started planning, going into mission mode.

"There's a hidden cache about seven miles east." Davon pointed at the map. "I can make the trip and be back in the afternoon with more meds. What do you think?"

Matt nodded. "Sounds like a plan."

I read through Deb's journal while Davon got ready. I never tired of it. I could almost hear her voice beside me whenever I read it.

Davon approached me. "I'll be back soon. Let Matt know if you need anything."

I closed the book. "I will. Be careful out there."

"I will." He touched his sheathed blade, then squeezed my hand. "I'll see you soon."

He approached Matt, who played solitaire on the table. "Take care of her."

"Of course. Stay alert out there. Soldiers may be searching the area."

They shared a handshake, and Davon climbed the metal ladder and exited through the hatch.

I sat at the edge of the bed. "Matt?"

"Yes?" He raised his head, his sparkling green eyes locked on mine. He ran his hand through his hair, attempting to move a defiant golden curl away from his face but failing miserably.

"How far from the city are we?" I clenched my fists together, fighting my inner turmoil while my uninjured leg bounced vigorously.

What if someone followed us out here?

"We're ten miles north. Still fifteen more to go."

I nodded as I calculated in my mind. It wouldn't take long to get there, but with my leg... "And are you sure we'll be safe there?"

He sat next to me. "I don't know. I won't lie to you. If the government is onto us, our whole system may be in danger. Davon and I have feared this for a while, and we've talked to Connor about engaging for years, but he keeps saying we need to be stronger and increase our numbers to have a chance at getting the city back. But if we stay put and they find us first, we lose everything we've built. Everything we've worked for." He rubbed the back of his neck.

"If there's so much to prepare for, why did you spend these last two years searching for me? Getting the city back is more important."

The citizens suffered daily. Many searched for a way out. And they spent their resources searching for me?

"This mission was much more. We promised Connor and Deb we'd find you, and while we focused mostly on that, we advanced our cause. In the last year alone, we saved over twenty runaways and kept the government away from our soldiers. We lost the checkpoint, but we made progress." He straightened. "As for myself, I'm glad we came across you. I believe it happened for a reason."

I wanted to believe him. To trust my reason to survive was to fulfill my oath. I willed myself to believe everything would be all right at the thought of meeting my sister again, of regaining my family. And speaking of family...

"How is Connor?" He wasn't just Deb's boyfriend. After my parents died, he was like a father to me.

Matt's eyes softened. "He's all right. You know they married, right?"

I widened my eyes. "They did?"

"Yeah." Matt grinned. "Three years ago, a couple of months after the attack."

I looked down at my hands. "I can't wait to see him."

"I'm sure he feels the same way."

I returned my gaze to him. "Thanks."

Matt's right eyebrow shot up. "What for?"

I extended my hand, and Matt took it. "For not giving up. For saving me."

He squeezed my fingers. "Always."

We ate lunch, and Davon still wasn't back.

"Do you think he's okay?" I asked Matt as we drank an afternoon coffee. My stomach roiled at the thought of something happening to Davon.

"Maybe he had to go farther out. Perhaps the cache didn't have antibiotics."

I closed my eyes. "Yeah. I bet that's it." But I didn't believe it for a minute. Something happened.

After an hour passed, Matt began to pace. I sat by the table, writing in my journal in an effort to keep calm.

The hatch opened.

Matt swiftly drew his revolver and aimed.

A sack fell to the floor, and Davon hastily came down, closing the hatch behind him. His face was covered in scrapes and bruises.

I struggled to stand but collapsed back into my chair.

"What the hell happened?" Matt said.

Davon placed the bag on the table. "I got the cache but was followed by two soldiers. I ran in circles until I lost them. I left them about three miles south and took the long way back here." He got the antibiotic vial and syringe and gave them to Matt. "Is this what we needed?"

"Yes, but let me take care of those cuts first."

He slapped Matt's hand away as he covered the huge gash on his forehead. "Tend to her first. I'll deal with my cuts."

Davon took me to the cot without a word. He gazed at me, then headed to the bathroom.

Matt gave me the third shot, which didn't hurt that much.

I glanced toward the bathroom. "Is he okay?"

He wrapped the gauze around my thigh. "He gets like that. I'll suture his cut when he comes out."

The afternoon was silent. After Matt stitched Davon's gash, we had dinner.

Matt went to sleep, and Davon put me to bed and sat on his cot. His gaze restless, he propped his elbows on his knees and covered the top of his head with his hands.

"How are you?" I whispered.

He let his hands drop and sighed. "I just want to get you home as soon as possible."

I wanted to assure him everything would be fine. "You'll get me there. I trust you."

He lay back and folded his arms behind his head. "I hope you're right."

Chapter 12

Davon

A week passed. We did as Matt suggested so Abi would get her strength back.

As soon as her wound healed from the infection, I started giving her therapies. It pained me to see her strained face as she took her first steps a few days ago. But she continued getting back to it daily. She was a fighter.

"How do you feel about getting out of here in the afternoons to start practicing? Are you up for it?" I stretched and flexed her right leg, trying to increase her range of motion.

A wide grin covered her face. "I'm in. I'm on the verge of going crazy in here."

I knew being trapped in a room brought back memories from her past. She told me about it a couple of nights ago, wanting to share her fears in the hopes of overcoming them. They'd taken root deep inside her.

"Perfect." I continued massaging the area.

She moaned and fell back on the cot. Her eyes closed as I loosened her muscles.

The sounds she made did things to me. I craved her presence. Her touch.

No matter how much I tried to deny it, it was there. It couldn't be helped. She felt like home. Someone with whom I could be myself, who got me. What killed me was all I was hiding from her. I was a coward. I knew she would run, and I couldn't risk losing her, losing someone I...

Taking a deep breath, I pushed those thoughts away. I couldn't put myself in that position again. I needed to concentrate on the task at hand and get her home. That was it.

Abi released another moan as I kneaded her calf.

I smiled. "You really enjoy this. I'm starting to believe you'll never say you've recovered just to get these."

And I wouldn't stop unless she asked me to.

She laughed and propped herself on her elbows. "You got me!"

"Well, I'm enjoying it too." I smirked at the glint in her eyes. "Pleasing you has become one of my favorite pastimes."

She widened her eyes for a second, then gasped as I increased the pressure on the sole of her foot. "Oh God."

I chuckled.

"Can I get one too?" Matt asked from the table where he was taking notes. "Abi seems to be enjoying it a little too much."

"Sorry, brother. There's no way I'll put a hand on your feet."

Abi and I laughed as Matt shook his head and continued writing.

I winked at her. "By the way, do you think Abi and I can go out in the afternoons to get some air and practice?"

"I think it'll be good if she gets to move more, but we need to help her up the ladder. Once she's out, she can use the hiking pole to walk. But keep the training moderate."

She pumped her fist and got off the bed, using the hiking pole as support. "Well, what are we waiting for?"

I waited on the upside with her pole as she started up. It was a slow process, but it was working. She put all her weight on the left foot to climb up each step, pressing on her right foot to sustain herself. She winced a bit at each step but kept going. Matt stayed below in case she missed a step, but she did just fine.

There was no easy way to find the safe house without knowing its whereabouts. The trapdoor that gave access to it was heavily covered with vegetation and camouflaged to appear as part of the ground. Its small control pad was hidden on the ground next to it.

We checked daily for guards and hadn't seen any in four days. Nevertheless, I came out armed in case we encountered any unwanted visitors.

Clean air filled my lungs as I helped her stand and gave her back her hiking pole. The air in the city was thick and covered by gray skies. Out here, everything was fresh. Clean. Full of color. The woodsy scent of trees, the chirping of birds, and the coolness of the wind invigorated me.

"I love this. It seems almost as if all that happened before was just a bad dream." She closed her eyes. "Thank you."

The light in her eyes as she took in the forest made it all worth it.

I wanted to show her a place I found while scouting. She'd love it. "Follow me. I found a place that has a clearing where we can practice. It has a hell of a view."

On our way, she asked about the safe houses, curious about the energy supply. Everything was powered by off-the-grid energy that came from harvesting tree technology. We had a team of engineers that specialized in the mass production of leaves with organic solar cells. They made sure we had enough energy to run the whole system. I didn't know the exact mechanics, but it worked. We had power.

When we reached the clearing, she gasped at the sight. Promissa... The whole city could be seen from this spot. We had at least an hour before the sun set.

"Show me your dagger," I said.

She unsheathed Jacob's blade.

"That's a sentry trench knife, perfect for stabbing and close combat." I took out the additional blade I brought for her. "This one is a Biltong pocket khukuri. It's perfect for you. Small, light, and easy to conceal, hence the name. It's used for slashing." I gave it to her. "It's yours."

"Really? You're just giving this to me?" Her gaze was drawn to the blade.

"I want you to have it. Just in case. I can't bear the thought of something bad happening to you because you're not prepared."

She watched me as I went past her to get to the clearing.

"Come on. We don't have much light left."

I showed her how to hold her dagger, slash, and evade attacks. Just the movements until she got enough strength to truly engage. Then I taught her how to hold the khukuri.

After an hour, we stopped practicing. It was enough for one day.

We sat to watch the sunset, our hands touching lightly. A heavy fog blanketed parts of the forest as the orange hue of the last sunrays covered the city. It was breathtaking.

My chest grew heavy. I was strongly aware of how close we were. I cast a side glance at her, catching her gaze.

She grinned.

Gorgeous. Her eyes gleamed, and her long hair fell in waves as the wind blew. The dark strands were softened by a coppery hue. I longed to run my fingers through it.

I couldn't help but cover her hand with mine as the desire to touch her became unbearable.

I was afraid she'd yank it away, but instead, she opened it, intertwining her fingers with mine. I sighed, caressing the side of her hand with my thumb. It felt right to share this moment with her.

She leaned against my shoulder. Her eyes were a blend of honey and emerald as she glanced at me. Her lips parted, and I narrowed the gap between us. I brushed her lips with mine before kissing the corner of her mouth and bringing our brows together.

The warmth of her skin on my mouth burned me inside as my body responded to her proximity. I wanted her so much but couldn't have her. I'd only cause her misery. She was still ignorant of my past, of whom I was. So I'd wait until there were no secrets between us. Until she knew my truth.

We walked back hand in hand and chatted about how ravenous we both were after the training session.

Back at the safe house, dinner was already served. Chili with beans.

"How did it go?" Matt said once we sat.

We exchanged glances. I couldn't understand it, but I'd never felt such a strong bond with anyone before. We understood each other on a different level. I wasn't sure if it was our dark pasts or our determination to bring down the NWG, but whatever the reason, it brought us together.

I was used to being in control, but with her... She had all of it.

"I gave her my pocket khukuri, and we practiced some moves. I think she'll be able to master it with practice."

"I love blades. Out there, they were my way of defense, especially daggers. But that khukuri is on another level." Abi took a spoonful of chili.

Her appetite was voracious, and if we let her, she'd eat both our plates. She looked healthier. If it weren't for the bullet she took, she would be in perfect condition already.

"Tomorrow we can practice with a gun. Who knows? Maybe you're a good shot," Matt said.

Abi's eyes widened. "I've never touched a gun before. I know I should learn to use them, but they make me nervous."

"Why?" Matt asked.

She closed her eyes briefly. "Bad memories."

Matt nodded. "I'll show you the basics—how to load the bullets, aim, and shoot. You never know when you might need to use one."

"I know. I want to learn. It's just... I'll deal with it." She pushed her half-eaten plate away and stood. "I'm tired."

She went into the bathroom.

Matt raised an eyebrow at me.

"I can only guess, Matt. In time, she'll tell us."

Could it have to do with how her friends died? She never told me the specifics.

She came out with a quivering smile and said good night. I didn't dare ask her about it. She reminded me of myself whenever my mind took a stroll down memory lane. If she needed space, that's what she'd get. When she was about to go to bed, she cast me a glance, and I went to her.

"Davon, I... Guns remind me of Jacob. Of the day I lost him." Her eyes were downcast as she fiddled with her bracelets.

I took her hand. "You don't have to explain. Take as much time as you need."

Her eyes were soft as she gazed at me. "No. I'll deal with it and train with Matt. I must move forward."

I couldn't help myself as I bent and kissed her brow, inhaling her fresh, floral aroma. She wrapped her arms around me and pulled me close. Her frame was so small, so delicate. Something reached within me and pulled at my heart, and I let myself go in her embrace. My soul flickered as darkness receded.

I held her close, hugging her head to my chest, and thanked the heavens for this gift. I could almost forget everything that was going on outside. In this moment, it was only us. Slowly, she ended the hug and took a step back. She smiled before getting into bed.

After washing the dishes and making sure she was asleep, Matt and I opened a bottle of whiskey and sat by the table. We kept our voices low to not wake her.

Matt crossed his arms. "Are you gonna tell me what's going on between you two?"

I shook my head. He knew me too well for his own good. I couldn't hide anything from him.

I sighed, glancing back at Abi. "I don't know. I haven't felt like this in a long time."

He slid his chair closer. "Like Elaine?"

"Stronger. I can't get her off my mind. It's like all that matters is her being safe." I set my drink on the table and paced.

"You've got it bad. And from what I've seen, I think she feels the same way. The way you seek each other out. I feel like a third wheel out here." He winked. "Maybe I should go on ahead and leave you to it."

I rolled my eyes. "Don't even joke about it. She's Deb's sister, for God's sake. How could I let this happen?"

I put both palms on the table, waiting for Matt's advice. In terms of relationships, I didn't know much. After I lost Elaine, I didn't take any woman seriously. We just took what was needed from each other and went our separate ways.

To feel again—I didn't want this. It was a road that always ended in pain.

Matt chuckled quietly. "So what? What does it matter if she's her sister? Do you truly think one chooses when or with whom it happens? No, brother. I know you're always guarding yourself, but it seems she broke through your walls."

Fuck.

I gulped down what was left of my drink. I was in deep shit. This was not part of the plan.

Chapter 13

Abi

"*February 2204: A month has passed since my sterilization, and I still struggle. Connor had his vasectomy too. We wanted children in the future, and sacrificing that dream wasn't easy. The government took it away from us. Keeping ourselves compliant for the sake of our mission was the hardest decision we've ever made.*" *(Deborah Davis's journal)*

Matt and I walked silently toward the clearing.

I needed an outlet for all the tension I'd been dealing with lately, and a good training session sounded perfect for that.

"Abi?" Matt's tone was solemn, almost apprehensive.

"Yes?" I tried to keep my voice calm.

He was not to blame for my outrage. No, it was the asshole who remained at the safe house. The one who broke through my barriers just to act as if it meant nothing.

"Why do you look as if you're about to murder someone?"

He approached me as I halted and twisted toward him. He took a step back.

I glanced down. "I'm sorry. It has nothing to do with you. It's Davon."

He exhaled loudly. "That idiot."

"I don't get it. That day in the clearing..." I raised my eyes to him. "We had a moment, but then he distanced himself as if it meant nothing. At first, I assumed I did something wrong, but the longer I thought about it, the less I understood. I didn't do anything to make him walk away."

"Come. Let's sit."

We sat at the same spot I'd shared with Davon five days prior.

Matt rested his elbows on his knees, his gaze fixed on the horizon. "Davon's a good guy. He's just had it tough and sometimes feels like he doesn't deserve to be happy. I'm not defending him. I'm only stating facts. Just know he does care. I'm sure of it."

I knew his past, like my own, tormented him. And like me, he chose to keep it to himself.

I looked down at my hands and fiddled with Deb's bracelet. "I care for him more than I thought possible."

And there it was. The truth of it all.

Matt covered my hand with both of his, like Deb would do when I was upset. "Do whatever it takes to get him to see. I've seen the two of you. You have something special. And it crushes me to see you waste it. To see you both drift apart because neither of you is willing to take the next step."

I shook my head and pulled away. "I'm not the type to express my emotions to someone who doesn't care enough to acknowledge them. I've already been through enough. This world. It's merciless. And I'm not going to take a chance on someone who isn't willing to fight."

"You had someone, didn't you?" His tone was kind.

I inhaled deeply. "Yes. Jacob." Saying his name still broke something inside of me.

"He died out there?"

"He was executed." My voice was so low he had to lean closer.

"I'm so sorry." He dropped his gaze. "I'll talk to Davon."

"No!" He needed to hear it from me. "I'll do it, but it won't be pretty."

Matt stood and slipped his hands into his pockets. "Please be patient with him. He can be a jerk sometimes, but he cares much more than what he shows." He offered me his hand. "Let's go. We have some shooting to do."

We went past the clearing and into an area that had an old, abandoned shack. Matt prepared it for the training by marking out areas around it and arranging random objects for target practice.

The gun was heavy even as I lifted it for what felt like the twentieth time. In the two hours I'd been here, only one shot had found its target, and it was in the middle of the goddamn shack. Impossible to miss.

"Abi, concentrate. You only have this shot left. I know you can make it."

The wind ruffled the tree limbs and howled across the barn. I swallowed and focused on the right-hand corner of the cabin. There was a small shed with an X painted in the center. Even though I shivered from the cold air, a bead of sweat streamed down my brow. I slowly let the air out and pulled the trigger.

The silencer muffled the sound, but the force of it always startled me.

"What the fuck!" I put the gun in Matt's hand and snatched my hiking pole. "I'm done." I hurried to gather my things.

We walked back to the safe house side by side. I was pissed. Whatever talent I possessed with blades was null when I took a gun in my hands.

"It wasn't that bad," Matt said.

I turned and crossed my arms. "Not that bad?" I raised my eyebrows. "I'm a disaster, Matt! You'd both die if your lives depended on me. That last one was less than twenty feet away. And you're saying it wasn't that bad?"

Matt laughed. "Okay, you're a terrible shot. However, everything can improve with practice."

I pursed my lips. "You don't even believe that, do you?"

He grinned. "At least you're a bit calmer. I feel sorry for Davon, though." He held up a tiny space between his thumb and forefinger. "Just a little bit." His smile faded. "Hear him out, please."

"I will if he's willing."

I continued down the path, my steps dragging as I fought back a sob from the wave of pain that hit me. Not just bodily pain but one that pierced deep within.

What was I going to say to him? How could I be patient when he was so stubborn?

I wanted to drill into him how much his actions hurt me. Every time he turned away from me, the pain seemed nearly physical.

If he knew how drained I was from the last few weeks. How hard I struggled to hide the physical toll these trainings were taking on me. I couldn't relax knowing we were stuck out here till I got better.

The only things that kept me going were my desire to see my family again and his unwavering strength.

I was a strong, independent woman. I'd been out there alone for years, years when I hadn't required a man by my side. Until Davon.

I didn't want this.

When did he become so important to me? Why did I let him take such a special place in my heart?

No matter how much I tried to pull away, to say, "Fuck Davon" and move on with my life, I couldn't. I cared for him. For his courage, pain, passion, flaws, and convictions. And if what Matt said was true, he felt the same way about me.

So why? Why was he shutting me out?

I couldn't take it anymore, so I rushed toward the safe house. To find my answers.

Chapter 14

Davon

I was alone in the safe house, studying the map to the base. Three days till the journey.

Abi's wound was healed, but the anguish lingered despite her efforts to hide it. A tiny wince or a barely audible moan was enough to tell me the pain was still there. Stubborn as hell, she sucked it down and kept going.

After our moment in the clearing, I decided to give her some space to heal, not only physically but emotionally. We never went out again to practice, and Matt took over her training. Denying being close to her was driving me nuts, so I took on the task of planning the journey.

It would take five, maybe six hours max to make the trip nonstop, but we had to rest because of her injury. For that, we needed a place to sleep near the eight-mile mark halfway through.

The cave.

I'd used it a couple of times while taking this route. It would work.

The trapdoor clanked open.

"I can make it down on my own," Abi said when I tried to help her. Once inside, she entered the bathroom.

No hello. Not even a glance.

My chest tightened at her dismissal. My mind raced, trying to figure out what had happened. We weren't talking much, but her icy attitude troubled me. It was a first.

I rubbed my neck as Matt came down, shaking his head.

"What's with her?" I asked.

He shrugged. "Why don't you ask her?"

"Did something happen out there?"

I stiffened as Matt went to the counter to get some water without answering.

The bathroom door opened, and Abi came out. She went to her cot, took her journal from the side table, and started writing.

What the hell?

"I'm going to take a shower." Matt took his stuff and went into the bathroom.

I sat on my bed and stared at Abi.

She continued writing as if I wasn't there.

"Abi?" Nothing, not even a twitch. "Abi, I'm talking to you."

At last, her gaze met mine, and she closed her journal. "Oh, you want to talk *now*?" She arched her eyebrow.

I had to resist the urge to back away. She was mad at me. I knew it in my soul. I'd never seen such a cold and condescending stare coming from her. "I..."

She never took her eyes off me as she put the book on the side table. "What?" She leaned on her elbows.

"What happened?"

"You really don't have a clue?" She frowned, searching my eyes. "Oh God." She rolled her eyes, blowing out an exaggerated huff, then covered her face with her hands.

"Please. Tell me." I had no idea what to do. What to say. I needed to fix this.

"You want me to tell you?" She pointed a finger close to my face. "You tell me! You suddenly became a different person. We don't talk anymore. When I come to you, you always look for something else to do. You're acting like a cocky bastard, as if the kiss we shared meant nothing. I've had enough!"

My body went rigid. I didn't deal with this kind of situation well, and all thoughts froze at that moment. At her harsh words. Her insulting gestures. My blood heated as I tightened my grip on the bed, trying to control myself and not lash out. I focused on her burning eyes.

I didn't like being put on the spot. The lack of respect. *Never let anyone talk to you the wrong way, son. You're the one in control.* I could almost hear his voice. Throughout my life, it was embedded in me. The need to maintain control. The power our name carried.

I relaxed my grip. I was not like him.

I held up my hands. "Abi, please. Give me some space, and we'll talk." I couldn't keep the edge from my tone.

Her eyes flickered, and she crossed her arms.

"I was trying to give you space." I softened my tone.

Her eyebrows squished together. "So you decide to stop talking to me. To ignore me. All because in your mind it would help me. Fuck you, Davon. Fuck you and all your bullshit!" She ran her hands through her hair. "Did you stop to think about how I'd feel? Do you know how hard it was for me to be open with someone? How much it took for me to relive everything I've been through and put myself out there? Knowing I could lose you like I did Jacob."

I gasped at her words. She had loved Jacob. Could she feel the same way toward me?

She wiped her face as she lay down on the bed, her back to me.

I didn't deserve her. "I'm sorry. I'm an asshole." I touched her shoulder, but she flinched away. "I'll fix this."

"Just leave me alone," she mumbled, and my heart crushed at the sound of her sobs.

I walked away and sat at the table, propping my forehead on my clenched fists. "What have I done?"

I didn't know how much time I spent sitting there until her cries went silent. I glanced back and saw her sleeping at last.

When Matt came out of the bathroom, we went to talk outside. He crossed his arms.

"I fucked up, all right!" I said.

Matt sighed. "I don't know why you're trying so hard to sabotage what you have with her."

I put my hands in my pockets and started pacing. "It's complicated. How can I be with her when I'm lying to her face? I feel like shit."

"We talked about it. We can't let her know about Deb's imprisonment. Connor ordered us to keep it secret, and even if we decided otherwise, once she knows, she'll want to get to the base as soon as possible, and we can't risk her. She needs to take it slow." He was so calm.

I envied his coolness in these kinds of situations. "I know. But that's not the only thing that troubles me. What will she do once she finds out who I really am? Will she ever trust me again?" I focused my gaze on him, silently pleading with him to help me.

He shook his head. "I wish I could help you with that one."

We went back inside, and I prepared Abi a sandwich and a strong coffee.

Matt cleaned his gun and took more ammo. We checked our perimeter daily, and today was his turn. I was certain sooner or later General Lavigne would send reinforcements to search deeper into the forest.

"I'm going now." Matt hugged me, slapping my back. "Happy twenty-eighth birthday, brother. I'm sorry you have to deal with this today."

I nodded. "I asked for it. Now I must man up and deal with the consequences. I'll fix it somehow."

He patted my shoulder. "I hope you do."

Abi woke sometime after, her eyes bloodshot. She went into the bath-room, and once she was out, lunch was already on the table.

"We need to talk." I motioned for her to sit. "Please."

A moment later, she stood beside the table and sighed as she sipped her coffee.

Our eyes met.

"There's no excuse for how I acted. It was never my intention to hurt you or make you feel like what we shared meant nothing. Because it's the opposite, and that's what scares me the most."

I struggled to find the right words. "There are many things you don't know about me. Things I'm not ready to share. Not because I don't trust you, but because I'm not sure how you'll react once I tell you. It's about my past. My father... I just need a little more time. Let me get you to the base. Once you're safe, I promise I'll tell you everything."

She took her seat and fixed her stare on me. "I don't ever want to see you pull away from me. Whatever you've been through, we'll deal with it together."

I wanted to believe her. I truly did. To imagine her understanding and accepting me for whom I was. But the feeling vanished the instant I envi-sioned her hearing my confession. The thought of her turning against me made me shudder. Her hatred focused solely on me.

I didn't want to lose her.

When Matt came back, I had already explained our plan to Abi. She was adamant about the time it would take to get there, as she was eager to see her sisters, but she accepted my decision after I explained the second half of the journey was a long hike.

"Hey! Did you make up?" Matt grinned, ignoring how awkward the question was.

I groaned and returned to the map.

He came closer. "Did he kneel? 'Cause if he didn't, I would make him start over again."

Abi giggled. She never tired of his teasing. I could swear she enjoyed how he drove me mad.

"Well, I'm glad you're back on speaking terms 'cause now we can celebrate," he said.

Abi gave him a quizzical look. "Celebrate what?"

"Big guy turned twenty-eight today."

Abi's eyes widened, her jaw dropping.

I cracked a smile.

She shook her head. "Now I remember you saying it was soon." She sighed and gave me a genuine smile. "Happy birthday."

Matt brought the bottle of whiskey and served three glasses. "To Davon, my brother and best friend. May this year be the one when you finally reach maturity and stop being such an asshole." He smirked. "Seriously, may you find happiness at last and achieve all you've longed for."

Every year he said the same words. But today...today they felt real.

We gulped our drinks in one swig, and Abi started coughing.

"Are you all right?" I patted her back. "Is this your first time drinking?"

"Yes." She blushed, her eyes glazing over. "Fuck, that was strong."

We laughed and chatted for hours.

Maybe this was gonna be a good birthday after all.

Chapter 15

Abi

*"March 2204: We're almost a hundred now, growing continuous-
ly, with people aiding us from within the city. Connor suggested
we put a name to our group, and I was thinking about the People's Revolutionary Front. Davon would take it to a vote this week." (Deborah Davis's
journal)*

Today was the day. Finally, we would go to Janus Peak.

How would it be to see my sisters again after three years?

Being away from Aunt Annie had to have helped Sarah. She needed her
meds, but to be always sedated and never in her right mind couldn't be
their true purpose.

As for Deb... Oh, how I wished to see her. How I fantasized about
talking till the sun went down and just being with her. I was overjoyed
she married Connor. He was a wonderful person. And, to think, he was
the rebellion's leader. His moral compass, self-awareness, and intelligence
made him perfect for the position.

"Hey, daydreaming again?" Matt waved his hands in front of me.

I chuckled. "Sorry. I'm excited about the journey."

"Understandable." He nudged my shoulder. "Ready to go?"

I closed my backpack after putting the last of my stuff in. I nodded, and
we climbed the stairs.

I found myself surrounded by the vibrant hues of autumn. The perfume of pine trees paired with the damp, earthy aroma of fall enveloped me. An orange-and-crimson canvas lay beneath me as the warm colors of the morning painted the horizon.

A cool gust of wind ruffled my hair, and I wished I had put it up as I struggled to tame my wild mass of curls.

Then I saw him, Davon, standing at the clearing, totally immersed in the map he held.

Even though everything was back to normal, the same question repeated itself in my mind. What was it about Davon's past that could change the way I saw him?

He could be a spy or an assassin. Perhaps he was a government soldier who deserted. But why would he be afraid of my reaction? I knew how the world worked, and many good people were forced to do awful things. It wouldn't be his fault.

I snooped on his map and startled him.

"And you say I'm always the one spaced out," I told Matt.

Davon frowned at us. "You're spending too much time with him."

We burst out laughing.

"Laugh all you want, but I'm still the one holding the map."

A grin appeared. He seemed to enjoy our banter as much as we did.

We walked for hours, stopping to rest every now and again. Even though I had my hiking pole, my leg hurt like crazy, so Davon and Matt alternated walking with me in case I needed help.

It was already afternoon when we stopped to check the map.

"The cave is close." Davon put the map away and moved ahead.

We followed and found the cavern about ten minutes later. It was deep enough to keep us out of sight, with just enough room for the three of us.

Davon headed out to scout the area as Matt and I set camp.

"It's gonna be tight, but it'll have to do." Matt put down a sheet for me to rest on.

He took my hiking pole. My legs trembled as I gripped him for support. I grunted as he helped me down.

"Is it hurting too much?"

"I'm just tired," I lied as we huddled together to eat some nuts and berries. I hugged myself below my hoodie to warm up since starting a fire was not an option.

"I'm glad you're talking again. It was driving me nuts being in the middle and unable to do anything about it." He rubbed his hands together.

When Davon distanced himself from me, it was a knife to my heart. As if an important part of me was missing. I got how he felt because for me it was the same. Scary as hell. With the constant danger we lived in, the last thing I wanted was to be close to someone. But I couldn't help it. My chest ached at the thought of losing him.

Matt bumped my shoulder with his. "You know, being close to someone can be frightening but good at the same time."

I stared toward the cave entrance. "Do you know why he won't open up to me?"

Matt picked up a rock and examined it, then stood and walked toward the entrance. "He's always been this guarded. All I ask is that you keep an open mind. His past haunts him. When he's ready, he'll share it with you. You're the only one in years he's trusted enough to let in. That's what scares him the most. Being vulnerable."

Outside, the leaves crunched. Matt pulled out his revolver, but he was too late. Two soldiers, a man and a woman, entered the cave. The woman kicked his gun out of reach, and it fired. I covered my ears. The bullet hit the wall next to me, my scream muffled by its echo.

I yelled as the man grabbed my neck and yanked me up, holding a dagger to my cheek. The cold metal cut my skin lightly as Matt fought the woman.

"Stop or I'll cut her."

Matt stopped and peered up. His gentle eyes were no more, as his cold, hard gaze was set on my aggressor. "I'll kill you."

The soldier behind me chuckled, pressing the edge of the blade against my skin. "The hell you will. Now, be a good boy, and stay put."

The woman forced Matt to stand facing me and pointed the gun at the back of his head. "Weeks searching, but at last we found you. You're going to pay for what you did, as are all your people." She pushed him at arm's length and cocked her gun.

"Stop! I know you want revenge for what they did to Peter, but General Lavigne will want to question them."

She grabbed Matt's curls and pulled him to her face. "Were you the one to pull the trigger? I can just kill your girl here, and we'd be even."

Matt's nostrils flared.

She sneered. "Oh, hit a spot there?" She aimed her gun at me.

His gaze was unsettling. He jerked his body and escaped her hold.

"Ah!" The cold edge of the dagger pierced my skin as the soldier behind me cut all the way down to my chin.

I didn't dare move. He tightened his grip around my neck. Warm blood dripped down my cheek.

"I wouldn't do that if I were you. Your girlfriend here might not make it."

Matt stopped, and the woman pushed him into a kneeling position.

"Bind her!"

As the man bound my hands, a shadow appeared behind the soldier who held Matt at gunpoint. She emitted a choked cry. A large blade, one I recognized, protruded from her stomach.

My breath stopped at the scene before me. Blood soaked her white uniform and pooled on the floor. Her eyes widened in pure terror as the blade was yanked out of her. She moved her shaking hands to the wound, her face ashen. Exhaling one last time, she collapsed. Dead.

That's when I saw him. His dark eyes narrowed, and his jaw tensed. His deadly gaze fixed on the man behind me.

Matt scrambled toward his gun.

Davon took a step forward, and I let myself fall to the side.

"What the hell?" were the last words that left my captor's mouth before Matt angled his gun and a loud boom reverberated around the cave. The man fell beside me. Blood gushed from his brow, his eyes wide and empty.

Davon ran over to me. He brushed my cheek gently. "Are you okay?"

"Yeah." It burned as if a hot rod was pressed against it.

He freed me and helped me sit. I peered at the cave entrance before returning my focus to him.

"They're all dead." He pulled me in. "Thank God you're all right."

Matt came to my side. His face was battered, especially his left eye.

"Let me look at her," he told Davon.

Matt shifted my face to the side.

I winced.

"It's deep. Let me get my things." He went to his bag.

I froze at his words and eyed Davon.

"He's going to suture the wound." Davon reached for his bag and took out a half-empty bottle of whiskey. "Drink. It's going to hurt."

A searing sensation ran down my throat as I downed half of the liquid.

Davon wrapped his arms around me to hold me still, and I turned my face to give Matt access.

I sobbed at the piercing pain and squeezed Davon's hands, holding on until Matt finished.

"All done," Matt said.

I finally relaxed.

"Stay here." Davon stood and nodded at Matt. "Help me with the bodies."

Time seemed to slow as they dragged the bodies out. When my adrenaline rush subsided, the world shifted around me, and I clutched my face, fighting the urge to puke. After they finished, Davon sat beside me, and the weight in my gut eased.

We finally settled and sat in a circle.

"I was on my way back when I heard the gunshot," Davon said. "I killed their scouts and rushed in."

"There were more?" I asked.

Davon took a swig of the whiskey and passed it to Matt. "Just two more. One kept watch at the cave's entrance, the other farther out."

Matt accepted the bottle. "They're too deep into the forest. We need to warn Connor. Strengthen our defenses."

Davon agreed.

I watched their exchange, then took the bottle from Matt and gulped down the last of it. We were leaving the city and entering another battleground. There was no mistake about it: they were coming for us.

"What's the plan?" I wanted to reach the base as soon as possible to see my family and start training. I hadn't told them yet, but I'd made my decision to join the army and fight against the regime. I couldn't just stand there and watch them fight for me.

"We leave at dawn. But for now, let's rest." Davon glanced at Matt. "I'll stand guard the first half of the night. You keep watch till dawn."

Matt nodded and sat with me as Davon walked outside.

"Try to get some rest. Tomorrow's journey will be difficult."

Matt was the first to fall asleep, curled into a corner.

I tried in vain to sleep, my cheek still burning. I must have dozed off after a while because when I opened my eyes, Matt was leaving the cave. I sat up.

Davon came to my side and wrapped his arm around my shoulders. "You're shivering." He drew me closer.

The closeness of his musky scent mingled with the woodland aroma sent a flush of warmth through my body.

In that moment, I could lose myself in his gaze, in those deep, dark eyes.

He blinked. "How are you feeling?"

I exhaled. "I don't know. It feels like we're never going to be safe."

"I know." He shook his head. "I'm sorry they hurt you. I'm glad I got here in time."

"You have nothing to be sorry about. It's not your fault."

He watched me in silence and brushed my uninjured cheek with the back of his hand.

My entire body burned at his warm touch. I closed my eyes, savoring the feeling.

"Let's rest. You need your strength." He lay back. "Come here."

I rested my good cheek on his shoulder.

As we stared at the cave's ceiling, I couldn't help thinking about the times Jacob and I would fall asleep imagining we were under the stars.

I glanced at Davon and caught him watching me.

"Everything good?" he asked.

"Yes. Just remembering my time at the tunnels. Jacob and I would lie down just like this and talk for hours, imagining we were free."

"Do you still love him?"

My heart skipped a beat. I remembered our long conversations. The nights when we lost ourselves in each other. His courage when mine dwindled. His devotion.

"He was my friend. My lover. I did and still do love him in some kind of way. But it's different now. I'll never forget what he did for me."

"I had someone I loved. Her name was Elaine. Six years ago, I lost her. I still think about her, but it's different now, as you say."

My heart thumped hard, as he'd never hinted at this before. "How did she die?"

"We were on a mission. It all went wrong, and a soldier shot her." He briefly closed his eyes. "I tried to get her to Matt, but when we arrived, it was too late. She died in my arms." A tear slid down his cheek.

I snuggled closer and put my hand on his chest. His words pulled at my heart. The pain he must have gone through. "I'm sorry."

He hugged me even tighter as silence surrounded us and we drifted off to sleep.

A soft caress. I opened my eyes.

Davon stroked my hair, his lips skimming over my brow. His reverent touch sent shivers down my spine.

"Morning." His voice was sultry. "I could get used to this."

I traced my finger over the edge of his shirt collar. His muscles tightened. He was breathtaking.

He pressed his forehead against mine.

I breathed deeply, controlling my urge to shudder as memories flashed before my eyes.

This was Davon. I wanted this.

I relaxed into him, and he pulled me closer, running his hand down my side and to my hip.

I bit my lower lip, longing for him to close the gap between us, to press his lips against mine.

To make me forget.

"Well, if you're done with your morning greetings, I propose we start moving."

We both turned to Matt. He grinned mischievously and left the cave.

Davon grunted, then sat up and rummaged through his backpack. "Here."

I took the protein bar he offered.

"Did you sleep well?"

Oh God. I fidgeted with my silver bracelet.

He sighed. "Don't overthink, Abi. Please."

I hadn't slept next to a man since Jacob. And even though my nightmares had dwindled recently, every night I still had at least some trouble sleeping. Last night, though, I don't remember waking up at all. And even after what happened, I was relaxed and full of energy.

"That's it. Now, how did you sleep?" His lips curved, his eyes alight.

I couldn't help but smile back. "I slept all through the night. It's been a long time since I've been able to."

"I know. Me too."

He stood and combed his hair with his fingers. Wavy hair that reached below his shoulders. So dark it was almost black. It was stunning.

He rubbed antibiotic salve on my cheek before helping me up. We gathered our belongings and went outside to meet Matt.

He handed Davon the map. "If we leave now, we can get there this afternoon."

Davon pointed to a trail. "We'll take this path and climb slowly."

"I can manage the more direct way. My thigh doesn't hurt that much." It was a lie, but I wanted to get there so badly.

Matt took the map back. "No, what Davon says is better. It's best not to risk it."

Davon came to my side, and we started on our way.

We hiked all morning and into the afternoon and eventually reached the mountain's slope, which was surrounded by trees.

"We're here." Davon had switched with Matt about halfway through and was now leading the way.

We made it. My pounding heart hammered in my ears.

Where is it?

Davon crouched ahead of us. Like the safe house, there was a trapdoor with a secret intercom system.

He was already talking to someone on the other end when we reached him. "We need to see General Harris."

Connor! I couldn't stay still, shifting from one foot to the other.

The hatch unlocked, and we went down two flights of stairs. It was still difficult for me, but Davon helped me. We found ourselves in a small, closed room that had a door with a camera. After a click, it unlocked.

I dried my palms on my cargo pants and shoved Davon aside, trying to get a quick look.

He chuckled.

"Welcome back, General," a tall, slim guard said. He rubbed the black stubble on his chin, then straightened his black-and-gray uniform. The letters *PRF* stood out on the right side of his shirt.

I gulped and jerked sideways, my heart in my throat. Davon was a general? Holy shit! I never thought him to be so high ranked.

"At ease, Gabriel. Is General Harris waiting for us?"

"He's aware of your arrival and is waiting for you in the command center."

The guard opened another door and stepped back as we passed.

Once inside, I stilled and glanced around. So many people. I clutched Davon's arm.

He grinned and took my hand, interlacing his fingers with mine. "Welcome to our home."

The underground structure had rows of steel doors on each side of the hallway. Each had a number and a small window. These must be the living quarters.

Davon let go as we reached the end of the hallway. The central room was a huge hexagonal-shaped area. Each corner led to a different corridor, six in total. Each hall had a letter on the topside: B, C, D, E, and F. We came in through hallway A. Everyone was moving toward hall E, entering through two huge doors to the right.

I frowned. "Where's everyone going?"

"To the dining hall." Matt beamed. "I want to see Aoki, but it'll have to wait."

"Sorry about that," I said as we entered hall F.

He shrugged. "No worries. We'll see him later, and you'll get to eat whatever masterpiece he cooked tonight."

Davon was unnaturally quiet and slipped his hands into his pockets as we moved through the complex, casting sidelong glances at me every now and then. We passed the armory and the training center on one side, the infirmary and the computer room on the other. I tensed, not knowing what to expect once we reached the command center.

Matt straightened as we approached the end of the hall.

Davon stopped just before we reached the door. "Matt, can you give us a moment?"

He nodded and went inside.

Davon took me aside. "Abi, please listen to me. Whatever happens in there, know everything I did was to protect you." His dark eyes searched mine.

I glanced toward the door and shifted my gaze back to him. "You're scaring me, Davon." I grabbed his arm. "Tell me. What are you talking about?"

What did he mean?

He grabbed my shoulder. "I can't say more, but whatever happens, please know I won't abandon you. You're not alone." He closed his eyes for a second, then stepped back as a guard took our stuff. "And I'm sorry...about everything."

I stood there, paralyzed. My mind raced, searching for answers. What was waiting for me in there? Was Deb truly okay? Was Sarah here?

Davon put his hand on my back, and we went in side by side.

His light-blond hair was cropped shorter than how I remembered it. He was built like a tank, much stronger than in his teens.

"Connor!"

I ran into him. My feet left the floor as he pulled me to him and held me tight.

"I can't believe you're finally here," he choked out as he put me down, brushing my cut. He furrowed his brow.

I waved him off. "It's nothing."

He moved aside, and my heart leapt. Sarah's green eyes locked on me, a smile on her pretty face.

"Sarah!" I launched myself into her arms.

We both laughed as we hugged each other.

Seeing her like this, so alert, was a first.

"God, Abi. I've missed you." She held me with her arms extended.

We both cried as we embraced again. I missed this. Family.

After a moment, I stepped back. "You seem different."

"I am. It took a long time to wean me off the meds, but I'm me again."
She gripped my hands. "I'm sorry I wasn't there for you. We lost so many
years."

"You don't need to apologize." I blinked. "Wait. You stopped taking
your meds? I thought you needed them."

Seven years and not a day had gone by without her taking them.

"I never did. They just wanted to keep me in line." There was a hard edge
to her voice.

I jerked my head back and gasped. "What? Why would they want that?"
A heaviness spread through me as I waited for her answer.

"Because they took away what I loved most and they knew I wouldn't
rest until they paid for what they'd done." Rage swirled in her eyes. "Sometimes I wish they just killed me then and there. It was a mercy, they said,
because Uncle Scott begged for my life. But what life? I was as good as
dead."

I grimaced. They took so many years from us.

I clenched my fists. "They'll pay for what they did to us. I promise."

As I gazed into her eyes, I couldn't help seeing a lot of Deb in her. That
silent anger I grew accustomed to after our parents died.

I stepped back and glanced around the room. "Where's Deb?"

Davon inched closer to me.

"Where is...?"

I studied Connor's unmoving stance, and that's when I noticed his
unshaven cheeks and sunken brown eyes. Distant. Empty. His pained
expression told me everything I needed to know.

My eyes welled up as I faced my sister. My stomach dropped.

"Where is she?"

Chapter 16

Abi

"*April 2204: Another encrypted message from Davon let us know our main community bunker would take some time to be ready, but we were very hopeful. He already had experts helping with repairs and technology for an off-the-grid community. I can't wait to see what it will look like when it's done.*" (Deborah Davis's journal)

A heavy ache descended into my heart, squeezing to the point of pain.

Sarah stepped toward me, shoulders slumped as she shook her head.

"Someone tell me where she is!"

No one looked at me. A grim expression was on everyone's face.

Davon's hand brushed my arm, and I jerked away.

"Don't you dare touch me!" Pure fire burned through my veins. I fisted my hands on his shirt and pulled him to me, his face a few inches from mine. "Tell me! Where the hell is my sister?"

His eyes were wide, pleading.

Each of my words threatened violence.

Connor gripped my shoulder. "Abi, please. Calm down."

I let go of Davon and faced him. "I will as soon as you tell me where she is."

"I ordered them to keep it secret until they brought you in. I wanted to be the one to tell you what happened," Connor said.

I growled. "Then tell me!"

Connor's eyes flooded with tears. "I'm sorry, but she got caught getting Sarah out."

I gasped and clutched my stomach. Bile shot up my throat.

Deb...caught?

The world crumbled around me. I backed away. It couldn't be. Didn't she take Sarah out right after my escape? It didn't make sense.

"Caught? The government has her?"

Connor nodded.

I scowled at him. "And you think keeping this from me was the right choice? Answer me!"

He averted his gaze.

I turned sideways. "And you, Davon?" My hands shook with rage. "Why did you lie?"

He flinched but held my stare. "I wanted to tell you. I swear. But we knew you would stop at nothing to get here. Risking your life."

I snarled. "That's bullshit! And you know it! You told me she was all right!" I pushed him away. "You said she sent you here!" I shoved him again.

He put his arms out in a placating gesture.

Matt came forward. "She did! Last time we saw her, she sent us to get you." Truth hovered in his eyes.

"And what the hell went wrong?" My vision blurred as I waited for an answer.

Matt reached for me.

"Don't." I moved away from him. "I trusted you."

He winced and stepped back, giving me space.

All this time waiting to see her, to finally reach her... I hugged myself and closed my eyes. My soul ripped open, and I let out an anguished scream. Tears burst from my eyes, and I covered my face. My sister was gone.

Sarah wrapped her arms around me, and I let my tears flow freely.

"She's gone." I sobbed. "What if she's—?"

"No. Don't even think about it. She's alive, and we'll get her back." She cupped my face and brushed away my tears. "We'll be together again." Her words were etched with determination.

I nodded, swallowing my doubts.

"We have a lot to explain. Let's sit," Connor said.

I took deep breaths to calm myself. If they didn't have a plan to get her back, I would get her myself.

"I'll go to the dining hall and get some food." Matt glanced at me.

I pinched my mouth and scowled.

He grimaced and mouthed, "I'm sorry." He left the room.

Coward.

"Davon, give us a moment," Connor said.

He moved to leave.

I narrowed my eyes. "No, I want you to stay. You kept this from me. The least you can do is give me some answers."

He lied to me, and I was furious. But he owed me an explanation.

Sarah and Davon sat next to me, and Connor used the last chair available opposite me.

He leaned forward. "We need to explain from the beginning, so please be patient. A lot happened in the last three years." He looked at Sarah. "Do you want to start, or should I?"

"I'll start." She sighed. "The day of your eighteenth birthday, Deb woke me and explained what she'd done. The guards came to take you to the facility, and the search became frantic. They gave us till noon to find you or else."

She exhaled hard. "Deb wanted me to leave with Connor and her, but knowing the government kept close tabs on me, I knew I couldn't go. So I convinced her to go without me."

Sarah glanced at Connor. "The patrols came an hour later. When I told them Deb was out searching for you, Aunt Annie said she'd seen her leave with her boyfriend and that I aided in your escape. They arrested me and asked the same questions daily: Are there more rebels? Who is your leader? What is your plan? I didn't have any answers, so they started to get more physical. It was hell."

She was shaking by the time she finished.

What had they done to her?

The government was an evil that devoured all. Each citizen had a different story about how the government threaded its claws through their souls, reducing them to shreds of what they once were.

I squeezed her hand. "I'm so sorry."

She wiped her eyes. "It's okay. Now I'm here. Safe."

Safe? Were we? Really?

I eyed Connor. "What about you? What happened after you got here?"

"Shortly after we arrived, the government attacked one of our bases. Hundreds of souls were lost." He hung his head. "We deployed all forces to protect the rest of our communities, and we couldn't rescue you in time."

I peered at Davon. His elbows rested on the table, his entwined hands concealing half of his face as he stared at Connor. He told me about this. The reason I was left behind.

Connor sipped his water. "After a few months, a team was sent into the city, but there was no trace of you or Sarah. After a year, Deb began to fear the worst."

He flexed his fingers. "We sent in one of our spies to get information from Electi's archives. He found a file on Sarah but nothing on you. When Deb read the file, she was shocked. The report related the real story about your parents' death and what happened to Sarah ten years ago."

I raised my eyebrows at Sarah.

She heaved a sigh. "I was pregnant at the time. The NWG had just implemented their new regulations, and I didn't want my baby to be born in Promissa. Carlos heard about a rebel group and was waiting for me in the forest to go find them. When I ran away, Mom and Dad went after me. They decided to help me escape, but as I was about to make it, a patrol opened fire. When Mom landed on me, the shots ceased. She wouldn't respond, so I crawled from under her to discover both her and Dad lying next to me, dead. They gave their lives for me."

This was the moment when our lives changed. When I saw the real face of the government. I was just ten at the time, but I remember it clearly. The knock on the door. Deb's scream after Uncle Scott told us what happened. Losing everything we called home in an instant.

Sarah paused. "They locked me up. I became violent and fought them every day. Wanting to avenge our parents. They kept me there for six months until Charlie was born. He was precious. He had Carlos's dark hair and my green eyes."

She smiled, but her face quickly grew solemn. "They moved me to another ward where we had a small room. They let me feed him and care for him, and we lived in some kind of normalcy until one day when I woke up, the baby was gone. There was no trace of him ever being there, and when the nurses arrived, they said there never was a baby."

Her face became ashen as a tear rolled down her cheek. She snatched my arm. "But, Abi, he was real. I cradled him in my arms, tended to him, and loved him with all my soul. They stole him from me. From that day on, they drugged me so I wouldn't be a problem. Then they took me home and left me in the care of Aunt Annie."

Hot tears flooded my eyes. *I have a nephew.*

Why would they take him away? Was it revenge? Or was the baby just a resource to be distributed to the highest bidder? The thought made me shiver.

Could there be more women in this situation?

All those lucid moments when she begged us to help her, to believe her... And we abandoned her.

Davon's hand reached for mine under the table, and despite my raging emotions, I found solace in his touch.

"I'm so sorry, Sarah. Sorry for not believing you all those times you tried to tell me."

"You don't have to apologize. They are the villains here. They destroyed us. But we will take it all back. And I *will* find my son."

I nodded and squeezed her hand. A silent promise that we would get Charlie back.

"And what about Carlos? Did he make it?"

"Yes. He's a soldier posted at one of the checkpoints. Didn't you see him on your way here?"

Davon tightened his fingers around my hand.

I tensed. The checkpoint.

"What?" Sarah pinched her eyebrows together. Her eyes darted from me to Davon.

Connor frowned. "How did you arrive without us knowing? It's been three weeks since we heard from checkpoint four. We were about to send out runners."

Carlos from the checkpoint was her Carlos. As horror set in, my voice froze in my throat.

There was a knock on the door, and all of us turned as Matt entered.

When he read the room, he inched back. "I'm sorry. I'll just leave this here." He put the food on a desk.

"I was about to ask why you didn't check in before coming. Please explain," Connor said.

Matt's gaze shot to Davon's, and he nodded.

Matt explained everything that happened. Our encounter with the patrol. Carlos's and Christina's execution. Our escape.

Sarah was shaking when he finished. "No. It can't be." Her gaze locked with mine. "Please tell me it isn't true."

I bit my lip. I had no words.

She shot to her feet, and the chair crashed to the floor. "He said he'd be safe!"

Connor shook his head and squeezed his eyes shut. When he opened them again, tears threatened to escape. "I'm sorry, Sarah."

She started hyperventilating.

I stepped toward her, and she collapsed.

Connor caught her before she hit the floor and carried her to a sofa as Matt rushed to help.

"Sarah! Can you hear me?" I shook her.

"Abi, give us some space," Matt said.

I didn't move an inch. I needed to be by her side.

Davon held my shoulders and pulled me back slowly. "Let's give them some space to work."

"Will she be okay?" I asked Matt.

Matt nodded. "The shock must have caused her blood pressure to drop. I'll take her to the infirmary. She needs some time to recover. You can come by later."

I gritted my teeth. "I'm going with her."

"There's nothing you can do to help her right now. I promise to take care of her and wait for you. Come by when you finish talking." He called a guard to help him carry her out.

Davon rubbed my back softly. "Are you okay?" His voice sounded small, so different from his usual strong tone.

Was I okay? Definitely not. "This was supposed to be a happy moment. Seeing my family again... You should've said something." I moved away from him. "I can't believe you hid this from me!"

"I know, and I'm sorry." He scrubbed a hand over his face. "I should've told you. Prepared you for this. Please."

He reached for me, but I stepped back, putting space between us.

You should have said something.

"Please follow me to my office," Connor said. "There's still much to explain."

We followed him to his office at the back of the command center. It was warm and inviting, with wooden panels surrounding it. Two shelves full of books and folders covered the right wall, and to my left was an antique wood bureau writing desk. It drew my attention because my father used to have one just like it. On top rested what appeared to be a detailed map of the bunker system. I brushed it as I passed by.

Connor sat behind his elegant wooden desk, and Davon and I occupied the two chairs opposite him.

Connor was the same age as Deb, twenty-seven. I remembered him as a more relaxed man, but here he seemed more demanding. Serious. He raked his hair back as his brown eyes locked on Davon. "I can't believe we lost Carlos and Christina." He wrote something on a paper and put it in an organizer to the left. "I'll assign a team to investigate. Someone must have disclosed their location."

Davon leaned forward. "I suspect the same. We need to launch a full investigation. Keep it close."

Connor nodded. He took a picture from his desk and handed it to me.

It was a beautiful picture of Deb and him taken in the forest. The light hit them at an angle, and their eyes were fixed on each other. Connor's blond hair was a bit longer. He wore a long-sleeved white shirt with a yellow tie and khaki pants. Deb looked radiant in a yellow day dress that accentuated her light-brown skin. Her black curls, longer than the last time I saw her, fell over her shoulder. And her smile... That was a treasure to see.

I gave it back.

A single tear slid down his face as he caressed the frame and put it back. "That was taken two years ago on the day we got married. It was a simple ceremony, just the two of us and our closest friends." He looked at Davon.

Connor reached across the desk and covered my hand with his. "I'm sorry for not finding you sooner. We tried countless times, but nothing ever went according to plan. And Deb, she suffered daily. When we thought they'd taken you, she wouldn't stop searching for answers. I'm glad Davon and Matt found you. It was a long mission, and I appreciate them." He nodded at Davon.

"She found us," Davon said. "She followed us for a month before showing herself."

"I'm glad she did." He rested his elbows on the desk, interlacing his fingers. "Two years ago, after we got the information on Sarah, Deb blamed herself. With this new intel, we started planning both your rescues. Knowing the government had nothing on you told us you were still out there, so Deb decided to send Davon and Matt into the city. Sarah's rescue was more complicated since she was held inside a secure facility."

Connor covered his face with his hands. After a moment, he lowered them. "We were trying to find a safe way to get Sarah back, but Deb lost it. Four months ago, she left in the middle of the night."

Winded, I tapped my foot, unable to stay still.

"Sarah explained a nurse would come daily to see her in the morning, afternoon, and nighttime, with medication and food. One afternoon, while Sarah was heavily sedated, Deb got into her cell, dressed as a nurse. She waited for the effects of the narcotics to wear off and took Sarah out of the cell by dusk before the nighttime nurse arrived."

His hands curled into fists. "We deployed a rescue mission a couple of days after Deb left. We thought we could catch her before she got in. When we arrived at the perimeter, the alarms went off. We thought we had triggered them, but, no, it was them. Gunshots rang out as Deb sprinted toward the forest with Sarah in tow. Deb went down as I ran toward her. She stumbled, her calf bleeding profusely. I had almost reached her when she begged me to take Sarah away and rescue you. Guards were almost on us, and I did what she asked and dashed into the forest with Sarah. I'll never forgive myself for leaving her. I would gladly give my life for her, but I understood. I'd do the same for my family."

Connor let out a strangled sob as tears trickled down his face.

They got her. Niles got her.

How could this be any worse?

I hunched over and massaged my nape.

I would give my life just to see all that man built burn to the ground. To see him gradually lose everything until there was nothing left in this world for him. To watch his empire crumble into dust.

"Do you know where they took her?" Davon rested his elbows on his knees.

"Yes." He hesitated. "We need your help. She's at Niles's high-security prison."

Davon ran his hands through his hair. "Fuck."

I frowned in confusion. "Wait. What exactly does Davon have to do with it?" It didn't make sense.

Davon bent forward and fixed his gaze on me. "There's something you should know about me. Something I've been dreading to tell you."

My thoughts raced as I looked at him, then Connor.

Connor sat back. "The floor is all yours, my friend."

Davon moved his chair closer and took my hands in his. Sweat beaded on his brow. "There's no easy way to say it, so I'll just go ahead. I couldn't say my last name when we met because you wouldn't have trusted me." He trembled, his eyes pleading. "My full name is Davon Niles. I'm Jordan Niles's son."

A lead weight settled in my chest. I jerked back, but he held me firmly. "No. It...it can't be. You can't be that bastard's son."

How can he be a Niles?

What kind of game was destiny playing with me? Me, the one who vowed to destroy everyone close to that man. Now I was faced with his son, the only man I'd dared to care about after so long. The man who had turned my world upside down and had given me back my hope.

I tried to calm my breathing. He was right. If he'd told me this before, I would have escaped or killed him in the middle of the night.

Hatred bloomed inside me as I recounted all the cruelty. The deaths. The times I promised to destroy his father.

But still...

I thought about our time together, trying to make sense of it all. I remembered our first conversation about his blade. When he wouldn't say more about his father. Every time he went silent after I asked about his past, about his family.

Matt said his memories haunted him.

Now I understood why he distanced himself from me, afraid that I'd run. He knew I hated his father. I told him about my vow to destroy him and everyone around him.

My hands shook as he held them, his pained eyes begging me to understand. "Please. Don't pull away from me. I'm not like him."

I forced down the pain and rage that threatened to break free. I knew in my heart he was nothing like him and remembered what I'd promised: *Whatever you've been through, we'll deal with it together.*

We needed to work through this.

I clutched his hand. "I won't run from you, no matter what."

His face softened as he relaxed.

Connor exhaled and straightened. "Davon has been here from the start. It took several years for us to trust him, but he's a valuable asset to our council and a friend to us all. He was the one who discovered the files on Sarah, after which he volunteered to be in your rescue operation."

"I read about Davon in Deb's journal, but I never expected him to be related to that asshole." I frowned at Davon. "What made you go against him?"

"Everything. He's ruthless. He controlled every aspect of my life and made me into a soldier. A weapon to use as he pleased. You have no idea what he's capable of, the things he made me do..." A vein throbbed in his forehead as he gripped the arm of his chair. "I followed some guys into that meeting when I was eighteen and joined the cause. That's when I vowed to stop him."

What had that bastard done to him?

I arched an eyebrow. "So how does it work? Do you still talk to him?"

He gave a slight nod. "I live a double life. I have a flat in Electi, which made your rescue mission more plausible. My father believes I work for him, and I contact him regularly. We sometimes leave evidence around so the intel I give him seems real and I can keep my cover."

"Being Jordan's son gives him access to high-security areas, which helps us in ways we never imagined," Connor said.

I crossed my arms. "Okay. I guess getting into that prison wouldn't be that hard for you, then?"

He shook his head. "It's the highest security prison in the city. Impregnable. Even I don't have clearance to enter it."

My stomach roiled. Could she be rescued? What if they found out who she was? What would they do to her?

Davon shifted his attention to Connor. "Have you heard about her? Do you have a plan?"

"Last time we heard, she was alive. We were waiting for you. You're the only one who can help us get her. An agent on the inside saw her and informed us your father has been visiting her." Connor hesitated, his eyes pleading. "I think he suspects her connection to the PRF. You know he's been hunting us for years. I'm not sure how much longer she has."

"Tell me what to do. I'll get her back, whatever it takes." Davon's chin trembled as he brought his eyebrows together.

What would he have to do to achieve this?

Connor stood. "We'll meet in a couple of days to discuss the plan." He came around the desk and shook Davon's hand. "Thanks again, my friend. I missed having you around. I'll call Jimmy in to tell him what happened. As for the rest of the community, I ask for your discretion."

Davon nodded.

Connor then took both of my hands. "Come by tomorrow morning. I want to show you around. Whatever you need, just ask. You're family."

After saying our goodbyes, he gave me a key to my apartment, and Davon and I headed out.

Chapter 17

Abi

"*July 2204: Today was Sarah's twenty-first birthday. Connor knew why my mood was solemn, as I would do anything for my family and keeping secrets from them was very hard. I especially suffered for Abigail. She was only eleven, and they were already planning her advancement into the facilities. A couple of years ago, I would have thought this was just a bad joke, but today it was a reality.*" (Deborah Davis's journal)

When we entered the infirmary, Matt was talking to a nurse.

I approached him. "How is she?"

"She woke up about half an hour ago, frantic. But we talked to her, and she's calm for now. You can go see her. She's still awake."

I started toward her cot, but Davon stayed behind. He told me on the way that he needed to tell Matt about the meeting.

"By the way, Abi," Matt said, "I think she should be kept under observation tonight. The nurse will stay with her so you can rest. She'll be in good care."

"Thank you."

I entered her room and sat beside her. "Hey."

Her eyes were crimson and surrounded by dark circles.

My heart ached. "I'm sorry."

She turned away. I gently stroked her hair, letting the silky, golden strands cascade across the pillow. Back at home, I used to spend hours brushing her hair. It always seemed to help her relax.

A silent sob left her. "We were supposed to have more time. This wasn't supposed to happen."

"I know." I covered her hand with mine. "Is there anything I can do to help?"

She closed her eyes for a moment. "You should rest."

"But I can stay and keep you company. You shouldn't be alone."

"I'll be all right. I need some time alone." She squeezed my fingers. "Come see me tomorrow."

I nodded, understanding she needed time to heal. Alone. "I love you. I wish there was more I could do."

"Having you here and knowing you're safe—that's enough." She gave me a half smile and patted my hand. "Go. I'll be fine."

I kissed her brow.

Matt and Davon were in the hall, deep in conversation.

"She took it well, but we still need to talk," Davon said.

He was obviously explaining what happened earlier.

"Davon's all right. Still an asshole, but you're both on the same level now," I told Matt as Davon shifted to make space for me.

He touched my arm lightly. Tentatively. "How is she?"

"Devastated. I don't know what else to do." I looked down, fumbling with my hoodie's cord.

"You're staying with her?"

I glanced up. "No. She asked me to go. Says she wants to be alone."

He nodded.

"Give me a moment." Matt entered the infirmary and came back with a paper bag. He handed it to Davon. "Did they give you an apartment yet, Abi?"

"Yes." I fumbled in my pocket and took out the key. It had a seventeen on top. "Here." I gave it to Davon, as I had no idea where to go.

"Is she with us?" Matt asked.

Davon read the number. "Yes, the room next to mine, opposite yours and Aoki's."

"That's good. I already had dinner with Aoki. That's yours." Matt motioned to the bag. "You must be starving."

My stomach rumbled. "We can eat at my apartment. I could use some food."

"Sure. Let's get you there," Davon said.

The three of us walked to my apartment, and Davon slipped the key in. It was a small room with plain white walls, a full bed, a sofa, a table, a kitchenette, and what I guessed was a small bathroom. My backpack was on the bed. Someone must have brought it in from the command center.

"My room is next door, number eighteen, and Matt's is opposite, number four." Davon set the food on the table.

Matt's apartment door opened, and a handsome man stepped out.

This must be his husband.

"You must be Abigail." He pulled his long black hair into a ponytail, then took my hand and kissed it. "Deb talked about you all the time. I'm so happy to meet you at last." He had Asian features and was strong but slim and the same height as Matt.

He let go of my hand. "I also wanted my boy back, so I couldn't wait for them to find you." He winked at Matt.

Matt kissed him. They made a stunning pair. "Abi, meet Aoki."

I grinned. "Nice to meet you."

He came closer. "I know you're worried, but Deb will be back with us in no time. I'm sure of it."

"Thank you." His words meant a lot to me.

Davon hugged him, patting his back. "Hey, man, good to see you again. Sorry I couldn't come by earlier."

"I'm just glad you're back. I'm sorry about Carlos and Christina." Aoki looked me over as Davon moved back beside me. "And you? Matt told me you got shot. Are you better?"

"Yes. It sometimes hurts a little, but I can walk without issues now." I noticed I was missing my hiking pole and had been walking without it for the whole time here. "Matt and Davon took good care of me." I glanced sideways. "I owe them a lot."

"You owe us nothing," Davon said.

An awkward silence fell.

"Well, I need to catch up with my hubby here if you know what I mean." Matt took Aoki's hand, and they crossed the hall.

"Have a good night," I said as they walked into their room.

"Oh, we will." Aoki winked at me and closed the door.

That left Davon and me standing alone just inside my apartment.

He cleared his throat. "I'm going to take a shower. I'll come back to have dinner. Does that sound good?"

"Heavenly." I hadn't showered in the last two days.

His eyes gleamed for a moment before he turned around and left the room. "See you in a few." He closed the door behind him.

There was a nightstand next to the bed, with a small device and a cube that looked like some kind of speaker. When I touched the device's screen, jazz music began to play through the cube. As the saxophone played a slow, deep melody, I closed my eyes and was transported back to before the regime when I listened to this with my father in his office. He was a huge fan of jazz.

I'd never seen anything like this before. I'd have to ask someone how it worked.

After my shower, I found the essentials in my room. I donned shorts and an oversized blue T-shirt. My body ached all over, so I went to the sofa to lay down for a bit.

Half an hour later, there was a knock on the door.

I sat up quickly. "Come in."

Davon's weightless gaze fell on me. White joggers hung low on his hips, and a gray T-shirt fit snugly around his torso. He appeared to be in good spirits as he walked to the table to set up dinner.

I stood and rubbed my tired eyes. "Thank you." A heaviness wrapped itself around my body as my mind took on everything that had happened.

"Are you okay?" Davon came to me.

I shook my head. "I don't know."

He hugged me tight, holding my head to his chest. "I'm sorry about everything."

Warmth flooded my body as his heart pounded against my ear. "I know."

He sighed, and his muscles relaxed beneath my touch.

My breath quickened. I could hear my own heartbeat as I broke the hug.

His intense gaze held me captive till he shook his head and sat. "We'll talk while we eat."

I took a moment to focus and sat by him.

He set a plate of rice with vegetables in front of me. The taste of spices filled my mouth as I took my first bite. It was warm and comforting.

"How's your thigh?" he asked.

"It hurts but no different than before."

He nodded and went back to his food.

The unique taste intrigued me. "Did Aoki cook this?" My voice sounded hoarse.

Davon slid a cup of water in front of me. "Yes. Isn't it good? This is Japanese curry. Matt's favorite." He continued devouring his plate.

Our day had been hard and long, and he surely was as exhausted and hungry as I was. We ate in silence, but we needed to talk.

"Why, Davon? Why did you hide this from me?" My chest ached. They had betrayed my trust, and it hurt like hell.

He fisted his fork and stopped eating, his head down. "There aren't enough ways to apologize, and even I can't seem to forgive myself for what we hid from you. I should have told you."

"I feel…" I dropped my shoulders and rubbed my eyes. I couldn't find the correct words for telling him how I felt. Betrayed, lost, overwhelmed. As I looked at him, a flood of emotions washed over me.

He toyed with his obsidian ring, and his Adam's apple bobbed as he swallowed hard, food forgotten. "I will earn your trust back. No matter how long it takes."

I nodded, then touched his ring. "Who gave you this?"

He let out a long, heavy sigh. "It was a gift from my mother. And him." He brushed his fingers over it. His initials were engraved in silver.

"It's beautiful."

We went back to eating, but the silence was killing me.

"Do you think we can get her back?" I asked. "I can't imagine the things she must be going through."

After years of the   government   granting them unrestrained control over the citizens, the officers out there were brutal with a sense of madness ingrained in them. That's what tyranny did: it created a barrier between individuals who once were the same. As Jacob once said, power destroyed everything.

I couldn't imagine how the officers inside the facilities were and the treatment the citizens were subjected to.

Davon pushed the curry around his plate. "I was thinking the same thing. I need to get in there as soon as possible. We can't risk her any longer."

I frowned at the thought of him going in there alone, even knowing he was our best option to get her back. "Do you think Connor will let me go with you?"

He choked on his food and coughed. "There's no way in hell I'm letting you come on this mission."

"You don't get to decide what I can or can't do." *He has no right.*

His eyes locked with mine as he put his fork down. "On the contrary. I'm a general here. Second only to Connor, the general of the army. If I say you stay, you stay."

Demanding. Commanding. This was not the man I met. This was the general of the PRF.

But I was no soldier.

I dug my nails into the table, pinching my lips together. "I'll go if I want to. She's my sister!"

He stood, palms outstretched over the table. "Do you have any idea of the danger you'll be putting yourself in? Out there in Electi, my father controls everything. Knows everything. I don't ever want him to see your face. Not even a glimpse."

I hadn't seen him like this since the day we met. But I didn't fear him anymore. I'd gone through too much to put up with his shit.

I mirrored him. "If you think for a moment you can control me, think again. It's my choice if I want to go. It's my fucking life, Davon. You don't get to choose for me. I want to be there for Deb. To save her from *your* father."

His hands clenched into fists, and he twisted away from me. He punched the door with a growl. His shoulders moved up and down.

I recoiled but conjured the courage to confront him. He wouldn't harm me, and I wasn't done. "Look at me! Do you think I'm weak? Do you think I need your protection? You have no idea what I went through out there. I fought again and again to survive. Alone. I was the one who fucking found you, for God's sake. And you. You decide to keep information from me. To lie to my face. And now you expect me to fall back and do nothing?"

My breath caught in my throat as he turned and took large strides toward me.

I backed away. My whole body trembled at his approach.

He stopped midstride and drew his eyebrows together. His eyes filled with concern rather than rage. He slowly approached and drew me to him, his face inches from mine.

"I've never believed you're weak. Don't you understand?" His eyes darkened. "I couldn't bear it if anything happened to you. When they shot you, I lost my shit. The thought of losing you…" He pulled back.

He closed his eyes, letting out a hard sigh. "I won't stop you if you want to come with me, but I'll keep trying to convince you otherwise until that day comes."

"Thank you," I whispered.

He opened his eyes. "Don't thank me yet." He brushed my cheek with the back of his hand. "I don't know what to do with you. You're too fucking stubborn."

I chuckled as he kissed my forehead.

He tilted my head toward him. His eyes captivated me, and I licked my lips at the thought of him narrowing the gap between us.

He stepped back and gave me the key to the apartment. "I'm next door if you need anything. No matter what time it is."

He was leaving. My heart wrenched at the thought.

"Please stay?" I said as he reached the door. I remembered last night. His warmth. The sense of peace he brought me.

He turned sideways and cocked his head.

"Don't take it the wrong way, please. I just don't want to be alone tonight. My mind won't stop going in circles."

He approached. "I can stay for as long as you need." He reclined on my bed, patting the space next to him. "Come."

My heart faltered for an instant. "To bed?"

His smile reached his eyes. "Don't worry. I'm exhausted. I promise not to try anything."

As I approached the bed, he shifted to make space for me. He put an arm around me and hugged me to his chest just like last night.

I relaxed into him. I could see the top of his tattoo exposed by his V-neck. I couldn't stop myself from touching it.

His muscles tensed. He gripped my hand and kissed it softly.

I pressed myself against him, and he pulled me closer. My leg instinctively bent on top of him.

Davon sucked in a breath as he held me. A flush of warmth spread from my core.

I thought I'd never want this, but he was different.

He brushed my back. "We should rest."

With a sigh, I curled into him, following his breaths as we both drifted into nothingness.

A knock on the door woke me. A warm, masculine scent enveloped me.

My breath hitched, but then I remembered Davon.

He held me sideways against his chest. I wanted to stay like this, cocooned in him, warm and safe, but I had to get the door. I tried to scoot away, but he pulled me closer.

When I looked up, he was watching me, gentleness reflected in his eyes.

"Morning, beautiful." He tucked a strand of hair behind my ear, making me shiver. Then he brushed my cheek with his thumb as his other arm hugged me close. "How did you sleep?"

In that moment, I noticed my left hand rested against his chest, a very naked and muscular chest. He must have taken off his shirt during the night. How I didn't notice was beyond me.

"Hey! Over here." He lifted my chin.

"Um, sorry. I'm going to get the door."

Davon chuckled, the vibration from his chest moving through my body.

"We can ignore it if you want to. Whoever it is will think you're away or in the shower." His sensual tone aroused something within me.

Something I thought I would never be able to feel again.

I wanted to stay wrapped in his warmth, but what if it was Connor? What if they were bringing new information? I untangled myself. "We need to answer. It may be important. And I need to get ready to go talk to Connor."

"You're right. While you get ready, I'll get us coffee and breakfast and bring it back here." He rose slowly.

I couldn't control the urge to look at him. His joggers fell beneath his waistline, and all I could see was his chiseled perfection. His hair was loose as he stretched and opened the door.

"Davon?" Matt's voice filtered inside.

"Morning! Is that for us?" Davon asked. "Smells good."

"Um, yes. I went with Aoki to help with breakfast, and since you weren't there, I tried your apartment. No one answered, so I came here." He glanced around Davon toward me. "Hey, Abi."

Heat seared my cheeks. "Hi. You can come in if you want to."

"No worries. I already ate. You two go ahead with whatever you were doing." Matt winked at me and gave Davon our food and coffee.

"Wait! It's not what it looks like!" I yelled, but Matt was already gone.

Davon closed the door. "What's not what it looks like?"

"Well..." I covered myself, feeling exposed, which made no sense since I was fully clothed.

He laughed softly and set the food on the table. "We're all adults here. There's nothing wrong with me staying over. No one will look twice."

"But they'll think we're together. Like *together, together.*"

He sat on the bed beside me. "Would that be so bad?"

"Davon?" My voice was just a whisper as he put his free hand on the nape of my neck.

"I'm done waiting, Abi. I've been wanting to do this for a long time." With that, he pushed his lips against mine in a soft, velvety stroke.

It was caring. Gentle. My heart threatened to jump straight out of my chest.

He coaxed my mouth open, and the moment our tongues clashed the kiss became deeper, urgent. I was drowning in him. In his scent, in his sweet taste mixed with the woody aroma of whiskey.

I arched into him as he moved his left hand up my T-shirt and brushed the side of my breast. I jerked, and he yanked his hand away, squishing his eyebrows.

I pulled it back to me.

He was safe.

He caressed me tentatively at first, and I moaned as he softly, gently grazed my breast again.

His lips trailed down my neck to my collarbone. Tasting. Nipping.

I gasped. My body burned from his touch.

He pulled away, and we touched our foreheads together, panting.

"I'm sorry," he said. "I…I couldn't help myself. I've been thinking about kissing you for weeks." He was still catching his breath.

I touched his cheek. "Me too."

He blinked, and a pleased smile curved his lips.

I slowly ran my hand down his chest. He closed his eyes, letting me explore down to his abs. His hard body shivered beneath my fingers as I reached his waistline. My center throbbed at the evidence of his arousal.

I looked up to find his hungry eyes on me. Gripping the back of his neck, I pulled him to me and kissed him hard. Having control made me feel elated, and his touch as he grabbed my hips became possessive, same as mine.

I didn't care about the past. Not at this moment.

I nipped his lower lip, and he groaned.

We let ourselves fall back onto the bed. Both exploring, touching, tasting. Our kiss grew feverish, desperate, as we pressed our bodies against each other.

I wanted him. Craved him.

There was a knock on the door.

Davon broke the kiss and let out a frustrated grunt. "Fuck."

"Miss Davis, General Harris asks for your presence in the command center in twenty minutes." The voice was muffled by the door.

As the footsteps receded, Davon kissed me again, this time soft and lingering. "You're so fucking beautiful." He caressed my hip, then moved off the bed. "We need to eat so you can get ready for the meeting."

I sat up.

He adjusted himself and leaned close to take the shirt he had discarded during the night.

I exhaled. "You're making this very difficult for me."

He grinned as he put his shirt on. "I'll go to my place and get ready. Be back in ten for breakfast. Sound good to you?"

"Sure."

He handed me a coffee. It was divine, just how I liked it.

"Sorry for taking you away from your caffeine. I know how much you need it in the morning."

He was so tall compared to me that his face was inches from mine as he knelt in front of me. He took my chin and kissed me again. Tenderly.

"Um, I think I found my addiction," he said.

After he left, I showered. I was putting my hair up when Davon knocked.

"Come in!"

I saw his reflection in the mirror as he kissed the back of my neck, sending goosebumps all over my body. He looked delectable in a white button-down shirt and gray jeans.

I leaned into him, unable to stop a moan from escaping my lips. He tugged at my ponytail, and I stilled.

The smell of cigarettes. The taste of blood. His evil sneer.

I sucked in a breath so hard I choked and jerked away, hitting the mirror with my shoulder. I blinked as I saw him. Davon.

"Abi? I'm sorry. Are you okay?" He took a step toward me but paused as I backed away.

God. What happened? It was him. He was safe. "I'm sorry. You did nothing wrong. I just...get flashbacks sometimes from my past. I..."

I hugged him.

He massaged my back and whispered near my ear, "It'll all be okay."

I moved back a little and caressed his hair. His soft, silky strands slipped between my fingertips.

He was safe. He was good.

I went on my tiptoes and kissed him. I needed to move forward.

My lips tingled as he deepened the kiss, and I responded with equal passion. After it, he held me gently and brushed his lips against my temple before going to the table.

Aoki had prepared grilled turkey sandwiches, and we devoured them.

Davon took the last bite of his sandwich. "I'll walk you to command. Connor left me a note. I need to check some maps and go out to ask the runners about what they've seen. We're launching a full investigation into what happened at the checkpoint."

"Okay. Be careful out there." I wiped my mouth with a napkin.

"Always."

We went to his apartment to get his khukuri. He had an incredible collection of blades across one wall. An antique red-velvet sofa was on the right. I'd never seen something so sophisticated in my life.

Davon stood beside me. "That's a Victorian chaise lounge. We found it in what today is Connor's office. No one else wanted it, so Deb agreed I could keep it."

"It's so elegant." I touched the soft material.

"Be right back. Make yourself at home." He trailed his fingers across my arm, then went to get his stuff.

Everything in the apartment had an antique vibe. Next to a bookcase was a small bar. There was nothing personal like photos. Only books, plenty of them. Most were about wars and martial arts. I browsed the titles, running my fingers across their spines. They seemed old, their colors fading.

"Do you read much?" He searched through his backpack. He took an old book out and put it on the shelf—*Osman's Dream: The History of the Ottoman Empire* by Caroline Finkel.

"I did before I escaped. It gave me a sense of peace. Once out there, I read Deb's journal daily. It gave me hope that one day I'd find a way to get here." I continued browsing his collection. "Where did you get all of these?"

"My father." He rubbed the back of his neck. "It's one of several hobbies we share. Books, blades, and antiques."

I shuddered inside when he mentioned his father. It was still difficult to accept his son was standing next to me, the polar opposite of whom I imagined Jordan Niles to be. I couldn't imagine him as a loving father. I had so many questions.

"It must be hard." I cast a sidelong glance at him. "Was he good to you in any way?"

"He was. He still is in his own unique way. It's just…" He shook his head. "It's almost as if he has two personalities. The affectionate father and the ruthless tyrant." He moved his weight from one foot to the other, rubbing his arm.

"You don't have to talk about it." I grasped his hand. "Are you ready to go?"

"Yes."

Chapter 18

Davon

November 2213

We were fifteen minutes late when we arrived at command.

Connor looked at us and frowned.

With a grin, I shrugged and had to bite back a laugh when he rolled his eyes.

Connor smiled at Abi. "Sorry to bother you this early, but I want to show you around the bunker, and my afternoon's busy."

She glanced at me and blushed. "It's no bother."

It's a huge bother.

"Morning." He shook my hand. "The maps are in the conference room. Remember to interview the runners. They must have seen something."

"I will."

Connor frowned again as I gave Abi a peck on the cheek.

"Can we meet at the dining hall for lunch?" I asked.

Her eyes brightened. "Sure. See you."

Connor was going to want to talk to me about this. I was certain. But I wasn't going to let him intimidate me.

What Abi and I shared scared me at first, but now I wasn't backing away. This morning, after the kiss, it all made sense. All the tension of the last couple of weeks left me as hope took its place.

Nevertheless, I couldn't forget her face as she backed away from me. Her horrified expression, as if she didn't recognize me for a second. That emotion was all too familiar to me, as I, too, kept memories to myself. Memories that would come to me from time to time and shake me to my core.

Whatever she remembered was terrifying if I were to judge by the look on her face. I needed to be cautious around her, as she was with me. She never pushed me, but when worse came to worst, I knew she would be there. Standing right beside me.

After she kissed me, I understood. It was her way of telling me she wanted me, of letting me know we could work it out.

Matt was already waiting for me in the conference room. I sat opposite him and opened the map to study the high-risk areas that needed to be checked around the perimeter of the city, especially the checkpoints.

"So...what's up?" He sounded chipper than usual.

I glanced up. "You have a good night?"

He lifted an eyebrow. "I could ask the same thing."

I chuckled. Of course he'd want to know the details.

"So...?" He tapped his fingers on the table.

"What?" I wasn't going to miss an opportunity to tease him.

"Just tell me, man!" His demand sounded more like a desperate plea.

I put the marker down. "We kissed."

He smiled. "I'm happy for you. She's good for you."

I narrowed my eyes. "Too good for me."

"You always do that, you know," he said as I continued marking the routes.

I clenched my teeth. "What, Matt? What do I always do?"

"Talk down on yourself."

I shrugged. "And what if I do? No matter how much I do here, that will never erase what I've done." I returned to the map, ignoring his pinched expression.

He placed his hand on the table. "Those aren't your sins. They're Jordan's. You can't go on like this. Blaming yourself for all he put you through. You deserve to find happiness."

He was always like this. Telling me how I needed to move forward and let my past be the past. But he knew my demons, as he was there when they were created.

Letting all that go was not an easy task. The memories were always there, lurking in the dark corners of my mind. Waiting to come back when I least expected.

"Whatever, man," I said, knowing he wouldn't let it go.

Matt shook his head. "Well, I'm happy you're giving it a chance. You both deserve it. I'm also glad you released some of that pent-up sexual tension. Sometimes I thought you would jump each other right then and there."

I grimaced. "It's not like that. I mean..." I rolled my eyes. "It is. But she's been through a lot, and I'll give her as much time as she needs."

"Wow."

"What?"

"You almost sound like *not* an asshole."

I threw the marker at him, but he dodged it. *Jerk.*

Matt leaned on the map. "So what's the plan?"

I focused on the task at hand. "Connor wants me to mark routes that may be compromised by the government's military. Tomorrow we'll meet with him to talk about increasing security in the perimeter."

"Do you think he'll act at last?"

"I think he doesn't have any other choice." I stood and rolled the map.

Matt followed me to see Nina at the center of operations. Everything that happened in the system ran through her. She was our right hand, a true genius. As head of operations, she managed all our missions and worked hand in hand with Connor, Jimmy, and I.

"Morning, Nina," I said.

Glued to her computer as always, she adjusted her glasses. Her brown hair was cropped on both sides, leaving a long blue-dyed strand that now hid her face. She moved it to her left as she fidgeted with her multiple earrings. I swear she never left that computer until the end of the day. A workaholic through and through.

"Yes, General." She clicked her fingernails against the table.

"I need a list of the runners and their assignments. Also, a location for Captain Thompson."

She started typing and handed me the list. "Jimmy. Sorry. Captain Thompson is bringing supplies from the farming and engineering bunker and training a new recruit on the routes."

"Perfect. Thanks." I turned to Matt. "We'll go to Jimmy first, then move on with the interviews."

We headed to the armory to get our bulletproof vests, then went out through hall D.

Matt led our way north. "Does he know about Christina?"

"Yes. Connor told him last night after Abi and I left. As for the rest of the community, he asked me to keep it quiet." Not that I agreed with that decision.

We were a close community, and hiding this from the citizens would only bring more chaos in the end. This bunker was mostly military, and the sooner everyone knew, the better prepared we would be for a threat. It was always the same with Connor, trying to keep everyone safe and calm, but we didn't live in that kind of society. This was a kill or be killed world, and we needed to be ready.

Raking his hair back, Matt stopped in his tracks. "It's gonna be hell when they find out. You know he's going to have us deal with it as always. I'm so fucking tired of his reluctance to attack. He keeps telling us our numbers are too low, but if we continue waiting, your dad's going to have the upper hand, and we'll be fucked."

This was not the first discussion we'd had about this.

After we lost the import base and Deb couldn't find her sisters, she became obsessed with getting them back, forgetting her job as our leader. She put her personal agenda first, endangering the community. As her friends, we all did what we could to help, but it was never enough.

I knew Connor, and he was trying to keep everything under control even though I was sure he was fighting his own battle. He carried a lot on his back, and I understood his reluctance to some degree. But something had to be done.

We got to the farming and engineering bunker just in time. Jimmy was about to leave with a young man by his side.

Wait. Is that...?

"Jimmy! Richard!" Matt yelled.

Both Jimmy and Richard faced us. Jimmy was training the boy we saved back in the city. He looked much healthier than when we left him a month ago. His dark-brown hair was no longer matted, and his skin was tanned in comparison to his pale complexion when we found him. He wore a runner's camo uniform. Many young people were assigned to this job, depending on their speed, agility, and endurance.

Matt shook Richard's hand and then hugged Jimmy. "I'm sorry for your loss. You should have taken the day off."

"Thanks, Matt, but it's better this way. It keeps my mind busy." He regarded me. "Morning, General Niles."

"Morning, Captain Thompson. I'm sorry about Christina."

He nodded.

My relationship with him was strictly professional. I couldn't put my finger on why, but there was something about him I didn't like. And I think it was mutual. We tolerated each other enough to do our jobs, but there was no friendship between us.

"Thank you. I was just heading for the energy bunker. Can I help you with anything?" He scratched his dirty-blond hair behind his ear as he shifted his weight from one foot to another.

I pushed my shoulders back. "We're launching an investigation as to what happened at checkpoint four. We wanted to let you know we'll be interviewing the runners to see if they've spotted government soldiers lurking around or anything suspicious moving in or out of the bunker toward the city."

He put his hands in his pockets. "Thank you for that. We need to find out how they got to them, if it was the government scouts or a slip of intel from our side." Tears welled in his eyes. "She didn't deserve to die like that." After a moment, he glanced at Matt. "What about Abi? Is she okay? Connor told me she was injured when you were attacked."

Matt nodded. "She's going to be fine. Her bullet wound is improving by the day, and her face will heal in no time."

Jimmy sighed. "I'm glad she's okay. I can't wait to see her."

I knew Jimmy and Abi had a past. That much he said when he objected to Connor's decision to send us in instead of him. But he was her friend, and I understood how much he meant to her. I tried to calm myself as a wave of jealousy washed over me.

"Hey, Davon, Matt. Long time no see. How's it going?" Steven waved at me from the garage. "Help me load the truck."

Our system had five bunkers, and each had two councilmembers in charge. Councilmember Steven Abrams ran the hydroponic farm system that fed us all, with Danielle Walters leading the food engineering process. Steven was a genius in his own way.

In the years we'd been out here, we'd found old vehicles and converted them into more efficient ones thanks to the energy bunker and the scientists. Most of our operations were done on foot, but at least once a month, some bunkers did supply runs using old roads to take their trade to the other communities so we all had what was needed. Other than that, runners were the ones to carry out regular runs the rest of the time.

"Can you finish here while I help Steven?" I asked Matt.

"Sure thing."

I turned to Jimmy. "We'll find out what happened out there."

He nodded.

I patted Richard's shoulder. "As for you, I'm glad to have you with us."

He straightened. "Thank you, General."

I walked to the garage.

Steven handed me a box. "How was everything out in the city? I see you've found new recruits."

"Yes, we did." I put the box in the truck, curious to know if Connor had told the rest of the councilmembers about the checkpoint.

The command center was the central bunker, with Connor leading the whole system as general of the army and me as his second. Deb had stepped back a while ago, letting others lead. Nevertheless, everyone knew she was the one who created the People's Revolutionary Front, the one who made it all possible.

After he closed the hatch, Steven removed his hat, raked his ash brown hair back, and wiped the sweat from his brow, then crossed his arms and rested his back on the truck. "I heard about the execution. That doesn't bode well for us. Do you know anything more about it?"

Had I received news from my father? That was the real question. Everyone knew who I was. The council accepted it, knowing all I'd done for the cause, but others still didn't trust me, mostly the newcomers. It didn't bother me. I wouldn't trust myself either.

"I don't." I leaned against the truck next to him and looked up at the sky. "But I will contact my father in a couple of days to check in. Our plan to lead them west worked. This took me by surprise also."

Steven kicked a rock. "We should start planning for a counterattack. I'm tired of waiting and hiding. Dani feels the same way."

I tilted my head. "I know. We have a meeting tomorrow. I'll talk to Connor. By the way, where's Dani?"

Danielle, or Dani for short, was like a sister to me. She usually would be out here, hyper and asking all sorts of questions as usual.

He grinned. "Oh. You know. Visiting Michael."

Michael was a councilmember of the science and technology bunker. Those two had been at it for years.

"Well, I need to leave, but tell her I said hi." I stepped away from the truck and shook his hand.

"Will do. Please let me know if you can get through to Connor. You have our full support." He gripped my shoulder. "We're ready when you say so."

At those words, hope surged within me. "Thank you."

I headed toward Matt, and we moved to an area where two runners were assembling caches. "Did you find out anything new?"

"Nothing out of the ordinary." He shrugged. "Just the usual runs."

Both runners stood and saluted. "General Niles."

"At ease. We're here to ask you some questions."

Their brows wrinkled.

"Whatever you need," the girl said.

"Perfect."

I'd learned this throughout my years of training with Dad. You always interrogated people alone to check their stories. If they didn't match, someone was lying. That was when things started getting ugly. At least in Electi.

"How's everything going lately?" I asked.

She eyed her partner as he left with Matt. "Everything's good."

I crossed my arms. "Seen anything out of the ordinary?"

She shifted her weight. "Like what?"

"A citizen walking about the forest at odd hours. A runner getting out without orders."

She shook her head. "No. I haven't seen anything like that."

"Are you sure?"

She nodded.

The leaves rustled. Matt was back.

"We'll leave you to it, then. Be safe," I said.

Matt moved east and I west to interrogate as many runners as we could. I reached command just before lunch. Matt was in the conference room. He sat at the table with his head resting on his hands. Something was wrong.

"What happened? Did you find anything?" I stood in front of him, palms on the table.

Matt glanced up. "I came back as soon as I talked to the last runner. She told me something that doesn't make sense."

"What is it?" My heart rose into my throat as I waited. Knowing Matt, this was bad.

His eyebrows lifted. "She said she'd taken a letter to the city dead drop a month ago."

I frowned. This was routine. Why would he worry about this? "That's not so strange. They could be taking instructions to our undercover agents in the city."

"Oh, I know. The strange thing is it wasn't in the common code used to sneak intel into the city. It followed a very complex cypher. One only used by one person." His stare was fixed on me.

My stomach dropped. I knew exactly who he meant.

What the hell is going on?

Chapter 19

Abi

"September 2204: Even though we took our classes together, Connor and I didn't have much time to talk. Soldiers were everywhere, guarding the halls, the dorms, even the classrooms. Classes were strictly government approved, and even teachers were closely monitored.

As teachers, we were obliged to teach the children about the supremacy of the elites and how they saved us. But that wasn't what was odd. It was the training they wanted us to teach, a new curriculum, one that was used only in the military, but they wanted to start using it on children. They would be handpicked for these classes and taken into a special facility. But for what purpose? We needed to tell Davon about it. See what he could find out."
(Deborah Davis's journal)

Connor took me to his office as Davon left. He handed me a coffee, then sat next to me.

"How are you?" He sipped his coffee, his tone casual.

"Still trying to make peace with everything." As a headache began to set in, I massaged my temples. Then I fixed my gaze on him. "We need to get her out, Connor. The longer she's out there, the more risk we're putting her in. Tell me what to do. I want to help."

"I understand your urgency. I feel the same. But we must do this right. We only have one chance. I already sent a team out to set up comms near the prison area so the extraction can go smoothly. We have one agent inside that prison, and he's in maintenance. Sometimes weeks go by without any intel, and that won't work."

I paused, trying to think of a better way to ask, but there was none. "I want to go with Davon on the mission."

Connor stiffened. "You're not ready. I'm sorry, but I'm not going to risk you."

So he thought I wasn't capable, same as Davon.

What's wrong with these men?

"Connor, with all due respect, I survived out there for three years. I think I can handle going back in undercover." I tried to keep my tone neutral. This was my brother-in-law but also the leader of the PRF.

"It's not the same. Niles is a calculating man. He'll see right through you. Also, you're not ready. You're still recovering." He leaned back in his chair.

"I can train hard. I can be ready." My voice cracked. "Please let me help."

He stared down at his coffee, then glanced at me, his gaze softening. "Believe me. I understand you better than anyone here. These past months have been hell, but I need to put the safety of the community first. Do this right. I've got no problem if you want to go on missions once you train. But going in now is out of the question."

I sighed. He wasn't going to give in.

He put the cup on his desk and grasped my hands. "We'll get her back. Trust Davon. He can do this."

"It's not a question of trust. I know he can do it. But this is also my fight, and I want to help." Tense, I pulled away.

He put his hands on his knees, his posture straight. "Then train, Abi. Train as hard as you can."

"I will." I'd do it until I was ready to head into the city.

Into battle.

After finishing our coffee, we headed out and paused once we reached the center of the bunker.

"This is the center of activity. Everyone needs to cross through here to get to their destination. We have four halls for living quarters: A, B, C, and D. Almost everyone in this community is a soldier except for teachers, cooks, technicians, and medical personnel. In this room, three emergency exits will open automatically if we fall under attack, and all are controlled by the command center." He pointed toward each exit. "At the end of each hall, we have guarded exits and a sniper room. There we keep watch for possible threats."

"Has this bunker ever been attacked?"

"Not yet."

We strode into hall E and paused in front of a door to our right.

"This is our school room," he said.

School?

He opened the door. A redheaded woman sat behind a desk with notebooks and materials scattered all over. Her small blue eyes focused on me as we entered. She adjusted her glasses, then stood.

"General Harris." She bowed her head slightly.

"Hello, Tammy. This is Abigail, my sister-in-law. I'm just showing her around our bunker." He motioned to Tammy. "This is our teacher. She came in from the city about a year ago."

I extended my hand to her. "Nice to meet you."

She took it in a firm handshake. "At your service. Would you like me to show you around?"

"That would be great," Connor said.

We followed her into another room. I gasped and covered my mouth as I shuffled back a step or two. Connor held me before I bumped into him.

Nine children sat in the classroom. All different ages, some even preschoolers, doing different activities. Assistants helped them complete their tasks.

Most students rose when they saw us, their eyes gleaming. "Good morning, Miss McGreggor. Good morning, General Harris."

"Good morning, students. Please help me welcome our visitors. General Harris has brought Abigail, a new member of our community, to meet you all. What do we say to her?"

The children stood taller. "Welcome to Janus Peak, Miss Abigail."

I couldn't help but smile as I swept my gaze around the room and landed on a pair of huge brown eyes. The small girl, who had dark hair, giggled as she read a book. Were these in vitro, or were some people here able to conceive naturally?

Connor moved to my side. "We rescued many before the government laid a hand on them. Therefore, all children here have been conceived naturally. We also have in vitro born, mostly teenagers. They take their classes at night along with any adult wanting to get an education. Our other teacher, Mr. Jackson, escaped the city on his own a couple of years back and has been with us since. He taught in the university before the war and took it upon himself to give higher education to those wanting to learn more."

"This is incredible," I said as we went back to the hall. "Do you teach still?"

A genuine smile filled his face, and he nodded. "I come in at least once a week, and we exercise in the training center. Deb used to teach here too. She loved it."

His words touched me deeply. I was glad he still practiced his profession and hoped Deb could go back to it after we rescued her.

The dining hall was next on our tour. It was mostly empty when we entered.

Aoki was near the back of the kitchen, and a woman was peeling potatoes on the kitchen island. She grinned as she focused her blue eyes on us. Taking a towel, she cleaned her hands and approached.

"Hello, Carol. How are you this morning?" Connor said.

"Busy as always, prepping for lunch. To what do we owe the pleasure?" she asked.

"This is Abi, Deb's sister."

Carol glanced back at Aoki. "Hey, Aoki, Abi's here to visit." She took my hand. "Great to finally meet you." She pointed her thumb at Aoki, who looked over the kitchen counter. "He's been talking about you all morning. Telling me all about how Matt saved you."

"Abi!" He gave me a hug. His eyes gleamed with mischief. "How was your night? Matt told me Davon..."

I widened my eyes and shook my head subtly.

He blinked at Connor. "Oh, hey, General. Didn't see you there." He extended his hand to him.

As if.

God, Matt and Aoki were made for each other.

Connor's brow creased, and he finished the handshake. "Morning, Mr. Ito."

"What brings you to my humble abode?" He opened his arms wide.

"Just showing Abi around Janus Peak," Connor said.

Aoki nodded and gestured for us to follow him. "Come. I'll show you around."

Carol went back to her task as we followed Aoki to the kitchen.

"This is where the magic happens," he said.

The scent of cooked steak from the ovens made my mouth water.

"Carol's my assistant chef. We serve meals at assigned times, three meals a day. If you need anything between meals, we have coffee and snacks available."

Metal tables filled the room, each sitting eight. There was a huge table in front of the kitchen counter where food was served.

My stomach growled. "This is awesome."

A satisfied smile curved Aoki's lips. "We aim to please."

"We should go on with the tour, Abi," Connor said.

I glanced back. "Oh, right." I turned to Aoki. "See you later!"

He waved goodbye, and I followed Connor to the hall. We paused in front of a door across from the dining hall.

"This is our club. We built it to have a place where we could relax and have fun."

I drew my eyebrows together. "A club?"

He gave me a half smile. "Sometimes I forget you were so young when the NWG took over. Clubs are places for adults to drink and dance. If you ever want to go, feel free to visit it."

I shifted to read a sign next to the door:

Club Underground

Open Thursday to Saturday

9:00 p.m. till morning

We walked to the end of the hall and passed through two double doors. My jaw dropped at the beauty of the elegant, rounded room. Dozens of plaques decorated the walls, the golden glow of a candle illuminating each name.

"This is our memorial center." Connor swallowed hard. "All these people died in the past decade. Most fighting for our cause."

An unnatural stillness claimed me. There were hundreds of candles lit. One for each soul.

Connor's stare was empty. "I know we need to act. We can't let this go on. But I can't find a way to protect everyone, and I don't want to lose more." He covered his face briefly, then pulled his hands away, sighing. "Davon's right. He's been right all along. Now we've lost Deb, Christina, and Carlos, and I feel our time's up…"

I squeezed his hand. It was at that moment that I understood his hesitation to attack. All these people had died already, and the fight hadn't even started.

How many more would be lost when the real war began?

After we took a moment to honor those before us, Connor led me back to hall F. I wanted to see Sarah before continuing the tour.

We entered the infirmary to find her and a nurse sitting in two armchairs, having coffee. She glanced at me and stood. Her face was devoid of any expression.

I hugged her tightly. She froze, but then her arms moved to my back, and slowly, so slowly, she hugged me back and began sobbing silently into my neck.

"Thanks for coming last night." Her chin trembled as she took a step back. She offered me a faint smile, but it didn't quite reach her eyes.

The nurse came toward us. "Hi, Miss Davis. Dr. Anderson left early but said to tell you she's recovered and is free to leave."

"You feel better?" I asked Sarah.

"Much better. I'm tired. That's all." Her eyes were swollen from all the crying.

"Do you want me to take you back to your apartment and stay for a while?" I didn't want her to be alone.

She shook her head. "Don't worry. I can get myself there. Please go on with your day." She glanced at Connor. "I'm sure you still have a lot to talk about."

"But Sarah..." I reached for her hand.

She took my hands in hers like she'd do before everything happened. Before my parents. Before the baby. To get me to listen, to understand.

"I'll sleep it off the rest of the day. I need to process everything. Come tomorrow morning after breakfast. It's number twelve." She kissed my temple. "Please. Let me deal with this in my own way. I'll see you tomorrow, okay?"

As tears threatened to fall from my eyes, I nodded.

Sarah went to get her stuff.

"She'll be okay. Give her time to adjust," the nurse said.

"Thanks for everything," Connor said. "Please make sure she gets back to her apartment."

"Will do, General."

Connor next showed me the armory, which was opposite the infirmary. They had every type of weapon imaginable—small blades, daggers, crossbows, longswords, guns, rifles...

I stood directly in front of the small blades.

"Everything you see here is a weapon option once you start training, but I see you like blades," Connor said from the threshold.

"Out there, blades were the only weapons I had. They kept me safe."

Connor approached me. "If you need to talk, I'm all ears." He took a wide stance, hands in his pockets as he scanned the blades.

I studied him. He was seventeen when my parents died. A lump formed in my throat as I remembered those following weeks. Deb would cry on his shoulder for hours. And sometimes he would sit with me to talk, helping me through the process. He had a good heart.

"A lot happened out there. Too much to recount, too many memories I wish would just vanish." I closed my eyes, trying to put it into words. "I carry with me two blades and the pocketknife Deb gave me when I escaped.

One knife is from Paul. He was a kid, beaten and taken by government guards six months after my escape. An innocent boy. The other one is from Jacob. We were together for three months before he was shot to death while trying to defend our friend. The pocketknife..." My voice broke.

The pain was still there, too close to the surface.

He put an arm around my shoulders. "I'm sorry, Abi. I wish we could've found you sooner. No one should suffer like you did."

I took a deep breath. "It's okay. It's no one's fault."

"It's not okay, and you know it. The plan was flawed. We should have known things could go wrong. Prepared for it." His brown eyes narrowed on my silver bracelet. He brushed it with his fingers as pain entered his eyes. "You kept it?"

I touched the golden heart. "Always."

We left in silence and entered the training center.

It was huge. The floor and walls were all padded, and it had different stations for training exercises. To the back of the room was a soundproof shooting room with a resistance training area next to it. A couple of bullseyes took up another wall, while a huge practice area filled the rest of the space.

A group of cadets was doing drills with a woman in front, leading them. Her black hair was braided to the side, reaching her waist. Her tanned skin dripped with sweat.

They noticed us, and all turned in unison in a salute.

"At ease, cadets," Connor said.

"Continue practicing the drills," the woman said as she approached us. "Morning, sir." She tilted her head toward me.

"Morning, Lieutenant Diaz. This is Abigail Davis." He motioned to her. "Lieutenant Diaz is in charge of training soldiers."

She extended her hand to me. "Nice to meet you, Abigail. You can call me Maria."

"Nice to meet you. I'm Abi." I shook her hand, her grip strong.

Her tank top revealed many tattoos. One caught my eye more than the others. It was on her right shoulder. A skull with a crimson serpent emerging from its eye socket. The remainder of her arm was full of red roses, thorns filling the stem that ran down to her palm.

"Lieutenant Diaz," Connor said, "Abi wants to train to become a soldier. I would like you to take charge of her training. She needs to be ready as soon as possible."

My heart swelled as he spoke those words.

"Yes, sir. You can count on it." She examined me. "Can you start today?"

I blinked. "Like, right now?"

"Sure. There's no better time than now."

I turned to Connor. "Can I?"

Connor nodded. "As long as you're careful. She's still recovering from a shot in the thigh."

Maria nodded. "That'll be no problem. We'll take it slow."

"Perfect. Can you give us a moment, Lieutenant?"

"Sure." She patted my arm. "I'll wait for you with the other cadets." She returned to her drills.

Connor took something out of his pocket. I covered my mouth. I recognized it immediately. My father's wristwatch. Black leather with a silver face and in the back his initials: "D. D." I'd forgotten it when I escaped and grieved over it for weeks, believing I'd lost it forever. It was his last remaining possession.

I trailed my fingers across the band. "Where did you find it?"

"Deb found it in your room when she was getting her stuff out to escape with me. She was holding on to it for you." He strapped the watch to my wrist.

I let out a sob. It still worked. I hugged him. "Thank you."

He took a step back and waved goodbye. "See you later, kid."

Chapter 20

Davon

Connor entered the conference room a moment after Matt dropped the bombshell. As soon as he saw our faces, he stopped.

"What happened?" He closed the door behind him and put his hands on the table. "What did you find?"

I hesitated as I glanced at Matt for reassurance. We didn't even have time to discuss Matt's findings before Connor arrived. We were in deep shit.

I stood by the glass wall. Everything moved as usual—Nina on her computer, soldiers going in and out with their orders, runners coming in from their assignments. All the same...except for me.

A desire to flee overtook me as my mind went to the worst-case scenario. Would Connor believe me? We'd been together for years, but a well-bred spy could remain in character for decades.

Connor's eyes narrowed at me. "What's going on, Davon?"

I flinched. "Matt found something. Well, he heard something from one of the runners."

Connor crossed his arms before shifting his focus to Matt. "Out with it. What did you hear?"

Matt rested his chin on his linked hands. "A letter."

"What about it?"

I paced again, unable to stand still.

Matt hesitated for a second. "A letter addressed to Jordan Niles."

Connor fixed his eyes on me. "From whom? No communications were scheduled to leave the peak."

I clenched my jaw and stopped pacing, facing Connor dead on. "From me."

Connor stepped back. He scraped his hair back. "We need to know everything. Who took it out? Who gave the order? Did it follow the cypher Davon uses when contacting Jordan?"

"I already have all those answers," Matt said.

Lips pressed together, Connor sat at the head of the table. "And?"

"The letter was dropped in the usual box of assignments that are left daily here at command. The runner didn't think twice, as usually these letters are put there by Captain Thompson, and took it to the dead drop near the city limits."

Matt sighed. "I went back to Jimmy to inquire about letters dropped in the past month. He told me they were the usual ones and one from Davon. He remembered it since it was left in his cubicle one morning. When he saw the cypher, he knew it was authentic and dropped it in the box."

I never used my smartphone for my father's missions. My justification was that it could be hacked. The true reason was we couldn't let him pinpoint my location. Because of this, I used the NWG's cypher, one my father created a long time ago, changing it as needed to keep the secrets safe.

I crossed my arms, squeezing my biceps. My chest tightened until it hurt. "I swear to you, Connor. I've never betrayed you and never would. You must believe me."

My mouth dried up as the seconds passed.

He raised his head and searched my eyes. "I believe you. But if word gets out..."

Oh, I knew what would happen. If this information got out of this room and the people tied it to the checkpoint incident, I would lose everything

I'd built. Because as it was, I was always standing at the edge of the line. One slip and no one would think twice about it. I would be considered a traitor.

We moved to his office and one hour later reached the same conclusions.

First, even though the contents of the letter were unknown, we believed it was related to checkpoint four's attack, as the timing was nearly the same.

Second, a government spy was among us. We told Connor about the group of spies that my father sent out. It had to be one of them. We'd taken a spy in and welcomed them to our base. A highly trained individual who was robbing confidential information from the system or had an accomplice inside helping them.

Only Connor, Maria, Jimmy, Matt, Sarah, and I had access to the bunker codebook, to which I attached the NWG cypher at the end. To send the letters, the spy merely needed to get their hands on that book. A book that was presently inside this office, locked inside the bureau.

As for the checkpoints, other than those of us with access to the code-book, only about a dozen runners knew their locations. We'd have to interrogate each of them.

At least the information was contained, and it wouldn't leave this room.

I let out a heavy sigh. "I've trained these spies. We're in big trouble. They're very skilled and discovering their identity will be hard work."

"I understand. As to why they haven't ratted you out yet, I have no clue. We'll have to proceed carefully. I don't want the spy to know we're onto them. Let's keep this between us. Don't tell anyone until we know more. Even Aoki," Connor said.

With a growl, Matt shot to his feet. "What the hell, man? Aoki couldn't have done it. He's been with us since the beginning. How could you possibly suspect him?"

Connor stood, making him step back. "Davon and you are at the top of that list. You could have planned everything from the start for all I know. Trust, friendship, and logic are the only things keeping me from believing that."

Matt took a seat, his mouth open.

Connor was right. It would have been simple to lie to everyone, build trust, and attack when the moment was right.

My heart twisted as I realized we'd always be the main suspects.

"I'm trusting you both because there's something that doesn't add up. All those who have been here since the beginning know our location. The exact coordinates of this base. I don't think any of you did this because the government would have already attacked. It must be someone who was brought in later. And until we know who that person is, we need to tread carefully."

His gaze swept over both of us. "In the meantime, I'll give orders that all the letters coming in and out of the bunker need to pass my approval. We'll reconvene tomorrow to decide how to move on from this and start planning Deb's retrieval."

"Understood." Matt left for the infirmary.

With everything that happened, I forgot about Abi. It was way past lunch, so I hurried to the door.

"Davon?" Connor said.

"Yes?"

He placed his journal in the safe on the right side of his desk, in which he kept a record of all PRF meetings and events. "What's going on between you and Abi?"

Fuck, I don't have time for this right now.

"Why do you ask?"

Glaring, he rose, knuckles against his desk. "Because she's my sister-in-law and I've seen how you've been looking at each other."

What's his problem?

I narrowed my eyes. "She's a grown woman, and she's more than capable of choosing whom she wants to be with."

Silence stretched between us.

Connor relaxed. "I need to know. Because you don't normally take any relationship seriously and I'm concerned about her. She's been through a lot."

This was what I got for fucking around. My own brother doubted me. How could he think I would betray his trust like this? I needed to make him see. "It's not the same with her, Connor. This isn't a fleeting thing."

He nodded. "Then go to her. You're late."

Chapter 21

Abi

"*October 2204: The bunker was up and running. The command center and half of the apartments were ready. We had people inside some facilities, watching closely, studying the behavior of students to determine whether they could be trusted or not, recruiting for the cause.*" (Deborah Davis's journal)

It was already 12:30 p.m. when I left the training center with Maria. My thigh ached, but Matt said that would last a couple of weeks.

We were ravenous and went directly to the dining hall. The room bustled with activity. Davon was nowhere to be found. Maybe his meeting was taking longer than expected.

Today's menu was mashed potatoes and steak. I followed Maria to a table, where Tammy, the teacher I'd just met, was sitting. Maria moved behind her and massaged her shoulders.

Tammy turned with a jump. Her eyes gleamed as Maria bent to kiss her briefly. Lovingly.

"This is Tammy. My girlfriend." Maria sat beside her.

"We met this morning. Good to see you again." I took the opposite seat, ready to dive into my food.

Tammy nodded. "Same here."

"Buen provecho," Maria said.

Confused, I glanced at Tammy. I was terrible at languages.

"Enjoy your meal." She opened her book, already done with her food. "That's what Maria's saying in Spanish."

"Oh. Gracias! You too." I bit into my steak, which was bursting with rich flavor. So good.

Maria looked at me. "I know we just met, but I'm curious. How did you manage to survive out there for so long?"

My stomach clenched. "I don't want to talk about it." If I could, I would erase those three years in a flash.

"Oh. Sorry." She fiddled with her food. "You want to become a soldier?"

"Yes, after being with Davon and Matt, I'm hoping to. I want to go out on missions." Hopefully sooner than later so I could help with Deb's rescue.

She raised her eyebrows. "Speaking of, how did it go with him and Matt? I mean, Davon's a good friend but stubborn as hell. He's got this 'I'm an asshole. Don't come near me' vibe around him." She chuckled.

A bark of laughter escaped me. "He's all right." I sobered, thinking about all he'd done for me in the last month. About his kiss. "He's a good man."

Tammy glanced at me, adjusted her glasses, and went back to her book. "Oh no. I know that look. Don't tell me..."

"Don't tell you what?" Davon's deep voice rolled through me like a warm wave. He put his arm on the back of my chair and kissed beside my ear. "Hi. Sorry I'm late. Let me get my food, and I'll be right back." He nodded to Maria and Tammy. "Hello, ladies."

Tammy stared after him as he walked away to get his food.

"Oh, right, you've never met him," Maria said. "That's General Niles, Davon for short. I sometimes forget he was out there when you got here." She grinned at me. "My admiration goes to you. I'd never be able to cope with him."

I laughed.

Tammy rose. "I need to go back to work. Nice seeing you again."

"Wait for me." Maria took her stuff and glanced at Davon, who was coming back to the table. "Time to leave. Spill the beans later, will you?" With a wink, she took Tammy's hand and walked away.

Davon sat beside me. "Did you wait long?" He dug into his food like a starved man.

"I just got here. Connor gave me the grand tour. This place is amazing." I bit into a piece of steak.

"I see you've met Maria. Who's the other girl?" His gaze followed them as they left the hall.

"Oh, that's Tammy, her girlfriend. We only met briefly." I sipped some water. "I trained with Maria for a while before coming here."

He jerked his head at me. "Trained with her?" He raised his eyebrows. "How was it? Maria is a beast on her training sessions."

"It was good. Connor told her to go easy on me since I'm still recovering. She showed me offensive drills, and we did some resistance training."

He frowned. "Did you ask him about coming with me?"

"I did. He said no. But that if I trained hard, he would send me on future missions. How did it go for you?"

He opened his mouth to speak but paused.

"Everything okay?"

He closed his eyes and touched his temple. "Yeah. It's just a lot. We have a difficult situation on our hands. We're still deciding how to work through it."

I cocked my head. "About the checkpoints? Deb?"

"Both, actually. Tomorrow we'll meet with Connor to walk through the details of the investigation and Deb's rescue. Both are high priorities right now. We need to decide before I leave how we'll approach each."

"I worry about you going in alone. I wish Connor would reconsider." I sighed, losing my appetite.

He lifted my fisted hand from beneath the table and interlaced his fingers with mine. "It'll be okay."

The common room was packed as always. Most ignored us, but some stared before continuing on their way.

"Did you see Sarah?" Davon asked as we crossed to our hall.

"I did, but she said she wanted to be alone."

He shook his head. "When I lost Elaine, I shut myself away and refused to let anyone help me. I nearly went insane with grief. Leaving her alone isn't a good idea."

As we approached his flat, his expression was downcast. "Go to her. Come by later if you want. I need some time alone to organize my thoughts. This morning was a little overwhelming." He yawned, bags under his eyes.

"Okay. I'll check on her and come back later." I put my hand on his cheek, and he leaned into it.

He softly grasped it and kissed the inside. A shiver raced down my arm.

"Her apartment is down the hall. The second to last on your left side," he said.

A minute later, I knocked on Sarah's door twice before she opened it.

"Oh. It's you." She had paint all over her face and clothing, and her hair was a mess. She sighed and let me in.

The scent of flowers caught my attention as I searched for its source. A vase of yellow wildflowers adorned her table.

"Jimmy brought those earlier. He wanted to pay his respects."

Jimmy... I almost forgot. I needed to find him.

Her apartment was cozy and full of art. The walls were covered with drawings of Deb and me. Of our parents.

Sarah stood in front of a canvas. She was a sketch artist, but this portrait was different. It was an oil painting of a man with short black hair and soft dark eyes filled with longing and affection. He was sleek, young, and attractive.

"Is this him?" It had to be, but I didn't remember him well.

"Yes. He was my everything." She stroked the image as a tear slipped down her cheek.

I touched her arm. "I'm truly sorry."

She bit her lip. "Every time someone goes out on a mission, we don't know when or if they'll come back. Every week he'd let me know if he was okay. I already suspected something was off when he missed his usual comm. He would've been the first to let me know about you. I was just so excited to see you that it didn't click. So much time lost, so little to make up for it. What am I going to do without him? How do I keep going?" Sobbing, she collapsed in my arms.

I held her close. "Oh, Sarah, I can't imagine what you're going through."

We sat on her bed and talked for hours. Sharing memories from her youth. Her relationship with Carlos.

We discussed her escape and how she suffered when Deb sacrificed herself. She explained Connor was lost in grief for a time after losing her and she'd taken Deb's place to assist him and help him get through it.

After experiencing the worst of the government's abuses, she worked with the newcomers to help them overcome whatever trauma they brought from the outside. Painting became more of a hobby after that.

When I was about to leave, she grabbed me. "Tomorrow night there'll be a memorial. Will you come?"

"Of course."

She looked down. "Good. And thank you."

I hugged her again. "I'm here for whatever you need."

After a hot shower, I decided to go to Davon's to unwind.

I stared at my reflection. I was still too frail to make a difference. I'd gained some weight, but my cheekbones were still prominent and the bags under my eyes heavy. I was better but still a mess.

All the information I'd gotten since yesterday played in my mind.

The urgency to get Deb back and the uncertainty of what could happen to Davon out there came forth, and I shook my head. Not having control over the situation was driving me mad.

I curled my hands into fists and rolled my shoulders back. I set my jaw and gazed at myself, ignoring my pain and doubts and concentrating on what was at stake.

I'll train hard and make myself strong for the ones I love.

I walked to his door and knocked.

"Coming!" He opened the door, wearing a white T-shirt and jeans. His feet were bare.

Handsome and casual.

"Hey." He gave me a peck on the lips and let me in. "How did it go?"

The smell of fresh cologne and his wet hair evidenced he'd just taken a shower. As soon as I entered, I saw an open book on the chaise lounge.

"It was hard but good." I sighed. "She said there's a memorial tomorrow."

"Yeah. Connor told me about it." He sat on the chaise and put the book away.

I took a seat beside him. "Are you better?"

"Still processing everything." His gaze seemed far away as he rubbed his forehead.

"Knowing how dangerous it'll be for you out there scares me, especially not being able to do anything to help."

"I've gone solo before, and we need to do it this way for it to work." He stroked my hand. "I'm not going to lie. I'm glad Connor said no to your going out there. At least for now. Dad's a very guarded man, more than me, and I need to tread carefully to get him to trust me enough to give me access to the prison."

What would Davon have to do to earn that trust?

"I wish you would tell me more," I muttered.

His brow wrinkled. "About?"

"Your past."

I was a hypocrite for asking with what I'd been keeping from him. But I would never truly understand him unless I knew what he went through.

Searching my eyes, he released a pained sigh and rested his elbows on his knees, his face in his palms.

"Please don't think less of me after this." He cast a sidelong glance at me.

I reached for him but decided against it.

He exhaled sharply. "Ever since I can remember, I trained with my father. He taught me everything from fighting and using blades to history and wars. It fascinated me. I loved him and looked forward to our long training sessions that always ended in his study to learn more about weaponry and war strategies. He was my hero." He raised his head.

His eyes glazed as he stared at nothing. "My last good memory of him was when he gave me my chaaklo. That was thirteen years ago. After that, I became his experiment. His weapon."

My throat tightened at his ragged breathing. This was wearing him down.

"I started training with his soldiers, long hours of fighting, of getting hit again and again until I learned how to defend myself. I can't recall how many times they beat me so hard that I lost consciousness. Only to get back up and continue. He was merciless, always wanting me to become stronger. Invincible." His gaze turned to ice. "Then came the brainwashing, one that was even taught at school."

I inhaled. "School?"

"Yes. In Electi, things are just as before." He confirmed what I'd always suspected.

I bowed my head. "How can people be so blind to it all?"

Davon clasped my hand. "You have no idea how much the people of Promissa have been denied. The gap that exists between us is immense. If it weren't for Matt, I would have fallen into their indoctrination, their hatred toward Promissa citizens."

I flinched back. "I don't understand. Matt? Is he also an elite?"

He gave a nod. "His father is the program director for the Genetic Enhancement and Population Control Program (GEPCP). The bond between Minister Anderson and my father was what brought us together. But, thanks to his mother, Matt had a different perspective. She's the Electi Medical Center's chief physician and has opposed the regime since the beginning. I doubt she'd still be with us if she wasn't so good at what she does. She's an exceptional doctor, one my father wants to keep in the NWG."

He fell silent for a moment. "Matt rescued me. He was there for me during my darkest hours. Even when my father..."

I squeezed his hand.

There was so much pain in his eyes. He closed them and shook his head. "Even when my father made me into a monster."

I frowned. "A monster?"

"Please understand. I didn't have a choice. At least, I didn't know I had one at the time. He made me do terrible things to get information out of his enemies in the most vicious and cruel way. I became his torturer. His assassin."

Images of a dark room filled with blood and terrified screams of pain came to mind, and I shuddered. I couldn't visualize Davon doing that. A man like him with so much heart. Was this what he feared? Having to go back to that?

"I've killed many. He wanted me to know what it felt like to take a life. Believing it was the ultimate thrill, to know you had the power to do so." A tear fell from his eye, then more as a sob escaped him.

He slumped forward, letting my hand go. I put my hand on his back.

He jerked. "Don't touch me. You have no idea. None. I...I don't deserve you. I'm the kind of person you should hate."

His words tore my heart. I wanted to help him, to show him what a wonderful person he was. To take away all his father had instilled in him.

I gritted my teeth as Jordan Niles came to mind. He destroyed his own son. His own flesh and blood. Hurt him to a point where he could no longer see himself worthy. What kind of father would do such a thing?

I longed to meet him face-to-face. To enact my revenge. Not only for what he did to us all but for what he did to the incredible man sitting beside me.

"Davon..."

He stood and walked away, his back to me. "Go. I want to be alone." His words were piercing. Final.

I crossed the room and wrapped my arms around him from behind. He flinched at first but then relaxed into me.

I drew him closer. "You're not a monster. Whatever he forced you to do, it's not who you are. I could never hate you."

"How? After all you've been through. I know there's much more that you haven't told me. Things you went through that you won't share. And it's all my fault, my own failure to fix all this." His tone was fragile. Broken.

"You haven't done anything to me. You're not one of them. You're one of us." As he turned in my arms, I gazed into his red-rimmed eyes. "Please don't pull away from me. I don't think I could take it."

He stared at me for a few seconds, then tucked me to his chest and kissed the top of my head. "I'll make up for all they've done to you until I'm worthy."

I pulled away from him slightly and looked into his eyes again. "You don't have to prove anything."

His lower lip trembled. "Thank you."

And in those two words, I knew he said so much more.

I stroked his hair and pulled him down to me. Just as my lips brushed his, a knock on the door made him pull away.

Davon's jaw clenched. "Who is it?"

"It's us." Matt's voice filtered in. "We brought food."

I trailed my fingers down Davon's neck. "Can't we just ignore them?"

A flush of warmth spread through my body as he tugged my waist to him.

"Hey, are you guys letting us in or what?" Matt yelled.

I shook my head as Davon grunted and went to the door.

Matt and Aoki entered. Aoki began setting the table.

"We thought something must have happened for you to skip dinner. Are you okay?" Matt said.

I smiled. "Yes, just glad you're here."

I sat next to Aoki, and he passed me a plate of sautéed potatoes with chicken breast. "This looks great. Thanks."

His lips curved upward, and he pulled his hair into a low ponytail. "Happy to serve. How did the rest of the tour go?"

"Fine. I got to train with Maria. She's great. Oh, and I also saw you have a club. I've never been to one."

"We should go someday." Matt winked at me. "You'll love it."

"I don't know. With all that's going on…" I did want to go, but I couldn't put Deb out of my mind. Or the knowledge that Davon had to go back into the city so soon.

Davon sat beside me, then took my hand. "We should make time to enjoy life a little. We're still planning the mission. A night out won't affect it. But only if you're willing."

I sighed. "I'm too anxious to think about something like that even if I'm dying to check it out."

Davon chuckled. "No pressure. We'll wait as long as you need."

We ate and talked about random stuff. No missions or rescues. Nothing about the government or the rebels. Just four friends having a nice time together.

When we finished, Davon went to his small bar and returned with a bottle of whiskey. He poured four glasses.

"Thanks," I said, grateful for him. For my new family.

Matt eyed the bottle. "Is this the whiskey you got from your father's personal collection?"

"You bet. A hundred-year-old bottle of scotch whiskey. At least something good I can get from that scumbag." Davon raised his glass in toast.

"To old and new friends and for these moments so that we can always make time for them. Cheers!"

"Cheers!" we said.

And we drank until we couldn't think any longer.

Chapter 22

Abi

"*November 2204: Ten people lived in the bunker permanently, keeping the place running. We had a new cook. He studied with Connor and me before the regime and decided to join us. He brought his younger brother, the first person brought in before the government got its hands on him. Davon also brought a new guy in. They were good friends, and he vouched for him.*" *(Deborah Davis's journal)*

My head throbbed as I opened my eyes. Davon slept behind me, his arm slung around my waist. I moved, but he held me in place, squeezing me tighter.

"Morning," he mumbled. He inhaled deeply, then brushed his lips against my neck.

I angled my head to give him better access and nestled into him.

He grasped the curve of my hip and pressed against me.

I knew what would happen if I wanted. I pushed the memories back into a corner. I wouldn't let them take this moment away from me. So I hid them: my fears, my doubts, my insecurities.

I opened my legs slightly, responding to his touch, as a surge of heat centered in my core at the hard proof of his arousal.

"You're shivering." He massaged my belly, and I waited for the flinch, but it never came.

He was driving me wild with need, distracting me from the pounding headache that had woken me. But I didn't want him to stop.

"I'm just a bit cold, and my head hurts a little, but I'm fine," I said.

"Let me take care of that." His lips lingered on the back of my neck and shoulders, his tongue languidly tasting my earlobe while his hand trailed up my side and grazed my breast.

I gasped.

His deep rumble did strange things to me as he shifted to rub my temple. "Anywhere else that hurts?"

I wanted to tell him everywhere just to feel his hands all over me. His searing caress. "No, but what you're doing helps."

He continued kneading and then stopped and got out of bed. "I'll get you something from the infirmary."

I missed his warmth right away. We were still dressed the same way as the night before. I guess I wasn't the only one who drank heavily.

He ran his fingers through his hair, tied it up in a bun, and put his shoes on. "I'll be right back. Wait for me."

I entered his bathroom to wash my face and grimaced at my reflection. Pale, sweaty skin and black circles under my eyes. I looked sick. I was sick.

I rushed to his bar, fighting the urge to vomit. I left a quick note and dashed to my apartment.

After retching my life out, I rinsed my mouth and turned on the water. I was dizzy and nauseous. I clung to the wall and let the hot water run down my face.

I finished my shower, wrapped my towel around my body, and stepped out of the bathroom to get dressed.

Davon stood next to the table. I froze. His exploring gaze sent shivers all over my body.

I must have left the door open in my rush.

He averted his eyes. "I'm sorry. I read your note and found your door open. I brought your medicine." He walked to the door.

God, this is embarrassing.

What if it was Matt or, worse, Connor?

"I'll go take a shower. Come when you're ready." He left.

Pulling out of the haze he put me in, I dressed. There was a note on my table next to a glass of water and pills: *Take these. —D.*

The smell of food made my stomach roil as I walked into Davon's apartment.

Aoki ate while grimacing and holding his head in one hand as Matt kneaded his neck.

"How was your night?" Matt asked me.

"I don't remember much, but my head's killing me." I groaned as the room shifted around me.

"Aoki isn't fond of alcohol either. He always has the worst hangovers."

"Morning," Aoki mumbled as I took a seat beside him. His voice was strained.

"Hey."

Davon kissed my head, then sat next to me. "Did you take the pills?"

"Yeah. Thanks."

He slowly slipped my hair band out and combed his fingers through my hair. I let out a moan as he massaged down to my neck. His hands were magic.

He put my hair band on his wrist.

I frowned. "Hey!"

"I'm doing you a favor. This will just make it worse." He winked.

I huffed.

Matt chuckled. "Are you ready for the meeting?"

Davon nodded. "Yeah, we need to start planning what to do about Deb."

"How long do you think you'll be out there this time?" Matt asked.

Davon hesitated. "A couple of weeks, a month at most. I'm not sure."

I forced down the fear that clawed at my heart. A few weeks could easily turn into months. His father could refuse to let go of him after what he told me yesterday, even after Deb's rescue.

Matt left with Aoki after breakfast to prepare for Connor's meeting. Aoki and I decided to spend the morning together while Matt and Davon met with Connor. We still hadn't had time to get to know each other. And what better way than over a hangover?

I smiled at the thought.

As I reached the door to leave, Davon stopped me. "Do you have a second?"

I nodded. Before I could speak, he spun me around, and his mouth covered mine in a mind-blowing kiss, his arm holding me firmly against him. We were both breathless when he finished.

His forehead touched mine. "I've been dying to kiss you since I saw you step out of your bathroom this morning."

"Why didn't you?" I ran my hand down his chest.

He closed his eyes and took a trembling breath. "Because I wouldn't have the strength to stop and you're more important than my needs."

Heat flooded my face.

He stroked my cheek. "You're gorgeous." He gently massaged my temples.

As the pounding in my brain subsided, I closed my eyes.

He brushed his lips against mine, sending tingles up my neck and arms. "I'll do my best to meet you for lunch, but the meeting could take longer than expected."

We stepped out into the hall to find Matt passionately kissing Aoki.

Davon cleared his throat.

With a grunt, Matt released Aoki. "See you later."

I went to Aoki, who leaned against the threshold, and Davon slapped my right butt cheek.

I stared at him. "Hey!"

"Sorry. Couldn't help it." He waved goodbye as he walked down the hall. Matt joined him, laughing.

Matt and Aoki's apartment had a minimalist vibe about it. Everything was either black or white.

Aoki sat on a white sofa and put a cold pack on his forehead. I gasped as a black-and-white cat walked between his legs. It was adorable.

"I didn't know you could have pets in here." I wondered if anyone else had them. "I'd love to have a cat someday."

"Ah, yes."

The cat leapt onto the sofa.

"This is Shirokuro."

The cat purred loudly as Aoki rubbed its ears.

"Shirokuro, meet Abi."

I sat next to the cat, and he walked onto my lap after sniffing my hands. I cracked a smile. "What does his name mean?"

"Black and white. It's from Japan."

"Have you had him for long?"

The cat closed his yellow eyes as I petted his neck.

"Since Matt left to rescue you. A gift to keep me company. Matt knows how much I hate being alone, so he brought him in."

I laughed as the cat hopped down and curled into a box that was a bit too tiny for him, but that didn't stop him.

"Did Matt give you anything for the headache?" I asked.

"He did, but I get these awful migraines, and most medicines don't work." He squeezed his eyes shut, resting his head back.

I moved closer. "Is there anything I can do?"

"Nah. Don't worry about it. I'll not let this spoil our day. How do you feel about seeing the sun for a while?"

"Outside?" I shrieked. For all I knew, they always kept in hiding. With the threat of the government, I wouldn't think of going out.

He groaned.

"I'm sorry."

"Don't worry." The corner of his mouth lifted. "Yes. Outside. We have two secured forest areas. Citizens would go crazy if it weren't for them. Didn't Connor tell you about this yesterday?" He put the cold pack on the table.

I shrugged. "Maybe it slipped his mind."

"Well, we have them at the end of hall B and D. We're free to go out, as they're guarded by snipers." He rubbed the back of his neck.

"That's amazing. Sure. I'd love to go out. I miss the forest." I jumped to my feet.

"Perfect." He put on his sunglasses. "Light is the enemy of migraines."

"But we don't have to go out if you're feeling sick."

"Sure we do. I'm not going to spend my free day hunkered inside my apartment." He went to the door. "Come on."

I followed. "Your free day?"

"Yes. I wouldn't drink if Carol wasn't there to cover for me. I'm always like this, yet the taste of whiskey warms me and relieves all my pent-up stress. Being so close to Davon, I'm sure you understand. It's difficult to be with a man whose job puts him in constant danger."

I hadn't considered it, but Aoki had it tough. Matt was always on missions as Davon's right hand. I stressed every time they risked themselves for my safety out there. And now, with this mission coming up, I was even more stressed.

As soon as I stepped past the threshold, a commotion caught my attention. I hurried to see what was happening, but people had already dispersed.

Aoki reached me, and we both stared at the bulletin board.

Memorial service for Christina Thompson and Carlos Rodríguez.
We invite family and friends to join us tonight as we say our final goodbyes.
May we never forget our mission.

"At last, he decided to tell the community." Aoki shook his head, fists clenched by his sides. "I don't understand Connor sometimes. It feels as if he's scared. Unable to take the next step."

Connor was family. But I understood Aoki's feelings. He was the general of the army. The man that, with my sister, created the People's Revolutionary Front, whose sole purpose was to take back what belonged to us by right. Our city.

He'd told me he didn't want to lose any more people, but that was impossible in war, and if the people chose to fight, he had no choice but to let them.

"Maybe he's tired of losing people and wants to take precautions to have a good plan. I mean, if we go in like we are right now, many will die."

"I know, Abi. But Matt and Davon have asked him time and again to let them plan a strategy, and he's said no countless times. They know we don't have the numbers, but we have people inside and a city full of fed-up citizens who would likely help us when the time came. If we do it right, we may have a chance."

Suddenly, it all made sense. I'd seen it, the angry citizens, even NWG soldiers like the one who saved Paul who might fight with us. We might have a shot after all.

We crossed over to hall D, and as we reached the end, Aoki tapped in a code. A door opened, and we signed our names on a log as a guard punched in another code and a hatch opened in the roof.

Natural light reached us, and the fresh scent of the woods filled the room. We went up the ladder and out to the forest. The dry leaf litter crunched beneath us as we walked toward a fallen tree and sat.

I hugged myself, closing my jacket. The cold wind chilled my skin. Aoki rubbed his hands together and blew inside of them.

Silence followed as we took in the view. It was stunning. Pristine. Untouched.

The horizon was filled with infinite forest and mountains with snow-covered peaks. The valleys were shrouded in mist. My heart swelled at the view, and I let my head fall back as I looked to the heavens. I was grateful for this moment.

Aoki hugged his knees. "I come here to unwind. Mostly by myself."

"How long have you been here?"

"Eight years. My brother and I have been here since the beginning before the bunker was finished. We were part of the first group to move in."

"Your brother?" I wanted to meet him.

He beamed. "Yeah, my younger brother. He's a guard."

"And Matt? Was he here by that time?" I always wondered about them. I knew very little about the process of constructing this community since Deb only mentioned it briefly in her journal.

A wistful smile crossed his face. "I met Matt that same year when Davon brought him in. I can still remember the first time I saw him. It seemed as if the entire world had gone black, and he restored its brightness." His eyes twinkled as he gazed at the horizon.

His love for him was palpable.

"When did you guys get married?"

"Seven years ago. Connor presided. It was a beautiful ceremony." He cocked his head. "But enough about me. What about you and Davon?"

Davon and I... How could I describe it? Something deep drew us together. Maybe our pasts or our painful memories. He gave me the courage to move forward.

"He makes me feel alive. Even with his dark past, he's kind, gentle, and full of dreams. He makes me feel like there can be hope after so much darkness."

There was a lot we needed to fix before we could finally be happy and get rid of the ghosts of our pasts.

What we had was intense. All encompassing, and it filled me to the core. He'd made his way into the deepest recesses of my soul where I wouldn't even dare to go.

"I'm glad for you two. I haven't seen him this happy in years." Aoki took my hand. "And how are you dealing with all that's happening?"

I took in the horizon. "I don't know where to start."

"It's not good to keep so much bottled up inside you. In the long run, it destroys you little by little."

He was right. The tightness in my chest worsened by the day. There were times when I couldn't breathe, only to find myself counting to ten to calm down.

Davon was someone I could talk to. He always listened and understood me like no one else. But I didn't want to put extra pressure on him, so I'd kept my feelings to myself recently.

I wanted to tell someone about my ongoing sense of powerlessness. I couldn't stop thinking about Deb's safety. Or the risk of losing Davon on this mission. I wished I could give Sarah more after all she'd been through and take vengeance for what happened to Paul, Jacob, and Bonnie. For all of the citizens who were lied to. Oppressed. But nothing could pass the lump in my throat.

I couldn't hold it in any longer and let my walls down. I sobbed loudly, shedding tears I had suppressed since I got here. Gentle arms embraced me, and I allowed myself to fall into them.

"There, there. Let it all out." Aoki's voice was soft.

So much feeling. So much pain. When my tears stopped, he pulled back.

"Do you feel better?" he said.

I nodded.

A kind smile curved his lips. "When you're ready to talk, I'm here for you. Okay?"

Lightness filled me for the first time since I got here. Like all that pent-up emotion had left me and all that remained was quiet. "Can we talk now?"

"Of course."

I told him everything. Every little detail.

Aoki listened, only nodding now and again.

After about an hour, we went back into the bunker. We were just about to enter our hall when a gentle voice stopped me. I recognized it immediately.

"Abi? It's really you?" Jimmy pulled me in. "God, I wanted to see you so bad. I'm so relieved you're here."

I relaxed into him and embraced him back, soaking in his fresh aroma, which mingled with spring and earth. I never thought I'd see him again. His embrace felt protective and full of emotion as he caressed my hair in an intimate manner. I had missed him terribly.

My heart ached as memories of our time together rushed in. He'd been there for me during my ups and downs. Happy tears streamed down my face.

"I...I thought they'd gotten to you. That I'd never see you again."

He pulled back. "I'm right here. I'm not going anywhere."

I gripped his hands while I attempted to keep the knot in my throat at bay. "I'm sorry about Christina."

"I know. Thank you." He gently rubbed away my tears.

I instinctively touched his hair. It reminded me of the dark sands of the desert I'd seen in books. I brushed his silken strands, which reached his shoulders, and smiled as his blue eyes took me in. He'd grown to almost the same height as Davon in our years apart.

"Are you going to be there tonight?" he asked.

"Of course."

For a moment, his captivating smile reminded me of old times, and a sense of peace washed over me.

"I need to go prepare Christina's eulogy." He took a step back and noticed Aoki.

Aoki lightly gripped Jimmy's arm. "Christina had a beautiful soul. She will be missed sorely."

Jimmy gave a nod. "Thanks." He glanced at me again. "See you tonight." He walked toward hall B.

"Were you close?" Aoki asked as we continued on our way.

I stared down, lost in my thoughts of the past. "We were."

He nodded, and we walked in silence until we reached their apartment.

Once there, he gave me some materials he used to meditate with when he felt anxious. It was a form of zen cultivation and mindfulness called *shakyo*. By hand-tracing sutras—sacred scriptures that contain the teachings of Buddha—I would be able to focus my mind. He gave me a book full of sutras and their meanings for me to trace.

I was to find a quiet place and sit in total silence with nothing but a piece of paper and a pen. Then I should give thanks and start tracing my sutras. Once finished, I had to close my eyes and thank myself for the moment. The technique would help me find stillness in my mind.

I did my first shakyo with him by my side, teaching me how it worked. I was nervous at first, but as I concentrated on it, my anxiety eased, and a new sense of peace filled my soul.

Chapter 23

Davon

"I hope today's different and he'll finally give us the go," Matt said as we made our way to the command center.

Matt wasn't a guy to lose his shit, but after what happened at the checkpoint, we were tired of excuses.

For the past five years, we continually urged Connor to hear us out and start strategizing to overthrow the New World Government. "We're not ready," he always said.

Change was coming, and it wasn't the good kind. Standing by and watching it all go to hell would accomplish nothing. We needed to act. Soon.

I understood his reluctance, but we had some things going for us that we couldn't ignore. Most citizens would fight if they had the resources to do so, and if we found a way to contact the rebel factions emerging around Promissa, we might be able to persuade them to fight alongside us.

We had sleeper agents inside the government and the military who would go to any lengths to bring the NWG down. We could use them to recruit and attack from within.

Even inside Electi, there were people who sympathized with our mission.

True, our numbers were small in comparison to the government's, but one-third of their forces were Promissa citizens stationed there because of their skills. They would help us. I was confident they would.

We just had to devise a strategy.

"This meeting is a good start," Matt said, always optimistic.

"I hope so."

A commotion in the common room caught our attention. People surrounded the bulletin board, some crying, others shouting. I grimaced at the notice announcing the memorial service that would be held tonight.

"What happened?" someone asked.

"Are we in danger?" another yelled.

Tears streamed down one woman's face. "When did this happen? Poor souls..."

Fear took control of the common room in seconds, unleashing chaos among those present.

"Everything will be okay. We're dealing with it," I said, trying to defuse the situation.

"How?" the club's bartender asked.

"We can't say more, but please trust us," Matt said.

Outraged and terrified, people demanded answers we weren't at liberty to share.

I held up my hands. "Everyone, please calm down. As soon as we have more information, we'll let you know immediately. As for now, we've enforced our perimeter, and no government soldiers have been sighted near the area."

People slowly nodded.

"Whatever is needed let us know, General. We're ready," one of my cadets said as she urged the rest of the people to disperse.

"This isn't good," Matt said.

My control slipped as anger clouded my senses, and I stalked toward command. Connor had to do something about this. The people needed answers.

I went through both doors without stopping and stormed through to get to his office.

"Have you seen what's happening out there?" I pointed toward the hall. "Are you just gonna sit there while everything goes to shit?"

Connor shoved his chair back and stood, his eyes deadly serious. "Stop now."

I took a step back at his imposing tone. I was about to argue back when Matt moved between us.

"Both of you will calm the fuck down now!" he said. "I'm also mad, but we're not solving anything this way. Let's sit and talk like rational adults." He sat, an expectant expression on his face.

"Fine." Connor grunted and took a seat.

"I'm not gonna sit back!" I was way too riled up to stay put.

Matt narrowed his eyes.

I growled. "I will not calm down. People out there are afraid. Hell, I'm scared. This is the first time in years a checkpoint has been breached, and we need to give them something."

Connor stared at me, his face devoid of emotion. "As you both know, I coordinated this meeting to talk about the letter we found yesterday, the events at checkpoint four, and Deb's rescue mission."

He sighed. "Davon, I understand your feelings. Mine are the same. If you think for one minute I'm not scared shitless, you're mistaken. We just lost two of our best. Ten more soldiers are out there guarding the perimeter, and we've only heard back from four of them."

Matt shifted in his seat. "Wait. They didn't check in?"

Our forces were highly organized and structured. If they didn't check in, something must be terribly wrong.

"Who are you sending in?" I asked, knowing Connor must have already sent someone to investigate.

"Anna and Pedro already left. They'll do reconnaissance and be back tomorrow. Depending on their report, we must act. We can't let everything we've built fall. It's not an option."

They were two of our best, and I trusted them fully.

"We should have acted sooner," I said under my breath.

Connor shot to his feet. "Don't you think I know that?" His voice thundered through the room. "Do you have any idea what I've been through? Deb wouldn't have peace until Abi and Sarah were safe. You know this. You were there. She couldn't think straight and went off without a word. Did you ever stop to think about how I felt after abandoning her in that facility, knowing she could be dead as we speak?" He slumped down into his chair. "I've failed you all."

Lost, enraged, and scared. As he reined it all in, I stared at the floor.

I knew how it was. Deb's anxiety attacks. The long fights in command as she demanded more action. She was our leader, and ignoring her was a hard task. Abi and Sarah's retrieval was prioritized, and that was it.

But the last thing he said was what shook me to the core. How would I feel if I had to abandon Abi and see them take her away? It would break me.

I wasn't sure how I would react. Perhaps I would do the same thing.

But war was different, and our decisions affected the lives of countless others. And they had to come first.

"We'll wait for their report and move on from that," Matt said.

We all agreed.

A knock on the door startled us.

Nina entered and stopped just inside the door, her gaze sweeping over us. She adjusted her glasses and straightened. "Sorry for interrupting. We just got intel from our man inside the prison. He saw Deb being moved. She's alive."

Connor closed his eyes and pressed his palms against the desk. "Thank God."

After a moment, he regarded Nina. "How was she? Did he say anything more?"

She stared down at her papers. "She's beaten up but still in high spirits. She fought and cursed through the halls."

Connor sneered. "They'll pay for this."

I faced Nina. "Thanks. Keep us informed of any new developments."

She bowed toward me and exited the room.

"We *will* get her out," I said as Connor sank into his chair, cradling his head in his hands.

We took a moment to calm down and started planning our strategy to investigate the letter and checkpoint situation. Connor was checking into everything that went in and out of the bunker in the last months and interviewing all the key players, starting with the runners and the soldiers who scouted the perimeter of the forest.

As for us, the ones with access to the cypher, we'd also be thoroughly investigated as well as our acquaintances. The problem was keeping everything casual so as not to alert the spy.

Nina's team would update our surveillance system and place more cameras in the hallways and near command, but that would take weeks.

As for Deb's rescue mission, we had two problems. One was getting me inside the prison, which would take some work with my father. The second was setting up more reliable comms in the city and near the prison area so I could communicate with command.

If what we suspected was true, my father believed me to be the one sending him the checkpoint intel, and that would work in our favor. As to why the spy used my name to send it, my answer was they knew it was the only way to get the intel out. And if that was true, this person was deep inside our system, already aware I worked as a double agent, a fact only a few of us knew.

But why hadn't they blown my cover yet? I tried to think of reasons but came up empty. Perhaps they were waiting till they had control of all checkpoints. Or maybe they wanted me to be with my father so they could arrest me. Whatever the reason, I couldn't shake the chill running through my body. I swallowed my fear and focused on the matter at hand—catching the spy.

"We have one chance at this, Davon. Once we get comms up, you move in," Connor said, back in his element.

Setting up comms would take about two weeks. Even though I was glad I could stay longer, my rooted instincts told me we needed to act soon. I was ready to leave at Connor's request. Nothing was more important than protecting the community and keeping Abi safe.

"I'll get everything ready in case you need me to get there sooner than expected."

Matt was late for his shift at the infirmary and left first.

Connor leaned against his desk. "Davon, do you have a minute?"

I was almost at the door. "Sure. What is it?"

"I wanted to ask about Abi. How is she taking everything?" His gaze was pained.

My heart twisted. "It's been hard on her. She's keeping it all in, and that's what worries me."

"Make sure you take good care of her."

I stiffened, my chest tightening. "I'll protect her with my life, my friend. Never doubt it."

"I would never expect anything less from you." He walked toward me and clasped my shoulder. "Sorry about yesterday. I wanted to make sure your head was in the right place. I'm glad it's you she's with. There's no better man I would pick for her."

I nodded and gripped his forearm. "Thank you."

He walked back to his desk. "Did you know she wants to train to become a soldier? To go out on missions?"

"Yeah. She'll be a great asset to our army. I worry about her safety. But I won't stop her." I shook my head and shifted my weight. If I could hide her and keep her safe, I would. But she was stubborn, and there was no way she'd stay away from it all.

"I don't like it either, but she has Deb's spirit. We have to get her ready and trust she'll be okay. Have you seen her fight?"

"Briefly, but she knows how to defend herself. And she does know how to handle blades. As for guns, that's a different story. She couldn't shoot a bullseye if you put it right in front of her. But I told Matt to train her anyway. You never know when she'll need to use one."

"Good. If she's okay with it, she can continue training with Maria in her defensive and offensive skills. You and Matt can take over her weapon training." He sat back in his chair.

"I'll talk to her. Anything else?" I glanced at the doorway.

"No, that's all. Thank you." He started organizing his paperwork.

"Please, if you hear anything, let me know immediately. I have a bad feeling about all this." A heavy feeling had settled in my chest since he told us about the checkpoints.

"Me too, but there's nothing to do but wait. Now go. I know you're anxious to get to her." He gave me a sly smile. "It's written all over your face."

I grinned. He knew me too well.

When I reached the common room, a sole person stood in front of the bulletin board. Her golden hair was so different from Abi's, but her expression was the same. Numerous times I'd seen the same empty stare on Abi's face as she remembered her past.

I stood beside Sarah, hands in my pockets. "Are you okay?"

Carlos was my friend, and he never lost faith we'd find Sarah. She was his everything.

She closed her eyes, tears streaming down her cheeks. "It's surreal to lose him like this. Death follows me everywhere."

I understood completely. The NWG was like a plague—everything it touched withered.

"I'm sorry. He was a good friend." I would never forget our conversations and how he always placed others before himself.

She bit her lip. "I don't want to lose anyone else."

"I promise I'll keep Abi safe and get Deb back. I'll not rest until I do."

"Thank you. Connor told me all you've done for this place, and I'm happy you're here." She dried her tears. "Are you going tonight? I'm on my way to the memorial center to get this in place." She held up a canvas.

I was curious about what it was but didn't want to intrude. "Yes. I'll be there."

I walked with her through hall E until we separated by the dining hall.

"I'll see you tonight." She continued toward the end of the hall.

I crossed the dining hall threshold, searching for Abi. She was seated at a table near the middle. Her eyes locked on me.

God, she was so beautiful. Her captivating eyes. Her unruly, naturally highlighted hair. It was like catching the first glimpse of sunshine after long, dark years.

What had I done to deserve her?

There was nothing I wouldn't do for her, to protect her. She was perfect.

Chapter 24

Abi

"*November 2204: We lost someone today. The first person from our group to be executed. Louis was a good friend and one of our classmates in this facility. We recruited him three months ago to be our tech guy, working to create networks between the facilities and the bunkers. He started working at a high-security facility as soon as he graduated and never came back. He was caught spying and was killed as an example to anyone who planned on rebelling. They made him a martyr.*" (Deborah Davis's journal)

After completing my first shakyo, I left Aoki's place in time for lunch. His migraine had gone from bad to worse, so he stayed to rest.

Davon was not in the dining hall, so I got my soup and took a seat at an empty table where I could see the entrance in case he arrived. I was desperate to know what happened in the meeting. When would the mission take place, and what was the strategy? The checkpoint executions also had me on edge, as I had a feeling Davon was keeping something from me.

Halfway through my lunch, he entered the dining hall. His black eyes fixed on me. His presence clouded everything around him, leaving me with only him to see. As he approached, he drew the sleeves of his gray sweater up. The tribal tattoos on his arms fascinated me.

"Sorry I'm late." He gave me a peck on the lips. "Let me get my food."

People murmured behind me. Something about me and the general. Not everyone knew who I was, as the mission to get me was kept under the rug. But now that we were together, I was a topic of conversation.

At first, I didn't understand why we were the talk of the community. But Aoki told me Davon hadn't dated in a while. That he was known as a hard man. Heavily guarded. He said Davon had changed, had come back different. More relaxed. Easygoing. And everyone saw me as the source of such change.

My racing thoughts came to a halt the instant he sat next to me. "How was the meeting?"

"A lot to plan still. Some checkpoints were due to check in and never did. Two of my best soldiers are out doing reconnaissance. Tomorrow we'll know more. As for Deb, we got intel midmorning from our informant inside the jail. He saw officers taking her to her cell." His features softened. "She's messed up but alive."

My heart seized. "They're torturing her."

"Yes. More so knowing she aided in an escape."

"When was the last time command heard about her before today?"

"Two months ago."

I gasped, picturing the despair Connor must have gone through at not knowing anything.

She was alone out there, suffering, and we couldn't do anything about it. My ribs tightened, and I straightened in an attempt to fight these troubling thoughts. I had to be strong.

"Connor already sent out teams to set up comms inside the city and near the prison's perimeter. Some spies will aid me once I'm out there. Everything will be ready within a week or two, but I think I should leave sooner. With everything that's happening, Father may grow impatient.

He's a very calculating man." He shook his head. "He may be waiting for me now to get the truth out of her."

A shiver ran through me. I already knew what his father trained him to be.

"Do you think he'll make you torture her?" I kept my voice low.

He dropped his spoon and covered his face with both hands, then raked his hair back. He placed his hands behind his neck, his head bent toward the table. "I'm 100 percent sure of it." He exhaled hard. "It's going to be hell."

No. This can't be.

Oh my God, he would torture her. My sister. There had to be another way.

From what he said to me, he was trained to be the best. She wouldn't survive it.

"You can't do this!" I grabbed his arm, forcing him to look at me.

He stared down at his hands. "There's no denying my father. And if I want to get inside, it's the only way. Connor already knows this."

The cold talons of dread clamped around my heart until I thought it would burst. "But what will you do?"

He pinched the bridge of his nose and closed his eyes. "I'll make it work. And I'll get her out safe, no matter the cost."

I swallowed hard, my eyes burning. But what would the cost be?

After lunch we decided to get ready for the memorial, each going to their own apartment.

I didn't have many clothes, so I wore black cargo pants and a black shirt. Someone knocked on the door.

"Come in!" I shouted.

"Hey!" Matt entered, dressed in a dark-blue shirt and black jeans. "How was your day?"

I brushed my hair. "Good. I had a great time with Aoki. Is he feeling better?"

"More or less." He sat on the couch and fumbled with the music box.

I had forgotten to ask Davon about it. "What is that? I've never seen anything like it."

"The engineers here have recreated most of the technology we had before the wars. This is one of my personal favorites." He grinned and put on some music, bobbing his head to the beat.

It was faster than jazz, and it had lyrics. I could make out the sound of a guitar and drums. I liked it.

"This is a Bluetooth speaker. It plays the music you pick on your MP3, which is this little thing." He grasped the small device that had the music list. "The music we got after hacking the net."

"I love it. I remember Father played music, but he had an old boom box and some of those discs from hundreds of years ago. They passed from generation to generation. He was a huge jazz fan."

"That's very cool. Aoki and I are more soft rock kind of guys. But Davon, he's hardcore. Metal's his favorite. How about you?"

My mind was blank. I liked jazz since Father used to listen to it, but Uncle Scott didn't have any music in his house. "I'm not sure. I suppose…" I bit my lower lip. "I didn't have music when I was young."

He sighed deeply. "Right. But don't worry." He pushed his shoulders back and placed a palm to his chest. "When it comes to music, I'm a genius. I'll teach you everything you need to know." He leaned forward, one hand on his knee, the other next to his mouth as if telling a secret. "However, don't tell Davon. Between you and me, he has no idea what great music entails."

I burst out laughing at his expression. It was dead serious, but his eyes twinkled with mischief.

He waggled his eyebrows. "About that, what's going on with you two? It's obvious you've been staying at each other's places. But I want to know from you."

I stopped midway through braiding my hair. "We're together. We haven't talked about it yet, but yes."

"Oh, it's official. Trust me. He hasn't been committed to anyone in years."

"Since Elaine, right?"

Matt's eyes widened. "He told you about her?"

"In the cave."

Matt sighed. "He lost her six years ago during a reconnaissance mission. The bullet perforated her liver, and by the time they got back, there was nothing we could do for her. She died within a couple of hours. He was in love with her, and after her death, he changed." He gave me a soft smile. "I'm glad he found you. He hasn't been this happy in years."

"I don't know what to think. About us, I mean. He's twenty-eight." I looked at him, waiting for his opinion on this.

I had been with Jacob, and we both were new to everything. But it was not the same with Davon. According to Aoki, he was much more experienced and had numerous lovers after Elaine, none of whom were serious. And even though both Matt and Aoki kept telling me this time was different, I couldn't help but wonder if he'd one day let me go. If this was only temporary.

"And what does age have to do with anything? If he's with you, he's all in. You should know how much you matter to him. How he looks at you."

"I hope you're right." Heat crept into my face. "I mean, all we've done is kiss. But he's intense."

He stared at me. "You still haven't been together, like really together?"

I lowered my gaze. "No."

"And how do you feel about it?" His voice was gentle.

"Well, I'm just... I don't know." I shifted my feet.

He sat forward. "What don't you know?"

"I'm not sure." I hadn't told a soul about what happened out there. I wanted to push past it and open a new chapter in my life. And for that, I had to tell Davon, but I didn't know how.

He tapped the spot beside him. "Come here."

I sat by him, and he started doing my hair.

"I don't know what's going on, but I think you should talk to him. Your feelings matter to us and to Davon especially." He finished my braid and turned me to face him. "I don't know what you went through out there. But you need to know we're here for you. That you can talk to us."

I sighed. It had been a long time since someone cared for me.

There was a knock on the door, and Matt went to open it.

"Hey, man." He shook Davon's hand, then put a hand on his shoulder. "Just having a little chat with your girl here. See you at the memorial."

As Matt closed the door, Davon raised an eyebrow at me. "Everything okay?"

"He came to ask about us."

Davon huffed. "Why does he have to be so...Matt?"

I chuckled as I took him in. Davon resembled a god, an Adonis. He wore black slacks and a black long-sleeved shirt, and his hair was tied back.

He approached me slowly. When he reached me, he grasped my right hip and pulled me to him. "And what did you say?"

I shivered with desire, my blood heating. "I told him we were together but that we hadn't talked about it." My insides twisted into knots, and I lowered my gaze. How was I supposed to talk to him about me? About us?

He raised my chin and kissed me slowly. A sweet, lingering kiss that made me tremble in his arms.

"Do you doubt this is real?" He trailed his lips down my face, brushing my jaw, then my neck. Not an inch of space separated us.

I was on fire.

"I know how I feel when I'm with you, but..." I took a step back. His closeness made it impossible for me to think straight, and we needed to have this conversation.

Straightening, I gathered my courage. "I feel safe around you, and, well, I want to be with you. But there's a lot you still don't know about me."

He came closer. "Tell me."

"Until a month ago, I was losing all hope. I lived in terror every single day, not knowing what would happen next. Not trusting anyone. Then you came along with Matt and changed everything. And you, especially you, made me feel something I had vowed to never feel again." I moved away from him as heat poured into my cheeks.

"We can talk about it. Please tell me." He stood behind me.

"After Jacob was killed, I promised myself not to fall for anyone else. We were only together for three months, and even though our relationship was new, my heartbreak was intense. Unbearable. Then something terrible happened, and I wanted to die. I never wanted to feel again. But you, you changed that. You slowly dug a place into my heart. Into my very soul. And I feel lost. Scared."

I trembled as he stepped in front of me.

"I'm sorry if this has been too fast. I'd never take advantage of you. If that's what you're worrying about, don't. We can take it as slow as you need." He stroked my cheek while looking deep into my eyes. "Believe me when I say this isn't a passing thing. I do care about you, and I want to get to know you better, no matter how long it takes. If you need more time, tell me."

"I don't need more time. I want to be with you, but there are some things that might make you reconsider if you want to be with me. If I'm worthy of you." I had to get to the root of the problem.

I was damaged. Dirty. A mess. Unworthy of love. I could almost feel the pain as if it just happened. The hollowness inside my soul.

He blinked, his jaw dropping. "You're way more than I deserve. How can you say that about yourself?"

I shook my head and looked down to hide my tears. Remembering. Shuddering from the memories.

His hands. His touch.

"Abi?"

Davon's voice brought me back to the present. I pushed my thoughts away.

"Listen to me. I don't know what happened out there, and I know you're still not ready to share it with me. But I'm here for you, and whatever you went through, whatever they did to you will never change how I feel about you. You're an incredible and strong woman, and you need to get that into your head. Nothing else matters, only what we feel. Believe me. I really want this."

I gazed at him through my tears. "Me too."

He kissed me.

We walked to the memorial hand in hand. People started to gather in the center of the room where chairs were set.

We went to Matt and Aoki.

Aoki leaned close, his face flushed. "Do you feel better? I've been sick all afternoon."

"Davon gave me some pills that did the trick, but I'm still a bit dizzy."

Davon frowned. "You should've told me. I would've gotten you something else."

I waved dismissively. "Don't worry. I'll be okay."

He grunted as we took our seats.

Jimmy sat next to Christina's picture and Sarah by Carlos's portrait.

Connor stood in the center. "If everyone would take a seat, we'll begin the memorial."

His booming voice caught everyone's attention, and everyone started sitting.

"Today we honor the memory of Carlos and Christina. They were true heroes who brought in countless people from the city. They aided our soldiers in their missions and were loved by their families and friends. Jimmy and Sarah would like to say a few words."

Sarah stood. "Carlos was my everything. I met him twelve years ago, and we started a family together that ended before it began. Of those twelve years, we were only together for two. I never thought I would see him again until I got here." A tear trickled down her cheek. "These past months were wonderful. He was loyal and true, never hesitating if anyone needed him. I'll never forget him. Today I light this candle in remembrance of his beautiful soul. May we never forget our mission."

She lit a candle on the wall next to his plaque: Carlos Rodriguez 2182–2213.

When Sarah went back to her seat, Jimmy took his place next to Christina's plaque.

Sorrow coated his features. "Christina saved my life and brought me here, giving me a chance to live a normal life. To have friends and experiences I wouldn't have had out there. She never stopped fighting for the ones in need and never wavered in her mission. I'll miss her always, as I'm sure many here will do. Her smile. Her jokes. Her light. She touched all our lives in a unique way. Today I light this candle in remembrance of her precious soul. May we never forget our mission."

He lit a candle next to her plaque: Christina Thompson 2185–2213.

Everyone rose and said in unison, "May we never forget our mission."

I glanced around as one by one people made their way to give their condolences. Davon stood still, his dark gaze centered on the two candles up front. Unblinking. I grabbed his hand, and he jerked toward me, waking from his haze.

We decided to walk around and give the others space since I planned to stay with Sarah afterward.

I blinked back tears as I gazed at the multitude of names and candles surrounding me, then shifted my gaze to Davon, who studied a plaque.

"Have all of them been killed by the government?"

His eyes misted. "Most. Some just disappeared."

"Did you know them?"

"All of them. Louis was the first one we lost." He pointed to a candle: Louis Patterson 2183–2204. "He was killed on this day nine years ago as an example to us all." He glanced at me. "As I told you, I've been here since the beginning. In one way or another, I've met each of these souls. This is why we fight. Many more die than people know about. Many suffer inside facilities, and we haven't been able to rescue them." His eyes burned with barely contained rage.

"I want to know more. Will you tell me?" As an elite rebelling against his own people, I knew this affected him greatly.

He nodded.

The room started to empty, and Davon and I stepped forward to give our condolences to Jimmy.

As I approached, he took my hands. "I wish she could've seen you. She worked very hard to help Deb find you."

My thoughts returned to that day. The blood puddle in the street. Her twisted body sprawled on top of it.

The injustice of it all made me tremble, and my eyes glazed over.

Christina had a bubbly personality and was always cracking jokes. She adored her brother and friends.

I squeezed his hands, and he hugged me. As he sobbed, his trembling breath crushed my heart. My eyes misted, but I fought back my tears. I needed to be strong for him.

We stayed like that for a moment before slowly letting go. His eyes were sunken in, puffy and crimson.

"I'm sorry for your loss," Davon said.

We both jerked sideways.

Jimmy shook hands with him. "Thank you, General. We all know the risks, but no one can truly prepare us for it." He put his hands in his pockets.

Jimmy looked at me. "Do you have time for lunch tomorrow?"

"Sure. We can do that."

"Good." He nodded, then kissed my cheek and left.

Davon's gaze followed him till he left the room. His expression was pinched, his muscles tight.

I furrowed my brow as he took my hand. "Let's go see Sarah."

She seemed oddly serene, Connor by her side.

I embraced her tightly and held her for a minute. "Do you want me to stay over tonight?"

She nodded.

"Okay, I'll get my stuff and go to your place."

With a nod, Connor whisked her away.

My heart was heavy. This place emitted a haunting peacefulness, but great desolation lurked inside these walls.

As we reached my apartment, Davon hugged me good night. "Breakfast tomorrow?"

"I think I'll stay with Sarah during the morning." I let my hand linger at his waist.

"Okay. Let me know if you need anything. Can we meet after you finish lunch?" He stepped back.

I nodded. "Sounds good."

His gaze drifted away for a moment before he turned to his apartment.

I grasped his arm. "Are you okay?"

"I will be. Don't worry. Go to your sister. She needs you." He touched my cheek, then went inside.

Chapter 25

Chapter 25

"*January 2205: Connor and I celebrated our nineteenth birthdays inside the facility, missing our friends. We'd found a storage room in my living quarters, and Connor would sneak in every now and then for us to be together. He'd found some booze in the faculty room. His stealth skills were terrific. We toasted for our mission, for the ones we'd lost, and for the new members.*" (Deborah Davis's journal)

It was nine in the morning when a knock on the door woke us. Sarah and I stayed up late, talking about random stuff, trying to forget about our troubles.

I stepped outside for a moment. "Morning, Matt."

"Here. I brought you breakfast."

I took the food. "Thanks."

It was weird Davon wasn't the one bringing it. I'd been thinking about him. He seemed distressed when we said goodbye.

"How's Davon?"

He looked down the hall. "I don't know. Haven't seen him. I checked on him last night to see if he wanted to come over, but he told me he'd stay in."

I shook my head. "After the memorial, something seemed off."

He let out a breath. "I'll check on him later. These events always rattle him. He feels somehow responsible for not being able to stop his father, given his position both here and in the government. I'll let him know you asked about him."

"Thanks."

I hated leaving Davon alone last night, but my sister needed me. Maybe I could go over to his apartment before lunch.

"Abi, I'm starving! Did Matt bring coffee?" Sarah asked.

I bid Matt goodbye and went inside. "Yes, he brought the good stuff. Let's dig in."

We talked for another hour or two, and then I left for my apartment. She lent me a book, and I read for a bit after a quick shower. I hadn't been able to get alone time in weeks and was craving a bit of calm. Silence.

I woke with the book on my face and my stomach growling. It was already 12:00 p.m. I must have dozed off.

I hurried to Davon's before meeting Jimmy, but there was no answer at his door. As I made my way to the common room, I heard shouting from Connor's apartment.

"Six more soldiers killed! We can't just sit here and do nothing," Davon yelled.

I stopped in front of the door, my insides twisting into knots. *God, what's he talking about? Six dead? What the hell happened?*

"Niles, stop and think about it. We still need more soldiers. We lack the resources to take on the government. We don't stand a chance."

I did agree with Connor in part, as I'd seen the government forces. Their numbers were astounding. I didn't have the details about the PRF army, and even though I had no doubt they were ready to fight, going in right now would be suicide.

But Davon wasn't asking to go in without a plan. His heart and mind were in the right place. He wanted to build an offensive because if we let them come to us, we would lose everything.

Davon growled. "I hate it when you use that name. It's bad enough I must carry it. I'm asking you to give us the go. Let Matt and I form a small group and begin strategizing. We have people inside already. We can easily start taking players out."

"It's too risky."

"And what's the problem with that? They've been at us for the last nine years, starting with Louis and all the others who have died. And what have we done? Nothing. We've done nothing to fix it. I'm tired of being stepped on. Others think the same. And we haven't even started to deal with all the people who are being abused and enslaved by the government and the elite. How long are we going to hide what we know from everyone? It's been two years since I found out about the program, and we've done nothing."

What's he talking about?

What program? What could Jordan Niles be doing?

My mind raced as I searched for answers, and then I remembered. The officer, the one who saved Paul, talked about a general and his orders to take the escapees back to the NWG. His partner had wondered why. Wouldn't it be easier to kill us?

I remember asking myself the same thing after the soldiers in the tunnels took the children away, saying they'd hit the jackpot. It almost seemed as if they needed us for something.

Were they using us for some kind of plan? An experiment? I wouldn't doubt anything from that man.

"I've done nothing because my wife's missing. How do I tell the people we're going to fight back if we can't even get someone as important as Deb back? She was the one who created all this, and many still see her as our leader." Connor paused for a moment. "Having her back will bring them hope. A will to fight."

"I know. That's why I want to start working on her extraction sooner than you propose. I'm not saying to go all in right now. I'm asking for you to give notice to the bunkers to start preparing. To be ready to strike at any moment. Let Matt and I go and check the prison's perimeter. Find possible escape routes and inspect the checkpoints that were breached. We need to know if the patrols are moving toward us."

After a moment of silence, Connor said, "Okay. You and Matt can go tomorrow. But don't engage the soldiers or enter the city under any circumstances. For now, let's keep this between us. Once we have a better idea of what we can do, we'll tell the citizens."

My heart stopped. Six people were killed, and they were going out there. Aoki's words repeated in my mind: *"It's difficult to be with a man whose job puts him in constant danger."*

"Please think about what I told you. I'll do everything in my power to get Deb back for you and for Abi. But we need to stop my father."

"I know, and we will."

Footsteps approached. I darted behind a corner. Davon left Connor's apartment and headed down the hall. After lunch, I would go to him.

He was a great soldier, but after all we'd been through and the threat from the NWG soldiers... What if the patrols got to them?

I clutched my arms to my chest. Staying behind while he was out there would be very hard indeed.

***

Jimmy waited at a table at the end of the room, a plate set for me beside him. "Hi, Abi. I'm glad you could come."

I sat. "Tacos today. I've been here only three days and am very impressed by the food."

Too many years of eating garbage. I took a bite, savoring the cheesy beef.

Jimmy chuckled as I wiped a bit of cheese off my chin.

He bit into his taco. "We have a network of communities, and we help each other out. I brought these tortillas yesterday from the agricultural site."

I nodded. "I like your system."

"It's definitely something we want to implement when we free Promissa. We have five communities collaborating. Imagine how much we could do in the city." He paused. "The heart of it all is Janus Peak. We provide security, personnel, and weaponry. People come here to train and are dispatched to other areas as guards or on missions."

"Everything you're saying is great, but I'm curious as to how you maintain peace. Who decides stuff in here?" I knew Connor was the general of the army, with Davon as second-in-command, but what about the other bunkers?

"Two councilmembers run each bunker, and no decision is made without a vote. It's like a cooperative. We all have a say in the decisions taken. The council is there to advise, protect, and maintain peace. But Connor and Davon are considered the leaders by all of us even though they never wanted it."

"And what about you? What's your role as captain?"

He frowned. "How do you know I'm a captain?"

"Oh, Davon told me."

"Ah. Niles." He raised an eyebrow, then continued eating.

What's that about?

"Well, as captain of the runners, I make sure everything runs smoothly between the bunkers. I answer directly to General Harris."

He took a sip of water. "But enough about me. Tell me about you, about the years out there. How did you do it?"

Oh, here it was. The topic everyone wanted to know about and the one I didn't want to remember. Sometimes I thought it was mere luck how I survived all those years without going crazy. It was a battle between surviving, losing hope, and thinking about ending it all.

The truth of it was I wished I could erase those three years. The beatings, the murders, the rapes, and the suicides. I became stronger, but it left scars. Not only the ones you could see but ones hidden beneath the skin. Ones that would never heal.

A fist closed around my heart, making it difficult to breathe, and I shut my eyes, pushing back all those memories.

Jimmy's hand covered mine, and I glanced up.

His blue eyes were focused on me. "Are you okay? You zoned out."

I sighed. "Yeah. Sorry. I do that often."

"Let's not talk about it right now and just enjoy our meal. Do you know what assignment you'll be doing?" He went back to his food.

Now, that I could talk about. "I already started training to become a soldier. I want to be out there and fighting."

"I don't like you risking your life out there, but I know you. Once you make up your mind about something, no one can stop you."

I chuckled.

The place was getting very crowded, and we had to raise our voices to hear each other.

"I never thought I would see you again, Jimmy. Not after what everyone said in the city. I wanted to rescue you. I even had a plan, willing to risk it all." If it wasn't for Deb, I would have been caught trying to get him back.

"I didn't know Christina was planning to get me out. Hell, I didn't even know about the rebellion. I wanted to send you a letter. But they wouldn't let me. Deb had her own plan." His gaze was fond. "Do you have something to do after lunch? We can go to the forest and talk some more."

"Oh, I'd love to, but I'm meeting Davon." I needed to talk to him urgently, especially after what I just heard outside Connor's place.

He nodded, his eyes begging. "Okay. What about tomorrow? Do you want to meet for breakfast? I have so much to tell you."

He always did that, even when we were children. Always getting his way.

"Maybe in the afternoon after lunch?" I wanted to have a quick breakfast and train during the morning.

"That sounds good." He clasped my hand. "I'm so happy you're here. I missed you."

"Me too." My heart swelled. Having him here meant a lot to me too.

"What's going on here?" Davon sat beside me.

Jimmy pulled his hand back.

I stiffened at his tone. Was I being watched now? "What do you mean what's going on? We're just talking."

Davon held a taco but didn't bite into it. "It didn't look that way to me."

What was he implying?

I ground my teeth as I tensed.

Jimmy stopped eating and stood. "Well, it was nice talking to you. We'll talk later."

Frowning, I rose. "Wait! You don't have to leave."

He waved me off and left without glancing back.

I glared at Davon. "What the hell's wrong with you?"

"Hello to you too." He eyed me. "The guy was obviously hitting on you."

I scowled. "Grow up! He's my friend, and we were just talking."

He shrugged as if he hadn't just been a complete asshole toward Jimmy or me.

I thrust my chin up and challenged his stare. I was not going to let him push me around. "You know what? I don't know what's wrong with you today, but I don't want to deal with your shit right now." I grabbed my plate.

He averted his gaze, his muscles bunching beneath his shirt.

I knew he was hurting and having a tough day, but I was not going to be as immature as him. "I'll be in my apartment. When you're ready to act like an adult, come see me."

I walked away, ignoring him as he called after me.

Who does he think he is?

I got to my room and slammed the door behind me as my blood heated. I paced around the room.

How could he think that of me?

I washed my face and picked up the book I started reading this morning. It was a romance, which I was not in the mood for, but I didn't have anything else, so I plopped onto the couch to read. I might as well do something while I waited. If he wanted to fix things, let him come to me.

A few minutes later, I flinched as Davon threw open his door and cursed. I tried to hear through the wall, but everything was quiet.

An hour passed.

"Abi? Are you there?" Aoki asked from outside.

I opened the door.

His brow furrowed. "Is everything okay? I saw you and Davon arguing and came as soon as I could."

I shook my head and jerked my thumb toward Davon's door. "I'm not sure what to think. He's never acted this way."

He crossed his arms. "What did he do now?"

"He acted all macho man when he saw Jimmy and me holding hands."

Aoki raised his eyebrows.

I rolled my eyes. "It's not what you think. He took my hand as he told me he had missed me, and I reciprocated. He's my best friend. It was nothing romantic."

He blew out a breath. "I get it, I do, but maybe the big guy doesn't. He's never liked him. Jimmy, according to Davon, thinks too highly of himself, although one could say the same about him." Aoki shrugged, and I chuckled. "But seriously, I'm not excusing him, but perhaps he snapped when he saw you two together. Before all of this, we all knew there was something between you two. Jimmy made that clear when he wanted to be the one to rescue you."

I gasped. "I had no idea he told you about us. But I don't see him that way anymore."

"Have you told Jimmy?"

After all these years and everything that happened, I turned the page. I didn't see him the same way as before. I only wanted to have my friend back, but what if he...? I shook my head.

Could he still have feelings for me?

He shook his head. "Forget what I said. You don't have to explain. Davon should have trusted you. He was wrong in the way he handled it. Let him cool off, and hear him out. I'm sure he's trying to get it together right now."

"Okay. But he better get on his knees. This time he really screwed up."

Aoki laughed. "Give him hell."

***

I dozed off after crying on my sofa, angry but also sad that the day had turned out this way.

A knock on the door woke me.

"Abi, can I come in?" Davon's voice was so low I could barely hear him.

My pulse accelerated at the sound of it. I closed my eyes and thought about the situation. I wanted to be the bigger person, so I'd hear him out.

I rose from the couch and made my way to the door.

"Please, Abi. Please let me in."

I opened the door and moved to the table, sitting with my back to him.

He entered, the clip-clop of his flip-flops stopping beside me. "Can I sit?"

I looked up. His freshly showered hair hung loose, and his eyes were sleepy. He wore a plain gray T-shirt and had his hands inside his denim pockets.

I shrugged.

"I brought some chicken fingers and fries for dinner. Here's some of your sweet nectar." He set a mug in front of me.

The scent alone had me drooling.

He took a seat in front of me, then served both our dinners.

"I'm not hungry." I begged my stomach not to growl.

"Have you been crying?" He reached for my hand, but I moved it away.

I ate a fry, then let my hand fall to my lap.

He hunched over. "I was a jerk. I'm sorry."

I pushed the food to the side so I could rest my elbows on the table, giving him my full attention.

He kept his head down but looked at me. "I'm sorry for crashing your lunch and for the way I handled myself. Jimmy and I don't see eye to eye, and when I saw him holding your hand, I snapped. I know he cares about you, and something came over me. I didn't stop to think what was happening or how my actions affected you."

I moved my hands closer to him but didn't touch him. "I know you've suffered. I know how you fight to keep your inner demons inside. But you can't expect me to stop spending time with him just because you don't like him. He's only my friend. You can't control my life, Davon." I struggled to continue. "It's as if you don't trust me. I told you yesterday I want to be with you. Only you."

"I know. I'll work on it. Please give me a chance." He reached for me.

After a moment, I put my hand on top of his. "It can't happen again. Okay?"

"It won't." He squeezed my hand. "Thank you."

I wanted him to tell me what he was going through. "Matt told me this morning that memorials put you on edge. I tried to visit you before lunch, but you weren't there. That's when I overheard the argument between you and Connor."

Davon's eyes widened. "Did you hear everything?"

I nodded.

He lowered his gaze. "Something happened yesterday. Three more · checkpoints were taken, six people killed. It was a bloodbath." His hands shook. "Matt and I will leave tomorrow night to scout the prison and checkpoint area."

"I'm sorry about your loss." I gripped his hand tighter.

"Don't worry. I'm okay." He released me and started eating.

He had to be hurting, the way his hands trembled and his voice cracked.

I decided to change the topic. "I know about your plan to infiltrate the system. He's right, you know. We can't just barge in. We don't stand a chance against their whole army."

His eyebrow hitched up.

"I get what you're saying, but you need to hear him out. He has worked with them as you have, training soldiers. We must work hand in hand because divided, we'll lose." I tapped my fingers on the table, thinking of alternatives. "Maybe we can prepare a proposal to start gathering intelligence and plan a series of attacks, but we need to lay it out in a way that Connor won't be able to refuse."

He jerked his head back. "Are you implying you want to be part of the group?"

"Of course I do. The things I've lived through... What I've witnessed... We must do something about it." I shook my head. "We don't stand a chance if they come to us. An offensive strike is our best option. We could sneak right in, and they won't see us coming."

We'd recruit as many people from within as possible. I was positive that with Davon's knowledge and Connor's expertise, we could pull it off.

He smirked. "You never cease to amaze me."

"What do you mean?"

"Your grit. It's no surprise I've fallen for you. You're too good for me." He watched me for a moment and returned to his food.

His confession almost caused my heart to leap out of my chest. Could he truly care that much about me? I wanted to say something, but nothing came out.

I had to tell him everything before I let him know how I felt.

For a brief period, there was silence.

"Are we okay?" he murmured.

I smiled. "We are."

"Do you want to start training tomorrow? I can show you how to wield your blades and teach you some offensive maneuvers."

I almost jumped off my seat. "Sure! I was planning to train with Maria, but I want to learn to use blades."

Davon chuckled. I loved that sound. I was happy to see him more relaxed. We still had much more to talk about, but this was a good start.

He nodded toward the coffee. "How is it?"

I took another sip. "Divine. Thanks."

"I'm glad." He stood. "I'll be leaving, then."

"I wouldn't mind your staying." I wanted him by my side.

He opened his arms. "Come here."

I went to him, letting myself relax in his embrace.

He lifted my chin. "I'm meeting with Connor and Matt about tomorrow's mission. It may take a while, and you're tired. I'll be here first thing in the morning. Deal?"

"Deal." I yawned.

He gave me a gentle kiss and groaned against my lips. "I'll miss you tonight."

"Me too."

He stroked my cheek and left.

I took a shower and let the water wash away everything that happened today. I hopped into bed, and my eyes drifted shut, but I couldn't stop thinking about tomorrow. And as I fell asleep, dark thoughts filled my mind.

Chapter 26

Abi

"*March 2205: Davon found countless communities already dispersed deep within the mountains. Many had already lived years outside, escaping before the New World Government took control of the city. Veterans of war or simply families willing to have a new beginning free from the hands of their oppressors. He had united all these people under the People's Revolutionary Front community and had achieved what we dreamed of—to create a united front to fight the system.*" (*Deborah Davis's journal*)

I'm alone in a dark alley. Footsteps approach me. I hide behind a dumpster, and a can clatters to the ground. My breath hitches as someone moves the dumpster away from me. A middle-aged officer in an NWG white uniform points his gun at me. I back up against the wall.

"Would you look at that? I found me a little princess," he says, grinning like a madman.

I look around. There's no way out. I curl my hands, my nails biting against the wall to the point of pain. I crouch into a corner and press my chin to my chest, closing my eyes. I'm trapped. I fucked up.

The man yanks me out by my hair. It hurts.

"No! Let me go!" I kick and punch, but it's futile.

He squeezes my neck and shoves me against a wall, then wets his lips. He kisses me hard. I thrash, but I can't get him off me. He presses himself against me, forces my mouth open, and pushes his tongue inside me. Nausea churns in my gut as the taste of cigarettes fills my mouth.

A metallic, coppery tang hits my tongue as I bite him, drawing blood.

He sneers. "Just how I like them. Feisty. Why don't we have a little fun before I take you in?"

He throws me into the opposite wall. My head slams against it with such force that my vision blurs.

I drop to the ground and scramble away, pleading for anyone to help me. No one comes.

"Shut up, bitch!" He punches my face so hard that my head snaps back.

I close my eyes, clenching my teeth at the stinging pain.

His intent is clear as he opens his trousers. He pulls my pants down as I struggle to get free, kicking against his chest, but he's too damn strong and holds me down. Crouching between my legs, he pries them open, then pulls up my shirt. He lowers his head to my breast and bites hard, breaking my skin.

I let out a guttural cry and shudder.

"Please let me go," I beg.

He ignores my cries and presses my hand against him. "Look what you did."

Bile rises to my mouth.

"I know you want it."

I shake violently, attempting to free myself from his grip.

He pins me to the ground.

I try to push him off me, but he's too heavy. I turn my head sideways and close my eyes, biting the inside of my cheek as he pushes against me.

His sinister laugh follows as he enters me. The pain rips me apart. I scream, but no one comes. I'm completely alone.

A violent knock woke me. Sweat coated my body. This was not the first time I relived that memory, but it didn't make it any less terrifying. It had been almost a month since my last one.

"Abi! Let me in!" Davon yelled frantically.

I glanced at my watch: 3:00 a.m. I rose and opened the door, and he pulled me into a hug.

He gripped my shoulders and peered inside. "Are you okay? You screamed, and I thought someone was attacking you." He caressed my face and dried my tears.

"I'm fine. It was just a nightmare."

Matt's door burst open, and he rushed across the hall. Aoki hovered in the threshold.

Matt stood beside us, his gaze darting inside my apartment. "Everything all right?"

I took his hands and squeezed them. "I'm good. It was just a nightmare."

I attempted to keep my voice as neutral as possible, trying to control my shuddering body as I reassured him. I glanced at Aoki, who looked at me with a concerned frown.

"Don't worry. I got it," Davon said.

Matt hesitated but stepped back. Without another word, he returned to his apartment and closed the door.

Davon led me inside. "That was a hell of a nightmare. You scared the shit out of me."

"I get those a lot. Don't worry." I took deep, controlled breaths to calm down.

He grabbed my hands. "Are you better now?"

I couldn't stop my fingers from trembling. "I think so."

"What can I do to help?"

I dipped my chin. Ever since they found me, my nightmares had mostly disappeared. Apparently, being alone triggered them.

"You can stay," I said.

We climbed into bed, and he caressed my back. No words were needed, just him.

I woke to his earthy smell and warmth. The nightmares didn't come back. I was tired, but at least I got a couple of hours of sleep. My leg rested over him as he held me close. His calm breaths told me he was still asleep.

My cheeks burned. Why did he have to see this side of me?

He stirred and stretched. "Mm, you smell like the sun. Like flowers in the morning sun." He pulled me close and opened his eyes. "Did you sleep well?"

"Yes." I sighed. "Thanks for staying over."

"Anytime." He kissed my forehead. "You really scared me. So many thoughts ran through my mind. I believed you were being attacked. You kept screaming 'Get off me' and 'Please' like you were begging for your life."

"I thought by being here, they wouldn't come back." It was so vivid. I could feel everything all over again. The coppery taste in my mouth, his weight as he pressed against me, the ripping pain... I shuddered.

He touched my cheek. "Let's not talk about it. What do you think about getting out of here for a while?"

My chest lightened. "To the forest?"

"Yes." He twirled a stray hair of mine around his finger, making me relax into him.

I kissed him on the nose. "I'd love that."

He brushed his lips against my temple. "I'll get the food and coffee, and we'll go out for a picnic, just the two of us."

An hour later, I donned a blue sweater over my tank top, adding a coat to go outside. The temperature inside the bunker was comfortable, but winter was approaching, and temperatures outside could drop suddenly.

I took my dagger and khukuri and put my hair in a high ponytail as I waited for Davon to come back.

A tap on the door signaled it was time to leave. His hair tied back, he looked fantastic as always, dressed in green cargo pants, a black V-neck shirt, and a leather jacket.

His gaze swept over me. "Someone got the memo. You look great in training clothes. You could do better with the hair, though, but I get it."

I slapped his chest playfully. "Stop that. I like it up, and you have to stop seizing my hair bands. I'm beginning to think you only want them for yourself and not because you like my hair loose."

His lips curved into a devilish smile. "On the contrary, I do prefer your hair down, but having something that belongs to you on me, well, that's a plus."

Warmth spread through me. This man made me forget how to breathe normally when he was this close.

I put my hands on my hips. "Well, you need to stop taking my stuff."

He pulled me closer. "I can't help it, Miss Davis. You're a sexy as hell minx trapped in a beautiful small body." He gave me a peck on the cheek. "Now, let's get out of here."

And with that, he left me to follow him, my mouth hanging open.

Davon led me through hall B.

We passed Tammy and Maria as they left their apartment. Tammy blushed and looked away.

Maria chuckled. "Good morning, Abi, General Niles. Excuse Tammy. She's very shy."

Davon narrowed his eyes at Tammy, then shook his head and flicked his gaze to Maria.

"Glad we crossed paths. Abi and I are going to the armory after breakfast to get her some training weapons and to see how she feels wielding some blades. I need the training center only for us this afternoon from 12:00 to 2:00 p.m. Can you arrange it?"

"Sure. Anything else?"

"No, that's all."

Maria continued down the hallway with Tammy.

Davon frowned. "Maria's partner, I feel like I've seen her before. Before all this. I keep trying to remember from where but come back empty."

I shrugged. "I don't know. Maybe she has one of those faces. I think she's harmless."

We reached the end of the hall. Davon entered a code on a pad in the wall. We moved into another chamber with an armed guard inside. As he examined us, he adjusted his glasses. His eyes reminded me of coffee.

He saluted. "General."

"At ease, Mark. I told you not to be that formal with me. You're my friend. We drink beer together."

"Sorry, General, I mean, Davon." Mark glanced at me. "Since you're with someone, I thought formalities were due."

"Oh, no worries. This is Abigail, but I think you already know that. Abi, this is Mark, Aoki's brother. He's been with us for eight years now and is a good friend."

I grinned. "Oh, Aoki told me about you. Nice to meet you!"

Mark extended his hand. "Nice to meet you too." His voice was honest and gentle like his brother's.

I shook his hand.

Mark smiled. He appeared the same age as Davon, with long light-brown hair. He was lean and muscular, a lot like Aoki.

Mark opened the hatch for us and let us out. "Be careful out there. After recent events, we need to be on the lookout."

"I know. We'll be careful. See you." Davon waved at him as we went out.

Light danced across the trees as the wind rustled through the leaves. A fresh pine scent reached me, and I took a deep, cleansing breath, taking in the sight. We stood on an escarpment at the mountainside. The view was spectacular.

A cooling breeze hit me, and I shivered and pulled my jacket around me. Maple trees and dogwood mixed with pine trees stretched through the scenery, an assortment of reds and oranges with a heavy fog resting below. From this altitude, an outline of the city was visible on the horizon, reminding me of our current predicament.

"Magnificent, right?" Davon took in the view. "This way."

We made our way through a heavily forested area and sat on a log. Davon started unloading his backpack onto a stone slab in front of us. He brought grapes, crackers, strawberry jam, and two metal mugs filled with coffee.

He handed me a mug. "Let's dig in. I'm starving."

We ate quietly and then lay back on the ground to gaze at the bright sky. The birds sang, and the trees creaked as they swayed. I could stay here for hours.

It made me remember the first time we held hands.

I shifted my gaze to him. "Thank you for this. For everything, really."

He was watching the sky, his arms folded behind him, cushioning his head. "You don't have to thank me for anything." He closed his eyes.

Images from my nightmare sliced across my brain. I needed to tell him even if it hurt like hell to do so. If I wanted this to work out, he had to know everything. "We need to talk about last night. I don't think I can keep this from you any longer. These nightmares I have—they're real."

He stiffened. His eyes locked with mine. "What do you mean?"

"Memories. Stuff that happened during my time out there. Some things I haven't shared with anyone." I fiddled with Bonnie's thread band. Even after her death, she helped me get through it. I found strength in knowing I'd survived, and because of it, I needed to fight back to stop this from happening to anyone else.

He sat up. "Did someone attack you while you were out there?"

I leaned against him and put my hand on his thigh. "Yes, someone did. Brutally."

His muscles tightened beneath his jacket.

I squeezed his leg. "Please. Just please hear me out. I don't want any secrets between us. But it takes a lot for me to say these words out loud. I've tried to forget about it for far too long, but it's impossible. I need you to help me heal."

He took a deep breath and nodded.

"The year after they killed Jacob and Bonnie was the hardest of all. Food was scarce, and I wasn't in my right mind. Breaking in to get what I needed became the norm, apartment buildings being my preferred target. I thought I was being careful, but someone alerted the government that there was a thief in the neighborhood."

Sweat trickled down my face even though the temperature was so low. "One night I was leaving a house, and there was movement in the alley. I hid behind a dumpster, but there was a clatter, and a patrol officer found me." I intertwined my hands to control my shaking.

Davon's eyes flashed. "What did he do?"

A tear slipped out. "I tried to stop him, but he was stronger than me, and he had a gun. He dragged me down the alley to a dead end and beat me, promising to take good care of me before he took me into custody." I glanced down as tears started pouring freely from my eyes.

Davon stared at me, his body trembling as if he struggled to hold on to his last shreds of control. But he gave me the time I needed to let it out.

"He..." I needed to say it. A torrent of tears fell as I took a gulp of air and whispered, "I was raped."

As the words left my mouth, my entire world blurred. My sobs became desperate, and my whole body shuddered.

Davon pulled me close and caressed the back of my head. "I'm here. You're safe."

I don't know how long we stayed like that, but he held me until my tears stopped.

Davon snarled. "I'll kill him."

I gripped his shirt. "I already did."

He sucked in a breath, and I pushed back enough to see his ashen face, his hard eyes.

"While he attacked me, I desperately searched for a way to kill him. I couldn't die, not like Bonnie. I searched and searched until I found it. My pocketknife. It must have fallen from my pants during the struggle. I used the last of my strength, the last of my energy, and stabbed him in the throat." My voice broke. "I'll never forget the gurgling sound he made. The metallic taste of his blood as it poured down on me. The satisfaction I felt as the light left his eyes."

Davon hugged me, his arms strong yet gentle. "That was too fast a death for what I would've done to him." He touched my face so lightly, as if he feared I would break. "You should have told me. You should have said something."

This was why I didn't want to tell him. I didn't want his pity or for him to treat me differently. I survived. I made it through. And that was enough.

I closed my eyes. "Please don't. I don't want this to change things between us. It's perfect as it is. But you had to know. I have scars, physical ones, ones that one day you'll see." I couldn't keep his gaze. Would he see me differently now?

"Nothing will ever change between us. We're together for good." He cupped my face. "I'll never forgive myself for not getting you out sooner. I'll never let anything like that happen to you again. I promise."

The last twenty minutes were spent between touches and sobs. I made him promise not to tell a soul.

I cuddled in his arms as we rested on the forest floor, and we talked about other things, random stuff.

After a while, we headed back to the bunker. Before we reached the door, I stopped. His eyes darkened as I gripped his waist and pulled him closer. He put a tentative hand on my hip.

We needed to put this behind us. I knew he was restraining himself, and I didn't want that. I needed him raw, strong.

"Please," I said.

He bent and nipped my neck, and I ran my hand down his chest. I closed my eyes, absorbing the sensation.

He slowly picked me up and held on to my thighs as I wrapped my legs around his waist. His mouth was on me in an instant. It was a ravenous kiss, not a soft one.

I moaned in pleasure and let myself go. It was all-consuming, and it was only us.

He playfully tugged at my lower lip with his teeth, then ended the kiss and set me down.

We were both breathless when we entered the bunker, hand in hand.

Chapter 27

Abi

"*M*ay 2205: Our insider got news for us today. The command center bunker was complete. Its name, Janus Peak, is in honor of our new beginning. It was inside a mountain, with four halls for apartments and two for offices and common places. It had an armory next to a large room that would be our training center. The other bunkers were underway and already producing food and energy." (Deborah Davis's journal)*

When we reached hall F, we entered the armory.

"Aren't these like the one you have in your room?" I stroked the handle of a sabre with a curved blade.

"Yes, amazing blades. This one is a talwar." He gave it a swing. "It's from the Mughal Empire. See the knuckle-bow hilt? It allows for a secure hold. Getting struck by this beauty can easily sever an extremity." He put it back and showed me the daggers and small blades. "I was thinking these might flow better for you. These daggers are for practicing purposes only."

I frowned. "I brought my dagger and khukuri. I thought we were training with those." I touched the hilt of my khukuri and pinched my lips. I really wanted to use it.

"We will once you dominate the training ones. We don't want to risk an injury. These daggers weigh almost the same as a genuine one. Their ends are flattened to prevent physical injury during practice." He glided his fingers across them.

I took a black dagger that had space for the knuckles in its handle, just like Jacob's. "This one feels like mine. What do you think?"

"That'll work." He moved to another wall and took a small khukuri blade like the one he gave me. "I prepared this one for practice. Be careful with it, though. I tried to smooth its ends, but it still has some edge. We'll start with the dagger, then move on to the khukuri. In a couple of weeks, you should be able to start training with your own weapons. Once you master the use of both blades in unison, the result will be deadly."

I looked at the weapons, eager to use them.

He chuckled. "I think I created a monster."

We entered the training center and stood in the middle of the practice area.

"We'll start by practicing how to move with a blade. I know we did it before, but you were injured. I want to see how you move now that you're mostly recovered. The key is to treat the blade as an extension of your body. Make movements consciously so you can dodge attacks and incapacitate your opponent." He removed his jacket.

I tossed my coat and sweater aside and put my left knuckles through the trench knife.

"Try to stab me," he said.

I twitched my fingers. "But what if I hit you for real?"

He shook his head. "I told you. These are training weapons. You won't hurt me."

I shrugged. "Okay, if you say so." I wiped my clammy hands against my clothes and locked my knees in a fighting stance, just like he taught me.

I attempted to stab him, but he took my forearm and twisted it, taking my dagger. My back hit his chest, and I couldn't move.

My heartbeat pounded in my ears, and the room swayed as my thoughts flashed back to the moment I was crushed against the wall.

I jerked and shook hard against Davon's grip, but he wouldn't budge.

"You need to learn to predict your adversaries' movements, or they'll have you under their control in no time." He let me go and gave me back my dagger. "Again."

We practiced for half an hour, and not once did I hit him. After a water break, he reminded me that in a real battle I could not rest and that we'd eventually increase training time. He was going to ask Maria to work on my resistance even more.

He handed me the khukuri. "Okay, hold it with your right hand since it's your dominant one."

After he showed me the slashing movement with his own blade, I attempted to strike him.

He put his arm up and grabbed my wrist, applying enough pressure to make me lose my blade. "Again."

As time progressed, we started learning from each other.

He followed my moves, and I caught up to his. It felt like a dance, each moving in response to the other. He flowed like the air, and his speed was difficult to match.

The khukuri became part of me like he said. I eased through the maneuvers, each drill better than the last, so I became bolder, seeking to get closer to him each time.

We were both spent when I slashed up to confuse him. As he defended, I targeted his abdomen. My khukuri hit.

"Fuck!" He winced, a hint of blood on his shirt. "Well done."

My heart lurching, I sheathed my blade. "Oh, I'm sorry. Are you okay?" I pulled up his shirt to see the wound.

He waved me off. "It's nothing. I'm more than okay." He gave me a big smile. "I'm very proud. Not many get to strike me during their first training. Some have never been able to."

I'd never seen anyone this excited about getting cut. I grinned at him.

The cut was on the left side of his abdomen, close to his obliques. It wasn't deep enough to need stitches, but it was about three inches long and was bleeding a lot. I cleaned the area and applied antibiotics, then wrapped a bandage around him. Other than wincing a little, he took it well.

Matt entered the room as we were leaving. He grimaced. "You chose him over me. Blades over guns."

I giggled at his wounded expression. He winked at me and slapped Davon's back.

Davon flinched, his features contracting.

He eyed Davon's shirt. "Wait. She did this to you?"

Davon nodded.

He laughed. "Oh, this is epic. You're a total badass."

Davon rolled his eyes. "If you both want, you can start training after we get back tomorrow."

Matt frowned at him.

"She knows about tonight," Davon said.

"Oh, okay. Well, we should be back early in the morning if everything goes according to plan. I can train you after our briefing."

Worry curled in my gut, but I pushed it away. "Sounds great."

After I had lunch with Davon and Matt, they both left to rest since their mission would take all night.

I went to my apartment and was about to rest a bit when someone knocked on my door. It was Jimmy. I pushed my palm against my forehead as I remembered we agreed to meet today.

"Come in. Give me a minute. I need to get ready."

He stepped in, and I rushed to the bathroom. When I came out, Jimmy was standing next to the bed, my family picture in his hands.

I stood beside him.

"You were such a happy family." He clenched his fingers around the frame.

I reached for his hand, and he relaxed. His eyes were glassy. Pained.

No words needed to be said. We had lost so much.

I took the picture from him and put it back.

Jimmy and I exited the bunker via hall D. In the eastern corner, we sat on a boulder. It offered an incredible view of the mountains, no city in sight. The cold wind whistled along the slopes.

He stared at my blades, which were sheathed on Jacob's belt. "Were you training today?"

"Yes. Davon was teaching me how to defend myself using blades. But we only used the training ones." I kicked the ground, still a little saddened at not using the real thing.

Jimmy's expression grew solemn. "So it's true. You're together."

I nodded. "We are. I thought everyone knew at this point."

Hurt flickered in his eyes for a second, then his deep voice broke the silence. "I'm always going from place to place and don't listen to gossip. I only got the vibes yesterday when he interrupted our lunch. We don't see eye to eye, but I never expected him to behave as he did."

"I already talked to him about it."

He huffed as he rested his elbows on his knees. I studied him. His hair took on a golden hue as the wind swept through it. He had striking features. His prominent chin and straight nose made him a very attractive man. I couldn't help but admire him as he fixed his gaze on the horizon. Nevertheless, I no longer felt that rush, that longing we had in our youth.

My thoughts drifted to Davon. He exuded raw, unadulterated strength. His piercing features had the power and intensity to devour you whole. When I was with him, there was nothing else. His presence dominated everything. But what mattered most was what was within him. His determination, loyalty, and courage eclipsed all else. Nobody could ever compare to him.

I sighed.

The silence that followed was so still I could make out the chirping of cardinals and goldfinches coming from the high branches of the pine trees, mixed with the low hum of insects.

"I don't understand how you can be with him. His arrogance is disgusting."

Blinking rapidly, I whipped around and stared at him. *What the hell?*

His eyes narrowed. "I hope he doesn't hurt you, 'cause if he does, I won't hesitate to put him in his place."

I gave him a pointed look. "You both need to put your disagreements aside because you two are very important to me." I frowned. "You don't know him at all. Why are you acting this way?"

He hunched over. "Forget about it. I'll try to be on my best behavior. But only because of you."

After a few silent minutes, we started talking, trying to put our disagreement behind us.

"Becoming a captain wasn't easy," he said. "Training sessions were long and hard, and I had to memorize all possible routes in, out, and around the system."

He told me about wanting to be the one to rescue me. They sent Davon and Matt instead since they could hide in plain sight inside Electi and Matt's clinic, making the rescue effort easier. He believed he would have found me sooner and still held a grudge against Connor for not letting him go.

I understood how he felt, being in the same spot when I thought he was taken. I fought daily with Deb, pleading with her to let me go look for him.

I told him about Jacob and Bonnie. About my vow to rescue Paul. But nothing else.

He asked about our escape from the city and cried as I described how we found Christina and Carlos and our own narrow escape. I held him as he let everything out, all the tears he'd never shed.

We stayed there until the shadows from the mountains marked the end of the day. Warm tones of dusk painted the horizon.

"If you need anything, let me know. Clothing, furniture, random stuff. I can send an order out and get you all you need to make you feel more at home," he said as the light started to fade.

"You'd do that?" I was used to living with little during my time out there, so I hadn't asked for anything.

"Sure. Write a list, and give it to me. I live in hall B, apartment five, next to Maria and Tammy. If I'm not home, slide it under the door. I'll make sure to get everything on your list as soon as possible."

When I gazed upon his profile, the sky was practically dark. "We should go."

"I'm glad we talked. I missed our conversations." He stood and helped me up.

"Me too. I never thought we'd be able to have this again."

He held my hand a little longer than expected, brushing his thumb along its back. Time stood still, and he took a step toward me. We were the only ones out here. A shiver ran through me. The way he held my gaze, the touch of his flesh against mine, brought back memories. He filled the gap between us, and just as his lips were about to touch mine, I stepped back, raising my hand to his chest to put space between us.

"I can't do this, Jimmy. I'm in love with him."

He needed to understand things were not like before.

He went still and turned away from me. "Sorry. It won't happen again."

I reached for him. I didn't want things to be weird between us. "Jimmy?" I pulled away as his arm twitched slightly.

"Don't worry about it. I understand."

I exhaled and slowly backed away. "I'll see you tomorrow?"

He nodded without looking at me.

My heart broke for him as I left him there. Alone.

Chapter 28

Abi

"*July 2205: Sarah's twenty-second birthday was today, and I got a special permit to visit her. Abi and I made her a red velvet cake, her favorite. Sarah didn't talk much, but she was happy today. Celebrating with my sisters made me realize the urgency of getting them out.*" (Deborah Davis's journal)

I knocked at Davon's around six. I frowned when there was no answer. We had dinner plans with Mark and his family. Maybe he was still in the shower. I tried the door, and it was open. Water vapor filled the room. The bathroom door hung open, the shower running.

I'd wait for him. I served myself a drink and sat on his luxurious chaise lounge. After what happened with Jimmy, I needed the drink.

When he turned off the shower, my heart thudded. I prayed he wouldn't be upset that I let myself in.

My breath caught in my throat as he stepped out the bathroom door, drying his hair and completely naked. I gazed over his nude physique, absorbing every single detail. His chiseled arms swathed in tattoos, the phoenix that covered his bare chest, his marked abdominals down to his... Heat flooded my face as I stared. He was perfect, raw, solid, and... I moistened my lips. My hands ached to touch, to explore. A picture of him firmly pressed against me, kissing me senseless as my fingers trailed over every inch of his body, flickered in my mind.

I turned away.

"I'm sorry. I... You didn't answer. The door was open, so I decided to wait inside," I said.

"Don't worry. You can look now. I didn't think my nakedness would bring such color to your face."

I shot him an irritated look.

His towel was wrapped around his waist, and I scanned the wound I had given him earlier. I frowned.

"I'll wrap it up, Abi. It doesn't hurt much." He took some clothing from his closet. "I'm sorry I overslept. This will just take a minute." He went into the bathroom and closed the door.

"Hey, Davon?" I yelled from the sofa, letting the warmth of the whiskey calm my nerves. "I wanted to ask you something."

"Sure. Give me a minute."

He exited the bathroom in black sweatpants, tugging his white T-shirt down as he approached the bed. "So what do you want to know?" He put on his sneakers.

"At the memorial, you said you'd tell me about the government and what they're really doing in the facilities. I want to know more about what's happening out there and about your bunker system. Jimmy explained some of it already, but it was vague."

Davon rolled his eyes at Jimmy's name but continued tying his shoes.

"I was wondering since we're having an early dinner, maybe you can tell me more about it tonight."

He put his elbows on his knees. "It'll have to wait till tomorrow because we're running tight as it is. Connor wants us to be ready to leave by nine tonight. As for our system, I can show you around the bunkers this week if you want."

He walked toward me. I was tiny compared to him. He stood in front of me and bent down. With one hand on the backrest and the other on my neck, he closed the space between us. His lips touched mine in a slow but heated kiss. I was breathless when he stood back.

"You taste delicious." He licked his lips and glanced at the empty glass. "You were drinking?"

I scowled at the mischievous glint in his eyes. "To calm my nerves!"

Again, talking without thinking. Too many years alone, and you started speaking your mind out loud just to hear a voice. I needed to stop.

I shot to my feet. "Let's go. They should be waiting already."

His soft chuckle followed me to the door, and we headed out.

Once in the dining hall, he waved toward the other side. This place was always full of life, everyone meeting to eat, talk, and have a good time.

Mark sat at a corner table next to Carol, Aoki's assistant. Beside her was the little girl I met at the school. She was a replica of her mother except for her eyes, which resembled her father's.

Mark did the introductions. "Abigail, Carol told me you already met. This is my daughter, Diane."

"Nice to see you again," Carol said.

Diane ran around the table and jumped on Davon. "Uncle D! You're back!"

We all laughed hard as he let out a gasp and caught her midair.

"How old are you?" I asked Diane as she combed Davon's hair with her small hands.

"I'm six." She beamed at me. "And you?"

"I'll be twenty-one in three days."

Davon raised an eyebrow at me. I shrugged. I guess I forgot to mention it.

I smiled at Carol. "She's beautiful. She looks just like you."

Diane giggled as Davon made funny faces. I'd never seen this part of him. So fatherly. It made me think ahead, and a pang of heartache washed over me. Could he still have children? Some people were okay with not having them. As for me, I always dreamed of having a family.

According to Deb, before the regime, people were already conscious of the resources and never had more than one or two children. The severe actions taken by the government were never necessary.

Looking at all these people surrounding me and knowing most of them wouldn't be able to conceive even if they wanted to broke my heart. Being part of the rebellion after a certain age also meant giving up on in vitro pregnancies since the government was in control of the facilities where the fertility storages were.

Davon took Diane to her seat. "Are you okay, Abi? You seem to be elsewhere."

I shook my head. "Sorry. Everything's okay. Just thinking."

He nodded. "I'll get our food."

"So, Abigail, what do you think of this place?" Mark asked.

"It's impressive, and everyone is so warm and welcoming."

It truly was a great place to be, with a true sense of community. What Deb, Connor, and Davon created was something else.

"Roast beef and mashed potatoes. Can't wait to dig in." Davon put the food on the table and sat beside me with a grin. He seemed relaxed, as if he didn't have a worry in the world.

Diane kept calling Uncle D, showing off as she ate. It was adorable. Her eyes were only for him while Carol kept trying to keep her daughter's area under control.

I watched the scene unfold, and for a moment, everything in the world seemed right. It made my heart swell.

"Are you okay? You haven't touched your food," Davon whispered in my ear.

My vision blurred as I cast a sidelong glance at him.

He cupped my cheek, his features softening.

"Thank you for bringing me here," I murmured.

He pulled me close. "Sharing these moments with you means everything to me. I've never felt more at home than now." He gave me a swift kiss before releasing me.

Everyone was quiet for a moment.

"Mommy, why is Uncle D kissing the princess like you and Daddy kiss?" Diane asked.

Carol hid a snicker. "Her name's Abi, honey, and don't bother Uncle D. Let them be."

Diane giggled. "I know! Uncle D loves Abi like Daddy loves you."

Everyone laughed.

Davon took her little hand. "You're very intuitive, Little D, and I love you for it. Now, finish your food, or I won't give you a piggyback ride back home."

At this, she beamed and ate all her food.

As for me, I had no doubt. I'd fallen completely and utterly in love with this man.

While Davon gave Diane a ride back to hall B, I slipped my list beneath Jimmy's door without him noticing.

We said our goodbyes and headed back.

When we reached my door, he hugged me. "I have to go, love."

"Be careful out there. Don't do anything stupid. Come back to me safe," I said.

"It's just a scouting mission. After the checkpoints, we'll inspect the prison perimeter and be back by morning."

Matt opened his door. "Oh, there you are. Ready?"

Davon kissed me tenderly. "See you tomorrow."

"Don't worry. I'll take care of him. We'll be back in a jiffy," Matt said.

My heart hammered as they disappeared down the hall.

Please let them be safe.

Chapter 29

Davon

An emptiness grew in me as I walked down the hallway. All that trauma, and she kept going. She was incredibly brave, and I loved her for it. If she only knew how much...

Matt's voice brought me back to the present. "Is she okay? That was a hell of a scare last night."

"Yeah. She's good. Just a nightmare." She made me promise not to tell a soul, and I respected her decision.

We entered the armory and donned our black uniforms with bulletproof vests.

"We need to be prepared. Even if Anna and Pedro didn't encounter any troops out there, it doesn't mean we won't find some." Matt reached for his Glock 19 and an MP5 submachine gun.

"Yeah, I'm bringing everything just in case." My chaaklo was safely sheathed by my side as well as my two Glocks.

When we entered command, Connor was waiting in the conference room. A map lay on the table with circles on each of the checkpoints that had been attacked. Another area was marked with small *X*s near the prison's perimeter.

Connor straightened. "Just in time. Thanks again for doing this. Your mission is to assess whether the peak is in danger or not. You'll visit the checkpoints to the south to see if there's any patrol activity. Just stakeout, no engaging. If you see patrols, note the number of soldiers and their weapons and location, and move on to the next one. After you're done, head northeast toward the prison."

He pointed at the *X*s. "I've marked a couple of spots for you to check. Pick at least two places that can serve as good extraction points for Deb's rescue. They need to be heavily forested, off-site, and at least two miles from the safe house. You should be done by six in the morning if you leave now. I expect you back by noon at the latest. If you're not back, I'll send a team to get you. Any questions?"

"No, sir!" we both said.

"Now go. Be safe."

Finally, Connor was in his element. The man who sparked our uprising. His ability to remain focused in any situation and to identify what was required and how to use it to our advantage never stopped amazing me. He was calculating, precise, and a true general when it came to warfare.

Today was our first step toward our offensive response and gaining the freedom we sought. We needed to gather as much intel as possible and report back. That's why, for me, going to Electi as soon as possible was a priority. I knew there was much more happening we didn't know about, and it was imperative to get that information back to Connor. This was our opportunity to build a strategic plan against the New World Government. I knew we couldn't just march in and face them. It would be suicide. We had to do it right—position our pieces and, when the king least expected it, strike.

We left through the hatch door hidden in the sniper room. As it closed behind us, we secured our backpacks and started walking. We had fifteen miles to cover and wanted to keep our strength for whatever waited for us out there.

In total, there were six checkpoints around the city. Only two were operational now, number one to the west and number six to the east, north of the prison. It was midnight when we reached checkpoint one.

We whistled our signal as we approached the area.

"Who's out there?" David whispered.

Matt and I came out of the foliage, hands up.

"It's just us. Everything okay? Where's Kim?" Matt asked.

"Everything's good. Kim's scouting," he said. "Did General Harris send you?"

I nodded. "We brought your sniper rifle. You need to be on the lookout and put into practice all you've learned. We're on high alert."

David inspected his rifle, making sure he had everything he needed. At only twenty-one, he was the best sniper we had.

He saluted. "Thank you, General, Matt. We'll make sure no one passes through here, whatever it takes."

"We'll send backup as soon as possible," I said before leaving.

Four of the five remaining checkpoints were lost, and we had to check each before reaching the prison. I sighed. It was going to be a long night.

Patrols covered the whole region surrounding the city, stretching one to two miles into the forest. Whoever leaked the intel seemed unaware of our base's location.

All those who were taken from the city were blindfolded and went through a screening process that took around two weeks. After undergoing interrogations and a psychiatric evaluation, their profiles and backgrounds were investigated. However, even after the process, there was no guarantee the person was true, as government spies were trained to enter under the guise of any average citizen.

We needed to act soon. Minister Lavigne, the general of the NWG army, was a seasoned soldier. Soon he'd send his troops into the forest. It was only a matter of time. And the clock was ticking.

After four hours, we finally got to the prison area.

As we moved through the zones Connor marked, we found the most secure one was near the psychiatric ward, south of the prison's main building. Three square watchtowers were placed along the perimeter, but their searchlights missed a spot between the buildings, creating the perfect escape route. The extraction would have to be done during the night, moving from the campsite to the space between the ward and the prison where no one stood guard.

"I think this might work. If you take Deb out that door over there, we may be able to wait between the buildings and make a clean escape. No one would notice." Matt pointed toward a door in the southwest corner of the main building that I presumed led to the lower levels of the prison.

The plan could work. But we still were blind to what was inside, and we couldn't plan based on speculation alone. Once I was in, it would all depend on me.

We moved along the forest's perimeter to reach our final location. It was 5:00 a.m. when we heard a struggle coming from checkpoint six. We ran toward the commotion. Gunshots fired, and our soldier went down, a bullet in his head.

"Leon!" Rachel screamed as an NWG soldier held her while another beat her. She was bloodied and hurt, unrecognizable.

Instinct took over as I charged straight toward her abuser with my chaaklo at the ready.

Matt followed me, guns out.

I jumped, slashing the throat of the one beating her in one swift move.

Matt's bullet hit the other soldier, killing him instantly.

As I helped Rachel up, another soldier came into view.

Shit. There are more.

I rushed forward.

Matt pushed me back. "Go! I'll cover for you. Get her to safety."

An overwhelming sense of dread tore through me as I clutched his arm, Rachel by my side.

He jerked away. "We don't have time for this. You need to go."

I hesitated. I couldn't leave him. There was no way he'd keep them at bay alone.

"Go! Now!" He took out his MP5 as a group of soldiers rushed toward us.

He was right. I needed to get Rachel to safety. We bolted. We were a safe distance away when we heard gunfire.

"Go to him. I can make it from here. I'll wait for you in the safe house." Rachel limped away.

I sprinted back as fast as I could. Adrenaline pumped through my system. I ran like never before, my calves burning from the effort, and reached Matt just in time to see a bullet strike his chest. He wavered as another one landed in his arm, knocking him down.

Time stood still. I couldn't breathe. Agony ripped through my chest. My best friend, my brother, was down. All our memories, our time together, flashed through my mind in that moment. I ran to him, forgetting about the soldiers and our impending danger. He couldn't die. I wouldn't allow it.

I tore his shirt open. The bullet was encrusted in his vest, a bullet meant for his heart.

"Don't touch it!" Matt flinched. "Something's broken." His face was pale, his eyes dimmed, his respiration shallow.

My hands were drenched in his blood. "Fuck!"

Matt's right side was soaked, and blood pooled on the ground beneath us.

I took my belt off and made a tourniquet at the top of his arm. He groaned as I tightened it.

A man riddled with bullets lay on the ground. A bullet cracked against the tree next to us. I bent over Matt, protecting him. The soldier was almost upon us when I grabbed Matt's pistol and shot the man twice. He collapsed, screaming in agony while clutching his abdomen. I stalked toward him.

"Please don't kill me. I beg you." He squirmed, hands bloody.

I growled. "There's no mercy for you. There never will be." I pointed the gun at his head and shot between his eyes.

"I hear more coming," Matt muttered.

I rushed back. "Can you walk?"

He grabbed onto me. "I'll try. Get us out of here!"

We dashed toward the forest, but Matt collapsed about halfway through.

He was losing too much blood. Whatever I did wasn't working. I shook him till his eyes opened. His unfocused gaze eventually fell on me.

"You can't die on me, Matt. Come on!" I lifted his unconscious body and sprinted away, my legs urging me to stop. Matt's weight was taking its toll on me, but I kept running.

When we arrived at the safe house, the sun had already risen.

Rachel kept the hatch door open while I carried Matt inside, his breathing faint.

"He took a bullet to his chest. The other hit his arm." My hands shook as I placed him on the bed.

Rachel was a nurse back in Promissa, and she immediately began working on him. She cut the sides of his vest. There was a large bruise on his chest. He would have died if it hadn't been for it.

I was rooted to the spot. My chest tightened until it hurt to breathe. *My brother.*

I blinked. "Can you do anything to help him?" My voice was strangled. This was Elaine all over again.

Rachel checked under his arm. "He's in shock and has lost a lot of blood. I don't see an exit point. Stay with him while I fetch the pincers to extract the bullet."

Please, God, let him be okay.

She came over with a field blood transfusion kit. "He needs blood. What's your blood type?"

"O positive. He's A positive. You can take whatever you need from me."

I sat in the lower bunk next to him as she cleaned my arm and put a constricting band around it.

She located my vein and hooked the tubing. "You need to mix this continuously. Maintain it below your heart."

She went to Matt and hooked up an IV saline bag. She glanced at me. "Remember to keep moving the bag. Can you handle it?"

I nodded. "Just help him. Please."

During my training, we were taught about this type of procedure. Transfusing fresh whole blood had its risks, but we were all tested regularly, and out here we didn't have much of a choice.

She slowly released Matt's tourniquet. The blood loss had reduced drastically, but it was still flowing, so she elevated his arm on a pillow and applied pressure until it decreased enough for her to work.

Please, God, let him survive this. I watched as she cleaned and examined the area.

"Is he going to be okay?"

"The bullet entered through his bicep and probably stopped at the humerus." She ran into the kitchen and brought back restraints. "I'm sorry. I'm going to have to bind him to the bed. He might wake in the middle of the procedure and cause himself harm."

"Do whatever you need."

After restraining his arms and legs, she inserted the pincers.

Matt opened his eyes wide and arched his back. His scream was deafening.

"Hold on, Doctor. Just a little bit more." She continued searching.

He glanced my way, tears streaming down his face.

"Try to keep still, Matt. Rachel needs to get the bullet out."

He clenched his teeth and closed his eyes. His features tightened.

"I got it!" Rachel extracted the bullet before suturing the wound. She gave him an antibiotic injection.

Matt blinked. "God, that was awful." His voice sounded raspy, but it was still full of mischief. "The next time you decide to torture me, let me know ahead of time. Now, could you please untie me?" He panted and gave me a weak smile.

I let out a faint chuckle. He was back. I removed his restraints.

"Thank you, Rachel." He recoiled. "I think my ribs are broken." He grunted. "And my humerus too. We'll need an X-ray to confirm."

"I figured." Rachel bandaged his arm and made a sling to keep it stable.

The blood bag was full, and she unhooked me. She went to the kitchen and returned with a bottle of water and a protein bar for me. "Take this. You need your strength."

I munched on the bar and drank some water. I was a little dizzy, and my muscles ached.

"You lost a lot of blood. We're ready for a transfusion. Should we proceed?" Rachel asked.

Matt nodded.

After an hour or two, the blood transfusion was running smoothly, and Matt was gradually regaining color.

Rachel assured me he was going to be okay but would need surgery. I'd have to contact Dr. Lewis, our surgeon, from the science and technology bunker as soon as we got to the peak.

We sat at the table while Matt rested.

I studied Rachel. "Are you feeling better?"

She held an ice bag to her fractured nose. "Yes. Thank you for rescuing me." She wiped a tear from her cheek. "I still can't believe Leon is dead."

"Me neither. He was a good man."

We stayed silent for a minute.

"We should get back as soon as possible, or Connor will dispatch a team to retrieve us. I don't want to endanger anyone else," I said.

We were already pushing it. It was 7:00 a.m., and it would take four to six hours to reach the peak in our current state.

"We need to hold out for at least two more hours until the transfusion is completed and he gets better," Rachel said.

I glanced at Matt's sleeping form. It would have to do.

Once there, I would contact my father. I needed to enter the city and find out who was doing this to us.

Three hours later, I helped Matt as we moved slowly toward the peak.

"Hell, this isn't how I expected things to go. Who the fuck could be doing this?" Matt's voice was low but threatening.

I scowled. "I don't know, but I'm going to find out."

Whatever it takes.

He cocked his head. "And how do you plan to do that?"

"I need to get to the city and check my father's archives. The names and pictures of the spies who are sent out must be there."

"And how exactly do you plan to do that? Those are heavily guarded."

I shrugged. "I'll find a way."

"What about Abi?"

"I'm sure she'll understand. She's the main reason I want to stop this threat but the only one who makes me want to stay. If I could take her with me, I would, but it's a whole other game once you enter Electi, and she could be in danger. I must go in alone."

"Aoki and I will watch out for her while you're away. Just make sure you come back."

I breathed a sigh of relief as I glimpsed Janus Peak in the distance. "I will."

Chapter 30

Abi

"February 2207: After completing three years inside the facilities, we were finally back. Uncle Scott got a special permit to let me stay at their home and help with the care of Sarah. Abi was sixteen, so she stayed with Sarah during the day while I worked, then her teachers would come in during the afternoon once I was back. Connor was sent to train soldiers in a facility that stood near the border with Electi, about ten miles east of us.

"As soon as we came back, Davon stepped down as leader of the community. We insisted for him to lead with us, but he wouldn't, deeming himself unworthy of such a position.

"He did a fantastic job while we were away. Five bunkers were ready, and after choosing their craft, each citizen was moved to the respective bunker for that specific trade. The councilmembers were chosen by votes.

"The People's Revolutionary Front Army had hundreds of recruits, and they had chosen him as their general. I don't know what we would have done without him." (Deborah Davis's journal)

All through the night I had bone-chilling night terrors. I saw Davon die in my arms multiple times after taking a bullet directed at me or getting shot while trying to get to me. I woke up crying and covered in sweat every single time, as if I had really lost him.

I couldn't take it anymore. It was six in the morning when I knocked on Aoki's door.

He opened it immediately. His hair was down, and dark circles hovered beneath his eyes.

"Are they back yet?" we asked in unison.

"Fuck." Aoki moved aside. "Come on in."

"Still nothing?" I asked.

"No. Connor gave them till noon to come back." He paced the room. "This doesn't feel right. I just know something happened."

I clutched my arms to my chest. I had the same feeling, but I focused on the facts and tried to stay positive. They would return. We needed to wait and trust they were okay.

"I'll get us something to eat. Is Carol running the kitchen today?" I asked.

"Yes, I asked her to." He gave me an apologetic look. "Sorry. I know this is hard on you too."

I took his hand. "No worries. We need to stick together."

He squeezed back. "I'm glad you're by my side today."

After breakfast, Aoki and I took some time to trace shakyos.

Aoki outlined a sutra. "Mark told me you met yesterday."

"Yes. He's a great guy." I kept at my parchment. Drawing sutras took a lot of effort, but it calmed my nerves.

"He is. My parents adopted him when he was a baby." His mouth curved into a half smile. "I was five at the time, so we became thick as thieves."

"He has a peacefulness about him. It reminds me of you."

He chuckled. "Oh, but you still haven't seen my wicked side." With a grin, he winked at me.

We laughed and talked for hours until there was a knock on the door. We both launched for it.

Maria stood there, her face grim.

Aoki pressed his fists against the door. "What happened? Are they back?"

She nodded. "They're back and safe. General Harris asked me to let you know they're waiting for you in the infirmary."

I clasped Maria's arm. "The infirmary?"

She held her hands up. "Please calm down. Everything will be okay."

My heart stopped for a beat, and Aoki and I exchanged glances. We dashed out of the apartment, heading toward hall F. We bumped into people but didn't stop until we got there.

I was the first to enter. Davon stood close to a stretcher where Matt lay. Another soldier held ice to her nose in the cot next to Matt.

Matt twisted in anguish as the nurse removed bandages from his right upper arm.

Aoki rushed toward him. "Matt? What happened?"

Davon glanced our way and ran toward me. As he hugged me, I touched his back and arms, making sure he was whole.

"Are you okay? Are you hurt?" I asked.

"I'm okay. Just tired."

I pressed my hand to his chest. "What happened out there?"

He covered my hand. "We caught a patrol ambushing checkpoint six. We saved one soldier but lost another. Matt covered our escape and was shot twice."

I gasped and looked at Aoki, who sat next to Matt while the nurse checked his wound.

Davon raked a hand back through his hair. "One bullet tore through his bicep and shattered his humerus. We already called a doctor in. He needs surgery."

I frowned, eyeing Matt's bruised chest. "And the other one?"

"It was aimed at his heart."

I covered my mouth, my heart plummeting.

Davon drew me close. "His vest protected him. He has a broken rib, but he'll be okay. Don't let your mind take you to a dark place."

My eyes welled with tears. "He could have died."

"But he didn't. We made it back." He held me till I calmed down.

I caught him stifling a yawn. "How about we eat lunch at your place, and then I'll leave so you can rest?"

"Stay with me."

I nodded before going to Matt.

"Hey." I brushed his hair. "Davon told me what happened. How are you doing?"

His green eyes looked tired and dull, but he smiled anyway. "I'll be fine. More so with Aoki pampering me."

I glanced at Aoki, who clutched Matt's hand with such tenderness that it made my heart swell. "And you? Do you need anything?"

His gaze never wavered from Matt. "No. We're okay. Thanks for everything."

I went to get lunch while Davon bathed. Ten minutes later, I walked into his apartment, and the woodsy scent and cozy lights welcomed me.

"I'll be out in a minute," Davon said from the bathroom.

I set the table as he came out barefoot, his gray joggers hanging low as he put on a blue T-shirt. His eyes were sunken as he devoured his pizza.

We sat in silence on his chaise lounge. He laid his head across my thighs, holding my left hand over his chest.

My fingers tingled as he played with them. He kissed my hand and closed his eyes.

I caressed his hair with my other hand, easing him to sleep. My eyelids grew heavy, and I drifted away, allowing Morpheus to carry me along with him.

Davon kissed my stomach as I awoke. "I definitely need to take more naps like this one."

I frowned and glanced at my watch. It was 6:00 p.m. We slept for five hours straight.

Davon rose and stretched as I headed straight to the bathroom. When I came out, he passed me a glass of whiskey.

"Thanks." I took a sip, letting its smoky flavor ease my tension away.

He sat on the couch and patted the spot beside him. "How do you feel?"

I slumped beside him. "Better now. I couldn't sleep last night."

His brow wrinkled. "Nightmares?"

I nodded. "About you. But enough about that. How about you?"

He put his arm around me. "Much better now."

I didn't believe for a second that he was all right. I would never forget how he trembled this afternoon as I hugged him. "You told me about what happened out there last night. But how are you really? How bad was it?"

He shuddered, then sighed. "I thought I'd lost him."

I straightened.

He raked his hair back and rubbed the back of his neck. "It was supposed to be an easy mission." He shook his head. "We're supposed to be ready for these kinds of situations, but watching him slowly drift away...it broke me." His Adam's apple bobbed as he swallowed hard. He swirled his glass, his expression solemn.

I put my drink down and cupped his face. "It's okay to be scared. You don't have to be strong all the time."

His eyes searched mine, and he covered one of my hands with his. "Thank you."

I relaxed again, resting my head on his shoulder.

He hugged me. "I'm sure Matt will be fine. He's strong."

I nodded.

"I know you have concerns about the government and, most important-ly, what we're dealing with. I figured now would be a good time to talk." He took a sip from his drink.

"I'd like that."

"But before I go any further, how much do you know about what's going on in the city?"

I pulled out of his embrace and sat sideways, legs crossed. *Where do I start?*

I gulped a large swig of whiskey. "I was ten when the New World Government implemented the regime. That same year, I lost my parents. We moved in with Aunt Annie and Uncle Scott. I don't remember much about how it was before. With the war, much of my life was spent hidden at home. Sarah and Deb had their friends and remembered more, but I only had my family, Jimmy, and the NWG."

I tucked my hair behind my ears. "Deb was everything to me. She taught me about the real face of the government. How everything was a fight for control. Nevertheless, she said we had to do as they said. My aunt focused solely on getting me ready for my advancement, and I was recruited to be part of the New World Facility for Advanced Individuals. The night before my eighteenth birthday, Deb helped me escape. And you know the rest of the story."

"You got stuck on the outskirts, unable to go back to the city or to leave."

I nodded. "Remember when I told you about Deb's journal?"

He raised his eyebrows. "Oh, I do. She shouldn't have given you some-thing so valuable. If discovered, it would have revealed the entire opera-tion."

I pursed my lips. "Well, I read her journal every night to stay sane, learn-ing what she knew about the government. Simply put, she explained they were controlling our lives with the pretext of solving a resource problem that didn't exist anymore. Their true goal was to have complete power over us and our city. Most of it I already imagined, but it still shocked me."

Davon looked away. "I remember on that first meeting being mostly clueless about everything that was going on in Promissa. We lived in a bubble back in Electi."

I frowned. "But how could you not know what was happening in Promissa?"

"Have you ever seen an elite in the city?"

We didn't leave the house much, but even during my three years outside, I never once saw anyone other than common city folks. I shook my head.

He grimaced. "This is because we don't need to go there. As I told you before, in Electi, everything is as before. We're surrounded by farmland, water reservoirs, and everything you would need for a life of leisure. Most elites don't even work but live life as they please while you do the work for them. There are no birth control laws. We have schools, cinemas, restaurants. Everything you had before the regime. The laws you follow don't apply to us."

My jaw dropped, and I stared at him. They lived in riches while we struggled to survive. I suspected as much but wasn't sure to what extent. "Does this mean you can have children? You never had the surgery?"

"I never did, same as Matt, who is the only other elite who lives here. Others who were taken in before reaching eighteen fall into the same group. Everyone here has access to education, contraceptives, and health care. As for myself, I've always taken oral contraceptives, and we're all subject to routine blood tests to make sure we're healthy."

My face burned. "I thought I was one of the few in this community who could have children. Seeing you play with Diane touched me deeply. I thought about how wonderful you were with her and wondered if you could ever have children of your own. But now..."

He tilted his head "Now?"

I waved dismissively. "Forget about it."

He chuckled. "What else do you want to talk about?"

I bit my lip. "Is there anything else I don't know about?"

He swallowed heavily after a little pause. "Yes. There's another thing. Two years ago, when I uncovered the truth about Sarah, I decided to dig for more information. What I found was worse than I imagined. The government has facilities for everyone who doesn't fit the system. I found one where they have young women from age fifteen and up who serve as surrogate mothers for the children of the elite. Other facilities have citizens who are forced to work around the clock, giving them only the necessary food and water so they can survive another day. All of them work—children, elderly. They're held in common rooms and share everything, with little to no privacy. That's their punishment for going against the system."

My stomach turned to lead. "But that's horrible. How many people are in there?"

"I don't know, but I'm sure there are even more programs we don't know about. When Deb and Connor were inside the facilities, there were talks about a new one where they'd teach a new curriculum to train children in the ways of war." He scowled. "I'm sorry for ever being part of that world. You have no idea how I feel when I go there, acting as they do to keep up appearances. I hate it."

I paused. "You told Deb and Connor, right? About these citizens who are being held inside those facilities?"

"Yes. I told them as soon as I came back, but they kept it from the rest of the community. That's the root of all our fights. We've waited too long, lost too much time. We should be strategizing, looking for a way to free them." He sighed and put our empty glasses on the side table, then stretched out and put his head in my lap again.

"Other than the ambush, did you find anything else last night?" I asked.

He took a deep breath and closed his eyes. "We found a possible extraction site next to the prison to get Deb out." He gazed at me. "Abi, there's something you should know. These attacks... We believe there's a spy within the community."

I flinched back. A spy among us?

He clasped my hand. "I might have to leave earlier than expected. I need to get to the archives that contain information regarding covert agents in Electi. We believe the spy doesn't know our exact location yet, but it's only a matter of time before they do. We need to figure out who it is before they get the intel out."

My hands trembled. This was far worse than I'd anticipated. No longer just a rescue effort but a race against time. And all our lives were on the line.

Chapter 31

Abi

"April 2207: Today Carlos radioed in that they found a girl near one of the inner checkpoints, dehydrated and in weak health. They tried to explain to her she was safe, but she was scared we were with the government. Carlos said she didn't look older than sixteen. If we didn't help her, the government would find her. We decided to send Matt and Mark there to get her, maybe talk some sense into the poor girl so we could take her in." (Deborah Davis's journal)

My back ached, and my stomach rumbled as I opened my eyes. The tingling in my feet responded to the weight that lay on top of my thighs. We must have fallen asleep while talking on the chaise.

Davon held my waist as I stroked his dark hair.

He breathed me in and exhaled long and hard, then pulled me close, his eyes twinkling. "Morning."

I smiled and shifted a bit to get the blood flowing to my legs. "Did you sleep well?"

"Like heaven. And you?"

I kissed him. "I just can't feel my legs, and my back is killing me. But, otherwise, I slept well." I laughed softly.

He sat up and stretched, his muscles straining against his clothes. "Stay there."

He pulled a chair over and sat in front of me, then patted his thighs. "Give me your feet."

He massaged from my calves all the way to my feet, knowing exactly where to touch and how much pressure to apply. I relaxed. It brought back memories from when he gave me therapies in the safe house, which seemed so long ago. I couldn't believe only a month had passed.

He focused on my legs, and I focused on him. He was beautiful inside and out. When he was on a mission, his eyes were always full of fire and determination. But in this moment, they were gentle.

This was surreal. How did I get so lucky?

He took a seat next to me and drew me onto his lap, then kneaded the back of my neck and shoulders.

I closed my eyes. "You don't have to do this."

His breath tickled my neck. "Of course I do. I'm the reason you're feeling sore, and I promised to take good care of you. Unless you want me to stop."

I moaned as he worked a spot in my back.

"I'm guessing you don't want that?"

I shook my head and sank into his chest. He hugged me.

My stomach chose that moment to interrupt with a loud growl.

He chuckled. "As much as I'd love to keep holding you, you need to eat and get ready for gun training. It's already eight thirty."

I jerked sideways. "But Matt's injured, and I thought after yesterday's events it would be canceled."

"I'll handle the rest of your gun training while he recovers, and Maria will take over once I'm gone. I'm not sure what's going to happen, but whatever it is, I want you to be ready."

I scooted off him, and he went into the bathroom.

When he came out, his face and hair were wet.

"When are you leaving?" I asked.

The question hung between us for a moment.

He sighed. "I want to leave by the end of the week. We can't keep losing people."

His departure sounded final. I knew he needed to go. For Deb's extraction. To find the spy. But it didn't stop my emotions from taking over.

My throat ached from the effort not to cry, and tears threatened to fall.

He crouched in front of me, his thumb stroking my cheek. "This is also difficult for me, but I don't have any choice. I'm the only one who can do this."

"I understand. Don't worry about me." I reined in my emotions. I had to be strong. For him.

He held my hands. "Impossible." He kissed my forehead. "Go to your place. Take all the time you need to get ready. I'll wait for you here."

I met him back at his apartment at 10:00 a.m. after a long and relaxing shower. He answered the door, looking refreshed. A towel hung by his neck, and he wore ripped jeans and a black shirt with a guitar that read, "Rock on."

This was the first time I'd seen him wearing something so casual.

I wrapped my arms around him, kissing him softly. "I really like this look on you."

He pulled me closer. I could feel all of him. My body heated instantly, melting in his embrace.

"Back at you. I'm tempted to skip breakfast."

I shuddered with pleasure as he nibbled on my neck. I was still dazed when he stepped away.

"But we both know you can't function without coffee." He smacked my butt. "C'mon. Let's dig in."

Two plates of pancakes rested on the table next to two mugs of coffee.

I took my place at the table. "Oh God, it's been forever since I had pancakes."

"Enjoy." He sat next to me. "By the way, the doctor operated on Matt last night. Everything went smoothly. He's recovering. His bicep's torn as we suspected, but there was no major nerve damage. His humerus was broken, but the doctor put it back together. Four months of therapy, and he'll be back to normal. As for his ribs, they'll heal with time."

Thank God.

I paused. "When can we see him?"

"We can go after breakfast. Then we'll train."

Fifteen minutes later, we entered the infirmary. Aoki was helping Matt sit up.

He grinned at us. "Hey. Now I'm bionic."

Aoki chuckled.

I shook my head. At the very least, he hadn't lost his sense of humor.

I approached him. "How are you holding up?"

Matt's expression grew serious. "It hurts like hell, but I'm good."

A tear slipped from my eye as I thought about how close we came to losing him.

He dried it with his thumb. "I'll be okay."

I raised an eyebrow at Aoki. "And you?"

He cocked his chin toward Matt. "I'm okay. No complaints here."

I relaxed as I watched them. They would be just fine.

Davon rested his hand on the bed's railing. "Are you sure you're all right? That was quite the scare."

Matt placed his hand on top of Davon's. "I'll be okay. Thank you for coming back for me and for everything else."

Davon squeezed Matt's fingers. "Always."

We stayed with him for a few moments, then Davon went to the armory to get our weapons.

I headed for the training center to work on some drills he taught me. As I started moving, my muscles relaxed. Sparring was like a dance—you had to hold a strong stance and attack with force, but the movements had to flow. I went into my own world while going through the movements.

Davon entered with a black duffel bag. "I see you started without me." He smiled and gestured toward the shooting room. "Come on. We'll do target training first, and then I have a surprise."

"Aren't you going to tell me about it?"

He didn't answer.

I huffed and reluctantly followed him. I hated surprises.

Foam walls surrounded the shooting room, with five lanes divided by glass partitions. Headphones and protective eye gear hung by each lane.

He showed me a black handgun. "This is the gun you'll be training with. It's a semiautomatic Glock 19, with a round capacity of fifteen bullets."

He passed it to me. It was heavy, but I'd worked with it before when I practiced with Matt out in the forest.

We donned the protective headphones, and I started target practicing. I was terrible at it. No bullet hit the target, not even the sides.

I put the gun down and threw my hands up. "God, I'm so bad at this."

He handed me another magazine. "We'll just keep practicing until you hit it."

Davon aimed with me and told me to ease the tension in my grip. I took the shot.

I hit the target's shoulder. "I can't believe it. I finally did it!" I needed to tell Matt.

Davon chuckled.

We went through three practice rounds, but I didn't have the same success handling it on my own.

"Concentrate, Abi. Imagine the enemy in front of you. Think about your life being in danger, and aim to kill."

I tried to relax as I imagined the guard who killed Jacob standing in front of me. His sick grin. His wild eyes. I let my rage flow into the gun as I steadied my breath and fired. Adrenaline rushed through me as I hit the target's chest.

Davon clapped. "Good. Now you need to do it like that every time. Out there you need to act quickly."

My pulse raced. Soon we'd be battling for our lives out there. It was inevitable. We were getting ready for war. Terror clawed at my breast at the certainty of it, and I hoped that in that moment, I'd be able to react and fire in the same way I did today.

"Now for my surprise. Follow me."

We entered a small room encircled by concrete walls. It had a window that ran from the middle of the wall to the floor and looked out to the forest. A metal stairwell led up to a trapdoor with a keypad on the side. When he opened the window, a cool breeze blew in. There was only enough room for two people.

He opened his duffel bag. "This is a high-precision, long-range M110 semiautomatic sniper rifle. It has a silencer and telescopic sight for extreme accuracy. Its range is about eight hundred meters."

I widened my eyes. It was a big weapon, and I couldn't imagine myself firing it. "You want me to use that?"

He gave me a reassuring smile. "Don't worry. I'll show you how it works. Now, do you see those places that are shining? Those are your targets. We placed them around the perimeter for this kind of training."

Light reflected from some trees when the sun hit them. Davon sprawled on the floor and taught me how to set up and stabilize the sniper, then passed it to me.

I shot five rounds, but none hit their intended targets. I punched the floor and tried again with no luck.

Why is this so difficult for me?

I followed his advice, but I still couldn't hit them.

I cursed under my breath and stood. "I'm done with this."

He squeezed my shoulder. "You'll get better at it as you keep practicing." He put the rifle back in the duffel bag.

We parted ways so he could go to the computer room. He had a briefing with Connor before lunch.

Once I reached the dining hall, Sarah called out to me. She sat with Jimmy, Maria, and Tammy.

Sarah stood and gave me a hug. She appeared much better than the last time I saw her. She wore her hair up in a messy bun, a loose strand falling to her side. Her eyes were more focused.

"How are you?" I asked.

"Much better, sis. A coworker is helping me deal with all that's happened, and since yesterday, I've been attending therapy sessions." She grabbed her food tray. "I'm sorry I can't stay. I have a briefing with Connor."

"Yeah, Davon is on his way there."

She faced Jimmy and the girls. "Well, take care, guys. Thanks for the time."

Jimmy rose and clasped her hands. "Remember, you're not alone. You're family."

Sarah offered him a half smile, her gaze darting between us. "It's great to see you two together again. It brings back memories."

Jimmy put his hands in his pockets and glanced at me. "It sure does."

My chest burst with warmth. This was my family, and only Deb was missing. A hollowness settled in my heart, but it was soon replaced by hope in knowing Davon would bring her back. Soon we'd all be together again.

As she walked away, Jimmy motioned for me to sit.

I'd decided to let what happened in the forest go. He already knew I was with Davon and would deal with his feelings in his own way.

"I'll go get your food." He pushed my chair closer to the table.

I nodded. "Thanks."

As he left, I regarded the girls. "Hey, guys, *buen provecho*."

"Thanks. You too!" Maria said. "How's everything?"

I rested my elbows on the table. "A lot is going on, but everything's good. And you?"

"I'm good. Connor has me working around the clock." She looked at Tammy. "When did I get back home last night?"

Tammy narrowed her eyes. "Three in the morning."

Maria took Tammy's hand. "Honey, I'm sorry. You know I can't disclose why, but he needed me. He did give me the afternoon off."

Tammy raised Maria's hand to her lips and kissed her knuckles. "At least. I've missed you."

My heart ached at their exchange. Many lives were affected by this, and many more would be when the real war began.

Jimmy returned with my tray and sat. "How was your morning?"

I took a bite of the stew, the warmth banishing the chill in my bones. "I was training with guns. I'm terrible, but Davon says I'll hopefully get better with practice."

"That's okay. It takes time to get used to them," he said.

Maria finished her bowl. "I see you and Davon are officially a couple."

My chest swelled. "Yes, we're together."

Tammy stared at me, her gaze surprisingly cold. The hairs on the back of my neck prickled. She gave me a smile that was a bit too sweet, and I looked away.

Jimmy rolled his eyes. "Apparently."

I huffed at his jealousy.

Jimmy had to do a run, so he left first.

I invited Maria and Tammy back to my apartment. When we arrived, there was a box in front of it. I picked it up and entered.

A folded note was taped to the top: *I got this for you. Early birthday present. Hope it all fits. —Jimmy.*

A variety of outfits were inside. Jimmy had good taste. He must have left it while I trained with Davon.

I hummed as I organized them in the closet. The girls giggled.

"He's such a good guy." Maria walked over to the table to have some oatmeal cookies Aoki had brought over yesterday.

Tammy followed suit.

My attention was drawn to Tammy. My senses were strongly aware that something was off. Why would she glare at me and then act as if nothing had happened? Was she hiding something? Did she have feelings for Davon? Or was it she didn't like me? I was curious about it, so I decided to dig into her past.

"Tammy, I don't know much about you. Connor told me you arrived about a year ago. But were you recruited or taken in as an escapee?"

A gentle smile curved her lips. "A recruiter contacted me at a facility, and I came in about a year ago. Out there teachers were tough on me because I questioned their education system. The banning of history class and the indoctrination of government curriculum made me sick."

I blinked. That was the most I'd heard about her since we'd met. Her answer didn't explain her actions, but maybe I was imagining things. "I remember being taught all that bullshit. Having people like you question the curriculum could make a difference in the city. Education is the best weapon against despotism." Her conviction and her courage to question the system signified what a true rebel was.

Still, I wanted to know more.

I glanced between them. "Did you guys meet right away?"

Blushing, Tammy winked at Maria. "Yeah. For me, it was love at first sight."

Maria chuckled. "We met as soon as you came in, in your screening. Remember?"

Tammy nodded. "It took me a month to convince you to give me a chance. Six months later, we moved in together." She adjusted her glasses.

She had lovely features. I could see how Maria was enchanted by her.

We continued snacking.

"Do you want to train with me tomorrow?" Maria asked.

A knock sounded on the door before I could answer.

I rose and opened it. Davon barged in, his expression grave.

A weight pressed against my chest. Something wasn't right. This wasn't like him. "Are you okay?"

He shook his head and glanced at the girls.

Maria stood. "Thanks for the cookies and the chat. We'll leave now."

After they left, we sat on the bed.

"What is it?"

He grimaced. "It's just as we feared. Everything went to shit."

Chapter 32

Abi

"*October 2207: After two weeks working undercover, Davon arrived today. His twenty-second birthday was yesterday, so we decided to surprise him. His face as we yelled 'surprise' was precious, his reaction not so much. He'd taken his gun out in defense, thinking something had happened. After he saw it was us, he relaxed, and we had a nice time. It was funny, though, the look on his face, even though he scared the shit out of us.*

"*He's always riled up like this. The moment he chose to aid us was the moment he chose mayhem over peace of mind. I hope someday he finds someone with whom he can relax and have some type of normality. He deserves it. He was indispensable to our mission, and I deeply appreciate him.*" (Deborah Davis's journal)

My heart leapt. "Tell me."

He stared down at his hands. "Matt and I found out about a letter that was sent out from the bunker about a month ago while we were still on the outskirts of Promissa. A letter addressed to my father from me."

My insides tightened. *How come I'm finding out about this now?*

I frowned. "But...how?"

He shook his head. "I never wrote it. That's when we started suspecting a spy was hiding in the community. We kept it silent until we could find out more. Today, when I went to contact my father, I found what I dreaded was true." He paused and took a deep breath, as if preparing to tell me something hard to swallow. "I found a coded message from him, thanking me for the intel on the rebel checkpoints."

I jerked back.

He gripped my hands, his eyes pleading. "Abi, you have to believe me. I would never do such a thing."

Many thoughts raced through my mind. Could he possibly be a traitor? Their training, as he stated, was excellent. My stomach twisted.

"Please. I would never lie to you."

But he had, and he was Jordan Niles's son after all. He taught others how to be spies. Bile rose up my throat, and I swallowed.

I looked at our joined hands and slowly glanced up. His eyes reminded me of the anguish I saw that afternoon when he discovered his friends had died. I thought about the conviction they showed whenever he talked about freeing Promissa. The rage that burned in them when he mentioned his father or the government. Their love every time we were together.

I pushed my doubts aside and squeezed his hands. "I'm sorry. You just caught me off guard." Even though I had a nagging uncertainty in the back of my mind, I shoved it away. I had to hear him out. "What did Connor say?"

"He trusts me. We've been working together for ten years in this community. But it's more than that. This spy doesn't know our exact location, or else they would've attacked by now. If it was me, they would know." He lowered his gaze. "The problem is your sister. She was there when we found the email."

He rubbed his cheek, which I just noticed was red. Did she slap him?

He shrugged. "I get her, you know. I wouldn't trust me either."

Sarah lost Carlos. She didn't know Davon much, and, in her eyes, his name could easily make him the enemy. Even though it crushed me since it would certainly create a barrier between us, I understood. I'd have to prove to her he wasn't the enemy. Make her understand.

"I'll help you clear your name."

He shook his head. "Please don't. I can't let you put yourself in danger. Especially once I'm gone." He looked pained, eyes downcast. "Connor's trying to keep this contained and to calm Sarah as we speak, but it's only a matter of time until the information leaks out to the community."

His fingers tightened around mine. "What I don't get is why they haven't told Father I'm a traitor. Wouldn't it be easier? Why keep this from him?" His brow creased. "It doesn't make sense."

My gut clenched. If he returned to Electi and his treason was revealed, he would be tortured or worse.

My flesh crawled as I realized the risk he would face out there. What would their next step be? Maybe if he didn't leave, he'd be okay. But what about Deb?

I scraped back my hair.

God, this is impossible.

I held him firmly. "I understand you're scared, but I want to help."

"Abi, if they see you as an obstacle, God only knows what could happen. I can't be out there, knowing you could be targeted. Please don't try to find the spy. Leave it to command and to me."

Did he believe I'd just let this go? See the man I loved be framed for a crime he didn't commit and do nothing?

"I'll try." The lie came out of my mouth so naturally even I believed it. There was no way I would sit back and do nothing.

"There's something else." His eyes were full of sorrow. "My father summoned me and appointed me a place on his council."

"What if it's a trap?"

"It could be, but I'll take my chances. I already talked to Connor about it. We have a plan." He brushed his thumb over my knuckles. "I'm going to move into the city in a few days. Indefinitely."

His last word echoed in my mind, and it went numb. I knew it would happen but not on his father's terms. Not as part of his council. Not with the risk of being uncovered. Once he went in, there was no certainty Jordan Niles would ever let him go.

He would just be gone with no return date. My chest was pried open, my soul left bare. I was going to lose him.

His warmth enveloped me as he hugged me tightly. Tears slipped down my cheeks.

Holding me at arm's length, he dried my tears with the back of his hand. "Talk to me, please."

He lifted my chin. "I'll be in the city for weeks, maybe months, but I'll find a way to get back to you. I promise. Give me some time, and trust I'll be working on it. But for now, there's no other option. No matter the scenario, this is a unique opportunity. Circumstances aren't on our side right now, so we must accept it and trust it will be okay."

It was true. This was our only option. But it didn't stop the emptiness from growing inside of me. This finality that once he exited the bunker, I'd never see him again. That once his father got his hands on him, I'd never get him back.

I peered into his dark eyes, burning his image into my mind. How long would it be until I saw him again?

I traced the stubble along his cheek and drew him closer. No words needed to be spoken. He kissed me hungrily, full of need.

I began to remove his shirt, and he pulled back.

"Abi, what are you...?" His dark, intense gaze pierced my soul. "Are you sure about this?"

My entire body longed for his touch. To connect with him in the most intimate way possible before he left. "Yes."

His fingers stroked the nape of my neck. "I promise I'll make it back to you."

I smiled. "I know you will."

I took off his shirt.

He had scars, remnants of his dark past. I brushed my hands over them and kissed each one. He trembled as I trailed my fingertips downward, following the outline of his tattoo.

So strong and hard, but his skin was so soft. He was perfect.

He cradled my head and consumed me in a passionate kiss. I tilted back slightly as he kissed my neck down to my shoulders.

The yearning to have him was overpowering. Warmth spread through-out my body as he ran his fingers up my side. He grabbed the ends of my top and pulled it off.

I covered my left breast, hiding my scar. A continuous reminder of the horror I went through.

His gaze held me as he slowly moved my hand away. "Don't shy away from me."

He caressed my breast, then peppered kisses all over the sensitive area. "You're so beautiful."

I shuddered with pleasure at his adoring touch and arched my body toward him, pleading for more. Heat surged in my core when he put his mouth on me. His stubble brushed across my chest.

I slipped my hand beneath the waistline of his pants.

A deep, shuddering breath escaped him, and he took my mouth in a frenzy, rocking against me.

I quivered as his fingers brushed my center.

"Relax. Let me love you."

He never took his eyes off me as he explored, the crescendo of his touch driving me mad with need.

My hips followed his movement, and I closed my eyes, burning inside. I panted with want as he knelt and tugged my pants and underwear down.

"Davon?"

He lifted me up on the bed, allowing my head to fall back on the pillow, then kissed my thighs and ever so slowly moved to my center.

I fisted my hands on the sheet, wriggling wildly. "Oh, Davon, please."

He pulled me against his mouth and moaned as he consumed me whole.

Grabbing his hair, I drew him even closer, greedily. The feel of his hot breath against me was my undoing. My body melted beneath him, as a flood of scorching pleasure swept over me, making time seem to stand still.

"Davon." I struggled to speak. "I..."

"Tell me, baby. What do you need?"

"All of you," I whispered.

I wanted to let go in his embrace, for him to fill me with his love and replace my ugly past with something beautiful.

His loving gaze raked over me. "Are you sure?"

This man was willing to stop, to let me choose. My heart swelled. How could I be so lucky?

I touched his cheek. "I am. Please make love to me."

Make me forget.

He stood and took off his jeans.

My breath hitched. He was magnificent.

He climbed onto the bed. His hair cascaded down, and his dark eyes swirled with desire. The press of his body to mine made me feel small but so safe, wanted. I couldn't believe he was mine.

He kissed me tenderly, lovingly.

My heart was close to bursting. God, I couldn't get enough of him. I gripped his hips and drew him to me, spreading my legs as he settled between them.

I gasped as he slid himself slowly into me. My core pulsed with heat, welcoming him. Finally, our bodies became one. I was whole again.

His eyes locked on me. "Are you okay?"

I smiled. "Better than ever."

His gaze was soft and piercing at the same time. "I've been dreaming of this moment."

My feelings were reflected in his eyes. Love at its purest.

I stirred beneath him, and he kissed me gently, moving slowly, giving me time to adjust. The rhythm intensified and we became lost in each other.

He grabbed my hips, deepening the connection. The heat of his breath as he nipped my earlobes sent a powerful current down my body.

I shuddered with need, and grasped his biceps, seeking the feel of his strength beneath my hands, clutching him tightly. I kissed his neck and chest, his muscles straining with each movement.

With each caress, with each touch, my pleasure grew until my world exploded, and wave after wave of ecstasy poured through me.

As his movements became erratic, he gazed at me passionately. "Abi."

He grunted in pleasure and came undone. I'd never seen anything so raw, so entrancing.

He continued moving, prolonging my bliss, caressing my skin until there was calm.

We were both spent when he eased out and raised himself on his right elbow, fondling my stomach and hips while lovingly kissing me.

He didn't need to say anything because I could sense it in his touch.

There was no question—he was mine, and I was his.

He embraced me while we both dozed off, savoring the moment.

I opened my eyes and took a deep, satisfied breath, still feeling the effects of our union. I stretched and examined my watch. It was eleven at night.

As Davon's sweet caresses and adoring touch replayed in my mind, I brushed his muscular chest and snuggled closer to him. He was breathtaking.

My thoughts returned to earlier, recalling our current situation.

Davon moved sideways, and I twisted away, trying to hide my tears.

He tilted my face toward him. "Look at me, baby. Don't cry."

We faced each other, shedding tears and basking in each other's presence.

He cupped my face. "I'll never let you go."

Chapter 33

Davon

November 6, 2213

I buried my nose in Abi's hair. Her leg rested on top of me, her hand against my chest.

She had been an enigma from the start, consuming all my thoughts. I craved her presence and would go to any lengths to be near her. To protect her.

Last night, when she covered her breast, my heart ached for her. I would cherish her until she no longer remembered what happened. Until that scar became a symbol of her strength. Of her resilience.

I held her close, so thankful to have found her.

Leaving her would tear me apart, but we couldn't waste this opportunity. Being a member of my father's council would grant me full access to sensitive information as well as clearance to enter high-security locations.

Connor and I agreed the PRF would make an official declaration and detain me in three days. I'd escape on the second day, putting the entire community on high alert.

That way maybe the spy would become more confident and let down their guard so we could discover their identity.

Dark thoughts filled my mind about what I would do to them once I found out who they were. I would break them slowly and use against them the same training they made me use on others.

Abi stirred, and I hugged her closer.

Her hand went to my hair, and she kissed me.

Her mouth was addictive. So sweet, so soft. I could never get enough.

When she ended the kiss, I caressed her side. "Happy birthday."

She opened her eyes wide.

I'd been waiting for this day since she slipped the information to Little D.

Connor gave us the night—at least one night—to pretend everything was fine and celebrate. Matt, Aoki, and I had planned it all.

Her gaze softened. "You remembered."

"Of course. We have a surprise for you, and I got you something to wear, but it's in my room."

She opened her mouth to speak, but I put a finger to her lips.

"Don't even try to find out anything more because I won't tell you."

She huffed, and I chuckled. I loved her face when I teased her, and right now she was pouting. Irresistible.

She straddled me, peppering kisses down my nose, lips, chin, and neck. My body responded to her instantly.

She smiled mischievously. "Is there anything I can do to convince you otherwise?"

Her smoldering mouth and delectable body were a huge temptation, but we needed to get ready. "As much as I want to act on this, we have to get ready. Connor wants to meet us after breakfast."

I kissed her cheek and slowly eased her off me, then sat on the side of the bed in search of my jeans.

She circled the bed and stood between my thighs, clutching my pants. "Is this what you're looking for?"

With her nude body in front of me, I couldn't help myself. I caressed her round breasts and took them as she moaned and ran her fingers through my hair. Her skin was so soft. So sweet. "We can always make him wait a little."

She giggled as I dragged her back into bed with me, bringing her on top. It was beautiful.

After we made love, we decided to split up so we could shower in our respective apartments, knowing we would never be ready otherwise.

Half an hour later, I knocked on her door with two packages in my hands.

"Come in!" she yelled.

Sarah gave me a cold look as I opened the door, her eyes narrowing.

"I have to go. Come by later." She embraced Abi. "And happy twenty-first birthday."

"Will you be coming tonight?" I said as Sarah walked past me.

She stopped beside the door. "I don't think so, but have fun." Her jaw tight, she turned and left.

Abi held a piece of paper, a smile on her face.

I came closer. "Are you okay?"

"Yeah. She came by to deliver this." She showed me the paper.

It was a sketch of the three of them standing in a field of wildflowers. Abi stood in the center, holding both Sarah's and Deb's hands as they stared at her with glee.

"It's stunning."

"This is Sarah in her element." She put the picture on her side table next to the one of her family she always kept close. "I'm sorry she left."

"Don't worry. We'll work through it." I pushed my worries away. "But enough about that. I brought you these."

She took my gifts and plopped onto the bed. "Two? When did you find the time for this?"

I shrugged and sat beside her as she tore open the large box. Her excitement revealed it had been years since she had received a birthday gift.

I rubbed her lower back softly. I couldn't contain my smile.

She squealed as she pulled my gift out—a small royal-blue tube dress with spaghetti straps that crossed in the back. Her gleaming eyes stirred something deep inside of me, and all the tension of the past day vanished.

I grinned. "I think it'll fit you perfectly."

Her eyes sparkled. "I love it! It's my favorite color."

I nodded. "I know. Once I wore a royal-blue shirt to a New Year's Eve party here at the bunker. Deb's eyes glazed over when she told me it reminded her of you because you liked that color. That was right before we left to find you."

"And you remembered?"

"It stuck with me because it's my favorite color too. Go on. Open the other one." I moved the small box on top.

She gasped and brushed her fingers against the silver necklace with a pendant of raw sapphire. She flung herself into me with a powerful hug, and I blinked in surprise.

"Thank you." She kissed my cheek and removed it from the box. "It's gorgeous. How did you—?"

"There's a mine to the southwest where people from import and construction go to get materials for occasions like this. People still want this kind of stuff."

She examined it. "What did you trade to get me this?"

"It doesn't matter. Give it here. Let's see how it looks." I clasped the necklace around her neck.

In truth, I traded my Scottish claymore, which had been passed down through my family. It was worth it just to see the joy on her face as she looked at herself in the mirror.

She turned and kissed me fervently before looking deeply into my eyes. She tucked a stray strand of hair behind my ear and caressed my stubble as she lowered her fingers down to my chest. "Thank you for last night, for today, for everything. I'm so lucky to have you."

My heart swelled at her words, and I covered her hand with mine. "I'm the lucky one. I don't know what I did to deserve you."

After basking in each other's embrace for some time, we left for breakfast.

The rich aroma of coffee and steak hit us as we entered Matt and Aoki's place.

"Hey, birthday girl!" Matt hugged Abi, wincing a little. "How does it feel, being a grown-up at last?"

Abi rolled her eyes as Matt barked with laughter.

Aoki came next, wearing his yin-yang apron, and kissed her hand. "Happy birthday! I made you something special and a strong coffee to start the day off. Make yourself at home while we get everything ready."

Aoki prepared a brunch for all of us to enjoy before the daily routine. Steak and eggs with sautéed potatoes.

They tried to appear content, but there was an unnatural stillness in the room. When everything occurred, Matt was in command. Aoki had been cleared before our last mission, so he also knew what transpired.

Matt came to the sofa where we sat. "For you."

Abi gasped as he put a delicate, tiny garden on her lap, with white sand on the bottom, succulent plants in a corner, and stones arranged throughout. A yin-yang replica of a gong stood in the center.

Aoki crouched in front of us. "Here." He gave Abi a tiny rake. "It's a Zen garden. You rake the sand and rearrange it however you want. It relieves tension and improves creativity and concentration. It's also lovely."

A tear slid down her cheek as she looked between us. "Thank you so much. I haven't received anything in a long time. This means a lot to me."

Matt handed her a tissue. "Don't cry. Let's forget about everything, at least for today. We have an exciting night planned."

Abi glanced my way and smiled, but her gaze carried so much worry. I patted her thigh.

"And what is it that we're doing tonight, Matt?"

"Tsk, tsk, tsk. Abigail Davis, those puppy eyes aren't going to work on me."

When she arched an eyebrow at Aoki, he stood abruptly. "I'll go get the food."

I laughed. Her charms clearly affected him.

After breakfast, we went directly to command. I asked Connor for this meeting so he could explain everything to Abi. I hoped she'd understand the finality of the decision since Connor was our general.

Abi's sadness was palpable. Her downcast eyes as we walked to command broke me.

I took her hand and held her back. "We can reschedule for tomorrow if this is too much."

"No, this is urgent. Don't worry about me. I can handle it." She squeezed my hand lightly before letting go.

"Happy birthday!" Connor hugged her as soon as we entered his office. "This is for you." He gave her a box.

Inside there was a uniform and a badge: Abigail Davis—Cadet—PRF.

She yelped and threw herself at him. "This is amazing! So can I go on missions now?"

"Maybe." Connor chuckled. "But you need to train more. Maria and Davon told me how much you've improved, so I'm making it official. Welcome to the PRF armed forces."

She nodded. "Thank you."

Connor sat behind his desk while Abi and I took our seats. "I'm glad you could come, and I'm sorry we have to talk about this today. As Davon informed you, yesterday's events have given us a once-in-a-lifetime opportunity to advance our cause. It's not what we wanted, but we'll take it. I want you to know I didn't make this decision lightly, but with the current threat and Deb's imprisonment, we have no other choice."

The room fell silent. Connor and I had been friends since the beginning, and the offer to join my father's council was uncharted territory. It was a dangerous scenario, and it could be a trap, but we didn't have a choice.

I didn't know how far I'd have to go or if I'd ever be able to escape my father's circle. Abi was aware of this, and it made everything much more difficult.

Would she ever forgive what I would put Deb through? Would she ever look at me as she did this morning, or would my actions tarnish all we'd built?

Hell, I didn't even know if I would be accepted back because if I didn't succeed in catching the spy, my exile would be final.

"We have two goals—to get Deb back and to find out who the spy is. The plan is to get Davon inside, and, hopefully, his position will give him access to the high-security prison. He'll keep us posted using channels we're still setting throughout the city. I've forbidden him from being in direct contact with the bunker to protect his mission, so all comms will be thirdhand."

Abi's expression faltered for a moment. I squeezed her hand.

"I understand this is difficult for you both, but I beg you to trust me. I'll give you as much information as I can, but this is a top-secret assignment, and some details must be kept private." Connor rested back in his chair. "Davon also asked me to keep you out of the loop for your own safety."

Abi's face flushed, her eyes narrowing. "It's one thing to ask me not to look for the spy, but keeping me in the dark? Why?"

I sighed. "I can't work if you're in danger. You've known since the beginning. Having you take part in this mission will put you at risk."

She scowled. "So you just decided for me without even asking and made Connor tell me, thinking I'd accept it quietly. Coward!"

God, she was right. I should've told her before.

"We'll talk about it later, but please try to understand. It's for your own protection and mine. Deb would have wanted this."

She clenched her jaw. "What the hell do you know about what she might think?"

I reached for her, but she pulled away. She hadn't acted this way since we first met.

Connor rubbed his brow. "Davon is leaving in five days. That's all I can give you. His treason will be made public in three days, and he'll be relocated to a cell."

Her eyes grew wide. "You'll arrest him? But why? Can't he just go?"

"It needs to be this way. The spy must think we believe he's guilty. We'll announce an investigation will be carried out, and Davon will flee the bunker on the second day following his arrest."

Connor lowered his gaze. "Once he leaves Janus Peak, we'll go on high alert. We'll increase the number of people working in the command center, hoping the spy will take advantage of this opportunity to get inside. We just need a slipup so we can catch them." He motioned to me.

"Today I'll send a message to Father, accepting his offer. After I escape, I'll go to checkpoint four, where soldiers will be waiting to take me to Electi. Command will be blind from then on until I can get word out. It'll take some time, so please be patient."

The energy in the room was oppressive. Silence reigned for a long moment.

Abi finally broke it. "Is that all?" she asked Connor.

He nodded.

She rose and gathered her stuff. Without even a glance at me, she exited the room, slamming the door behind her.

Shit.

This wasn't how I expected things to go.

"Good luck, my friend. You'll need it," Connor said.

I raked a hand through my hair. "No shit."

I went to her place. We didn't have much time left together, and I wanted her to understand. I knocked and called her name, but there was no answer.

"Trouble in paradise?"

I spun around. Aoki leaned against his doorframe, holding his cat.

I had to find her. "Have you seen her?" I gritted my teeth.

"I haven't. Sorry." Aoki stepped into his apartment. "Come in. Tell me what happened."

I rushed inside and sat on their plush white sofa, my elbows resting on my knees as they shook uncontrollably. "Connor and I explained to Abi what would happen, and she lost it."

Aoki sat beside me.

Shirokuro hissed at me and ran away. I swear that cat hated my guts.

"What exactly did you try to explain?" he asked.

"That I would be imprisoned in three days and the mission would be confidential because I didn't want to endanger her."

Aoki blew out a breath and sank deeper into the sofa, his arms behind his neck. "Wow. What did you think her reaction would be?" He raised his eyebrows.

I shook my head. "I fucked up, didn't I?"

Aoki patted my back. "That you did, brother. That you did."

I was new to this relationship thing, but he and Matt had been together for a long time, so he might be able to help me. "What should I do?"

"The problem was in the approach. You should've discussed it with her privately. She's an adult, and if she wants to risk herself for you, it's her choice. Putting her on the spot made her feel vulnerable, and maybe she felt you didn't trust her. You need to apologize and let her get everything out. Try to understand her situation here."

"Fuck, I'm such an idiot. How did I not see this coming?" I bit my lip. "Where do you think she went? My mind's a mess right now. I can't think straight."

He twisted his lips and stared at the ceiling. "Well, if Matt did something like that to me, I'd seek refuge in my kitchen. It's what I enjoy doing the most, and it would take my mind off him."

I closed my eyes. Then it came to me. The ideal place for her to let off some steam.

I stood. "I know where she is."

"Good luck, man!" Aoki said as I walked out the door. "You'll need it."

Chapter 34

Davon

The sounds of shuffling and fighting met my ears as I entered the training center, which was to be expected at ten in the morning.

Maria fought three soldiers at once. She was very skilled at hand-to-hand combat and a force to be reckoned with once you gave her a weapon. She squatted between the cadets and landed one on the floor with a low side kick.

As another cadet attempted to assault her, she pivoted, smacked her in the face with an elbow strike, and then shoved her back with a front kick. The third charged from behind. Maria delivered a roundhouse kick to his jaw, sending him straight to the floor. Setting her foot on his throat, she pinned him to the ground. I clapped as she wiped the sweat off her face.

It was that simple and quick. This batch of recruits would learn from the best. She never stopped surprising me.

"Cadets, continue your exercises." Maria approached me. "To what do we owe your visit, General Niles? Are you training the cadets today?"

"Lieutenant Diaz." I stepped closer, hoping to keep our conversation private. "Have you seen Abi around?"

She raised her eyebrows and put her hands on her hips.

"Please tell me. I need to talk to her." I was pleading. Desperate.

She nodded. "I was training the cadets, but I did hear someone entering the shooting room."

"Thank you." I started walking toward the room but looked back at her. "Please don't let anyone in. That's an order."

She grinned. "Good luck."

I put on ear and eye protection and entered the room. I stood on the threshold while Abi fired repeatedly at her target, never hitting it.

She needs a lot more practice.

Her bullets ran out, so I removed my ear protection and approached her. She needed to know I understood. That I would talk to Connor and include her in this.

She was stubborn as hell, and I was certain even if I said no, she'd find a way to be a part of the mission, either by endangering herself and walking in alone or by persuading her brother-in-law to let her in.

Given Deb's handling of Sarah's situation, I preferred the latter. Connor would take care of her and turn her into a damn good soldier capable of dealing with the hazards and challenges of this mission. She was family to him, and her welfare was his priority. I could go, knowing she'd be safe.

With a jolt, she whipped around. Her gun was aimed at my head in less than a second. Her breathing under control. Her grip strong.

I grinned. My girl had fucking quick reflexes.

Her piercing gaze was fixed on me, and I took a step back, hands up.

When she realized it was me, she lowered her weapon and removed her ear protection. "What the fuck is wrong with you? I could have shot you. Get the hell out!" She slipped her earmuffs back on and aimed for the target.

I quickly put on my earmuffs and crossed my arms as I waited next to her. This time she hit the target. She lowered her gun, then removed her protectors and placed them in front of her.

I pressed the button to move the target closer. "I don't think your target can take any more of your rage."

She'd hit the victim's chest several times during this final round. I couldn't decide whether to be worried or proud.

Her eyes welled up. "What are you doing here, Davon? Aren't you planning a *secret* mission?"

Ouch, that was direct. I stepped toward her, but she withdrew, keeping her distance.

"I'm sorry." I tried to touch her arm, to get her to talk to me.

"Don't touch me!" She batted my hand away.

I cringed. I had the feeling I was about to get an onslaught.

"Did you ever stop to think how it would make me feel? To be left in the dark during your time away?" She was in my face, screaming her heart out. Thank God this was a soundproof room.

"I'm sorry. I didn't think—"

"Oh, that I know! You didn't think at all! What did you believe? That having Connor tell me everything would make it better? That hearing it from him would make me accept it? Did you believe we would be lovey-dovey afterward, as if nothing happened? Fuck you, Davon! Do you have any idea how much you hurt me by not having the balls to tell me to my face? By again making me feel weak? Don't you trust me to be capable?" She scowled, her eyes burning through me.

"Of course I trust you. I'm so, so sorry about everything." I needed her to understand.

"Apologizing won't make it right. You have no idea what I'm going through. To know we need to get Deb back and you're the one leaving. Knowing the man I love will be sent to collect her in a matter of days, risking his life out there!" She covered her mouth, her eyes wide.

I stiffened. What we had was strong, and I'd fallen deeply in love with her. Last night, I had let all my feelings out when I made love to her. But to hear her say it. It changed everything.

She backed into the wall. "I'm sorry. I mean, it just came out."

I moved closer and pulled her into an embrace. "I love you too, Abi."

She froze, then a sob left her as she relaxed into me.

"Let's go somewhere private."

I took her hand, and we walked back to my apartment. I let her in ahead of me, and she stopped.

I hugged her from behind and kissed the curve of her neck. "I'm very sorry. I'll take care of it. I know I hurt you. I'm a coward, and there's no excuse for what I did. This is all new to me, and I sometimes feel as if I don't know how to act. The need to protect you overpowers everything else, and I didn't pause to consider your feelings."

"But that's the problem. I don't need protection. I understand how you feel. I know what you've been through. But I'm not a fragile doll you need to keep locked in a safe place. I know how to take care of myself. I did it for a long time before you entered my life, and you need to have faith in me. I'm nervous as well. Concerned about you going in. At what your father will put you through. But you don't see me trying to stop you."

She was right on point. It was true. She'd never asked me to stay. Never even hinted at it.

My arms sagged. "You're right, but it doesn't mean I'm going to stop protecting you. I know you're a soldier now, and I'll put my faith in your strength and training. Just assure me you won't put yourself in danger to protect me. Promise me if you see everything has fallen apart, you'll flee and save yourself."

She shook her head, her back still to me. "I won't ever run away. Know if I see you're in danger, I'll charge right in to save you. I'll never stand by again to watch the man I love suffer and die. I'll never stop fighting for our freedom even if it means my death. You can accept or reject that. In any case, it's how it'll be."

She rendered me speechless with her words. The conviction behind them. I would give my life to protect her, and she would do the same for me. "I can, and I get it. We're the same, you and I." I kissed her neck again. "I love you for all that you are and for the man you make me be."

She twisted in my arms and hugged me fiercely. "Please don't push me away. Don't keep me in the dark. For three years, I was shrouded in it, and I can't go through that again."

I swallowed hard. "I won't. I promise I'll do everything in my power to get back to you." I tried to hide my fear, this dreadful feeling that I wouldn't be able to return to her.

I rubbed the back of her head, finally feeling her relax, hoping I was wrong.

"I'm guessing Deb explained in her journal that this bunker was the first one we occupied, making it the center of operations," I asked Abi as we walked toward the dining hall for lunch.

She nodded. "She wrote about how you found the maps that led you to it. And how you found the other bunkers, expanding your community even more. I've always wondered where you got them."

I cocked my head in her direction as I remembered my childhood.

"When Dad took over Promissa, he relocated his seat of power here and brought in files from all of his eastern coast territories. He stored them in a room next to his study, which I enjoyed sneaking into while Mom organized Dad's stuff. I'd open boxes that, by the looks of it, had never been opened before and spent countless hours studying the journals and maps I discovered."

No servants were allowed in his study, so Mom took it upon herself to organize his belongings. He'd go insane when he returned, unable to find anything, but his love for her was so strong he never fought about it and instead embraced her quirks.

"When we were looking for a location for establishing the rebellion, I remembered a particular map I cherished, one I'd stolen from Father when I was just a kid. That was my thing. Anything I found interesting, I took till I had a modest collection of journals, maps, books, weapons, you name it. Dad didn't mind. He'd chuckle at my antiques, knowing I kept them hidden. He never looked twice, encouraging me to grow more like him every day."

"Wow. So your dad's the reason the rebellion got stronger. Kind of ironic, isn't it?"

"Definitely." Someday I'd have to thank him personally for all he'd done for us, just to see the look on his face.

"Is this the only bunker with soldiers?" Abi asked as a group of cadets passed us.

"No, we have soldiers all around the system. They train here and are assigned a post."

We'd been training countless soldiers for the last five years, preparing our armed forces. Over five thousand rebels, between soldiers and spies, were ready to engage if needed. And that wasn't accounting for all the citizens and soldiers of the NWG that we could rally toward our cause. It was a modest amount in comparison to the thousands in the NWG armed forces, but if we did it right, we could use it to our advantage. We had to be smart about it and recruit them to fight with us.

I opened the door to let Abi inside the dining hall. We got our food—white rice with shredded beef—and sat at an empty table.

"This is the only bunker that accepts new residents from the city. They're blindfolded to keep our location a secret, and we interrogate them, mostly about their past—family, housing, life before the wars. We have people working in the city archives who confirm if what they're saying is true."

She looked up in delight as she took her first bite.

Her appetite proved to be my undoing, and I kissed her cheek, finding it irresistible.

She squeezed her eyebrows and tucked a loose hair behind her ear before returning to her food. "You'll have to do a better job of it."

I chuckled. "I know. We need to reevaluate. It clearly isn't working."

"And what happens after they pass the interrogation?" she said between bites.

"Typically, the process takes a week or two, and at the end, they're given a choice. They can either start working straight away or enroll in a program to learn an occupation of their choice. When they complete the curriculum, they must enter the trade. If a person doesn't enjoy their employment, they can always change jobs if the one they want is available. You work hard, and you get a place to live, food, water, energy, clothing, and an education."

"It sounds a lot like what the government is doing."

"Yes, it does. The difference is that here you choose your trade and, regardless of career, if you give back to the community, you get the same rewards as everyone else." And it was still operating after nine years. We didn't think it would work and questioned our ability to pull it off, but it did.

She arched her eyebrows. "How do you get everyone to comply? You must have troublemakers."

I sighed. "Sometimes we do."

Abi frowned. "And what happens to them?"

"They must leave the community. But once you do, there's no turning back. Not to Promissa. Not to Janus Peak. We can't take the chance." It was a tough decision, but it needed to be done.

She stopped eating. "Where do they go?"

I grimaced. "We blindfold them and take them about one hundred miles north. We give them goods that will last many weeks and point them toward a large metropolis five hundred miles to the north of that point. When I was a kid, I recall my father talking about it and seeing it on maps. It's known as Empire City. I'm not sure what it's like or if they welcome immigrants, but it's the closest to us. There are more cities to the west, but they're farther away and more difficult to reach by foot."

I rubbed my eyes, my insides twisting. About a dozen citizens had taken the journey, and there was no way of knowing if they had made it.

She wrinkled her brow. "So there's no guarantee they'll arrive safely or that the city will be under a good government?"

"Not at all, but we do explain the risks."

She stared at me for a moment and went back to her meal. We stayed silent for a couple of minutes.

I swallowed. "I'm proud of where we've gotten, but we can't stay this way forever. While I'm on the mission, I'd like Matt and you to start strategizing, and he'll keep me posted. We have yet to decide when, but Matt will have to join me in Electi eventually. We've always worked together, and Father will wonder why he's not around. I'll tell him Matt is undercover and will join me whenever possible. That way he can move back and forth and keep you up-to-date."

She nodded. "It makes sense, but what will happen in the meantime before Matt gets to you? How will you communicate with us?"

"For the first months, we'll have to use time drops, which we're putting in place right now. That way if something happens before Matt arrives or if I'm trapped and unable to leave my father, we can still communicate between the city and Janus Peak."

I shuddered at the possibility of being unable to escape my father's grasp.

Abi wrapped her hand around mine. "Everything will be all right. We'll make it work."

I intended to tell Abi about tonight after lunch, but we'd decided to keep it a surprise for her. Everyone was invited, but one of the most important guests chose to skip the party after yesterday.

We went to the infirmary to see how Matt was doing, as he started his therapies today.

"Is life back to normal in paradise?" he asked.

I ran my fingers through my hair. I should have expected Aoki to inform Matt.

Abi stared at me with a puzzled expression.

"I went to your place to look for you, and Aoki heard me."

"By that, he means he was yelling and nearly breaking down your door. After hearing what Davon did, Aoki put him in his place by telling him he acted like an asshole." Matt grinned.

"It wasn't like that!" I flashed him a glare that indicated I'd get him for this later.

"Okay. Go ahead and tell us how it went." He raised an eyebrow, his eyes twinkling with mirth.

I ignored him. "Aoki asked what happened, and the moment I told him, I realized how badly I'd screwed up. He told me to look for you at a place you'd find comforting, which led me to the training center."

Abi nodded. "Give my thanks to Aoki, Matt."

I shook my head. Abi and Matt had an amazing connection. They always found a way to get to me whenever they got together.

He laughed. "I will. What brings you here?"

"We were taking a stroll around the bunker. Davon hasn't told me anything about tonight, so I'm following him around in the hopes that he'll let it slip." She rolled her eyes.

I elbowed her. "So that's the only reason you've stayed with me all this time?"

Matt smirked. "I would tell you, but the big guy wants to wait. What time are we leaving tonight?"

"I was thinking of meeting at my place around nine," I said.

Abi pursed her lips and crossed her arms, her features tense. "Either you tell me this second about tonight, or I'm not going anywhere."

"Oh, I nearly forgot. You know the people you told me to invite. They're coming. We're going to have a blast!" Matt winked at me.

Abi twisted around to leave, but I took her arm in mine and walked away with her with a wave at Matt.

"Hey, Davon," Matt said. "Make sure you're both presentable and prepared when we arrive. We don't want any shocks when we get there."

I grumbled while Abi laughed her ass off.

"You'll look fantastic in what I got you," I said as we neared Sarah's apartment.

She cocked her head and giggled. I could see the gears turning in her head.

"I know exactly where you're taking me. We're going to have a great time!"

I shook my head. "I really wanted it to be a surprise."

"Where else would I go with that dress? You're taking me to the club! I can't wait to see you dance."

God, give me strength. "Really? That's the first thing that comes to mind?"

She stopped in the middle of the hall. "And what else would I think about?" She rested her palm against my cheek, then kissed me sweetly while standing on her tiptoes. "Tonight we dance."

I was at a loss for words. She banged on Sarah's door. When Sarah opened it, I froze. I could still feel the force of her slap.

Sarah's gaze locked on me as she straightened her shoulders and pressed her lips together. "Hello, Abi. Davon."

Abi's mouth opened and closed quickly. She knew there was nothing she could do. Sarah clearly did not want me there.

I realized it was time to go and kissed Abi's cheek. "I'll see you tonight."

Chapter 35
Abi

"*August 2209: Our club's inauguration is this afternoon. Davon was very helpful in bringing in the booze and picking music to play. Some engineers created a lighting system and linked it to our power grid. Since the government had abolished all rights for leisure activities, we wanted to do this as a way of rebelling against the system. Being here filled my soul with joy. I'd be able to move here soon and bring my sisters with me. One more year...*" (Deborah Davis's journal)

I looked at Sarah after waving goodbye to Davon. "Hey there, sis."

"Come in." Her hug was longer than usual. "Thanks for coming."

We sat on the sofa.

"Abi, I asked you to come here so we could talk about what happened yesterday. I have faith in Connor. I'll give Davon the benefit of the doubt. But until I see proof, I'll keep suspecting him."

"But Sarah..."

She raised her hands. "Before you continue, I know you're together. It's no secret. That's why I know my opinion matters to you. I'm doing my best to offer you as much as I can, but please try to understand."

"I get what you're saying. I had my doubts, believe me, but I was there with him. He was destroyed. There's no way in hell he did it, and it's not because we're together since we weren't at the time."

I took her hands in mine and gazed into her emerald eyes. "I understand how tough it is to trust him, knowing who his father is. But there's a lot about him you don't know. What he's gone through. The way he lives to atone for his previous mistakes. He couldn't have sent that letter."

Sarah shook her head.

"We'll get the evidence you need, and we'll find whoever killed Carlos." I snarled.

I would clear his name and find out who the spy was.

"I'm sorry you can't understand what I'm saying. I wish things were different." She bit her lip. "Will you still come to see me after this?"

"Of course. You're my sister. Let's just not talk about it." I would never leave her. "Switching topics. Are you coming tonight?"

She avoided my gaze. "I want to, but I can't deal with Davon right now."

I fought the impulse to lash out at her, knowing she wouldn't come no matter what I said.

"He got me a dress, you know. I was wondering if you had any shoes that match with royal blue. Also, I'd love it if you could style my hair."

She went to her closet. "Here." She gave me a pair of black sandals adorned with gold thread. They were stunning. And ideal for dancing.

"Thanks." I put them on. They fit perfectly.

"You're welcome. Now, what to do with your hair?" She started playing with it, arranging it in different styles. "I can shorten it to add bangs. How does he like it?"

Her question caught me off guard. Knowing she cared put me at ease. Maybe we'd be able to get through this after all.

"Anything as long as it's loose. I like it that way too, but I wanted to try something new."

She tapped a finger against her chin. "How about a half-offside braid? That way it would be styled differently but still flow."

"Sounds perfect. Thanks. And sorry for earlier. I know you care enough to give us a chance, and that should be sufficient."

Her smile was tinged by a hint of sorrow and something else—regret. "You're my sister, and you're clearly in love with him. Your happiness means everything to me." There was something about the way she said it that touched my heart.

We went to my room to get ready. Sarah finished my hair at 8:50 p.m.

"All done," she said. "You look beautiful."

"Thank you. This means a lot to me." I wrapped my arms around her. "Are you sure you don't want to come?"

"I'm sure. And happy birthday." She withdrew and held my arms. "Now go. Have fun!"

Aoki and Matt's door opened right after Sarah left. Both looked fantastic. Matt was dressed in black ripped jeans. His muscles seemed ready to burst from his black shirt, which had a semi-open collar that exposed a little skin. A black sling held his right arm in place. Aoki, on the other hand, had donned gray narrow-fit slacks and a purple long-sleeved shirt. They made an attractive couple.

They whistled as they glanced at me.

"Whoa, Davon is going to die when he sees you. You look great!" Matt seized my hand and spun me around.

Aoki grinned. "He certainly will. I'm hoping he doesn't decide to lock you in his room and skip the club."

I laughed nervously.

"Come. Let's get your man," Matt said.

Aoki pounded on Davon's door.

"Coming!" he called.

A second later, the door opened. Davon was devastatingly gorgeous. He was dressed in dark-blue jeans and a black long-sleeved shirt that was rolled up to his elbows. His collar was partially open, revealing his pecs. The way the shirt and jeans hugged his body was deliciously sinful, every muscle straining against the fabric. He wore black boots and had his hair up in a man bun. His stubble made him look more handsome than usual.

He was studying me with his hands in his pockets but quickly grabbed my waist for a kiss. I surrendered to him as he angled me closer with his hand behind my neck, deepening it. For a moment, we were the only ones in the world.

"Aoki, you've got to step up your game. How about we leave them alone and return to our apartment?" Matt asked.

"That sounds like a great plan," Aoki said.

We paused and turned to see Aoki embracing Matt from behind, both grinning.

"Let's go!" Davon took my hand and led us to the club.

"Oh, by the way, Mark and Carol decided to go ahead and get us a table," Matt said.

How many people did they invite to this thing?

My body tingled with anticipation. As we made our way down hall E, I was almost bouncing with glee. The music's vibrations flooded the hall.

Once we entered, the club was bursting with people dancing to loud house music. The air was stuffy as Davon clutched my hand, trying to get us past the crowd. The music pounded through my body, urging me to hit the dance floor. Laser lights and smoke filled the space. Couples danced as if no one was watching. Their sensual moves filled the area.

"Matt!" someone said from a table to the right.

Matt bypassed me, and we followed him toward the voice. I tried to make out who was calling as we hurried to our table.

"Surprise!" they all said in unison.

My vision blurred. Carol, Mark, Jimmy, Maria, Tammy, and even Connor. They were all here. For me. A cake stood in the center of the table, surrounded by drinks.

I glanced at Davon, whose eyes glowed. Placing a hand on his chest, I tiptoed and whispered in his ear, "Thank you."

He gripped me tightly, tilting his head to reach my ear. "You deserve all of this and much more." His gentle tone made my heart skip a beat. He let me go. "Now go and say hi to your friends."

Everyone beamed at me.

I gave them a bright smile. "Thank you so much!"

Davon took a seat.

Jimmy came to me. "Happy twenty-first birthday."

I embraced him. "I'm glad you came."

He returned the hug, lifting me off the floor. "How could I have missed this?"

I smiled and stepped back.

Connor was the next to come and kissed me on the cheek. "Happy birthday."

"Thank you for being here."

He pressed his hand against my cheek. "I promise we'll all be together next time." His voice broke.

"Hey, Abi!" Carol hugged me from behind. "I can't wait for all of us to dance tonight! It's been a long time since we took the night off."

Davon drew a chair between Jimmy and him, and I sat between them. To have both put aside their differences to be with me on my birthday meant the world to me.

Congratulations continued as Aoki put a tequila bottle in front of me next to a small plate with lemon slices and a salt dispenser.

A club employee began filling up shot glasses.

Matt stood, glass in hand.

Davon snickered. "Here he goes."

"The usual toast speech," Aoki said.

"Davon and I set out two years ago to find a girl who'd gone missing. I didn't have much hope, but this guy over here seemed dead set on finding her. He was relentless in his pursuit, and no matter how many times I urged him to let up, he refused. We never found her. She found us. This brave woman defied all expectations, shocking us with her determination to live. She refused to give up." Matt lifted his glass, and everyone else did as well. "To my sister and my friend. To Abi!"

"To Abi!" they all said.

Tears streamed down my cheeks as Matt mouthed, "I love you, girl."

Everyone at the table licked their salted hands and drank, then took a lemon slice and bit into it. The tequila's heat dissipated as soon as I bit into the lemon.

I coughed.

"The second one goes down smoother." Davon served us both another one. "To us!"

I raised my glass to his. "To us!"

I kissed him, and we drank together.

We talked for a time before eating the cake and singing "Happy Birth-day." I hadn't had cake in a long time, and the amaretto flavor was delicious.

After about an hour, most headed for the bar or the dance floor.

Connor and Jimmy left in a rush, saying they needed to handle some-thing in command. We tried to follow, but Connor ordered us to stay and enjoy the night.

As Davon drew me toward the bar, Aoki and Matt remained at the table, immersed in conversation.

Carol and Mark had already left, and Maria and Tammy were drinking by the bar.

"Two whiskeys on the rocks," Davon said as the music became louder, the rhythm faster.

He grabbed the drinks and led me to the back, pushing a glass into my hand.

He placed me against the wall and leaned onto me. "You look ravishing. It took everything I had not to bring you back inside my place. Fuck the club." He kissed me after taking a sip of his drink.

My senses were overwhelmed by the smoky flavor of the whiskey combined with his heady taste.

He paused the kiss to murmur against my lips. "Drink up. I promised you a dance." He clinked his glass with mine, a sexy grin on his face.

I sipped my drink. Warmth spread throughout my body, and I relished the flavor. We began to move to the rhythm, allowing ourselves to be immersed in the music. All the bodies grinding against one another on the dance floor intensified the feeling.

As the music blasted through the room, I gulped my drink as quickly as I could, then took Davon's hand and led him to the dance floor.

When we reached the center, I raised my hands and danced. The ecstatic atmosphere compelled me to lose myself as he began touching and kissing me all over. I turned and swayed as he held my hips, every inch of his body pressing against my back. I twisted and trailed my hands from his chest to his abs, then grabbed his waist and drew him closer. I kissed him passionately as we moved against each other. The entire world vanished in that moment, and it was just the two of us.

I looked over at our table. Matt and Aoki were kissing, then Aoki whispered something into Matt's ear. They moved toward us.

Matt winked at me. "We're leaving."

I wasn't sure how long we danced, locked in our own little world, but I savored every moment.

Then the sirens went off.

Chapter 36

Abi

"*March 2210: All our bunkers were completed at last after years of hard work. This was a top priority for the council, to get everything up and running. In six months, all would be ready to carry out our plan and get Abigail and Sarah out of the city.*" *(Deborah Davis's journal)*

The whistles! They're coming!

Loud sirens blasted all around us.

No. I shook my head violently. I'm at the bunker.

People kept pushing me, and I crumpled to the floor and covered my head.

Where's Davon?

Screams surrounded me as I tried to get up. I couldn't breathe. The pressure in my chest built until my vision blurred. Someone kicked my thigh, and I cried out in agony as intense pain shot through my side. Tears slid down my face, but I kept searching. I had to find him.

"Abi!"

My heart hammered against my ribcage. It was him.

"Davon?" I stood at last, trying to get my breathing under control, and glanced around but couldn't see a thing. "I'm here!"

Darkness, smoke, lights, and music mixed with the piercing sound of the sirens drove my senses into overload. "Where are you?"

A strong body bumped into me. "Come on," he yelled.

We ran to take cover. My back hit the wall, and Davon covered me, protecting me as people continued running by us.

His muscles bunched up against my hands as I held on to his biceps.

"Are you hurt?" he said into my ear.

The pain was excruciating, but I kept my voice calm. "I'm okay. And you?"

He sighed and pulled me closer. "I'm good. We need to get out of here." He took a step back and kept me close.

Some people fled to the club's exit, while others, like us, sought refuge in the vacant areas.

"What's happening? Is it an attack?" I trembled in his arms.

"That siren signals a lockdown." Davon's gaze darted across the room. "Something terrible must have happened for Connor to sound them. Stay close to me. We're going to command."

He took my hand, and we ran to the exit. My leg still burned from the kick, but I pushed forward. The club was nearly empty at this point. We hurried into the common area.

Soldiers attempted to keep order, helping people get by. Despite their efforts, there was chaos everywhere.

We skimmed the walls, avoiding the crowd, and soon reached hall F. We bumped into Aoki.

"What the hell are you doing here?"

Matt ignored Davon as he opened the infirmary.

"You're going to fuck up your arm."

People who waited outside, injured in the commotion, started filtering in.

Aoki grabbed Davon's arm. "Let him be. He said he needed to come. To assist Rachel, Mary, and Dr. Lewis. There was no stopping him, so I brought him here. Do you know what's going on?"

Davon shook his head. "No, we're on our way to command. I'll let you know as soon as I talk to Connor."

We rushed past them. Soldiers were entering the training center.

Maria, still in her leather dress, screamed orders. "Get your weapons, and be ready. We'll await General Harris's orders inside." She pointed at two soldiers, one of them Mark, who still wore the same clothes from the club. "Go to the exits. Check if they're secure."

A single soldier with a long gun stood vigil as we proceeded through the generator room.

The door to the computer room was slightly open, and there was noise within.

My lungs burned, my chest close to bursting as we dashed inside command. Connor stood behind Nina, who hastily typed on her keyboard in her pink pj's. Jimmy was next to Connor, his gaze fixed on the footage displayed on Nina's three monitors.

Davon ran to Connor's side, and I followed. Among the more than twenty camera feeds, a couple of black squares stood out.

Connor punched the desk, making Nina jump. "There's no footage? Fuck."

"What the fuck's going on?" Davon asked.

"Let's go into my office. I'll explain everything." Connor took the lead, with Davon close behind.

Jimmy grabbed my arm. "Are you okay?"

I nodded. "What happened?"

He shook his head and lowered his gaze. "Let's go inside."

He took my hand and brought me to Connor's office, where Davon was already deep in conversation with him. I was limping.

Davon gave me a quizzical look.

"I'm all right," I mouthed.

Connor told him something I couldn't make out, and Davon's expression darkened.

"Killed? How did you discover the body?" Davon's voice sounded frantic.

"What? Someone was killed?" I yelled.

The room shrank around me.

Jimmy squeezed my hand. "A maintenance worker was doing his rounds and found the body in the generator room."

Davon's fiery gaze shifted to him. "Who's the victim?"

Jimmy let out a loud exhale. "Richard."

Davon sagged back into a chair, and I gasped.

The boy he saved.

We went over the details, and Connor escorted us into the generator room. A guard remained outside.

The kid was lying on the floor, his bulging eyes bloodshot. Dark bruises covered his neck.

Connor crouched behind him. "We believe Richard was strangled, but we'll know for sure after the autopsy."

The spy had made their first kill. It was a gruesome picture, one that would stay with me forever. Whatever Richard knew died with him.

I stepped back and bumped into Davon. My chest tightened as the vision of Jacob lying dead on the ground raced through my head.

"Stay strong, love," Davon murmured.

Connor started giving orders. "Jimmy, gather the runners, and inform them of what happened. As for the rest of the community, we'll explain this happened near the bunker and that security measures were put in place as a precaution. Each citizen will be questioned. We need to know if Richard was seen by anyone before he was killed."

Jimmy took a challenging stance. "I think we should tell everyone the truth. How can we let the citizens move freely with an assassin on the loose?"

I choked down my rising fear. Jimmy didn't know about the letter pointing to Davon as a traitor or the scheme to get him out. Connor feared for Davon's safety, worried Jimmy wouldn't believe his innocence and could act rashly once he knew about it. Once Davon was arrested and safe behind bars, Connor would tell him about the plan, and, hopefully, he would understand.

"I agree with Jimmy. Until we have more information, we need to keep everyone safe," Davon said.

Connor pinched his eyebrows together. "Okay, we'll make an announcement tomorrow. Effective immediately, no one is to enter or exit the bunker unless ordered by us."

Jimmy pushed his shoulders back. "Thank you, General. After the announcement, I'll gather my most trusted runners to begin interrogations. Will that be all?"

"Yes, Captain. You're dismissed."

Jimmy fixed his gaze on Davon. "Keep her safe."

Davon nodded, and Jimmy exited the room.

Connor sighed, rubbing his brow. "Davon, do you know what this means?"

A look passed between them, and I understood.

I shook Davon. "You can't do it. You can't take the blame."

Davon shut his eyes. His throat bobbed as he swallowed.

"No. Please. There's no way you can come back from murder," I said.

Connor's eyes narrowed. "Then, whatever it takes, we have to find the spy."

Richard lay on the floor. He stared at me, his brown eyes wide as two words escaped his mouth: "Find them."

I snapped my eyes open, shaken by the nightmare.

We came back to Davon's apartment at 4:00 a.m. after Connor told us we would regroup for breakfast at his office. There was too much to do and not enough time.

As I slept in Davon's arms, the one thought that crossed my mind was his taking all the blame and being unable to return to us. The fear took root deep inside me as soon as I learned he'd be charged with treason and murder.

His breathing paused for a second, and he hugged me against his chest.

"Talk to me, baby." He massaged my neck, unknotting all the pent-up stress I held there.

I couldn't talk. My emotions were too close to the surface.

He turned me. As our gazes connected, my tears dropped. He kissed them away, then pushed his lips to my mouth in a tender, caring kiss.

"I'm hurting too, love. I'm not sure if the danger inside is worse than the danger outside."

He shed a single tear, then another. He sobbed silently and leaned toward me, putting his head on my belly.

The next morning, we arrived at the training center before anybody else. We danced around each other, slicing and stabbing, releasing our rage from the night before. The more we trained, the more our motions grew in rhythm, my body fluidly responding to his attacks. After an hour of sparring, Davon led me outside through the hidden exit in the command center. Connor had cleared us last night.

A cool wind met us as we reached the summit. We faced the city as we'd done numerous times since we first met.

Davon held my hand. "We'll breach their defenses and fight together till we destroy them. We'll get through it and bring them to their knees for what they've done."

As we stood there, facing our enemy, I knew we'd make it. We'd do it together.

Connor waited for us with three mugs of coffee and some donuts. He had multiple letters in front of him and was searching through a logbook, writing down names on a list. He lifted a finger to ask for a moment.

"We're starting with people who have arrived in the past three years, but there's still a chance it's someone who's been with us longer. Let's hope that's not the case." He closed the logbook and narrowed his eyes. "We still have no idea how this was done. Why was Richard in the generator room? Why did the spy kill him? The assembly will be hell. I hope you're ready. We haven't been in a situation like this since the import base attack."

Davon leaned forward, one elbow on his knee, his other hand resting on the desk. "I propose giving them something to focus on other than the murder. Maybe tell them we'll start preparing for an offensive attack. That we've put together a team to infiltrate the administration and begin laying the groundwork for the real battle. Most here are soldiers and will be able to cope with the threat in that way. We need only to keep the lockdown for two more days. Once they have the culprit, everything will be better, and we can move forward with the plan."

"You're really going to make Davon take the blame for Richard?" I asked.

"There's no other option. We must take steps to restore people's sense of safety. If the spy believes we suspect Davon, discovering them will be easy. I'm convinced they will take the chance and attempt to enter the system." Connor interlaced his fingers on the desk. "I understand how difficult this is for you, but you won't be alone, and Davon can handle it."

"I wanted to talk about that Connor," Davon said. "I want to take Abi with me."

My heart skipped a beat.

Connor's eyes widened. "I don't think that's a good idea."

Davon clasped my hand. "I'm not leaving her here after yesterday's attack. She's too close to me, and the spy is aware of it. She'll be their next target."

As we exchanged glances, Connor exhaled loudly. "I see what you're saying. But know that she, like you, will be viewed as a traitor. We'll need to give her a new identity. I'm sure Nina can find a way. Maybe she's your liaison in the city. Your informant." His gaze darted between us. "Are you prepared to deal with that?"

Davon squeezed my hand.

I nodded without taking my eyes away from him. "I am."

"Then it's done. You'll help him flee and go with him into Promissa. I'll tell Nina to begin working on your profile and paperwork right away. As for today, I need you both to deliver these letters to the bunkers ASAP." He passed us four letters. "They're addressed to each of the councilmembers. Inside I detail orders to get everything ready for an imminent attack. After you finish in the bunkers, please go to the dead drop near the city."

Connor gave a sealed packet to Davon. "You're going to leave this in there. It's notifying our spies about our plan. It's coded, and, hopefully, if it's intercepted by an NWG agent, they won't break it since I used our initial cypher. The one we created when we first formed the rebel group. You know that one isn't in any book, and it's only taught to our most trusted spies."

Davon slipped the letters and the envelope into his jacket. "We'll get this there before the end of the day."

"The assembly will begin in the late afternoon. Be here by five. I want you by my side." Connor went to the door.

"Understood," Davon said.

We followed him and stepped outside.

"Please be careful out there," Connor said.

I glanced back at him. "We will."

Chapter 37

Abi

"*April 2210: Davon was training our armed forces with Connor. Their goal—to take down the regime. We didn't know how long it would take for us to be ready, but we were positioning our pieces. We needed numbers, but most of all, we needed a strategy.*" (Deborah Davis's journal)

We left Janus Peak after donning our vests and selecting our weapons. It would take the entire morning and part of the afternoon to get the letters to each bunker, and we hoped to arrive on time.

"Why didn't you tell me earlier? About me going with you," I asked as Davon led the way.

He continued walking. "Last night, I ran through all possible scenarios, and in most of them, you would be in danger. At least with me, I'll be able to protect you."

I shook my head. "Don't take this the wrong way 'cause I'm ecstatic to come with you. But I've already told you I don't need your protection. I need you to focus on completing the mission. I want to be there for you but as support. Don't think I'll be just sitting at your place as you work your ass off. Once we go back, I'll talk to Connor about it. I want to make myself useful."

He stopped in his tracks. "Okay. But I'm your superior on this assignment. You'll obey my commands. Understood?"

I blinked. I realized what he meant now that I was a soldier. "I do."

Our first stop was the import, construction, and storage bunker, which was thirty miles away from the city, five from us. I gave Davon a questioning glance at the military vehicles transporting materials.

Davon entered a security code in a hatch. "At first, this bunker was mostly used for smuggling produce from the city, but we're now completely self-sufficient. Now they're in charge of constructing everything the communities require. All the vehicles and weaponry you see were already inside the bunkers when we discovered them. They were used long ago during wars by our ancestors. We fixed them so they're energy efficient and have been using them ever since."

A massive man approached and shook Davon's hand. He was bald with a full auburn beard that was graying in some spots. I straightened as he studied me.

"General Niles, what brings you out here?" he said.

"Good to see you, Seth. This is Abigail Davis. As to why we're here, Connor sent us. Something happened," Davon said.

"Nice to meet you, Miss Davis."

I shook his hand. "Please call me Abi."

He gave a nod. "Please come in. Let's go to my office and talk privately."

We followed him down a wide hall with rooms on either side. It was a long walk, and it took us maybe five minutes to come across what appeared to be a massive storage facility.

The deafening sounds of the equipment filled the room. People on one side worked on wood and metal. At the far end of the enormous space was a storage area filled with furniture, tools, and electronics. To the right was a garage with Hummers and motorcycles.

We entered an office with a large table in the center and several maps placed on top. Two desks were positioned in opposite corners of the room.

At the left desk, a woman was going over some files. Her gaze locked on Davon. Her grin made my stomach twist into knots.

As jealousy took root in my mind, I couldn't help but think something had happened between them.

"Hello, Katherine. This is Abigail Davis," Davon said.

Tall and powerful with beautiful ebony skin, she gave him a heartbreaking smile as she stood. Her black hair was shaved short, emphasizing her symmetrical facial features. Her hazel eyes never left Davon. She disregarded me and kissed him on the cheek, stroking his arm.

I tensed and clenched my fists by my sides. Rage heated my blood as I imagined yelling at her to get her hands off him.

Davon took my hand, making it clear we were together. She stared at our clasped hands and surveyed me with a disdainful look.

"I've missed you, Davon. It's been too long." Her remarks held more weight than she let on.

"A lot has changed in the last two years," Davon said, composed as always. "Matt and I found Abi. She's been with us for about a month, training to join our military forces."

"It's a pleasure to meet you, Miss Davis. I hope you find our community to your liking." Her fake smile made my blood boil.

Two could play this game. I grinned. "Same here, Miss...?"

"*Ms.* Williams. Katherine Williams, councilmember." She looked at Davon as if I didn't exist. "If you're here, something must have happened."

Davon nodded and reached inside his jacket for the letter. "This is addressed to you. Orders from Connor. A new development is forcing us to act sooner than we anticipated."

Katherine stiffened as she read it. "A spy? Inside Janus Peak?"

Seth took the letter. "Sad news indeed. Wasn't he the young runner in training?"

Davon dipped his head. "Yeah. We took him in about a month ago."

Seth frowned. "Have you considered the possibility that he may have been working with the spy?"

"We don't have any concrete evidence. Maybe he was in the wrong place at the wrong time. Jimmy is conducting interrogations as we speak."

"We'll begin preparations. Please inform General Harris we'll be ready for whatever is needed." He slid the letter into his pocket.

Katherine crossed her arms. "We've already begun organizing, and I was about to send a report to General Harris. I'd like to hear your thoughts on it."

"Sure. I'll take a look at it," Davon said.

Katherine returned to her desk.

Davon pulled me aside. "I know you have some questions. Please have faith in me. We're in this together."

Were they previously in a relationship? The thought made my stomach turn. He never mentioned her to me, only Elaine.

Could she be one of his lovers? Aoki did mention he had been with women, just nothing serious.

I couldn't help it as I shifted my gaze to her, then back to Davon.

"Please trust me," he said.

Seth approached me. "If you want, I can show you around while they work."

I released Davon's hand. "Go do your thing."

"Thank you, Seth. We'll keep it brief, as we're on a tight schedule." Davon stared at me for a moment, then went to Katherine's desk.

I followed Seth out but not without one last glance. Davon stood next to Katherine, going through her paperwork.

"Ms. Williams and I are in charge of this modest community. She oversees logistics, while I supervise the mechanical and civil engineering area."

As we approached the workshop, he handed me ear and eye protection. The room was filled with approximately twenty stations where people worked on various materials. Some with circuitry and motors, others on wood and metal. We exited the area and removed our protective gear.

"What are they working on?" I asked.

"Here we build and repair generators for the energy bunker. Others come from the science and technology bunker and are teaching workers how to build computer systems. We need better communications for the war to come and as many able hands as possible."

"The war to come…" I said, catching the finality of his words.

"Davon and I have been friends for a long time, and most of us share his views on the inevitability of war. All the councilmembers respect him, and even if he denies it, we regard him as one of our leaders. We respect and follow General Harris's rules and have been waiting for this moment, for his orders. We've been moving forward as needed, mobilizing people and resources."

I gritted my teeth. "I'm glad it's happening at last. We need to take control back. So many suffer out there, trapped in the system."

He focused his blue eyes on me. "How was it out there?" His tone was solemn.

A torrent of memories rushed through my head. I closed my eyes and inhaled. "It was hell."

"I'm sorry." Seth moved closer to me. "I lost my twin sister, Sissy, on a mission five years ago. As we helped a group of escapees flee, a patrol ambushed us and shot her down. I wanted to go back, but it was too risky for the others, so I kept going. Not a day goes by without my thinking about her. I don't even know if she made it."

I grasped his hand, understanding his grief. "If she's still alive, we'll get her back. I'll make sure of it."

He studied me for a moment, then straightened. "Thank you."

He showed me the garage and storage room. Some Hummers were equipped with bazookas and were being loaded with even more weapons.

"General Harris began transporting weaponry from the command center to the other bunkers two days ago. We oversee their mobilization. He's sending troops over to help our military cover more ground."

Dozens of vehicles were being filled with weapons.

"It's actually happening," I said.

"There's a shipment going out to the science and tech bunker. Let's go see Davon. Maybe you can hitch a ride and get there faster."

I followed him toward the office, but some workers called him as we were about to enter.

"It seems I'm needed elsewhere, but please tell the general to get a ride up there. It'll save you some time." He took both my hands in his. "It was a pleasure to meet you, and you're welcome here anytime."

I hesitated by the door at the sound of Davon's raised voice.

"I already told you I'm with Abi now. What we had is over."

Someone shuffled.

"But we shared so much," a seductive voice said. "Come on. Don't tell me that little girl can make you feel as I did. You know you can take me any way you want to. Why stop when she doesn't need to know?"

My blood boiled. I clenched my fist around the doorknob, ready to give her hell.

"You're right in one aspect—she doesn't compare to you."

I froze.

"She's much more than you ever could be. I won't tolerate you ever treating her like you did today. We're over and will never go back to those times. Keep that in mind, and don't ever bring it up again. You'll treat her with respect."

I opened the door. She was standing just a foot away from him.

He glanced my way and walked toward me, then pulled me into a quick kiss. "Let's get out of here."

Her eyes were frigid as I shot a venomous glare at her. She would not give up on Davon. I was sure of it.

We walked out of the office and stood outside.

"How much did you hear?" he said.

"All I needed to."

He dipped his chin. "Before I left to find you, Katherine and I were lovers. That's all. There was no emotion involved. You must believe me."

"How long were you together?" I asked, my tone serious.

He took my chin in his palm. "That's not important."

"How long?" I raised my voice. I wanted answers.

He lowered his gaze. "A year."

I inhaled as the reality of their situation set in. One year was a long time.

He grimaced. "We ended things way before I left. I never loved her, and we were never officially together. We just fooled around, nothing else. I was clear with her from the beginning. We were just two consenting adults having a good time."

I moved away from him. Nausea stirred in my belly. Would he do the same to me?

He gripped my hip and drew me to him. "I adore you. I've never felt this way about anyone in my life. You have to believe me."

I covered his cheek with my hand and stared deeply into his dark eyes. There was no deception in his words.

"Okay. Let's get out of here."

We hitched a ride and reached the science and technology bunker in no time. We were met outside by soldiers who took the cargo inside.

"General Niles." A soldier saluted as we walked toward the entrance.

"At ease, Major General Li. Are Simmons and Hernandez around?" Davon asked.

"They're at the labs overlooking the pharmaceutical area. I can take you there." He was shorter than Davon by maybe half a foot and had Aoki's build. A longsword with an exquisite jade hilt hung by his side.

"There's no need. I know my way. By the way, Yuxuan, meet Abigail Davis."

"So it's true. You found her." He gave me a slight bow. "An honor to make your acquaintance. Councilmember Davis was always talking about you."

I shook his hand. "Thank you, Major General Li."

"Please call me Yuxuan. Deb's family, and that makes you the same."

My breath hitched at hearing this from a man I just met. "Thank you."

As we went inside the bunker, Davon said, "Yuxuan works with us at the peak, but he was sent here to train more soldiers. He's an honorable and noble man, sworn to protect our people by any means necessary. He was very close to Deb. Did you see his weapon?"

It was a beautifully crafted sword. "I did. I've never seen one like that before."

"That's a *jian*, a double-edged Chinese blade. Li's family was of Chinese ancestry, and he inherited that family heirloom. He's a black belt in kung fu and teaches the martial art to the soldiers who are interested. He was my teacher." Davon straightened, a proud smile on his face.

I frowned. How did such a warrior end up here? "How long have you two known each other?"

"Well, that's an interesting story. About six years ago, we found him living inside this bunker. He fought in the wars and lost his family along the way. He was alone, and his spirit was broken. We never knew where he came from. His past continues to be a mystery, but he did tell me about his sword, knowing my profound interest in blades. After meeting us, he decided to help us create our dream and became a great aid in building our army."

To be alone without hope, waiting for someone to find you while the world was restructured. A profound sense of kinship grew in me as I twisted to see Yuxuan outside, giving orders to the soldiers. How much had he lost?

Davon opened a double door at the end of the hall to a room bustling with people. All wore white lab coats and moved around different hallways. He took my hand as we headed to the right and went through another door into a laboratory full of science equipment.

In the back room, there was a small woman, maybe in her fifties. Her red hair was tied up in a ponytail, and she peered through a microscope.

Davon, still holding my hand, cleared his throat.

She jumped in surprise and adjusted her glasses. "Hey, Davon, great to see you!" She stood and stared at our clasped hands. "At last… You got yourself a girl. I'm glad!"

She came to me, her energy infectious. "You got yourself a hunk and a good man. Don't let go of him. He's a treasure!"

Davon grinned. "Jess, you exaggerate. This is Abigail Davis."

Her eyes widened. "I heard you'd found her. I can see the resemblance."

"How's everything going?" Davon asked, changing the topic.

"You know, same as always. Finding new ways to care for our people. Did you come here to show me your girl?"

He chuckled. "No, Jess, I come with orders from Connor."

Her brow wrinkled. "Is it finally happening?"

Davon handed her the letter.

She perused it. "This is terrible, but we all knew it would happen eventually. Let me get Michael."

She left the room for a few moments and returned with a man around Davon's age. He had tanned skin, and his dark hair and stubble resembled Davon's, except his hair was trimmed short.

"Davon!" They clasped forearms and hugged. "Hey, man. How are you? These past few weeks have been hell."

"I'm okay. Thanks." Davon gave him an appreciative nod.

Michael approached me. "Jess told me you're Abigail. I'm sorry you came back to find such an impossible situation."

I shrugged. "Don't worry. This is just how the world is."

He patted Davon's back. "Tell Connor he can count on us."

"Thank you."

"Are you visiting all of the bunkers?" Michael asked.

"Yes. Why?" Davon asked.

Michael removed a box from a drawer, then came to us. "I'd owe you one if you could give this to Dani. I won't be able to visit, and I'm afraid we won't be seeing each other for some time."

"Sure, man. I thought you would've moved in together by now." Davon placed the gift and note in his backpack.

"We thought about it, but we're both too attached to our jobs to leave, so we stuck with the long-distance relationship. Normally, she spends a week here, and I go over there for another week, but things have been hectic, and it's becoming more difficult by the day." He glanced down at his empty hands.

"I'll take it over to her and explain." He gripped Michael's hand. "See you later."

Jess hugged Davon. "It was great to see you. Take care out there."

We moved to leave and quickly reached the threshold.

When we left the room, Davon briefly covered his face with his hands before pulling them away. His arms dropped to his sides.

His eyes were glazed. I wanted to reach for him, to comfort him, but he took a deep breath and walked away. That's when I realized why Connor had sent us on this mission—so Davon could say goodbye to his friends.

Chapter 38

Davon

Fuck. This was hard. It wasn't until I was leaving Jess and Michael's bunker that it hit me. This might be the last time I saw them before the war to come. These people who helped me build this system and with whom I had an unshakable bond were preparing for war.

How many lives would be lost while taking the city? How long would it be until we saw each other again, knowing what my future held?

Abi gripped my hand as we exited, and we made our way to the farming and engineering bunker.

"Can we stop for a moment?" She rested her back against a tree, gripping her chest. Her respiration was short and quick, her eyes unfocused. "I...I can't..."

I gave her space and held her at arm's length. "I think you're having a panic attack. Breathe with me. Slow and steady."

We both sank to the ground as she began to weep.

"It's just...too much. All of this, people...and the war to come." Her tears fell as she shook uncontrollably.

My ribs seemed too tight as I held her quivering body, my own thoughts growing dark.

What if we didn't catch the spy? Would I ever be able to see my family again?

My throat burned at the prospect of losing everything I'd worked for. I hadn't had time to truly think about it, to grasp the finality of it all.

We sat on the forest floor, staring at the sky, until her breathing calmed. Her hair was tangled and wild, her eyes a soft hue of green as the light struck them.

"Thank you," she said. "I love you."

I kissed her slowly. "You're my everything."

We ate a quick lunch and continued on our way, reaching the next bunker in the early afternoon.

Steven greeted us and nodded after reading Connor's orders. He was one of the most devoted individuals I'd ever met. Whatever was asked of him, he would do. No questions asked.

Abi was curious, and he took us on a tour of the laboratories. He explained the cell culture process used to grow and mature animal cells, eliminating the need to raise farm animals. She was entranced by the science behind it.

We moved on to the subterranean farms that produced fresh grains and vegetables. Steven explained how by using hydroponic technology and LED lighting powered by our own renewable solar energy grid, they could produce fresh food.

The bunker's vertical farm was equivalent to two and a half acres and produced more than fifty harvests per year. The process was soil free and used less water than outdoor farms. It was carbon neutral and used no pesticides.

What Steven and Danielle did here was amazing. We reached Dani's office to find her engrossed in paperwork as usual. She managed the distribution of food and clothes, so her work never dwindled.

Steven alerted her to our presence as we approached. "Dani, Davon and Abigail Davis are here to see you."

She pushed her chair back to stand. "Davon! It's been too long." She hugged me tightly, as was her habit.

I returned her embrace, grinning. This woman, like Matt, brightened every room she entered.

She grasped Abi's hands. "Happy to meet you. Can I call you Abi? Davon told me all about you. I'm glad he finally found someone."

I bit back a laugh. Dani was a free spirit and said exactly what she felt, no filter.

Steven widened his eyes and looked between us.

Abi blinked. "Um, sure. Nice to meet you too."

The truth was I had written Dani a letter to let her know I was back and to tell her about Abi. Knowing her, she must have yelled with joy when she read it. She was always pushing me to get into a relationship, concerned I was such a loner.

"Speaking of relationships." I offered her the box from Michael. "Here you go. This is from Michael."

She ripped the paper wrapping and gave a dreamy sigh as she saw its contents. "He's such a romantic."

I chuckled and shook my head. I'd miss her terribly.

Steven gave Dani the note.

"What's this?" After reading it, her whole demeanor shifted. "Fuck." She handed it back to Steven. "We'll make do. Are you okay?"

Dani knew everything about my father and my life before this. She knew that even though I wanted all he'd constructed destroyed, there was a glimmer of hope in a dark corner of my soul. A belief that my father would fix things. That this could all be settled without going to war.

"We all knew it would come to this," I said.

She squeezed my arm. "If you need anything, I'm here. Come over next week. I'll make your favorite chicken Alfredo dish." She glanced at Abi. "You can come too. I can't wait to get to know you better."

My throat ached as I swallowed my tears. "Sure. We'll be here."

"I'll let you know as soon as I set the date." She hugged me once more. "I'll see you then."

I took deep breaths to keep my tears from falling.

Abi held my hand, and we walked away quietly.

The energy bunker was our last visit. Councilmember Faez received us. He managed the manufacture of organic solar cell leaves, while DeLuca oversaw the energy collection, conversion, and grid connection. It was a complicated system, but it was one of the most crucial. They were also in charge of the underground water system, making sure everything was in working order.

Faez's and DeLuca's relationship with me was entirely professional. They saw me as their general and went about their business. Both extremely intelligent and quiet, they spent most of their time secluded in their laboratories.

They agreed to begin preparations immediately after reading the letter.

It was 1:00 p.m. when we left the bunker.

"All right, Abi. We'll take the package to the dead drop and turn back."

The dead drop was roughly seven miles outside of Promissa. I opened the underground hatch, swiping the dirt away, to find a note. Another one addressed to my father from me...

My heart nearly stopped as I read it:

Dad,

I found the last rebel checkpoint on the western side of the city's perimeter. Kimberly Milton and David Martinez, according to my informant, are guarding this location. Be aware one of them is a sniper and will be on the lookout for an attack.

Davon

My hands shook as I struggled to keep my control from slipping.

Abi's eyes were wide. "What? What does it say?"

It was in the NWG's cypher, so she couldn't read what was written.

I shook my head. "It's a letter. From me to my father."

"I don't understand. Wasn't Connor supposed to watch for these?"

I folded the letter. "I'm lost here. We need to go back to command."

I was about to place the parcel into the hatch when footsteps sounded from all around us. I quickly slid the packet back into my rucksack along with the letter I discovered.

This was one of several dead drops used to deliver information to our people in Promissa. Spies delivered messages addressed to my father to a government time drop on the city's outskirts. Someone must have followed one of them into the forest.

The location was compromised.

My stomach dropped, and I pulled up my hoodie to cover my face.

"Get your gun out. There may be soldiers." I shook Abi's shoulders. "Listen to me. We need to get back into the forest. You see movement, you shoot. Understood?"

Her face flushed, she nodded and removed her firearm from the holster. We began moving toward the trees.

"Stay right where you are!" a soldier said from behind us.

Others came out of the foliage.

"Run!" I yelled.

We raced toward the forest, dodging as soldiers emerged from all sides, their bullets creating cracks in the trees around us.

A man approached from the left and knocked Abi down. As he tried to restrain her, she clawed at him, thrashing like a wild beast.

I shot him in the head without blinking and helped her up.

She shoved me to the side and fired at a man coming for me. Three shots until she hit him in the head. He fell, dead.

The bullets kept coming as we darted to the right toward an opening. My lungs burned from the exertion.

Abi cried out.

I stopped and saw her blood-stained hands. She clutched her side.

No. Not again. I couldn't lose her, not like this.

A heartbeat later, I pulled her shirt up to see where it hit, but she smacked my hand.

"It's just a graze. We need to keep going." She ran ahead of me.

I'd have to trust her. With no time to lose, we went uphill until we reached a cliff. We had no escape, and the soldiers were right on our tails.

I crouched. "We need to make our way down."

Abi followed suit. "Is it safe?"

"We have no other option."

It was a steep drop, and my legs stung as the jagged rocks scratched me. I slipped, but I gripped the edge of a rock and kept going down. Abi was following in my footsteps. My feet touched the ground. There was a small rock platform hidden inside the mountain.

I waited for Abi, but she slipped just as she was about to reach me. I slid to the edge and grabbed her arms, her legs swinging in midair. She gazed over the edge.

"Don't look down. Focus on me." My heart was racing, and her hand was sliding.

Please God.

"Davon?" She could hardly focus on me, her eyes wide in terror.

"Abi, I need you to help me. See if you can reach the wall. I won't let you fall."

I was on the verge of losing her, but I kept holding on even as my limbs began to hurt from fatigue.

She swung for a few seconds until her feet struck the wall and she lifted herself toward me. Adrenaline surged through me, and I yanked her up with all my strength until she was in my arms. We hugged and moved within the mountain, both of us out of breath.

"Fuck, I thought I'd lose you." I pulled her to me and kissed her fiercely, clinging to her as if my life depended on it.

"They must be nearby! Search the area!" a soldier said.

We scrambled back.

As the footsteps faded, I lifted Abi's shirt. It was only a graze. I sighed in relief, then cleaned and bandaged the wound as best I could.

She looked up. "What are we going to do?"

"We're going to stay here for a while. They'll surely continue searching till nightfall and then go back to the city." I knew how they worked. They'd get backup and expand their perimeter. This area was lost.

She nodded.

My chest swelled with pride. "Thanks for saving my ass out there."

The corner of her mouth curved up. "Same here. We make a pretty good team."

"We definitely do." I wrapped my arm around her. "We'll be just fine out there."

We stayed there till nightfall. I wouldn't risk it until I was sure they were gone. I climbed and searched the area before throwing a rope to bring Abi up.

We rushed back, desperate for the warmth of the bunker. We had a long way to go.

Hours later, we arrived at the peak and began our ascent. Footsteps crunched ahead of us, and we came to a halt. I took a defensive stance with my khukuri and Abi with her trench knife.

"Abi?" a voice said.

Abi shifted around me. "Jimmy?"

He emerged from behind a tree, and Abi threw herself at him. He embraced her and closed his eyes.

I tightened my jaw as he held her, but their relationship was strong. I could tell she needed him as well.

As I approached them, I sheathed my blade.

Jimmy's gaze darted from Abi's bloodied shirt to me. "What happened? We've been searching for hours."

I moved closer. "We were surrounded by soldiers as we attempted to leave a packet at the dead drop. A bullet grazed her abdomen, but she'll be okay. We hid until we were certain they'd left." I took Abi's hand and continued our ascent.

We arrived at command just before midnight.

Sarah was the first to meet us, with Connor close behind.

With a gasp, Sarah snatched Abi's hand. "What happened? You're hurt."

Abi shook her head. "It's nothing. Soldiers attacked us. A bullet grazed my side, but Davon already took care of it."

Sarah touched Abi's face. "You should have someone at the infirmary look at it."

Connor frowned at me. "Soldiers? Where?"

"They were waiting for us at the dead drop. We fought our way into the forest, taking two down on our way," I said.

"Davon shot one, and I got the other. We ran and hid on a hillside," Abi said.

Connor glanced between us, then at Jimmy. "Call your runners back for the night. Tomorrow morning I'll send soldiers out there to guard the perimeter. That was a close call."

With a reassuring smile to Abi, Jimmy left.

Sarah narrowed her eyes at me. "What happened out there?"

I ground my teeth. "What are you implying?"

She glared at me. "Exactly what you're thinking. After all, you're a Niles." Her words carried venom.

I clenched my jaw. "What the hell is wrong with you? You think I'd do this to her? I love her, for fuck's sake, and I almost lost her tonight." My vision blurred.

Eyes blazing, Abi stepped between us. "We were there together. He nearly got killed. You need to stop this nonsense."

"Nonsense?" She crossed her arms and pursed her lips. "I don't believe a word he's saying." She glowered at Connor. "And you! How could you send her with him without asking me?"

Connor rubbed his brow. "Listen very carefully. You must deal with whatever suspicion you have toward Davon. Don't you think if he wanted to hurt her, he would've done it by now? Abi's her own person, and she can make her own decisions."

Sarah scowled. "I don't have to trust him. I can't wait for him to leave. You'll see. When we're attacked, he'll be the reason. The one who set us up."

Abi clenched her fists.

I took her hand. "Let her be."

She twisted toward me. "She has no right to act like this."

I sighed, knowing she wouldn't let it go.

Abi moved closer to Sarah until she was only a few inches away. "I've been patient, but I'm done. Do you honestly believe I'd be standing here if not for him? When I found them in the city, I was as good as dead. He brought me back, fighting his way to get me to safety. Tonight he shot the soldier who attacked me. He's been there for me since the beginning. How can you think so lowly of him? Just because of his name..." Her nostrils flared as she took a decisive step back. "And, just so you know, I'm leaving with him."

I flinched as she said it, bracing for her sister's outburst.

"What?" Sarah shouted, her chest heaving. "You're not going anywhere with him. It's a trap."

Abi grabbed my hand. "I'm going, and that's final."

"What the hell?" Sarah shifted her gaze to Connor. "Did you know about this?"

Connor crossed his arms. "I did. And, once again, it's her decision. They're both adults."

Sarah growled. "I'm not allowing you to leave, Abi."

Abi's grip on my hand tightened as she took a sideways stride into the hall, avoiding Sarah. "Watch me!"

We walked away without looking back.

Chapter 39

Abi

"October 2210: This will be my last note, as we're preparing to extract Abi from the city. She turns eighteen in a week, and I need to get her out before the advancement ceremony. She was accepted into an advanced facility to work with the elites. I couldn't accept that or let the government claim her." (Deborah Davis's journal)

While tending to our scratches and my wound, Matt told us the assembly went smoothly and the people, especially after learning about the murder, had been extremely supportive and committed to help with the bunker's protection. A curfew was imposed, and interrogations were scheduled to begin the following day. Armed soldiers were stationed throughout the hallways, with snipers ready to secure the perimeter. Citizens were allowed to walk around in order, with each hall having a specific time for citizens to exit their apartments.

We were gripped by worry as we examined everything that had transpired and planned our next steps once we arrived in Electi. Nina left my paperwork in my apartment. My name would be Gabrielle Jones. My designated position was secretary to Matt in his city clinic and informant to Davon. We'd just have to get used to my new identity.

We'd take up residence in Davon's penthouse and arrange a meeting with his parents. There he would present me as his city informant and partner. It was critical for me to get to know his mother in order to meet important people and climb into society, and it was even more vital for me to gain his father's trust. Davon was concerned about that last bit, knowing the evil that lurked within him, but I promised I'd be cautious.

As a member of his father's council, his role would be to plan Deb's rescue and gain access to classified files concerning spies and their current missions. My job would be to establish ties within Electi and recruit supporters for our cause. I'd also operate as a liaison between the spies in Electi and those in Promissa, keeping them busy recruiting and preparing for the final phase—war. If I got recruited as a government informant, Davon said I could play a significant role in determining who the spy hiding in Janus Peak was.

We decided to change my appearance since there were files on me in the government archives and Davon didn't want to risk it. There was a slight possibility his father had opened my file to study Deb's past and family. I'd trim my hair and dye it dirty blond. I'd wear glasses too.

After a long, sleepless night, we arrived at Connor's apartment at 5:00 a.m. to deliver the letter we found on the drop. Sarah's outburst cut our time short, and we forgot to give it to him.

Connor swung open the door. Red-rimmed eyes greeted us as he went back to his sofa.

"Care to explain why you're here this early?" He looked like hell.

Davon handed him the letter we discovered.

Connor read the contents and folded it back. "Thank God you found this in time. This is even worse than we expected." He sighed and gave me the letter. "Save it."

He regarded Davon. "The autopsy results are back. Richard was strangled."

God, who could do such a thing?

Davon tightened his fists by his sides. "What do you think happened?"

"I have no idea. Maybe he found something he shouldn't have or saw someone leaving with that letter. Hell, maybe he worked for the government this entire time, and he wanted out. Who knows? I don't know what to think anymore."

Connor rubbed his hands together, a dark stare engraved on his features. "Tell me, Davon, do you think our position has been compromised?"

"No. I still believe they're unaware. But they're getting closer. Less than ten miles away from the energy bunker. It won't be long until they discover it and take over one bunker at a time. We need to send in even more troops and strengthen our defenses."

Connor nodded. "I meant to pay you a visit and discuss the arrest. Today's the day, and we had a plan, but I just thought of another one that would work better." He glanced at me. "I'll need your help with that."

My heart thumped against my ribcage. What would I have to do?

"Everyone knows you're practically living together, so you'll return to Davon's apartment after this meeting. The original plan was to use the email Davon received, but the letter you're holding works better. This is how it'll go. He'll leave for an early training session, and you'll say you found the letter next to his bed. Since it's cyphered, you'll take it to command, thinking it's one of Davon's regular communications. Because we're on high alert, the letter will get inspected, as it's procedure, and we'll find the information to incriminate him."

I gulped. "You're going to make me turn him in?"

How can he make me do this?

"It makes sense. If it comes from you, it'll be more credible," Davon said. "Connor plans to arrest me today, using either the email or the letter as evidence. The letter adds to the authenticity. It gives us an advantage and puts the spy on edge."

Connor drummed his fingers on the arm of his chair. "I'll be at command by 9:00 a.m. Bring the letter to me."

He gave us both a mournful look. "I'll miss you both once you're gone. Use today to have one last day of calm because we have no idea what awaits you out there. At 7:00 p.m., you'll both walk into the dining hall, and officers will enter after you're seated. This arrest needs to be public. We'll take Davon in, and you'll act surprised. People need to see you devastated."

"I don't think I'll need to act that out." The moment they took him away, I would crumble even though it wasn't real. The judgment. The rejection. It would destroy him.

Davon clutched my hand closer, his black gaze fixed on me.

"Once Davon has been apprehended, I'll explain everything to Jimmy. He needs to know as captain of the runners. I think he'll trust me, but we need to keep an eye on him. He's never trusted Davon, not completely."

Breathing out, Connor went on. "You'll spend a day in the cells, and Abi will visit you there to keep up appearances. On the second night, Nina will set up a loop on the cameras. That's when you'll flee. Use command's hidden exit. No one will notice your escape until the morning, allowing you enough time to get far from us and closer to the city."

Connor stood. "If everything's clear, you can go to Davon's apartment and carry out the plan."

"We're clear. Thanks for everything. Please know we'll work hard to recover Deb and clear my name. This will work." Davon hugged Connor.

"Take care out there, brother. We'll talk again soon."

As we entered Davon's room, I placed the letter on the bedside table. We went to bed without saying anything as fatigue took over, collapsing into each other's embrace.

"Love, please wake up."

Davon's soft caress on my cheek woke me. When I stretched, the bed was empty. As I opened my eyes, he was crouching by my side, already dressed in his training gear.

"Good morning." He brushed my hair away from my face. "It's eight thirty."

With a jolt, I sat up. I needed to be in command by 9:00 a.m. "Fuck, I have to go."

Davon gripped me firmly, his head resting on my lap. He inhaled me as I stroked the top of his head.

I knelt on the floor and kissed him. We both knew everything would change in a matter of hours. As we held each other, the uncertainty of what was to come flooded my mind with anguish. We could talk about it, plan every single step, and there still was no guarantee it would go as we wanted. I closed my eyes and prayed for us to be able to do this.

The moment was broken by a knock on the door. As I entered the restroom to change, Davon went to see who it was.

After washing my face, I rested my hands on the bathroom sink and assessed my appearance. I was pale and had dark circles under my eyes. I slipped on black yoga pants and a blue top and quietly opened the bathroom door just enough to see Matt and Davon deep in conversation.

"Tonight's the night. How is she taking it?" Matt asked.

I peered through the gap. Matt stood close to the door, while Davon leaned against the wall.

"As well as I am." Davon's gaze darted across the room. "Promise me you'll look after her if something goes wrong and she can't come with me."

I clutched the doorframe. With everything going on, I couldn't help but worry about the same thing.

"Everything will be okay. But if that happens, we'll keep her safe," Matt said.

Davon buried his face in his hands. "Fuck, man."

Matt hugged him. "This isn't a goodbye. We'll see each other soon. Be careful out there."

The moment was private, a goodbye between brothers.

The bathroom door squeaked, and they both faced me.

"Hey, Abi." Matt approached and embraced me. "I'll miss you."

My body started shaking, and I sobbed.

"Stay with us tonight."

I nodded.

Matt returned his gaze to Davon. "I'll wait for you outside."

Davon kissed my forehead, then trailed his lips down my face until he reached my lips. "I'll be back at eleven. Wait for me."

My heartbeat quickened as I stroked his chest. "I'll be here."

I reached command at 9:05 a.m. The place was bustling with people. Connor stood next to a table, studying a map.

"Connor, Davon forgot this, and I think it may be important." I handed him the letter.

A couple of heads turned our way in question.

With a puzzled expression, Connor examined the letter. "I wasn't made aware of this. Did he say anything?"

I shook my head, acting confused.

"Thanks. I'll make sure this gets out today. Anna, Pedro, come to my office." He turned his back on me.

I left the room, dread crashing into me.

After breakfast, I headed back to Davon's, arriving with about fifteen minutes to spare. I walked around his room, inhaling the woodsy scent and brushing my hands across his weapons. I showered and sat on the chaise lounge, only a towel covering me.

The door rattled as Davon stepped in. His breath hitched as he took me in. He closed the door, flung the keys at the table, and took off his shirt.

"Don't move, love," he said softly.

As he kneeled on the floor, his pupils were lost in the depth of his intense and dark gaze. He gripped my thighs and closed the distance, causing me to sag against him.

He nipped and licked, his gaze fixed on mine. My moans were the only sounds in the room, and I trembled beneath his touch, needing more. I pulled my hips up toward him, aching for him to go on.

Pleasure grew inside me as he increased his rhythm. It was too much, too intense, and I tilted my head up as the world shattered around me, and I buckled against him. Hard. "Davon!"

He gathered me in his arms and carried me to bed. I took in the image of his sculpted figure as he stood shirtless and took off his jeans.

He crept toward me, held himself up, and slipped into me gently. "I love you so much."

He kissed me, brushing his tongue against mine in a tender caress. "I love the feel of your soft skin against my body." He clutched my hips as he drove into me at an excruciatingly slow speed. "Your moans as you come undone."

I gasped as I took in all of him, savoring the sensation as he began thrusting in a stronger rhythm.

I gripped his biceps and lifted my hips, allowing him deeper.

Pure hunger swirled in his eyes as they locked onto mine.

The moment was so raw, so pure. We made love slowly and thoroughly, taking time to explore each other. A fire ignited in me with each caress, and my body shivered. Each kiss, each word, pushed me closer to the edge. Suddenly, everything inside of me clenched, and I screamed his name. The force of it ran all through my body.

After a couple of strokes, he groaned and found his own release.

My body continued to pulsate around him as he collapsed on top of me.

He slid his fingers down my side while propped up on one elbow, which sent tingles down my spine, then kissed me passionately while holding my hips.

"I love you," I said as he hugged me to his side.

We both fell into blissful sleep as one.

A while later, we made love for a second time, then showered and got ready to head for the dining area.

Before we left, he pulled me to him and kissed me hard.

Time seemed to slow as our brows touched. We remained still, holding each other.

A huge weight lay on my chest, and each breath became harder than the next. The sapphire necklace Davon gave me hung around my neck.

He brushed it with his fingers. "I promise everything will be okay."

"I know." I buried my face in his chest.

One dark thought after another ran through my mind until all I wanted was for us to run away and forget about everything. What if this was the last time I got to hold him?

I forced those thoughts away and took a step back, peering deeply into his eyes, taking him in.

I would be strong, and the plan would work. Everything depended on it.

Chapter 40

Davon

Abi and I strolled hand in hand toward the dining hall, each step harder than the last. Back in my apartment, the way she held me felt too final. Right then and there, I began to doubt our plan would work, but I had to hold on to the idea it would and trust this was the way to go.

I squeezed her hand as we reached the dining hall, willing my strength to reach her.

Aoki and Matt sat at a table and motioned us over after we got our food. I took in my community, one we'd built as a family, and prepared for what was about to come. The place was crowded as we made our way to the table, and I hoped the spy was among them. A lot relied on it.

We tried to keep the conversation light, but a sense of gloom grew between us. Matt's usual humor was replaced by a solemn expression, while Aoki stayed unusually silent. Abi kept touching my thigh, her chin quivering. It was heartbreaking to see my family suffer. We ate in silence until a group of soldiers stepped inside. Invisible hands squeezed my chest, stealing my breath as I prepared for the inevitable. They stood behind me, and Connor entered the room.

Everyone fell silent.

"General Davon Niles, you're under arrest on suspicion of murder and treason to the People's Revolutionary Front." Connor motioned to the soldiers. "Take him away."

I frowned and struggled against their hold. "Connor, what's the meaning of this?"

"Yeah, he couldn't have done it," someone yelled from the back of the room.

"Let him go!" Abi wrestled with a soldier to get to me.

Matt held her back, Aoki frozen in place, as they placed handcuffs on me and escorted me out.

People crowded around me.

"Traitor!" someone at the back of the room shouted.

"This can't be true," another said.

"Just like his father," someone muttered behind me.

I winced at how readily they used my name against me. Even though I expected it to happen, the deep hurt that each of their words inflicted cut into me.

"I'll kill you," Jimmy said as Maria held him back. "I'll fucking kill you, you son of a bitch." His eyes were set on me, his intent clear. If he had a chance, he would do it.

My eyes remained on a single person. Her features were shattered, and tears streamed freely. She wasn't acting. She was in agony. As her gaze fell on me, I silently promised her everything would be fine.

Pedro threw me inside one of the holding cells in the command center. "Fucking traitor."

He punched me hard, and my head hit the wall behind me.

"You fucking killed them all. Our people. And all while keeping a straight face. How could you?"

He struck me again, this time breaking my skin. Blood dripped from my eyebrow.

"All this time, playing with us. Waiting to strike. I can't believe I fell for your act." He came for me, but someone held him back.

"Stop it!" Mark struggled against him. "He has rights, Pedro. You need to calm down."

Pedro spat in my face. His spit was more powerful than his fist. He was my friend. We spent years training together. And in an instant, all of it was forgotten. I wiped my brow as he walked away. An emptiness settled within me.

"Are you okay?" Mark crouched beside me, helping me to my cot.

"Yeah." My head throbbed.

"I believe you, brother. You would never betray us." He wiped the blood from my face.

"Thank you, my friend."

My chest felt lighter, and his words gave me hope. I didn't think I could have endured Mark's thinking the worst of me. He, like Matt and Aoki, was my brother.

"I must go now. I'm set to guard the hall. Maria sent me to make sure you were all right. She also believes in you." He stood and entered the code to close the automatic gate. "Stay strong."

Cement walls surrounded me, the metal gate my only view to the outside. A toilet and sink were in a corner. A moldy smell filled the cell as I lay on my cot. The next thirty-two hours would be vital to our plan. I closed my eyes and tried to rest.

Someone mumbled my name. When I opened my eyes, Aoki was standing outside the cell, holding a paper bag.

"Hey, man, I brought you some food."

I rubbed my eyes and approached him. "What time is it?" My voice was raspy.

"It's 4:00 a.m. Here." He passed the bag and water through the bars.

I sipped the water and examined the bag's contents. A sandwich with fries. "Thanks. How's she doing?"

He shook his head. "After they took you, she kept wanting to come see you. Matt calmed her down. She's resting."

"Thanks for letting her stay with you. I don't want her to be alone." I took a bite from the sandwich.

Aoki nodded. "She'll visit tomorrow. As for me, this is goodbye." He extended his arm inside the cell. As I took it, he pulled me into a hug, the cold bars between us. "Take care out there."

My throat burned. "I'll miss you, brother."

"You'll make it back to us. We'll win this thing." He smiled gently and walked away.

Always the optimistic one.

As I watched his retreating figure, I prayed they would all be safe.

I didn't get much sleep after Aoki's visit. Footsteps sounded along the corridor, and the lights switched on. When I caught sight of Abi, I pressed my forehead against the cold metal bars.

She stepped toward me, and I kissed her hard, the bars unable to keep us apart.

We held on to each other. Her flushed face and reddened eyes spoke volumes. We stood with our brows together.

She brushed the side of my face, and I flinched. "What happened?" she asked softly.

"Nothing." I kissed her palm. "Don't worry about it. How are you?"

"Good." The shadows under her eyes told a different story.

"I brought you toast and a cup of coffee." She handed me the bag, which I placed on the floor. "Matt said he'd pay you a visit tonight. Connor will only allow visits for a maximum of five minutes." She was attempting to keep the conversation light, as a guard stood a couple of yards away.

I drew her to me, wanting to feel her warmth.

She held my face and kissed me again, then whispered, "I'll see you later tonight. Be ready. Love you."

"I love you too." I stroked her hair and removed her hair band, letting her tresses loose. I put the band around my wrist. "I'll hold on to this for you."

She smiled before stepping back and leaving.

The day went by slowly. I received visits from Maria and Mark. They both believed in my innocence and were perplexed as to why Connor was doing this to me.

Connor also came to visit but later at night. He explained everything to Jimmy, but he was convinced I was the culprit. He believed Connor was biased because of our friendship. I feared this might happen, knowing we didn't see eye to eye. It would take time for him to trust us, but I was sure he would understand eventually.

We said our goodbyes, and he made me swear I would protect Abi with my life.

A guard brought me food and water for lunch and again at dinner.

Matt stopped by a few hours later to assure me everything was going as planned. I reminded him about the letter, the one I wrote after my training yesterday. He'd give it to Abi if anything went wrong.

I couldn't sleep after Matt left and paced back and forth, my mind too riled up to rest. The sooner I met my father, the sooner I could free Deb and access the databases to expose the spy. Once I uncovered them, I would not hold back. The fucker would suffer.

I wrapped my fists around the metal bars. It was all his fault. Since the checkpoint massacre, my loathing for Dad had grown tremendously. I yearned to punish him for all he'd done. This was our first move. Now the game would truly begin.

Chapter 41

Abi

Aoki highlighted my hair, and Matt helped me hide a package in the seams of Davon's backpack, one I hoped he'd find if we got separated. We all sat, waiting for my time to leave, the energy in the room constricting.

As I stood to pick up our stuff, Matt followed. "Abi?"

I spun around.

He wrapped me in his arms. "Wait for me. I'll get to you soon." He held my shoulders.

He'd never looked at me this way. His piercing green eyes made me shudder.

"Be careful with Jordan. He can be very manipulative and is a real charmer, but when the time comes, he will not hesitate. If he finds you out, he *will* harm you."

My heart stammered at his warning. "I'll be careful."

"Follow Davon's orders. He knows what he's doing and won't let any harm come to you."

"I will."

He held my face and kissed my brow. "I love you, girl. You can do this."

Aoki took Matt's place. He kissed my hand, just like when we first met. Always the gentleman.

"Remember to keep being you. You're ready for this. Make us proud, and protect our brother. He can be difficult at times, impulsive at others.

Keep him sane. Don't let him stray too far. If he finds himself in a dark place, be his light and show him the way back."

My insides twisted at his words. At what he was asking of me. Davon could lose himself, trapped under his father's claws. I needed to support him, to make him see there was still good in him.

Just as I was about to leave, Sarah came by. She cried her eyes out, desperate for me to stay, but I kept strong. I was not a child anymore. I hugged her goodbye and went on my way. I would miss her dearly, but this was my reality. What I needed to do.

My soul ached from not saying goodbye to Jimmy. He didn't believe Davon was innocent, so Connor opted to keep him in the dark about my leaving to make sure everything went as planned.

At 3:00 a.m., the lights went off. I rushed to the prison hall, carrying both our backpacks, which were loaded with weapons, paperwork, food, and water for the trip.

Davon was already out, and we ran to each other. A startling lightness coursed through me as he claimed my mouth in a swift but heated kiss.

He held my face in his hands, his gaze serious and demanding. "Let's get out of here."

I handed over his backpack.

We ran out of the jail hall and into the command center.

The guard was asleep at the entrance. Matt and Aoki mixed some cookies with sleep medicine and gave them to her after dinner. She was sleeping like a log.

We both pulled out our guns from our backpacks as we reached the hidden exit and climbed the metal ladder out the hatch and into the darkness. When we saw everything was clear, we dashed into the forest. Adrenaline surged through me as I followed Davon. We ran and ran and never looked back.

The night was chilly and quiet as we continued on our way. Almost four hours down, four to go. We alternated between running and walking, taking ten-minute breaks every hour to hydrate and eat protein bars.

As the sun rose, the crisp air of the forest cleansed my soul. We cracked jokes as we walked, keeping ourselves awake.

A branch snapped behind us. We jumped. A lone figure walked out with a gun aimed at Davon. He pushed me aside and reached for his weapon.

"Don't even think about it, you son of a bitch!"

I flinched, my heart plummeting. *Jimmy?*

"You fucking traitor! You murdered my sister! Your friend! How long have you been working on this? Is this some sort of sadistic game to you?" He approached us. "I've always had my suspicions, but I chose to think you were with us. Yet you're just like your father. You'll pay for her death as well as all the others you've killed."

Davon held up his hands and stepped back, taking me with him. "Jimmy, please calm down."

"Shut up." He faced me. "Abi, come to me. I know you think he's innocent, but he's simply too good at his job. He's a spy. Always has been. You've known me for far longer. You know I'd never harm you."

My body trembled. "Jimmy, please let us go."

He extended his hand. "Let's go. I won't tell anyone about what happened tonight, and I'll keep you safe."

I shook my head. I couldn't believe this was happening, as I was just beginning to think everything would be fine. "I'm going with him. He's not guilty."

"How can you defend him?" He aimed the gun at Davon. "You brainwashed her!"

"Please, Jimmy, listen to me," Davon said.

"You have nothing to say to me!" He took a step closer. "You think I'm afraid of you? You murder my sister, take Abi, and want me to show you mercy. I'm not Connor, and I don't believe your nonsense. You die here, tonight."

I stepped in front of Davon.

"Abi, for the last time, come with me. Now."

His angry tone made me take a step back. He'd never talked to me like this.

I couldn't take it any longer. Tears streamed down my cheeks. I raised my hands. "Please, Jimmy. Please understand. There's someone... Someone inside is doing this."

Jimmy smirked. "He's been lying to you all."

I continued toward him.

Davon grasped my arm. "Stay here. He's not himself."

I leaned toward him. "Please. Let me try to get through to him. He'd never hurt me."

Davon relaxed his grip, his gaze on Jimmy. "I trust you, but be careful."

I moved closer to my childhood friend. His gaze swayed between me and Davon, but he kept aiming at him.

"Connor explained everything to you, Jimmy. You know we have to get to the city to find the spy." I reached him.

"Lies!" Jimmy seized my arm and forced me behind him.

A cracking sound filled the forest. Davon collapsed.

My heart shattered as his body fell limp on the ground. An earsplitting scream left me. I shoved Jimmy away and rushed to him.

No! I can't lose you too!

"Davon!" I slid to the ground by his side and clutched his wounded shoulder.

He grunted. There was blood everywhere.

Not again! Not again!

I could hear my own heartbeat as I tried to stop the bleeding, but nothing was working.

"I'm okay." His voice was muffled.

"You aren't. What can I do?" My hands trembled. I couldn't lose him. Not like this.

Footsteps approached. Davon shoved me to the side with his uninjured arm.

Jimmy stood a few feet away. His gun was aimed squarely at Davon's head.

Davon backed away from him, unable to draw his gun.

My mind flashed back to Jacob sitting there as the guard shot him. His empty eyes staring back at me.

Time stopped. The intent in Jimmy's eyes was clear. He would pull the trigger.

My stomach dropped. For a moment, I saw Davon's dead eyes looking back at me, his cold body splayed on the ground, blood gushing from his head. Nausea hit me fast.

No. Not this time.

Without a thought, I pulled out my gun and squeezed the trigger. The sound of the bullet echoed around us. Jimmy tumbled to the ground. I kicked his gun away as he clutched his leg in anguish.

"How could you? How could you choose him over me?" he asked, his voice pained.

I took a step between them. On one side, my love. On the other, my friend. I went to Davon and removed his sweatshirt while he moaned in agony.

I searched my rucksack for bandages and a tourniquet belt. I wrapped it around his shoulder and secured it tightly. The blood wouldn't stop, so

I tightened it even more. The flow slowed, and I cleaned and dressed the wound. He groaned and closed his eyes.

Once done, I touched Davon's forehead with mine and thanked the heavens.

He held me and whispered next to my ear the worst word I could hear at that moment: "Stay."

I jerked back, mouth open.

"He won't make it on his own."

I glanced at Jimmy, who tried to tie his belt at the top of his thigh. As a puddle of blood grew beneath him, his lips were pale.

Shaking my head, I looked at Davon. "No. You're coming with us. We'll take care of you."

I shivered as I struggled to hold it together. This couldn't be our good-bye. Not when we were so close.

He ran his fingertips down my cheek, and I leaned into his touch. He was pale and in pain, but he still grinned and kissed me sweetly, tenderly. Through it, we were both drinking each other's tears.

He buried his face in my neck and pressed my head to his good shoulder, his breathing ragged. "Please be safe."

As I held him, my tears flowed freely. "I love you. I'll make it back to you. I promise."

No more words were needed. I helped him stand and put the pack on his good shoulder.

He softly kissed the back of my hand before pulling my lips to his. "We'll see each other soon. Trust me."

Those words. The same as Deb's before I escaped.

A heaviness settled in my chest, and my heart ripped open as he walked away. I took long, deep breaths, clutching my chest. My throat burned as my heart shattered into pieces.

One to two more hours, and he'd make it to the entry point.

Let him be safe. Please give him strength.

I went to Jimmy.

"You let him go?"

I didn't want to hear his voice, so I focused on knotting his tourniquet. "I'll never forgive you for what you did tonight. You were supposed to get it. To trust me."

"But he..."

I glowered at him. "He's the hero here, the one fighting for us all. He took the blame, knowing most people would believe him guilty. So he could leave, free Deb, and find the spy. I don't care if you believe me or not because I'm only doing this for the sake of our memories and because he asked me to."

"Abi..."

"Let's go."

I helped him up, slung his arm around my shoulders, and started heading back to Janus Peak.

My life was in an endless cycle, as again I was left behind. But this time I would not rest until we obtained what we wanted. Our liberty. And for that, I'd become a rebel unbound.

To be continued...

Thank you for reading *Rebel Unbound: First Book of the Promissa Trilogy.*

Follow Davon as he uncovers the truth and dives into his father's world in *Rule of the Elite.*

Please follow my author pages. Reviews are greatly appreciated.

Goodreads:

https://www.goodreads.com/author/show/49079198.E_R_Phoenix

Amazon:

https://www.amazon.com/author/erphoenix

Acknowledgements

I'd like to thank everyone who encouraged me to start writing again, particularly my husband, David. You are my everything, trusting in me no matter how many times I drifted off track. Even when I doubted myself, you were there to keep pushing me forward.

To my son David and two daughters, Karina and Mariana, for their unwavering faith and support during my journey. Thank you, Karina, for bearing with me and reading that initial copy to assist me fill any plot holes and edit the grammar as best you could. You were extremely helpful, and I will always be grateful for your time.

To my friends who knew this was my dream and supported me along the way.

To my parents and siblings for understanding and supporting me on this path.

I want to express my gratitude to three professors: Professor Nieves, Ms. Baez, and Mrs. Perez. I appreciate your encouraging words during my childhood, teenage, and adult years, which motivated me to take on this challenge.

To my brother-in-law, Rei, for taking the time to make such lovely art for my page.

To Miranda Miller, my editor. Thank you for helping me shape this debut work into what it is now. You were extremely valuable throughout the process, and I learned a lot from you. Thank you.

To Christian Bentulan for his fantastic cover artwork. It warms my heart to see my ideas expressed so beautifully. You're an excellent artist.

Thank you to everyone who read my debut work and allowed me to transport you to my world. Thank you for joining me on this adventure.

To everyone who has experienced oppression, brutality, and injustice. Never give up battling and remember that nothing and no one can change who you are within. You are strong and unique, and justice and goodness will always triumph over evil.

Finally, to myself from ten years ago. In January 2023, when pondering continuing my book, I discovered not only the two chapters I'd written, but also a letter I wrote about my life on the same date ten years before, in 2013. In that letter, I urged myself to keep fighting for my passion to write, even if life kept pulling me away from it, and to remember my dream and return to it.

Thank you all and I hope you enjoyed my book.

About the author

E. R. Phoenix is a full-time novelist born and raised in Puerto Rico. She's enthusiastic about the environment, freedom, human rights, and societal justice.

Dystopian fiction is her favored reading and writing genre. She combines this with romance, particularly when love appears suddenly in a dangerous setting and is impossible to resist. Her tales are filled with action, danger, suspense, steamy romance, and individuals who would stop at nothing to defend their cause.

She's worked as a middle/high school science teacher and as a personal trainer. When she's not writing, she spends most of her time reading and being with her family. She loves dancing, hiking, watching anime, going to the beach, and playing videogames.

E.R. Phoenix is best known for her Promissa Trilogy books.

She currently lives in Vega Baja, Puerto Rico.

Keep in touch with E.R. Phoenix via the web at:

https://amazon.com/author/erphoenix

https://www.goodreads.com/author/show/49079198.E_R_Phoenix

https://www.facebook.com/erphoenixauthor/

https://www.instagram.com/e.r.phoenix/

https://www.tiktok.com/e.r.phoenix/

www.ingramcontent.com/pod-product-compliance
Lightning Source LLC
Chambersburg PA
CBHW060242030726
47493CB00025B/1574